PONTIFEX, SON AND THORNDYKE

LECTOR HOUSE PUBLIC DOMAIN WORKS

This book is a result of an effort made by Lector House towards making a contribution to the preservation and repair of original classic literature. The original text is in the public domain in the United States of America, and possibly other countries depending upon their specific copyright laws.

In an attempt to preserve, improve and recreate the original content, certain conventional norms with regard to typographical mistakes, hyphenations, punctuations and/or other related subject matters, have been corrected upon our consideration. However, few such imperfections might not have been rectified as they were inherited and preserved from the original content to maintain the authenticity and construct, relevant to the work. We believe that this work holds historical, cultural and/or intellectual importance in the literary works community, therefore despite the oddities, we accounted the work for print as a part of our continuing effort towards preservation of literary work and our contribution towards the development of the society as a whole, driven by our beliefs.

We are grateful to our readers for putting their faith in us and accepting our imperfections with regard to preservation of the historical content. We shall strive hard to meet up to the expectations to improve further to provide an enriching reading experience.

Though, we conduct extensive research in ascertaining the status of copyright before redeveloping a version of the content, in rare cases, a classic work might be incorrectly marked as not-in-copyright. In such cases, if you are the copyright holder, then kindly contact us or write to us, and we shall get back to you with an immediate course of action.

HAPPY READING!

PONTIFEX, SON AND THORNDYKE

RICHARD AUSTIN FREEMAN

9 789353 366834
ISBN: 978-93-5336-683-4

First Published: -

LECTOR HOUSE

LECTOR HOUSE LLP
E-MAIL: lectorpublishing@gmail.com

PONTIFEX, SON AND THORNDYKE

BY

R. AUSTIN FREEMAN

CONTENTS

PONTIFEX, SON AND THORNDYKE

CHAPTER I:

DESTINY IN AN EGG-CHEST

(Jasper Gray's Narrative)

A crab of mature age and experience is represented by an ancient writer as offering advice to his son somewhat in these terms: "My son, I have observed in you a most regrettable tendency to walk with ungraceful and unbecoming sidelong steps. Pray endeavour to conquer this pernicious habit and to adopt a straightforward and direct mode of progression."

Excellent advice! Though the gait of the existing generation of crabs leads one to fear that it failed to take effect.

The ancient parable was brought to my mind by the cigarette that I was lighting; for I had been the recipient of some most excellent paternal advice on the subject of cigarettes, coupled with the same on Irish whisky. My revered parent had, in fact, actually removed a choice Egyptian from his mouth the better to expound the subject; and, pointing to the accumulated ends on the hearth and the half empty bottle on the mantelpiece, had explained with his admirable lucidity that these unsubstantial gauds were the inefficient substitutes for bacon for breakfast.

And yet I smoked. I did not consume Irish whisky, though I was perhaps restrained by reasons that were economic rather than ethical. But I smoked cigarettes; and recently I had started a pipe, having made the interesting discovery that the paternal cigarette ends were capable of reincarnation in a pipe-bowl.

I lit my cigarette and reflected on life and its problems. I was at the moment seated on a folded sack in an up-ended two-wheeled truck or hand-cart. In that truck I had conveyed a heavy bale of stationery from my employers, Messrs. Sturt and Wopsall, to a customer at Mile End; after which I had drawn the empty truck into a quiet yard, up-ended it and taken my seat in it as aforesaid. Since that day I have sat in many a more luxurious seat; in club divans, in hansom cabs, yea! even in the chariots of the mighty. But never have I found one quite equal to an up-ended truck with its floor turned to windward and a folded sack interposed between its tail and my own. There is much to be said for the simple life.

At this time I was just turned seventeen, and needless to say, I was quite poor. But poor boy as I was, there were many things for which I had to be thankful. In the first place I enjoyed the supreme advantage of having escaped education--or rather, I should say, the particular brand that is supplied by the State. Other boys of like indigence were hauled off to Board Schools, where they contracted measles, chicken-pox, ringworm and a most hideous accent, which would cling to them and, socially speaking, damn them hopelessly for ever, even though they should subsequently rise--or sink--to millionairedom.

From this curse I was exempt. My accent was that of the upper middle-class, my vocabulary that of the man of culture; I could manage my aitches and express myself in standard speech. If the present was meagre, the future held untold potentialities; and this was the priceless gift of circumstance.

My father was a clergyman; or rather, I should say, he had been a clergyman. Why he had ceased to be a clergyman I never knew, though I associated the cessation of pastoral activities directly or indirectly with his complexion. When I knew him he was what he called a classical tutor and other people called a crammer; and the "crammees" being mostly of humble station, though ambitious, his income was meagre and precarious even at that.

But he was a wonderful man. He could construe the most difficult passages from the ancient authors and work out intricate problems in spherical trigonometry, when, from causes which I need not dwell upon, the functions of his legs were in temporary abeyance; on which occasions he would sit on the floor, for the excellent reason--as he lucidly explained--that "the direction of the force of gravity being geocentric, it was impossible to fall off." Yes, he was a remarkable man, and should surely have attained to distinction in the church. Not, to be sure, that you can conveniently sit on the floor to conduct morning service; but what I mean is that a man must be accounted more than ordinarily gifted in whom, once more to adopt his admirable phraseology, "the effect of alcoholic stimulation is merely to induce motor inco-ordination unaccompanied by psychical confusion."

I must not, however, allow mere family pride to lead me into digressions of unreasonable length. To return to the present incident. The cigarette had dwindled to about an inch and a half, and I was beginning to consider the resumption of locomotive activities, when a man stopped at the entrance of the yard and then slowly advanced towards me. I thought he was going to order me to move on. But he did not. He sauntered down the yard, and, halting opposite the truck, surveyed me attentively until I became quite embarrassed and a little annoyed.

"Want a job, young feller?" he asked at length.

"No, thank you," I replied. "I've got one."

"So I see. Looks a pretty soft one, too. How much do they pay yer for sittin' in that truck?"

Of course it was no concern of his; but I was a civil youth and replied simply: "Ten shillings a week."

"And are they going to give yer a pension?"

"They may if I sit here long enough," I answered.

He pondered this statement thoughtfully and then resumed: "Sure yer don't want a job? Wouldn't care to earn five bob, for instance?"

Now this was a different matter. Five shillings was half my weekly wage. I was not pressed for time, for I had run all the way with the loaded truck and was entitled to loiter on the return journey.

"'What sort of job is it?" I asked, "and how long will it take?"

"It's to carry a case from Mansell Street to Byleses Wharf. Take yer about 'arf a hour."

"Very well," said I. "Five shillings is agreed upon, is it?"

"Five bob it is; to be paid on delivery. You cut along to Mansell Street, right 'and side next door to the 'bacca shop what's got the image of a nigger outside. I'll just mizzle on ahead and tell 'em you're coming."

He turned and left the yard at a much more sprightly pace than that at which he had entered, and immediately vanished from my sight. But he evidently discharged his mission, for, when I arrived at the house indicated, a seedy-looking man accosted me.

"Are you the bloke what's come for that case of eggs?"

"I've come for a case that's to go to Byles Wharf," I replied.

"That's right," said he. "And mind you're careful with that there case. J'ever hear about Humpty Dumpty what sat on a wall?"

I replied that I was quite familiar with the legend.

"Very well," said he. "There's two thousand of 'em in that case, so you go slow and don't get a-joltin' 'em. We don't want 'em made into omlicks before their time. Now then; just hold that truck steady."

As he spoke, two men came out of the house carrying a large, oblong case on the top side, of which was pasted an enormous label inscribed, "Fragile. This side up." I steadied the truck by its pole and they slid the case into position with extraordinary care while the seedy person stood by to superintend and admonish. Having settled it securely, they wiped their hands on the backs of their trousers and retired into the house, when the seedy one administered a final caution.

"Remember what I told yer, young covey. Don't you go a-gallopin' that there case over the cobbles or a-bangin' it aginst lamp-posts, and you'd best take the back ways so as not to get run into by fire-ingines or sechlike. D'ye ogle?"

I assured him that I ogled perfectly and he then requested me to skedaddlle; which I did with the air and at the pace of one conducting a modest funeral.

But my circumspect manner and elaborate care seemed only to invite assaults from without. In Upper East Smithfield a van, attempting to pass me at a wobbling canter, caught the corner of the precious case a bang that was enough to have turned the whole consignment into "omlicks"; and any that remained whole were like to have been addled by the van-driver's comments. Then in Pennington Street a man came running round a corner with a barrowful of empty casks; and I only escaped being capsized by turning quickly and receiving the impact of the collision on the back of the case. And, finally, an intoxicated Swedish seaman insisted on accompanying me down nearly the entire length of Old Gravel Lane, performing warlike music on the end of the case with a ship-wright's mallet.

As I turned into the gateway of Byles Wharf I looked anxiously at my charge, rather expecting to find some oozing of yellow liquid from its joints. But no such traces of its stormy passage were visible and I ventured to hope that the packing was better than I had been led to believe. Just inside the yard I encountered, somewhat to my surprise, the seedy stranger of Mansell Street, with another even seedier.

"Here you are then, young covey," said the former. "I hope you've been careful with them eggs."

I assured him that I had been most careful but I did not think it necessary to mention that some other people had not. After all, you can't mend eggs, so the less said the better.

"Very well," said he; "you stay here a minute while I go and see if they're ready."

The two men went away and disappeared round the corner of a shed, leaving me holding the pole of the truck. Now the act of standing still and holding the pole of a truck soon becomes monotonous, especially to a youth of seventeen. Half unconsciously I began, presently, to vary the monotony by working the pole up and down like a pump-handle. That couldn't hurt the eggs, and it produced a measured creak of the truck-springs that was interesting and pleasing.

Suddenly there smote on my ear a hoarse and muffled voice, which exclaimed fiercely: "Keep still, can't yer!"

I stopped instantly and looked around me. I had not noticed anyone near, and I didn't see anyone now. Could there be a ventriloquist hiding somewhere in the yard? The idea set my youthful curiosity aflame. I couldn't see him. But perhaps I could induce him to speak again and then I might locate the sound.

I renewed my application to the pump-handle with increased vigour, and the truck-springs squeaked joyously. The experiment was a perfect success. At the fourth or fifth squeak a savage but muffled voice exclaimed, rather louder than before: "Keep still, I tell yer, yer young blighter!"

The mystery was solved. There was no doubt this time as to where the voice came from. It came from inside the case. Eggs indeed! And then I thought of the Swedish sailor and I am afraid I grinned.

The joy of a youth of my age at this romantic discovery may easily be imagined. Instantly my mind began to evolve speculations as to the identity of the imprisoned man. He seemed to take his incarceration in a philosophic spirit, though the Swedish mariner must have been a trial, to say nothing of the other incidents. But at this point my reflections were cut short by the reappearance of the two seedy strangers.

"Now, young shaver," said my original employer; "bring them eggs along this way."

He preceded me round the corner to the quay, alongside of which lay a barge with a hoisting tackle rigged from the end of a mast-derrick. There I was directed to halt and my two friends proceeded to lift the case tenderly out of the truck.

"Now you can mizzle," said the seedier of the two.

"I want my five shillings," said I.

The man put his hand in his pocket and produced a half-crown, which he presented to me. I examined it critically and held it out to him.

"This is no use," I said. "It's pewter. Besides, I was to have five shillings."

He was about to argue the point when the other man broke in impatiently: "Don't play the goat, Jim. Give the cove his dibs"; on which the first man produced--from another pocket--five shillings of undoubtedly official origin. I pocketed them after careful scrutiny and offered him the "snide" half-crown. But he waved it aside magnanimously.

"You can keep that," said he. "'T'ain't no good to me if it's a wrong 'un. And now you can cut your lucky."

My "lucky" took me about a dozen yards along the quay, where I drew up behind a pile of bales to watch the progress of this stirring drama. The barge's tackle-rope had a sling hooked on the end, and this was now carefully passed round the case. The fall of the rope was put on the mast-winch, and, when all was ready, the word was given to "heave away." The men at the winch according hove away. The pawls clinked merrily, the rope tightened, the case rose clear of the ground and swung out like the bob of an enormous pendulum.

And then came the disaster. The barge was secured to two mooring-posts and was about ten feet away from the quay, so that the derrick had to be hauled over by guy-ropes. But the case had not been properly balanced in the sling; and no sooner had it swung clear of the edge of the quay than it began to slip through the rope loop.

"Look alive!" roared someone on the quay. "She's a-slippin'!"

One of the men left the winch and rushed for the guy-rope. But it was too late. Slowly, inexorably, the case slid through the loop and fell with a resounding plop! into the water.

An agonised yell arose from the quay and a furious stampede among the onlookers. The bargees snatched up boat-hooks and setting-poles and scrambled along the deck. But, alas! A swift tide was running, and the case, gyrating and dancing like a cork in a mill race, was out of reach before the first boat-hook could be got over the side.

A barge's dinghy was made fast at the foot of a ladder hard by. Abandoning the truck, I slithered down the ladder, closely followed by a barge-boy, and we met in the boat with mutual recriminations. But there was no time to argue. The boy cast off the painter, and snatching up the paddle, dropped it in the transom-notch and began to scull furiously down stream. Ahead of us, we could see the case dancing along on the tide, turning round and round, vanishing and reappearing among the tiers of shipping. Presently, too, I saw another boat start in pursuit and recognised my two friends among its occupants.

But the case had got a flying start and pursuit was difficult among the crowded shipping. We were beginning to overhaul it when it disappeared behind a cargo steamer, and when we next saw it, it had been neatly snared by a couple of ropes and was being hoisted by hand through the gangway of a little Welsh schooner that was just hauling out of the tiers. The barge-boy and I approached the schooner on the off shore side and climbed on board unnoticed; for the other boat, containing my seedy acquaintances had just arrived on the in-shore side. My employer proceeded to state his claim. "Hi, Captain! That there's my case."

The captain leaned over the bulwark and regarded him with an affable smile.

"D'y'ear," my friend repeated. "That case belongs to me."

The captain's smile broadened. "Belonged," he corrected blandly.

"What d'yer mean?" demanded the seedy one. "You ain't going to try to stick to my property?"

The captain maintained his affable manner. "This is a case of salvage," said he.

"Git out," rejoined the other. "It's a case of eggs; and they're my eggs."

"Did you lay 'em yourself?" enquired the captain (a good deal nearer the mark than he thought). The question seemed to irritate my seedy friend, for he replied angrily: "Never you mind 'oo laid 'em. You just hand that case over."

At this moment there came a diversion. One of the sailors, who had been closely examining the case as it lay dribbling on the deck, suddenly started back, like a cat who has inadvertently smelt a hedgehog.

"Golly wores!" he exclaimed. "There's some-think alive inside!"

"Hey! what's that?" demanded the captain.

"There is, sir, swelp me! I 'eard it a-movin' about."

The captain looked sharply over the bulwark. "Here you, mister!" he sang out, "you haven't been sitting on those eggs, have you?"

"Sittin' on 'em? What d'yer mean?"

"Because they seem to have hatched themselves and the chickens are running about inside the case."

"Yes, and they're usin' the most shockin' langwidge, too," said an elderly seaman who had been pressing his ear to a crack in the case.

This report, reaching the occupants of the boat, caused very evident dismay. But my late employer made a last effort.

"Don't talk nonsense," he said, sulkily. "Pass that case over and I'll pay what's doo for salvage in reason."

"Not me," replied the captain. "I'm goin' to broach that case and see what's inside."

The effect of this decision was rather curious. The men in the boat consulted together hurriedly; then their craft was turned about and rowed away rapidly in the direction whence they had come.

Meanwhile the captain and his myrmidons proceeded to operate on the case. Producing one or two small crow-bars, they neatly prised up the lid and threw it back; when there rose from the case, some what after the fashion of the obsolete toy known as "Jack-in-the-box," no less a person than the man who had originally chartered my truck. He stepped out sullenly and confronting the group of grinning seamen, remarked, in, perhaps justifiably, emphatic terms, that he had had enough of that mode of travelling for the present.

The captain looked at him attentively, and he looked at the captain; and then ensued a whispered conversation between them, which was interrupted by one of the crew remarking:

"Looks like the police boat, don't it?"

The passenger turned and stared wildly in the direction indicated. A police gig was approaching slowly but doggedly over the strong tide; and besides the amphibious officials were two men in civilian garb who sat in the stern-sheets and kept their eyes ominously glued on the schooner.

The passenger bobbed down behind the high bulwark and gazed about him despairingly; and suddenly his eye lighted on me.

"Here, boy," he said, "get into that case."

"No thank you," said I.

He dived his hand frantically into his pocket and brought it out with a shining, yellow burden that clinked musically.

"Here, boy," he pleaded. "Here's five quid for you if you'll get into that case and let 'em nail it up."

Five sovereigns! It was a fortune to a lad in my position. And there really was no particular risk. I examined the coins--I was a fairly expert judge of money from my occupation, which often included "payment on delivery"--and found them genuine; and I succumbed. Stowing the money in an inside pocket, I stepped into the case and hunched myself up so as to occupy comfortably the rather limited accommodation.

"Don't you drop the case into the water again!" I said.

"Right-o, Sonny!" the captain answered. "We'll handle you carefully. Now there, look sharp!"

The lid was clapped on, a few smart but not noisy blows of a hammer drove home the nails, and I began to earn my magnificent wage. The interior of the case was unpleasantly damp and stuffy, though a sufficiency of air and a few streaks of light came through the chinks of the lid. Sounds from without also reached me freely and consisted, for the present, chiefly of suppressed laughter from the sailors and admonitions from the captain.

"Stow that chap down in the lazarette, Fred," said the latter; "and you men, don't stand about laughing like a lot o' fools. Get that tow-rope ready for the tug. Here comes the police boat."

There was a pause after this with some scuffling about the deck and a good deal of sniggering. Then I heard a sharp, official voice. "What's this case, Captain?"

"I don't know," was the reply. "Belongs to those men that you see running up them steps. They hooked it when they saw your boat coming."

"That's Jim Trout," said another voice; "and Tommy Bayste with him. What's in the case, Captain?"

"Can't say. Seems to be something alive in it."

"There!" said the first official. "What did I tell you, Smith. It's Powis right enough. We'd better get him out of the case and clap the darbies on him."

"Not on my ship, you won't," said the captain. "I can't have any criminals let loose here just as I'm hauling out to go to sea. You'd better take the case ashore and open it there."

"Gad!" exclaimed Smith; "the Captain's right, Sergeant. We'd better drop the case into the boat and take it ashore. Powis is an ugly customer to handle. He might capsize us all into the river."

"That's true," agreed the sergeant. "We'll take him as he is if the Captain will have the case let down into our boat."

The captain was most willing for certain private reasons not entirely unconnected with the lazarette. I heard and felt a rope sling passed round the case and my heart was brought into my mouth by the squeal of tackle-blocks. For a few seconds the case swung horribly in mid-air; then, to my unspeakable relief, I felt it subside on to the floor of the boat.

A good deal of laughter and facetious talk mingled with the measured sound of the oars as I was borne away. Suddenly the sergeant laughed out boisterously like a man who has had a funny idea. And apparently he had.

"I'll tell you what, Smith," he chuckled; "we won't open the case till we get to Holloway. We'll take it right into the reception ward. Ha! Ha!"

The joke was highly appreciated by Mr. Smith and his colleagues--a good deal more than it was by me; for I had had enough of my quarters already--and they were still in full enjoyment of it when another voice sang out: "Keep clear of that tug, West. She'll be right on top of us. Hi! Tug ahoy! Look out! Where the dev--"

Here there came an alarming bump and a confused chorus of shouts arose. The case canted over sharply, there was a fearful splash, and immediately, to my horror, water began to ooze in through the cracks between the boards. Two or three minutes of dreadful suspense followed. A loud churning noise sounded close at hand, waves seemed to be breaking over the case, and I had a sensation as if my residence were being dragged swiftly through the water.

It didn't last very long. Presently I felt the case run aground. Then it was lifted on to what I judged to be a barrow; which immediately began to move off over an abominably rough road at a pace which may have been necessary but was excessively uncomfortable to me.

Hitherto very little had been said. A few muttered directions were all that I had been able to catch. But now a newcomer appeared to join our procession, and I began to gather a few particulars of the rescue.

"Any of the coppers drowned, d'ye think, Bill?"

"Not as I knows of. I see 'em all a-crawlin' up on to a dumb barge."

"Where's the tug now?"

"Islington, I should think. We left 'er on the mud with 'er propeller goin' round like blazes."

"What are you going to do with Powis, Bill?"

"We're going to shove the case into Ebbstein's crib and then nip off to Spitalfields with the barrer. And we've got to look slippery, or we'll have the coppers on our heels, to say nothin' of them tug blokes. They'll be wantin' our scalps, I reckon, when they find their craft on the mud."

This conversation was by no means reassuring. I was certainly out of the frying-pan but it remained to be seen what sort of fire I had dropped into.

Meanwhile I carefully stowed my treasure in a secret receptacle inside the back of my waistcoat and braced myself as well as I could to resist the violent jolting and bumping caused by the combined effects of speed, indifferent springs and an abominably rough road. It was during a readjustment of my position after a more than usually violent joggle that my hand, seeking a more secure purchase on the wet surface, came into contact with a small body which felt somewhat like a flat button. I took it between my fingers and tried by the sense of touch to determine what it was, but could make out no more than that it was hard and smooth, flat and oval in shape and about half an inch long. This did not tell me much, and indeed I was not acutely interested in the question as to what the thing might be; but eventually, on the bare chance that it might turn out to be something of value, I deposited it in my secret pocket for examination on some more favourable occasion. Then I wedged myself afresh and awaited further developments.

I had not long to wait. Presently the barrow stopped. I felt the case lifted off and carried away. The light ceased to filter in through the cracks of the lid and was replaced by a curious, sour smell. A muttered conversation with someone who spoke very imperfect English was followed by another brief journey and then the case came to rest on a wooden floor and the smell grew more intense. A confused jabbering in an uncouth foreign tongue seemed to pervade the foul air, but this was soon interrupted by the unmistakable English voice that I had heard before.

"I'll soon 'ave it open, Ebbstein, if you've got a jemmy. That's the ticket, mate. Look out, there, inside!"

The beak of the jemmy drove in under the top edge; one or two quick jerks dislodged the nails, the lid was lifted clear and I popped up as the last occupant had done. A swift, comprehensive glance showed me an ill-lighted frowsy room with a coke fire on which a tailor's "goose" was heating; a large work-board on which were piled a quantity of unfinished clothing, and three wild-looking women, each holding a half-made garment and all motionless like arrested clockwork figures, with their eyes fixed on me. Besides these, and a barrel filled with herrings and cut cabbage floating in a clear liquid, were the two men who confronted me; of whom one was a common, stubbly-haired English East-Ender while the other was a pale, evil-looking foreigner, with high cheek-bones, black, up-standing hair and a black beard that looked like a handful of horsehair stuffing.

"Blimey!" ejaculated the Englishman, as I rose into view; "'t'aint Powis at all! Who the blazes are you?"

"Who is he!" hissed the foreigner, glaring at me fiercely, "I will tell you. He is a bolice spy!" and his hand began to creep under his coat-skirt.

The Englishman held up his hand. "Now none o' that, Ebbstein," said he. "You foreigners are so bloomin' excitable. Tell us who you are, young un."

I told them all I knew, including the name of the schooner--the Gladwys of Cardiff--and I could see that Ebbstein rejected the whole story as a manifest fable. Not so the Englishman. After a moment's reflection, he asked sharply: "How much did he give you for getting into that case?"

"Five shillings and a duffer," I replied promptly, having anticipated the question.

"Where's the five bob?" he asked; and I indicated my left trouser's pocket. Instantly and with remark able skill, he slipped his hand into the pocket and fished out the three coins.

"Right you are," said he, spreading them out on his palm; "one for you, Ebb, one for me and one for yourself, young un," and here, with a sly grin, he returned me the pewter half-crown, which I pocketed.

"And now," he continued, "the question is what we're to do with this young toff. We can't let him run loose just now. He might mention our address." Ebbstein silently placed one finger under his beard; but the other man shook his head impatiently.

"That's the worst of you foreigners," said he; "you're so blooming unconstitootional. This ain't Russian Poland. Don't you understand that this boy was seen to get into that case and that the coppers'll be askin' for him presently? You'd look a pretty fine fool if they was to come here for him and you'd only got cold meat to offer 'em. Have you got a empty room?"

"Dere is der top room, vere Chonas vorks," said Ebbstein.

"Very well. Shove him in there and lock him in. And you take my tip, young feller, and don't give Mr. Ebbstein no trouble."

"Are you going away?" I asked anxiously.

"I'm going to see what's happened to my pal; but you'll see me back here some time to-night."

After a little further discussion, the pair hustled me up the grimy, ruinous stairs to the top of the house and introduced me to an extraordinarily filthy garret, where, after a brief inspection of the window, they left me, locking the door and removing the key.

The amazing folly of the ordinary criminal began to dawn on me when I proceeded to lighten the tedium of confinement by examining my prison. I was shut up here, presumably, because I knew too much; and behold! I was imprisoned in a room which contained incriminating objects connected with at least two different kinds of felony. An untidy litter of plaster moulds, iron ladles, battered pewter pots and crude electrical appliances let me into the secret at once. For, young as I was, I had learned a good deal about the seamy side of London life, and I knew a coiner's outfit when I saw it. So, too, a collection of jemmies, braces, bits and skeleton keys was quite intelligible; these premises were used by a coiner--presumably Mr. 'Chonas'--and a burglar, who was possibly Ebbstein himself.

I examined all the tools and appliances with boyish curiosity, and was quite interested for a time, especially when I discovered the plaster mould of a half-crown, very sharp and clear and coated with polished black lead, which seemed to correspond with the 'Duffer' in my pocket. The resemblance was so close that I brought forth the coin and compared it with the mould, and was positively thrilled when they proved to be one and the same coin.

Then it suddenly occurred to me that Ebbstein probably had forgotten about the moulds, and that if he should realise the position he would come up and secure his safety by those "unconstitootional" methods that he had hinted at. The idea was most alarming. No sooner had it occurred to me than I resolved to make myself scarce at all costs.

There was not much difficulty at the start. The window was fixed with screws, but there were tools with which to unscrew it; and outside was a parapet. I began by sticking the end of one jemmy in a crack in the floor and jamming the other end against the door; which was as effective as a bolt. Then I extracted the screws from the window with a turn-screw bit, softly slid up the bottom sash and looked out. Exactly opposite was the opening of a mews or stable yard, but it was unoccupied at the moment. The coast seemed quite clear, the house was not overlooked, and the parapet ran along the whole length of the street. Arming myself with a two-foot jemmy, I crawled out on to the broad gutter enclosed by the parapet, shut the window and hesitated for a moment, considering whether I should turn to the right or the left. Providence guided me to the left, and I began to crawl away along the gutter, keeping below the parapet as far as possible.

As I passed the dormer window of the next house, curiosity led me to peep in; but at the first glance my caution fled, and I rose boldly to press my face against the glass. I looked into an unfurnished room tenanted by one person only; a handsome--nay a beautiful girl of about my own age. Her limbs were pinioned with thinnish rope, and she was further secured with the same rope to a heavy chair. A single glance told me that she was no East-End girl; she was obviously a young lady; and my premature knowledge of the seamy side of life enabled me to hazard a guess as to what she was doing here.

She had already seen me and turned her deathly pale face to me in mute appeal. In a moment I had my big clasp-knife out, and, thrusting it up between the sashes, pushed back the catch; when I quietly pulled down the top sash and climbed over into the room. She looked at me with mingled hope and apprehension and exclaimed imploringly:

"Oh! Take me away from this dreadful place--" but I cut her short.

"Don't speak," I whispered; "they might hear you. I'm going to take you away."

I was about to cut the rope when it occurred to me that it might be useful, as there seemed to be a considerable length of it. So I untied the knot and unwound the coils, recoiling the rope and throwing it round my neck. As the young lady rose stiffly and stretched herself, I silently carried the chair to the door, where I stuck its low back under the handle and jammed the back legs against the floor. No one could now get into the room without breaking the door off its hinges.

"Can you follow me along the parapet, Miss?" I asked with some misgiving.

"I will do anything you tell me," she answered, "if you will only take me away from this place."

"Then," I said, "follow me, Miss, if you please," and climbing back out of the window, I reached in and took her hands to haul her up after me. She was an active, plucky girl, and I had her out on the gutter behind the parapet in a twinkling; and then, having softly shut the window, in case it should be noticed from outside, I crouched down in the gutter and motioned to her to do the same.

In the gathering dusk, we began to crawl slowly away, I leading; but we had advanced only a few yards when I heard her utter a low cry, and at the same time felt her grasp the skirt of my jacket. Turning back, I saw her peering with an expression of terror through a hole in the parapet that opened into a rain-hopper, and, backing as best I could, I applied my eye to the hole, but failed to see anything more alarming than a woman on the opposite side of the street, who was looking at the houses on our side as if searching for a number. To be sure, she was not a pleasant-looking woman. Tall and gaunt, with dead black hair and a dead white face, and pale grey eyes that struck a discord with her hair, and were not quite a match in colour--for the left eye looked considerably darker than the right--she impressed me somehow as evil-looking and abnormal with a suggestion of disguise or make-up; a suggestion that was heightened by her dress. For she wore the uniform of a hospital nurse, and I found myself instinctively rejecting it as a masquerade.

Still, unprepossessing as she was, I could see nothing terrifying in her aspect until my companion whispered in my ear: "She is coming to fetch me." Then I vaguely understood and shared her alarm. But the greater the danger, the greater the need to escape as quickly as possible. Accordingly, with a few whispered words of encouragement, I started forward again, crawling as fast as the confined space permitted. I looked up at the windows as we passed, but did not venture to peep in; but near the end of the row, I made out on one the words "To let," written with soap or whitewash, and on this, I raised my head and looked in. The appearance of the empty room with its open door confirmed the inscription, and I made bold, after a cautious look round, to slip back the catch with my knife, lower the top sash and enter. A very brief inspection showed that the house was really empty, so I returned, and quickly helping my protégée in through the window, slid up the sash.

While we were exploring the empty house, the young lady told me her story. That very morning her governess had left her for a few minutes to call at an office, and while she was waiting in the Strand, the woman whom we had just seen had come to her to tell her that the governess had been run over and taken to the hospital. She was then hurried into a cab by the nurse and driven to the house in which I had found her.

There was no time, however, for detailed explanations. We were by no means out of the wood yet. All the outside doors, front and back, were locked, and though I could have broken out with the jemmy, it was not a very safe plan on account of the noise that I should make. But there was another plan that looked more feasible. This particular house had no back yard, but gave directly on a narrow court; into which it would be fairly easy to drop from the first-floor window by the aid of the rope.

No sooner had I conceived the idea than I proceeded to execute it. Raising the bottom sash of the back first-floor window, I passed the cord through the bars of the fireplace.

"Shall I go first, Miss?" I asked. "The rope is rather short, and I had better be there to catch you if you have to drop."

She agreed eagerly, and, after a careful look up and down the court, I took the doubled rope in my hand, climbed out of the window, and, slipping down easily until I was near the ends of the rope, let go and dropped on the pavement.

Looking up, I saw the young lady, without a moment's delay, seize the rope and climb out of the window. But instead of grasping the two parts of the rope together, she had taken one in each hand, which made the descent much less easy; and as she apparently held one part more tightly than the other, the more loosely-held part began to slip up as the "bight" ran through the bars of the grate above. Finally, she let go with one hand, when the released end flew up and she came down "by the run" holding on to the other. I stepped forward as she dropped the last few feet and caught her without difficulty; and as I set her on her feet, the rope came down by its own weight and fell in a confused coil on top of us. Half unconsciously, I picked it up and flung it round my neck as I glanced about in search of the exit from the court.

At this moment a man came, treading softly, round a bend of the narrow passage; a foreigner, evidently, and so like Ebbstein that, for a moment, I really thought it was that villain himself. He stopped short and looked at me with scowling inquisitiveness. Then, suddenly, he seemed to recognise the young lady, for he uttered a sort of snarl and stepped forward. At the sound she turned and saw the man; and the low, trembling cry that she gave, and the incredulous horror that froze upon her face, will be fresh and vivid in my memory though I should live for a century.

"You shall come back with me now," the wretch exclaimed, and rushed at her with his foul hands spread out like talons. My gorge rose at the brute. The blood surged noisily in my ears and my teeth clenched tightly. The jemmy in my hand seemed to whirl aloft of itself. I was dimly aware of a strong muscular effort and a dull-sounding blow; of a limp fall and a motionless figure on the pavement. Perhaps the man was dead. I didn't know and I didn't particularly care. At any rate I did not stop to ascertain. Taking my companion by the hand, I drew her swiftly down the court, grasping the jemmy tightly and quite ready to use it again if need be.

We were obviously in great danger. Even as David, when he went down into Ashdod, we walked in the midst of enemies. There were few people in the ill lighted street into which we emerged, but those few eyed us with sinister glances and whispered together ominously. We walked on quickly but without appearing to hurry, and presently turned into a street that was quite deserted save for a hansom cab that had drawn up outside a small public house. I stepped forward joyfully, remembering the golden bribe that I could, and would willingly, offer for a safe passage; but my companion suddenly seized my arm and dragged me into a deep doorway.

"Don't let him see us!" she exclaimed breathlessly. "He is the man who brought me here, and he is one of them. I heard the nurse call him Louis."

We pressed back into the doorway and I watched the man putting on the horse's nose-bag. He certainly was a villainous-looking rascal; pale, black-eyed, with crisp, curly, black hair; the very opposite of the English horsey type. When he had secured the nose-bag, he turned and entered the public house; and at the same moment I made up my mind. Advancing quickly, I deliberately took off the horse's nose-bag and threw it down.

"Jump into the cab!" I said to my companion; flinging the coil of rope and the jemmy down on the foot-board; and she stepped in without a word. I led the horse forward a few paces clear of the house, and then I climbed quickly to the driver's seat and took the reins. My experience of driving was small, but I had driven our van once or twice under the carman's supervision, and knew how to handle the 'ribbons'. A gentle shake of them now started the horse at a walk and I had just plucked the whip out of its socket when there rose from the direction of the court a shout of alarm and a confused noise of many voices. I shook the whip, and the horse broke into a trot. The voices drew nearer, and, just as I turned the corner, a loud yell from behind us announced that the cabman had discovered his loss. I gave the horse a sharp cut and he broke into a canter.

On we rattled through one after another of the short and narrow slum streets, turning the sharp corners on one wheel and shaving the treacherous posts; and always the roar of angry voices seemed to pursue us, gathering in volume and seeming to draw nearer. The cab swayed, men leaped aside with curses, women and children sprang from the kennels screaming, windows were flung up and people yelled at us from doorways. And still the roar from behind seemed to draw nearer; and still I sat with clenched teeth, grasping the reins convulsively and thinking only of the posts at the corners.

Presently we entered a longer street and I whipped up the horse afresh. At the end of this street we came out into a broad road and I took a deep breath. Now I knew where I was: Commercial Road East. Ashdod was behind us with the gibbering crowd of our enemies. I lashed the horse into a gallop and rattled gaily along the broad road, westward. The police might stop me if they pleased; I cared not a fig for them. My lady was safe from those vampires, and that was all that mattered.

As we approached Whitechapel High Street, I stopped and raised the trap to ask where I should drive my fare. The address she gave was 63, Dorchester Square; and having obtained this, I drove on once more. But I went more soberly now that the danger was over and avoided the main streams of traffic. Years of experience in the delivery of parcels had made me almost as familiar with London as a fully qualified cabman, and I threaded my way through quiet squares and by-streets with no difficulty beyond that of driving the cab straight and keeping clear of other traffic. In less than an hour I turned into Dorchester Square, and, slowing down to read the numbers, at length drew up before a large house.

I climbed down quickly, and, snatching off my cap, helped my fare to alight. She stood by the cab, still holding my hand and looking earnestly into my face; and her eyes filled.

"I want to thank you," she said with a little catch in her breath, "and I can't. But my mother will. I will send someone out to hold the horse in a minute."

She ran up the steps and rang the bell. The great door opened. It was opened by a tall footman who seemed to be prematurely grey; in fact his hair was perfectly white, though he looked quite young. He stared at the young lady for a second or two as if stupefied; then he let off a most undignified yell. "Miss Stella's come back!"

So her name was Stella. A pretty name and a fit one for a lovely young lady. But I liked not that footman. And the great house, with its unfamiliar pomp, cast a chill on me. I felt a sudden shyness, which may have been pride.

Why should I see her mother? There was nothing more to do. "Miss Stella had come back," and there was an end of it.

I led the horse a few yards farther on to a lamp-post and taking the reins, which had fallen down, I secured them to the post with what our packer calls a clove hitch. Thriftily, I gathered up the coil of rope from the footboard--the jemmy had jolted off--and then I walked away across the Square.

I looked in at Sturt and Wopsalls, though the premises were shut. But the foreman, who lived there, told me that my truck had been brought home by the police; and when he had heard my story he advised me to leave all explanations to him; which I did. Of course I said nothing about the young lady.

To my revered parent I was even more reticent. Experience had taught me to maintain a judicious silence about any pecuniary windfall until some periodical financial crisis called forth my savings. But he was singularly incurious about the details of my daily life. Even the coil of rope which I brought home on my arm, drew from him no comment or question. And as the frugal supper was on the table and we were both pretty sharp set, conversation tended for a while to be spasmodic, with the result that the story of my adventures remained untold.

CHAPTER II

TREASURE TROVE

(Jasper Gray's Narrative)

IT was not until I had retired to my room for the night and taken the unusual precaution of locking the door, that I ventured to turn out the secret pocket at the back of my waistcoat and inspect the almost unbelievable wealth that the day's adventures had yielded. Indeed, so incredible did my good fortune appear that nothing short of a minute and critical examination of each coin separately would convince me that the windfall was a glorious reality.

But a reality it was; and as I laid out the shining coins on my dressing-table, my eyes travelled over them with something approaching awe. Five golden sovereigns! Wealth beyond my wildest dreams. As I recall the ecstasy with which I gazed at them I can understand the joys of the old-fashioned miser. The paper vouchers which pass as money in these later, degenerate days hold no such thrills.

And what a fortunate inspiration that secret pocket had been! The sewing of it on had been but a mere boyish freak with no defined purpose; for nothing more valuable than an occasional stray silver coin had ever come into my possession. Yet, but for that invaluable pocket, the five sovereigns would have gone the way of the two half-crowns. And thus reflecting, I was reminded of the little object that I had picked up in the egg-chest and dipped my fingers into the recesses of the somewhat irregularly shaped pocket. The object, when I at last discovered it in a sunken corner, appeared to be a little oval glass plate, flat on one side and rounded on the other, and about half an inch in length. As it was coated with dirt, I carried it to the wash hand-basin, and, having tenderly bathed and wiped it, brought it back to the candle. And then I received another thrill; for, holding it up to the light, I found it to be of a beautiful deep, clear green colour, whereupon I instantly decided that it must be an emerald. But more than this: as I looked through it with the rounded side towards me, there appeared, as if in its very substance, but actually engraved on the flat side, a little castle, such as one uses in playing chess, and above it the tiny head of some animal which seemed to combine the characteristics of a donkey and a crocodile, while, underneath the castle, in the tiniest of lettering, were the words, "Strong in Defence." Evidently this emerald had dropped out of a seal or a signet ring.

I knew all about seals, for Sturt and Wopsalls were accustomed to secure small parcels for the post in this way; and occasionally the packer had allowed me to perform this interesting operation, having instructed me in the proper method and how to prevent the wax from sticking to the seal. But the warehouse seal was a big, clumsy, brass affair, quite different from this delicate little engraved gem. Hence it is needless to say that I was all agog to make a trial of my new treasure; and, failing any more suitable material, I made a number of experimental impressions on samples of wax from the candle before returning the gem to its secret hiding-place. Then, having bestowed my golden windfall at the bottom of a drawer filled with miscellaneous clothing--mostly outgrown--I went to bed, gloating happily over my sudden accession of wealth.

Throughout the following day--it was a Saturday, I remember--the consciousness of my new opulence never left me. I seemed to walk on air. For the first time in my life I was a capitalist. If I had chosen--only I was not such a mug--I could have gone quite extensively 'on the bust' or brought something really expensive. It was a delightful sensation, and it cost nothing so long as I kept my capital intact.

But even more than my treasure of gold was the mysterious emerald a source of joy, to which the uncertainty as to its value contributed not a little. I had read somewhere that the emerald is the most precious of stones, even more precious than the diamond. And this was quite a good-sized stone. Why it might be worth a hundred pounds! I had heard of diamonds that were worth more than that. True, it was probably some other person's property, and the circumstances in which I had acquired it strongly suggested that it was stolen property. But what of that? I had not stolen it, and I was fully prepared to surrender it to the rightful owner if ever he should appear. Meanwhile it was mine to possess and enjoy, and I made the most of it, halting from time to time in unfrequented places to fish it out of its hiding-place and hold it up to the light, revelling in its gorgeous colour and the quaint little castle and the preposterous little donkey or crocodile or whatever he was, magnified by the lens-like convex back of the gem.

Presently I became possessed by an overwhelming desire to see those mystic figures embodied in wax--real wax; sealing-wax. A survey of my pockets, revealing the presence of several pennies, and my arrival opposite a small stationer's shop in Chichester Rents, settled the matter. I went in and demanded a stick of sealing-wax. The presiding genius, a dry-looking elderly man, rummaged awhile among some shelves at the back of the shop, and at length produced a cardboard box which he laid on the counter and in which I perceived a number of sticks of black sealing-wax.

"I'd rather have red," said I.

"M'yes," said he, giving the box a sort of reproachful shake, "I seem to have run out of red for the moment. Won't black wax do?"

I was about to say "No," when I observed a portion of a broken stick in the box, and my habitual thrift suggested the chance of a "deal."

"How much for that broken piece?" I enquired.

He looked at the fragment disparagingly, picked it out with much deliberation and laid it on the counter.

"Make you a present of that," said he; and taking up the box, turned his back on me as if to avoid my grateful acknowledgments.

I went forth gleefully from the shop with the little stump of funereal wax in my pocket and a growing urge to make a trial of it. But there are three factors to a sealing operation; the seal, the wax and the document or letter. The first two I had; and even as I was searching my pockets, and searching in vain, for some letter or envelope which might form a plausible subject for an experiment, Providence, or Fate, in a playful mood, supplied the deficiency. Just as I was about to cross Fleet Street, a spectacled gentleman, who looked like a lawyer's clerk and carried in his hand a large sheaf of letters, blundered hastily out of Middle Temple Lane and collided with another hustler who was proceeding in the opposite direction. The shock of the impact dislodged one of the letters from his hand, but, unaware of his loss, he hurried away eastward. I ran across the road and picked up the letter, but by the time I had secured it, he had disappeared into the crowd. However, there was no need to pursue him. The letter was stamped and obviously ready for posting. All I had to do was to walk down to the post office and drop it in the box.

With this intention I had turned eastward and was threading my way among the crowd when, happening to glance at the letter in my hand, I noticed that the flap of the envelope was very insecurely stuck down. The letter, as I had already observed, was addressed to a Mr. Brodribb, at New Square, Lincoln's Inn. Now, if Mr. Brodribb lived in Lincoln's Inn, he was probably a lawyer, especially as the letter had come from the Temple; and if he was a lawyer, the letter possibly contained important and confidential matter. It was highly improper that such a letter should be insecurely fastened. The least that I could do was to close the envelope as securely as was possible. And since mere gum had been tried in the balance and found wanting, the obvious proceeding was to seal it and make it absolutely safe.

No sooner had I conceived the idea than I set about its execution. Darting down Inner Temple Lane in search of a retired spot, I turned to the left beside the church, and, passing Oliver Goldsmith's grave, came to a monument provided with a shelf which would serve the purpose to perfection. Here, with no one to observe my proceedings (though, indeed, they were innocent enough and even meritorious) I laid the envelope, the box of matches, the wax and the seal. Very carefully and methodically I melted the wax until I was able to deposit a nearly circular patch on the flap of the envelope. Then, giving it a few moments for the excessive stickiness to subside, I laid the precious seal daintily in position and made steady pressure on it with my thumb.

The result was perfect, even to the microscopic markings on the castle; so perfect that I was loath to part with my work. Again and again I gloated over the beauty of its jet-like polish and the clean-cut device as I walked slowly down Fleet Street until I reached the post office, where, reluctantly I dropped the letter into the yawning mouth of the box. However, if I must needs part with the finished work, I retained the means of repeating it indefinitely; nor, to do myself justice, did I neglect my opportunities. Every parcel to which I could get access went forth enriched as to its exterior with a supplementary impression on the parcel wax, and a couple of ponderous rolls of cartoon paper which I conveyed in the truck to Studios in Ebury Street and at Chelsea, arrived at their destinations adorned with one or two black seals in addition.

It was late in the evening when I reached home--for Saturday was little different to me from other days excepting that it held the promise of Sunday. I was rather tired and uncommonly hungry. But, to a strong and healthy lad, mere fatigue is not unpleasant, especially with an immediate prospect of unrestricted rest; and my hunger was mitigated by the comfortable consciousness of a pound of streaky bacon in my pocket, the product of a trifling honorarium tendered by the Ebury Street artist. That bacon was dedicated to future breakfasts, but still at a pinch (and pinches were not infrequent in our household) it might be made to yield a highly acceptable supper.

However, as I toiled up the noble staircase that mocked our poverty with its faded, old-world magnificence, my nose informed me that the bacon could be reserved for its legitimate function. A savoury aroma on the second-floor landing, waxed in intensity as I mounted the "third pair," offering suggestions that I hardly dared to entertain. But when I opened the door of our sitting-room, my doubts were dispelled and my wildest hopes received glorious confirmation.

I recall very vividly the picture that greeted my eyes as I paused for a moment in the open doorway. Beside the fire, seated in the old Windsor arm-chair and clad in his shabby dressing-gown, behold Pontifex (my revered parent--Pontifex Maximus on occasions of ceremony, shortened to Ponty in familiar conversation) delicately adjusting something that reposed in a frying-pan and murmured softly, exhaling a delicious fragrance. I sniffed and listened in ecstasy. More grateful than the odours of myrrh and frankincense was that delightful aroma; sweeter to my ears that soft, sibilant murmur than songs of Araby. For they conveyed, without the clumsy intermediary of speech, the entrancing idea of scallops; and lest any faintest misgiving might linger, there in the fender was ranged a goodly row of twelve empty scallop-shells.

As I entered, Pontifex looked up with a smile compounded of welcome, triumph and congratulation. We were strangely different in many respects, but on one point our souls were tuned in perfect unison. We both had a gluttonous passion for scallops. It could not often be indulged, for the bare necessaries of life consumed the whole of our joint financial resources. Our ordinary diet--largely consisting of Irish stew--was supplied under a slightly ambiguous contract by the lady on the second-floor. But she was an indifferent culinary artist, and we did not trust her with such rare delicacies as scallops, or even with bacon. These called for more subtle treatment, and besides, the very process of cooking them was a feast in itself.

While Pontifex, with consummate artistry and an air of placid satisfaction, tended the scallops, I proceeded to cut the bread and butter in order that there might be no unnecessary delay. And as I thus busied myself, my mind became half-unconsciously occupied, in the intervals of conversation, with speculations on the train of circumstances that had produced this unlooked-for festivity. How came Pontifex to be able to buy these scallops? Only that morning funds had been so short that it had been doubtful whether they would run to butter. Could Ponty have received an unexpected payment? It might be so, but I doubted it. And as I weighed the probabilities--and found them wanting--a horrible suspicion began to steal into my mind.

Concerning my golden windfall I had, for sound economic reasons, kept my own counsel. But the "snide" half-crown I thought might be allowed to transpire, so to speak, in the form of a booby-trap for poor old Ponty; to which end I had that very morning planted it on the corner of the mantelpiece, experience having informed me of my respected parent's habit of snapping up any unconsidered trifles in the way of specie. It was a foolish joke, but I had taken it for granted that as soon as Ponty had the coin in his hand, he would see that it was a counterfeit. I had made no allowance for the difference between his eyesight and mine or our respective experiences of "snide" money. And now it looked as if my joke had failed disastrously. For I now remembered having noticed when passing a fish-monger's shop on my way home, that scallops were marked two shillings and six-pence a dozen. Of course, it might be only a coincidence. But a sensible man looks askance at coincidences; and the suspicious fact remained that a half-crown had disappeared and two and sixpence worth of scallops had unaccountably made their appearance.

However, I refrained from spoiling poor Ponty's enjoyment of the feast by raising the very awkward question and I even managed to dismiss it from my own mind. So we had a banquet that a Lord Mayor might have envied. The scallops were cooked to perfection and served tastefully in their native shells; and when those shells had become once more empty and I had brewed myself a pot of tea while Pontifex mixed an uncommonly stiff jorum of grog and lit a cigarette, we experienced that sense of luxury and well-being that comes only to those who have to count their coppers and whose rare banquets are seasoned by habitual hard living.

But the question of the "snide" half-crown had to be disposed of, for if it had purchased those scallops, then the scallops had been virtually stolen; and if it had not, it must be lurking in Ponty's pocket, an element of potential danger. Thus, I reflected on the morrow as, in accordance with our Sunday morning routine, I shaved Pontifex, laid the table, fried the bacon and made the tea. Accordingly, as soon as we were seated at table, I opened fire with a leading question, which Pontifex received with a waggish air of surprise.

"So that was your half-crown!" he exclaimed. "Now why did that very simple explanation not occur to me? I tried to remember how I came to put it there but my memory was a complete blank. Naturally, as I realise now."

"So you annexed it and busted it on scallops."

Pontifex smiled blandly. "Your inference," he remarked, "illustrates the curious fact that it is sometimes possible to reach a correct conclusion by means of perfectly incorrect reasoning. The connection which you assumed between the Treasure Trove and the scallops though false in logic was true in fact. But as to your use of the colloquialism, 'busted', I would point out that even as omelettes cannot be made without the breaking of eggs, so scallops at two shillings and sixpence a dozen cannot be eaten without the expenditure of half-crowns."

"Precisely. That was how I established the connection."

"Assumed, my son," he corrected. "You did not establish it. You will note that your middle term was not distributed."

"If the scallops were the middle term," I rejoined, flippantly, "they were distributed all right. We had six each."

"I mean," he said with a deprecating smile, "that you fell into the common confusion of the undistributed middle. You confused the generic half-crown with a particular half-crown."

"Oh, no I didn't." I retorted. "I wasn't born yesterday. I know that the generic half-crown is made of silver. But this particular half-crown was made of pewter."

Pontifex suddenly became serious. Laying down his knife and fork, he looked at me for several seconds in silent dismay. At length he exclaimed: "You don't mean, my son, that it was a base coin?"

"That is just what I do mean. Rank duffer. Made out of a pewter pot. Chappie probably prigged the pewter pot to make it."

Pontifex was too much overcome even to protest at my vulgarisms of speech. Still gazing at me in consternation, he exclaimed tragically: "But this is terrible, Jasper. I have actually committed a gross fraud on that most estimable fish monger! Unwittingly, it is true; but a fraud nevertheless." (It was characteristic of Pontifex that he refrained from any suggestion that my idiotic booby-trap was the cause of the disaster. No man was more sensible of his own faults or more oblivious of other people's).

"Yes," I agreed, "you undoubtedly sold him a pup. Precious mug he must have been to let you. But I suppose, as it was Saturday night, he was pretty busy."

"He was. The shop was crowded with buyers. But, my son, we shall have to make restitution: though, really, in the present circumstances of--ah--financial stringency--"

He explored his various pockets, which appeared to be rich in truncated fragments of lead pencil, in addition to which they yielded a small bunch of keys, a pen knife with a broken blade, a sixpence and three half pence. These treasures he regarded disconsolately and returned them whence they came. Then he turned an enquiring and appealing eye on me. He knew, of course, that I had received my wages on the previous day but delicately refrained from explicit allusion to the fact. However, as the entire sum reposed untouched in my pocket, in the form of four half-crowns and the fishmonger had to be paid, I produced the necessary coin and pushed it across the table. Usually, I was a little chary of handing money to Pontifex, preferring to pay our debts myself. For Ponty's ideas on the subject of meum and tuum were a trifle obscure--or perhaps I should say communistic--where my property was concerned, and the establishments of the tobacconist and the spirit merchant exercised a fatal fascination. But he was scrupulous enough in regard to strangers and I had no misgivings as to my present contribution safely reaching its proper destination. Accordingly, when I had furnished him with the means wherewith to make restitution to the defrauded fishmonger, I considered the incident of the "snide" half-crown as closed.

But it was not, as I discovered when I arrived home on Monday night. The fishmonger, it appeared, had communicated with the police, and the police were profoundly interested in the coin, which they recognised as one of a series which was being issued in considerable numbers by a coiner whom they had failed to locate or identify. In consequence, Pontifex had been requested to ascertain from me how the coin had come into my possession and to communicate the information to the fishmonger for transmission to the police.

Now, in my mind, there was little doubt as to the source of that half-crown. It had come from the work shop or studio of the mysterious artist who had been referred to as 'Chonas'. But my experiences under the too-hospitable roof of Mr. Ebbstein had begotten an unwillingness to be involved in any affair connected with that establishment. I am not peculiarly secretive, but I have a habit of keeping my own counsel. 'Chonas's' proceedings were no concern of mine and I was not disposed to meddle with them. Wherefore, in reply to Ponty's not very eager enquiries, I stated simply and quite truthfully, that I had received the coin from a man who was a total stranger to me. This answer satisfied Pontifex, who was not acutely interested in the matter, and once more I assumed that I had finished with that disreputable coin. And once more I was mistaken.

CHAPTER III:

A MYSTERY AND A DISAPPEARANCE

(Dr. Jervis's Narrative)

THERE are some--and not a few, I fear--of the dwellers in, or frequenters of London to whom the inexhaustible charms of their environment are matters of no more concern than is the landscape which the rabbit surveys indifferently from the mouth of his burrow. For them the sermons in stones are preached in vain. Voices of the past, speaking their messages from many an ancient building or historic landmark, fall on deaf ears. London, to such as these, is but an assemblage of offices and shops, offering no more than a field for profitable activity.

Very different from these unreflective fauna of the town was my friend Thorndyke. Inveterate town-sparrow as he was, every link with the many-coloured past, even though it were no more than an ancient street-name, was familiar and beloved, never to be passed without at least a glance of friendly recognition. Hence it was natural that when, on a certain Tuesday morning, we crossed Chancery Lane to enter Lincoln's Inn by the spacious archway of the ancient gate-house, he should pause to glance round the picturesque little square of Old Buildings and cast his eyes up to the weathered carving above the archway which still exhibits the arms of the builder and the escutcheons of the ancient family whose title gave the inn its name.

We were just turning away, debating--not for the first time--the rather doubtful tradition that Ben Jonson had worked as a bricklayer on this gateway, when we became aware of a remarkably spruce-looking elderly gentleman who was approaching from the direction of New Square. He had already observed us, and, as he was obviously bearing down on us with intent, we stepped forward to meet him.

"This meeting," said he, as we shook hands, "is what some people would describe as providential, if you know what that means. I don't. But the fact is that I was just coming to call on you. Now you had better walk back with me to my chambers--that is, if you are at liberty."

"May I take it," said Thorndyke, "that there is some matter that you wish to discuss?"

"You may, indeed. I have a poser for you; a mystery that I am going to present to you for solution. Oh, you needn't look like that. This is a genuine mystery. The real thing. I've never been able to stump you yet, but I think I'm going to do it now."

"Then I think we are at liberty. What do you say, Jervis?"

"If there is a chance of my seeing my revered senior stumped, I am prepared to stay out all night. But I doubt if you will bring it off, Brodribb."

Mr. Brodribb shook his head. "I should like to think you are right, Jervis," said he, "for I am absolutely stumped, myself, and I want the matter cleared up. But it is a regular twister. I can give you the facts as we walk along. They are simple enough, as facts. It is the explanation of them that presents the difficulty.

"I think you have heard me speak of my client, Sir Edward Hardcastle. I am the family solicitor. I acted for Sir Edward's father, Sir Julian, and my father acted for Sir Julian's father. So I know a good deal about the family. Now, yesterday morning I received a letter which was sealed on the outside with Sir Edward Hardcastle's seal. I opened the envelope and took out the letter, naturally assuming that it was from Sir Edward. Imagine my astonishment when I found that the letter was from Frank Middlewick, your neighbour in the Temple."

"It certainly was rather odd," Thorndyke admitted.

"Odd!" exclaimed Brodribb. "It was astounding. Here was Sir Edward's private seal--the impression of his signet ring--on the envelope of a man who, as far as I knew, was a perfect stranger to him. I was positively staggered. I could make no sense of it; and as it was obviously a matter that called aloud for explanation, I slipped the letter in my pocket and hopped off to the Temple without delay.

"But my interview with Middlewick only made confusion worse confounded. To begin with, he didn't know Sir Edward Hardcastle even by name. Never heard of him. And he was perfectly certain that the seal wasn't put on in his office. He had written the letter himself--I had already observed that it was in his own handwriting--but the envelope was addressed and the letter put in it by his clerk, Dickson, after the copy had been taken and the entry made in the index. Dickson states that he put the letter in one of the ordinary envelopes from the rack and he is quite certain that, when he closed it and stuck the stamp on, there was no seal on it. Of course, there couldn't have been. Then he took the letter, with a number of others, and posted it with his own hand at the post office in Fleet Street."

"Did he check the letters when he posted them?" Thorndyke asked.

"No, he didn't. He ought to have done so, of course. But it seems that he was in a deuce of a hurry, so he shot the whole lot of letters into the box at once. Careless, that was. A man has no business to be in such a hurry that he can't attend to what he is doing. However it doesn't matter, as it happens. The post-mark shows that the letter was actually posted there at the time stated. So there's no help in that direction."

"And what about your own premises? Who took the letter in?"

"I took it in myself. I was strolling round the square, having my morning pipe, when I saw the postman coming along towards my entry. So I waited and took my batch of letters from him, and looked them over as I strolled back to the house.

This one with the seal on it was among the batch. That is the whole story. And now, what have you got to say about it?"

Thorndyke laughed softly. "It is a quaint problem," said he. "We seem to be able to take it as certain that the letter was unsealed when it left Middlewick's office. Apparently it was unsealed when it was dropped into the post office letter-box. It was certainly sealed when the postman delivered it. That leaves us the interval between the posting and the delivery. The suggestion is that somebody affixed the seal to the letter in the course of transit through the post."

"That seems quite incredible," said I. "The seal was the impression of a signet ring which couldn't possibly have been in the possession of any of the post office people, to say nothing of the general absurdity of the suggestion."

"Mere absurdity or improbability," replied Thorndyke, "can hardly be considered as excluding any particular explanation. The appearance of this seal in these circumstances is grotesquely improbable. It appears to be an impossibility. Yet there is the devastating fact that it has happened. We can hardly expect a probable or even plausible explanation of so abnormal a fact; but among the various improbable explanations, one must be true. All that we can do is to search for the one that is the least improbable, and I agree with you, Jervis, that the post office is not the most likely place in which the sealing could have occurred. It seems to me that the only point at which we make anything resembling a contact with probability is the interval between Dickson's leaving the office and the posting of the letters."

"I don't quite follow you," said Brodribb.

"What I mean is that at that point there is an element of uncertainty. Dickson believes that he posted the letter, but, as he did not check the letters that he posted, it is just barely possible that this one may have in some way escaped from his custody."

"But," objected Brodribb, "it was certainly posted at the place and time stated. The post-mark proves that."

"True. But it might have been posted by another hand."

"And how does that suggestion help us?"

"Very little," Thorndyke admitted. "It merely allows us to suggest, in addition to the alternatives known to us--all of them wildly incredible and apparently impossible--a set of unknown circumstances in which the sealing might credibly have happened."

"That doesn't seem very satisfactory," I remarked.

"It is highly unsatisfactory," he replied, "since it is purely speculative. But you see my point. If we accept Dickson's statement we are presented with a choice of apparent impossibilities. Middlewick could not have sealed the letter; Dickson could not have sealed it; we agree that it appears impossible for the postal officials to have sealed it, and it is unimaginable that the postman sealed it. Yet it left Middlewick's hands unsealed and arrived in the postman's hands sealed. Thus the apparently impossible happened. On the other hand, if we assume that the letter passed out of Dickson's possession in some way without his knowledge, we are assuming something that is not inherently improbable. And if we further assume--as we must, since the letter was posted by somebody--that there was an interval during which it was in the possession of some unknown person, then we have something like a loop-hole of escape from our dilemma. For, since the assumed person is unknown to us, we cannot say that it was impossible, or even improbable, that he should have had the means of sealing the letter."

I laughed derisively. "This is all very well, Thorndyke," said I, "but you are getting right off the plane of reality. Your unknown person is a mere fiction. To escape from the difficulty you invent an imaginary person who might have had possession of Sir Edward's ring and might have had some motive for sealing with it a letter which was not his and with which he had no concern. But there isn't a particle of evidence that such a person exists."

"There is not," Thorndyke agreed. "But I remind my learned friend that this perfectly incredible thing has undoubtedly happened and that we are trying to imagine some circumstances in which it might conceivably have happened. Obviously, there must be some such circumstances."

"But," I protested, "there is no use in merely inventing circumstances to fit the case."

"I don't quite agree with you, Jervis," Brodribb interposed. "As Thorndyke points out, since the thing happened, it must have been possible. But it does not appear to be possible in the circumstances known to us. Therefore there must have been some other circumstances which are unknown to us. Now the suggestion that Dickson dropped the letter (which, I understand, is what Thorndyke means) is not at all improbable. We know that he was in a devil of a hurry and I know that he is as blind as a bat. If he dropped the letter, somebody certainly picked it up and put it in the post; and I agree that that is probably what really occurred. I should think so on grounds of general probability, but I have a further reason.

"Just now I said that I had told you the whole story, but that was not strictly correct. There is a sequel. As soon as I left Middlewick, I sent off a reply-paid telegram to Sir Edward asking him if his signet ring was still in his possession and if he had sealed any strange letter with it. In reply I got a telegram from his butler saying that Sir Edward was away from home and adding that a letter would follow. That letter arrived this morning, and gave me some news that I don't like at all. It appears that last Tuesday--this day week--Sir Edward left home with the expressed intention of spending a couple of days in Town and returning on Thursday afternoon. But he did not return on that day. On Friday, Weeks, the butler, telegraphed to him at the club, where he usually stayed when in town, asking him when he would be coming home. As no reply to this telegram was received, Weeks telegraphed next day--Saturday--to the secretary of the club enquiring if Sir Edward was still there. The secretary's answer informed him that Sir Edward had stayed at the club on Tuesday night, had gone out after breakfast on Wednesday morning and had not returned since, but that his suit-case and toilet fittings were still in his bedroom.

"This rather disturbed Weeks, for Sir Edward is a methodical man and regular in his habits. But he didn't like to make a fuss, so he decided to wait until Monday night, and then, if his master did not turn up, to communicate with me. As I have said, up to the time of his writing to me, Sir Edward had not returned, nor had he sent any message. So the position is that his whereabouts are unknown, and, seeing that he has left his kit at the club, the whole affair has a very unpleasant appearance."

"It has," Thorndyke agreed, gravely, "and in the light of this disappearance the seal incident takes on a new significance."

"Yes," I hastened to interpose, "and the assumed unknown person seems to rise at once to the plane of reality."

"That is what I feel," said Brodribb. "Taken with the disappearance, the incident of the seal has an ominous look. And there is another detail, which I haven't mentioned, but which I find not a little disturbing. The seal on this letter is impressed in black wax. It may mean nothing, but it conveys to me a distinctly sinister suggestion. Sir Edward, like most of us, always used red wax."

On this Thorndyke made no comment, but I could see that he was as much impressed as was our old friend and as I was, myself. Indeed, to me this funereal wax seemed to impart to the incident of the seal an entirely new character. From the region of the merely fantastic and whimsical, it passed to that of the tragic and portentous.

"There is just one point," said Thorndyke, "on which I should like to be quite clear. It is, I suppose, beyond doubt that this is really Sir Edward's seal--the actual impression of his signet ring?"

"You shall judge for yourself," replied Brodribb; and forthwith he started forward towards his entry (hitherto we had been pacing up and down the broad pavement of the square). He preceded us to his private office where, having shut the door, he unlocked and opened a large deed box on the lid of which was painted in white lettering: "Sir Edward Hardcastle, Bart". From this he took out an envelope, apparently enclosing a letter and bearing on its flap a small seal in red wax. This he laid on the table, and then, extracting from his pocket wallet another envelope, bearing a similar seal in black wax, laid it down beside the other. Thorndyke picked them up, and, holding them as near together as was possible, made a careful comparison. Then, through his pocket lens, he made a prolonged inspection, first of the red seal and then of the black. Finally, producing a small calliper gauge which he usually carried in his pocket, he measured the two diameters of each of the little oval spaces in which the device was enclosed.

"Yes," he said, handing the envelopes to me, "there is no doubt that they are impressions of the same seal. The possible fallacy is not worth considering."

"What fallacy do you mean?" asked Brodribb.

"I mean," he replied, "that if you would leave one of these impressions with me for twenty-four hours I could present you with an indistinguishable facsimile. It is quite easy to do. But, in the present case, the question of forgery doesn't seem to arise."

"No," agreed Brodribb, "I don't think it does. But the question that does arise, is, what is to be done? I suppose we ought to communicate with the police at once."

"I think," said Thorndyke, "that the first thing to be done is to call at the club and find out all that we can about Sir Edward's movements. Then, when we know all that is to be known, we can, if it still seems desirable, put the police in possession of the facts."

"Yes," Brodribb agreed, eagerly, "that will be much the better plan. We may be able to do without the police and avoid a public fuss. Can you come along now? It's an urgent case."

"It is," Thorndyke agreed. "Yes, we must let our other business wait for the moment. We had no actual appointment."

Thereupon, Brodribb drew the letters out of the envelopes, and having deposited the former in the deed box, which he closed and locked, bestowed the latter in his wallet.

"May want the seals to show to the police," he explained as he slipped the wallet into his pocket. "Now let us be off."

We made our way out of the square by the Carey Street gate and headed for the Strand by way of Bell Yard. At the stand by St. Clement's Church we picked up an unoccupied 'Growler', and, when we had jammed ourselves into its interior, Brodribb communicated the destination to the cabman, who looked in on us as he closed the door. "Clarendon Club, Piccadilly."

The cabman thereupon climbed to his box and gave the reins a shake, and our conveyance started forward on its career towards the west.

"I take it," said Thorndyke, "that Sir Edward wears this ring on his finger?"

"Not as a rule," Brodribb replied. "It is an old ring--an heirloom, in fact--and it is rather a loose fit and apt to drop off. For that reason, and because he sets a good deal of value on it, Sir Edward usually carries it in his waistcoat pocket in a little wash-leather case."

"And what is the ring like? Is it of any considerable intrinsic value?

"As to its intrinsic value," replied Brodribb, "I can't tell you much, as I have not been told and don't know much about jewels. But I can tell you what it is like, and perhaps you can judge of its value from the description. The stone, I understand, is a green tourmaline of an unusually fine colour, flat on the front, which, of course bears the engraved device, and convex at the back. The ring itself is rather massive and ornamented with a certain amount of chased work, but the general effect is rather plain and simple. What should you say as to its value?"

"Principally artistic and sentimental," Thorndyke replied. "A tourmaline is a very beautiful stone, especially if it is cut so as to display the double colouring--which, apparently, this one was not; but it is not one of the very precious stones. On the other hand, a green tourmaline might easily be mistaken by a person who had no special knowledge for an emerald, which is, in certain cases, the most precious of all stones."

"In any case," said I, "it would be worth stealing, and certainly worth picking up if it happened to be dropped."

The discussion was interrupted by the stopping of the cab opposite the club. We all alighted, and, as Thorndyke was paying the cabman, I followed Brodribb up the steps to the hall, where our friend presented his card to the porter and asked to see the secretary. Almost immediately, the messenger returned and ushered us to the private office where we found a small, grave-looking gentleman standing beside his desk to receive us.

"I am extremely relieved to see you, Mr. Brodribb," the secretary said when the necessary introductions had been made and the purpose of our visit stated. "I had the feeling that I ought to communicate with the police, but you understand the difficulty. The club members wouldn't like a public fuss or scandal; and then there is Sir Edward, himself. He would be annoyed if he should return to find himself the subject of a newspaper sensation. But now," he smiled deprecatingly, "I can transfer the burden of responsibility to your shoulders. Is there any information that I can give you?"

"If you have any," replied Brodribb. "I have seen your letter to Weeks, Sir Edward's butler."

"Then I think you know all that I have to tell. But perhaps there is something more that--" he broke off undecidedly and looked from Brodribb to Thorndyke with an air of vague enquiry.

"Could we have a look at the bedroom that Sir Edward occupied?" Thorndyke asked.

"Certainly," was the ready, almost eager response. "I will go and get the key."

He hurried away, evidently all agog to pass on his embarrassments to Brodribb and be clear of them. When he returned with the key in his hand, he invited us to follow him and preceded us along a corridor and up a back stairway, to another corridor at a door in which he halted to insert and turn the key. As the door swung open, he stood aside to let us pass, and, when we had entered, he followed and closed the door after him.

For a minute or more we all stood silently glancing around and taking in the general aspect of the room; and I could see that the distinctly uncomfortable impression that the appearance of the room produced on me was shared by my companions. Not that there was anything unusual or abnormal in its aspect. On the contrary, the room had precisely the appearance that one would expect to find in the bedroom of a gentleman who was in residence at his club. And that was, in the circumstances, the disquieting fact. For thus had the room been lying in a state of suspended animation, as one might say, for close upon a week; a fact which every object in it seemed to stress. The neatly-made bed with the folded pyjamas on the pillow, the brushes, nail scissors and other little toilet implements on the dressing-table, the tooth-brush, nail-brush and sponge on the wash-stand; all offered the same sinister suggestion.

"I take it," said Thorndyke, voicing my own conclusion, "that Sir Edward wears a beard?"

"Yes," Brodribb replied.

"Then, since he had no razors, and all his travelling necessaries appear to be here, we may assume that he took nothing with him."

"Yes, that seems to be the case," Brodribb agreed, gloomily.

"Which implies," Thorndyke continued, "that, when he went away, he had the intention of returning here to sleep."

The implication was so obvious that Brodribb acknowledged it only with a nod and an inarticulate grunt. Then turning to the secretary, he asked: "Did he leave anything in your custody, Mr. Northbrook?"

"Nothing," was the reply. "Whatever he had with him and did not take away is in this room."

On this, Thorndyke stepped over to the dressing-chest and pulled out the drawers, one after another. Finding them all empty, he transferred his attention to a suit-case that rested on a trunk-stand. It proved to be locked, but the lock was an artless affair which soon yielded to a small key from Mr. Brodribb's voluminous bunch.

"Nothing much there," the latter commented as he held up the lid and glanced disparagingly at a few collars and a couple of shirts which seemed to form the sole contents of the case. He was about to lower the lid when Thorndyke, with characteristic thoroughness, took out the collars and lifted the shirts. The result drew from our friend an exclamation of surprise; for the removal of the shirts brought into view some objects that had been--perhaps intentionally--concealed by them; a large and handsome gold watch and guard, a bunch of keys, a tie-pin, set with a single large pearl and one or two opened letters addressed to the missing man. The latter, Brodribb scanned eagerly and then replaced with an air of disappointment.

"Family letters," he explained. "Nothing in them that is of any use to us. But," he added, looking anxiously at Thorndyke, "this is a most extraordinary affair. Most alarming, too. It looks as if he had deliberately removed from his person everything of intrinsic value."

"Excepting the ring," Thorndyke interposed.

"True, excepting the ring. He may have forgotten that, unless he had intended to use it--to seal some document, for instance. But otherwise he seems to have jettisoned everything of value. I need not ask you what that suggests."

"No," Thorndyke replied, answering Brodribb's interrogative glance rather than his words. "Taking appearances at their face value one would infer that he was intending to go to some place where personal property is not very secure. That is the obvious suggestion, but there are other possibilities."

"So there may be," said Brodribb, "but I shall adopt the obvious suggestion until I see reason to change my mind. Sir Edward went from here to some place where, as you say, personal chattels are not very safe. And where a man's property is not safe his life is usually not safe either. What we have seen here, coupled with his disappearance, fills me with alarm, indeed with despair; for I fear that the danger, whatever it was, has already taken effect. This is the seventh day since he left here."

Thorndyke nodded gloomily. "I am afraid, Brodribb," he said, "that I can only agree with you. Still, whatever we may think or feel, there is only one thing to be done. We must go at once to Scotland Yard and put the authorities there in possession of all the facts that are known to us. This is essentially a police case. It involves the simultaneous search of a number of likely localities by men who know those localities and their inhabitants by heart."

Brodribb assented immediately to Thorndyke's suggestion, and when he had taken possession of the derelict valuables and given Mr. Northbrook a receipt for them, we shook hands with that gentleman and took our leave.

At Scotland Yard we had the rather unexpected good fortune to learn that our old friend, Superintendent Miller, was in the building, and, after a brief parley, we were conducted to his office. On our entrance, he greeted us collectively and motioned to the messenger to place chairs for us; then, regarding Thorndyke with a quizzical smile, he enquired: "Is this a deputation?"

"In a way," replied Thorndyke, "it is. My friend, here, Mr. Brodribb, whom you have met on some previous occasions, has come to ask for your assistance in regard to a client of his who is missing."

"Anyone I know?" enquired Miller.

"Sir Edward Hardcastle of Bradstow in Kent," Brodribb replied.

The Superintendent shook his head. "I don't think I have ever heard the name," said he. "However, we will see what can be done, if you will give us the necessary particulars."

He laid a sheet of paper on the desk before him, and, taking up his fountain pen, looked interrogatively at Brodribb.

"I think," said the latter, "you had better hear the whole story first and then take down the particulars. Or I could supply you with a full account in writing, which would save time just now."

"Yes," Miller agreed, "that would be the best plan," but nevertheless he held his pen in readiness and jotted down a note from time to time as Brodribb proceeded with his narrative. But he made no comments and asked no questions until that narrative was concluded, listening with the closest attention and obviously with the keenest professional interest.

"Well," he exclaimed, as Brodribb concluded, "that is a queer story, and the queerest part of it is that sealed letter. I can make nothing of that. It may be some odd chance or it may be a practical joke. But there is an unpleasant air of purpose about it. We can hardly believe that Sir Edward sealed the letter; and if he didn't, his ring was in someone else's possession. If it was, it may have been lost and picked up or it may have been stolen. There's an alarming lot of 'ifs' in this case. Do you know anything about Sir Edward's habits?"

"Not a great deal," replied Brodribb. "He is a quiet, studious man, rather solitary and reserved."

"Not in the habit of attending race meetings?"

"I should say not."

"Nor addicted to slumming?"

"No. I believe he spends most of his time at his place in Kent, and, apart from books, I think his principal interest is gardening."

"Ha!" said Miller. "Well, that leaves us pretty much in the dark. If a man was proposing to attend a race meeting, he might naturally leave his more valuable portable property at home; and the same if he was bound on some expedition into the slums, or if he expected to be in some sort of rough crowd. At any rate, the fact remains that he did turn out his pockets before starting from the club, so we can take it that he had in view the possibility of his getting into some shady company. We shall have to find out a bit more about his habits. What is this butler man, Weeks, like?"

"A most intelligent, conscientious, responsible man. He could probably tell you more about Sir Edward's habits than anyone. Would you like him to come and see you?"

"We've got to see him," Miller replied, "to fill in details, but I think it would be better for one of our men--unless I can manage it myself--to go down and see him at the house. You see, we shall want a full description of the missing man and at least one photograph, if we can get it. And we may want to go over his clothes and hats for private marks and Bertillon measurements."

"For Bertillon measurements!" exclaimed Brodribb. "But I thought you required the most minute accuracy for them."

"So you do if you can get it," replied Miller. "But, you see, the system depends on what we may call multiple agreements, like circumstantial evidence. It isn't a question of one or two accurate measurements but of the coincidence of a large number with no disagreements. If we should find an unrecognisable body with legs and forearms, thighs and upper arms about the same length as Sir Edward's; and if the chest and waist measurements were about the same as his and if the head would fit his hats, the hands would fit his gloves and the feet would fit his boots, and if there was no disagreement in any one measurement, then we should have established a very strong probability that the body was his body. It is surprising how much information an experienced man can get from clothes. Of course, I am speaking of clothes that have been worn and that have creases that mark the position of the joints. But even new clothes will tell you quite a lot."

"Will they really?" said Brodribb, in a slightly shocked tone--for, despite his expressed pessimism, he was hardly prepared to consider his client in the character of a body. "I can understand their use for comparison with those on the--er--person, but I should not have expected them to furnish measurements of scientific value. However, I think you have Weeks's address?"

"Yes, and I will just jot down one or two particulars--dates, for instance."

He did so; and when he had finished, as our business seemed to be concluded, we thanked him for his interest in the case and rose to depart. As we moved towards the door, Brodribb turned to make a last enquiry.

"Would it be admissible to ask if you think there is a reasonable chance of your being able to trace my missing client?"

Miller reflected awhile, assisting the process of cogitation by gently scratching the back of his head. "Well, Mr. Brodribb," he replied, at length, "I'm like the doctor, I'm not fond of guessing. The position is that this gentleman is either alive or dead. If he is dead, his body must be lying somewhere and it is pretty certain to come to light before very long. If he is alive, the matter is not so simple, for he must be keeping out of sight intentionally; and as he is not known to any of our people, he might be straying about a long time before he was recognised and reported. But I can promise you that everything that is possible shall be done. When we have got a good photograph and a description, they will be circulated among the police in all likely districts and instructions issued for a sharp look-out to be kept. That is about all that we can do. I suppose you would not care for us to publish the photograph and description?"

"I don't think it would be advisable," Brodribb replied. "If he should, after all, return to his club, it would be so extremely unpleasant for him--and for me. Later, it may be necessary, but for the present, the less fuss that we make, the better."

The Superintendent was disposed to agree with this view; and when Brodribb had once more promised to send full written particulars with a special impression of the missing seal, we finally took our departure.

CHAPTER IV:

MR. BRODRIBB'S PERPLEXITIES

(Dr. Jervis's Narrative)

DURING the next few weeks we saw a good deal of Mr. Brodribb; indeed, his visits to our chambers became so frequent, and he became so acutely conscious of their frequency, that he was reduced to the most abject apologies for thus constantly intruding on our privacy. But we always received him with the warmest of welcomes, not only for the sake of our long-standing friendship but because we both realised that the warm-hearted old lawyer was passing through a period of heavy tribulation. For Mr. Brodribb took his responsibilities as a family solicitor very seriously. To him, the clients whose affairs he managed were as his own family, their welfare and their interests took precedence over every other consideration and their property was as precious and sacred as if it had been his own.

Hence, as the time ran on and no tidings of the missing man came to hand, the usually jovial old fellow grew more and more worried and depressed. It was not only the suspense of waiting for news that kept his nerves on edge, but the foreboding that when the tidings should at last come they would be tidings of tragedy and horror. Nor even was this all; for, presently, it began to transpire that there were further causes of anxiety.

From chance phrases of rather ambiguous import we inferred that the baronet's disappearance bade fair to create a situation of some difficulty from the legal point of view; but as to the nature of the difficulties we were unable to judge until a certain evening when Brodribb at last unburdened himself of his anxieties and entered into explicit particulars. I do not think that he started with the intention of going into details, but the matter arose naturally in the course of conversation.

"I suppose," he began, "we could hardly expect to keep this horrible affair to ourselves, but I had rather hoped that we might have avoided scandal and gossip, at least until something of legitimate public interest occurred."

"And haven't we?" asked Thorndyke.

"No. There has been a leakage of information somewhere. Police, I suspect, unless it was someone at the club. It would hardly be Northwood, though, for he was more anxious than any of us to keep the affair dark. Anyhow, a notice of the disappearance has got into at least one newspaper."

"Which newspaper was it?"

"Ah, that is what I have been unable to ascertain. The way in which I became aware of it was this: a man--a relative of Sir Edward's and an interested party--called on me a day or two ago to make enquiries. He said that he had heard a rumour that Sir Edward was missing and wished to know if there was any truth in it. I asked him where he heard the rumour and he said that he had seen some obscure reference to the matter in one of the evening papers, but he couldn't remember which paper it was. I pressed him to try to remember for it struck me as most remarkable that he should have forgotten the name of the paper, he being, as I have said, an interested party. I should have expected him to preserve the paper or at least have cut out the paragraph. But he persisted that he had no idea whatever as to what paper it was."

"It was, as you say, rather odd," commented Thorndyke. "If it isn't an indiscreet question, in what respect and to what extent was he an interested party?"

"In a very vital respect," replied Brodribb. "He thinks that he is the heir presumptive."

"And do I understand that you think otherwise?"

"No. I am afraid I am disposed to agree with him. But I am not going to commit myself. Meanwhile he shows signs of being damned troublesome. He is not going to let the grass grow under his feet. He began to throw out hints of an application to the court for leave to presume death; which is preposterous at this stage."

"Quite," Thorndyke agreed. "But, of course, if Sir Edward doesn't presently turn up, alive or dead, that is what you will have to do; and having regard to the circumstances, the Court would probably be prepared to consider the application after a comparatively short period."

"So it might," Brodribb retorted, doggedly. "But he will have to make the application himself; and if he does, I shall contest it."

Here he suddenly shut himself up, dipping his fine old nose reflectively into his wineglass and fixing a thoughtful eye on the empty fireplace. But somehow, his abrupt silence conveyed to me in some subtle manner the impression that he would not be unwilling to be questioned further. Nor was I mistaken; for, after a pause, during which neither Thorndyke nor I had made any comment, he broke the silence with the remark: "But I've no business to come here boring you two fellows with a lot of shop talk--and my own private shop at that."

"Indeed!" said Thorndyke. "Are we then of no account? I rather thought that we were to some extent concerned in the case and that, to that extent, we might regard your shop as our shop."

"He knows that perfectly well, old humbug that he is," said I. "And he knows that nothing but our superlative good manners has restrained us from demanding full particulars."

Mr. Brodribb smiled genially and emptied his glass.

"Of course," said he, "if you are so polite as to express an actual interest in the civil aspects of the case I shall take you at your word. It will be very helpful to me to talk matters over with you, though I really hardly know where to begin."

"You might begin," said Thorndyke, "by filling your glass. The decanter is on your side. Then you might tell us what your objections are to this claimant, whom you admit to be the heir presumptive."

"I don't admit anything of the kind," protested Brodribb as he filled his glass and pushed the decanter across the table. "I merely agree that his claim appears, at the moment to be quite a good and well-founded one."

"I don't see much difference," said I, "between an heir presumptive and a claimant with a well-founded claim. But never mind. You object to the gentleman for some reason. Tell us why you object to him."

Brodribb considered the question for a while. At length he replied:

"I think, if you are really interested in the state of affairs, it would be best for me to give you a short sketch of the family history and the relationships. Then you will understand my position and my point of view. I need not go back in detail beyond Sir Edward's father, Sir Julian Hardcastle.

"Sir Julian had two sons, Edward and Gervase. As the estate is settled in tail male, we can ignore the female members of the family. On Sir Julian's death, Edward, the elder, succeeded; and as he was already married and had one son, the succession was, for the time being, satisfactorily settled. The younger son, Gervase, married his cousin, Phillipa, a daughter of Sir Julian's brother William. There was a good deal of opposition to the marriage, but the young people were devoted to one another and in the end they made a run-away match of it."

"Was the opposition due to the near kinship of the parties?" I asked.

"Partly, no doubt. There is a very general prejudice against the marriage of first cousins. But the principal objection of the young lady's people was to Gervase, himself. It seems--for I never saw her--that Miss Phillipa was an extremely beautiful and attractive girl who might have been expected to make a brilliant marriage, whereas Gervase was a younger son with very little in the way of expectations. However, that might have passed. The real trouble was that Gervase had acquired some bad habits when he was up at Oxford and he hadn't shaken them off. Plenty of young fellows tend to overdo the libations to Bacchus during their undergraduate days. But it is usually mere youthful expansiveness which passes off safely when they come down from the 'Varsity and take up their adult responsibilities. Unfortunately, it was not so with Gervase. Conviviality passed into chronic intemperance. He became a confirmed drinker, though not an actual drunkard.

"I may as well finish with him, so far as his history is known to me, as that history complicates the present position. I may have given the impression that he was a waster, but he was not, by any means. He was a queer fellow in many respects, but, apart from his tippling habits, there was nothing against him. And he must have had considerable abilities, for I understand that he not only graduated with distinction but was reputed the most brilliant classical scholar of his year. In fact he became a Fellow of his college and after his marriage I believe he took Orders, though he remained at Oxford in some teaching capacity. I don't know much of his affairs at this time. It wasn't my business, and Sir Edward did not talk much about him; but so far as I can gather, his career at the University came to a sudden and disastrous end. Something happened, I don't know what it was but I suspect that he got drunk under circumstances that created a public scandal. At any rate he was deprived of his Fellowship and had to leave Oxford; and from that time, with a single exception, all trace of him is lost--at least to me. But he must have felt his disgrace acutely for it is clear that he cut himself off entirely from his family and went virtually into hiding on the continent."

"What about his wife?" I asked.

"She certainly went with him into exile, and though she never communicated with her family at this time, I think there is no doubt that, in spite of all his faults, she remained devoted to him. That appears plainly in connection with the single reappearance which I mentioned, of which I heard indirectly from Sir Edward. It seems that a friend of the family who had known Gervase at Oxford, came across him by chance in Paris; and from his account of the meeting it would seem that the poor fellow was in a very sad way. His appearance suggested abject poverty and his manner was that of a man who had received some severe shock. He had a bewildered air and seemed to be only partially conscious of what was going on around him. He gave no account of himself in any respect save one; which was that he had lost his wife some time previously, but he did not say when or where she died. He did not seem to have any distinct ideas as to place or time. The fact of his loss appeared to occupy his thoughts to the exclusion of everything else. In short, he was the mere wreck of a man.

"The friend--whose name I forget, if I ever knew it--had some idea of helping him and trying to get him into touch with his family; but before he could make any move, Gervase had disappeared. As he had given no hint as to his place of abode, no search for him was possible; and so this unfortunate man passes out of our ken. The only further news we got of him was contained in a notice in the obituary column of The Times some twelve months later which recorded his death at Brighton. No address was given, and, I am sorry to say, neither Sir Edward nor I made any enquiries at the time. I cut the notice out and put it with the papers relating to the estate, and there, for the time being the matter ended."

"There was no doubt that the notice really referred to him?" Thorndyke asked.

"No. He was described as 'The Reverend Gervase Hardcastle, M.A. (so apparently he had taken orders), formerly Fellow of Balliol College, Oxford,' and his age was correctly given. No, I think there can be no doubt that the notice referred to him. Of course, I ought to have looked into the matter and got all the particulars; but at the time Sir Edward's son and wife were both alive and well, so it looked as if there were no chance of any question arising with regard to the succession."

"It is not known, I suppose," said Thorndyke, "whether Gervase had any children?"

"No. There were no children up to the time when he left England. But it is possible that some may have been born abroad. But if so, since we have no knowledge whatever as to where he lived during his wanderings and don't even know in what country his wife died, we have no date on which to base any enquiries. As a matter of fact, both Sir Edward and I assumed that, at least, there was no son, for if there had been, we should almost certainly have received some communication from him after Gervase's death. That was what we assumed, but of course we ought not to have left it at that. But now we had better pursue the course of events.

"Gervase's death, as recorded in The Times, occurred sixteen years ago. Six years later, Sir Edward lost both his wife and his son--his only child--within a few days. A malignant form of influenza swept through the house and brought Sir Edward, himself, to the very verge of the grave. When he at length rose from his bed, it was to find himself a childless widower. This altered the position radically, and, of course, we ought to have made such enquiries as would have cleared up the question of the succession. But Sir Edward was, for the time, so broken by his bereavements that I hardly liked to trouble him about a matter which had ceased to be his personal concern, and on the few occasions when I raised the question, I found him quite uninterested. His view was that there was nothing to discuss; and assuming, as he did, that Gervase had died without issue (in which assumption I concurred) he was right. In that case, the heir presumptive was undoubtedly his cousin Paul, Phillipa's brother; and as Paul Hardcastle was an entirely eligible successor, Sir Edward made a fresh will bequeathing to him the bulk of his personal property.

"That was the position ten years ago. But four years ago Paul Hardcastle died, leaving only one child, a daughter some twelve years of age. Once more the position was altered; for, now, Sir Edward's near kin were exhausted and the new heir presumptive was a comparatively distant cousin--a grandson of Sir Julian's uncle, one David Hardcastle. On this, Sir Edward revoked his will and made another, by which about three quarters of his personal property goes to Paul Hardcastle's daughter, in trust until she shall reach the age of twenty-one and thereupon absolutely. The remaining fourth, apart from certain legacies, goes to the heir of the estate, that is to David Hardcastle."

"And supposing the young lady should die during her minority?" Thorndyke enquired.

"Then the property goes to the heir to the title and estate."

"Does the personal property amount to anything considerable?

"Yes, it is very considerable indeed. Sir Edward came into a comfortable sum when he succeeded, and his wife was a lady of some means; and he has been an excellent manager--almost unduly thrifty--so there have been substantial accumulations during his time. Roughly, the personalty will be not less than a hundred thousand pounds."

"That," I remarked, "leaves some twenty-five thousand for the heir to the title. He won't have much to complain of."

"No," growled Brodribb, "but I expect he will complain, all the same. In fact, he has complained already. He thinks that the whole of the money should have gone to the heir to enable him to support his position in suitable style."

"So," said I, "we may take it that the gentleman who called on you was Mr. David Hardcastle?"

"You may," replied Brodribb.

"And we may further take it that the said David is not exactly the apple of your eye."

"I am afraid you may. It is all wrong, I know, for me to allow my likes and dislikes to enter into the matter. But I have acted for Sir Edward and for Sir Julian before him, and my father acted for Sir Julian and his father, Sir Henry, so that it is only natural that I should have a deep personal sentiment in regard to the family and the estate."

"Which," said I, "brings us back to the original question; What is the matter with David Hardcastle?"

Brodribb pondered the question, consciously controlling, as I suspect, his naturally peppery temper. But with no great success, for he, at length, burst out: "I can't trust myself to say what I feel about him. Everything is the matter. He is a changeling, a misfit, an outlander. He doesn't match the rest of the family at all. The Hardcastles, as I have known them, have been typical English landed gentry; straight-going, honourable men who lived within their income and paid their way and did their duty justly and even generously to their tenants.

"Now this man is a different type altogether. His appearance and manner suggest a flash bookmaker rather than a country gentleman. My gorge rose at him as soon as I clapped eyes on him, and I don't fancy I was any too civil. Which was a tactical mistake, under the circumstances."

"Is he a man of independent means," asked Thorndyke, "or does he do anything for a living?"

"I have never heard that he has any means," replied Brodribb, "and I do know that he is occasionally in pretty low water, for there are several loans from Sir Edward outstanding against him. As to his occupation, God knows what it is. I should say he is a sort of cosmopolitan adventurer, always on the move, prowling about the continental watering-places, living on his wits, or the deficiency of other people's. A distinctly shady customer in my opinion. And there is another thing. In the course of his travels he has picked up a foreign wife; a Russian woman of some sort--may be a Jewess for all I know."

"What an inveterate old John Bull it is," chuckled Thorndyke. "But we mustn't be too insular, you know, Brodribb. There are plenty of most estimable and charming Russian ladies; and even if she should be a Jewess, surely you would not deny that she would belong to a very distinguished and gifted race."

Brodribb grunted. "The Lady of Bradstow," said he, "should be an English lady, not a Russian or a Jewess. Besides, this person is not an estimable and charming lady, as you express it. She had to hop out of Russia mighty sharp in consequence of some political rumpus--and you know what that means in that part of the world. And a brother of hers was I believe, actually tried and convicted."

"Still," I urged, "political offences are not--"

"Are not what?" interrupted Brodribb. "I am surprised at you, Jervis, a member of the English Bar, condoning crime. A lawyer should revere the law above everything. No, sir, crime is crime. A man who would compass the death of a Tsar would murder anyone else if it served his purpose."

"At any rate," said Thorndyke, "we may sympathise with your distaste for the present claimant; but, as you say, your feeling as to his suitability or unsuitability for the position is beside the mark. The only question is as to the soundness of his claim. And that question is not urgent at the moment."

"No," agreed Brodribb, "not at this moment. But it may become urgent in twenty-four hours. And this fellow thinks that the question is settled already. As he talked to me in my office, his manner was that of the heir just waiting to step into possession."

"By the way," said Thorndyke, "I understand that he knows exactly how Sir Edward has disposed of the personal estate. How did he come by that knowledge?"

"Sir Edward gave him all the particulars as to the provisions of the will. He thought it the fair thing to do, though it seemed to me rather unnecessary."

"It was the kind thing to do," said I. "It will have saved him a rather severe disappointment. But what are you going to do if he shows signs of undue activity?"

"What the deuce can I do?" demanded Brodribb "That is the question that is worrying me. I have no locus standi; and the beggar knows it. Practically told me so."

"But," I objected, "you are Sir Edward's man of business and his executor."

"I shall be the executor," Brodribb corrected, "when Sir Edward dies or his death is proved or presumed. So long as he remains alive, in a legal sense, my powers as an executor have not come into being. On the other hand, my position as his solicitor gives me no authority to act without his instructions. I hold no power of attorney. In his absence I have really no locus standi at all. Of course, if he does not turn up, alive or dead, some arrangements will have to be made for administering the estate and carrying on generally. But the application for powers to do that will be made by the legally interested party--the heir presumptive."

"And supposing," said I, "Sir Edward should be proved to be dead--say by the finding of his body--your powers as the executor of the will would then come into being. In that capacity, would you accept David Hardcastle as the heir?"

Mr. Brodribb regarded me speculatively for some moments before replying. At length he said with quiet emphasis, and speaking very deliberately: "No, I should not--as matters stand at present." He paused, still with his eyes fixed on me, and then continued. "A very curious thing has happened. After my interview with Mr. David, realising that the question of the succession might become acute at any moment, I did what I ought to have done long ago. I set to work to clear up the circumstances of Gervase's death and to try to settle the question as to whether there had been any issue of the marriage, and, if so, whether there could possibly be a son living. I began by looking up that cutting from The Times that I told you about. As I mentioned to you, no address was given. But there was the date; and with that I thought I should have no difficulty in getting a copy of the death certificate, on which, of course, the address would be stated, and at that address it might be possible to start some enquiries.

"Accordingly, off I went to Somerset House and proceeded to look up the register of deaths for that date. To my astonishment, the name was not there. Thinking that, perhaps, a wrong date had been given, I looked up and down the entries for a week or two before and after the given date. But there was no sign of the name of Gervase Hardcastle. Then I settled down to make a thorough search, beginning ten years before the date and going on ten years after. But still there was no sign of the name. I noted one or two other Hardcastles and got copies of the certificates corresponding to the entries, but the particulars showed them all to relate to strangers.

"Then I went down to Brighton and personally called upon the local registrars and got them to overhaul their records. But the result was the same in all the cases. There was no record of the death of Gervase Hardcastle. Now what do you make of that?"

"Mighty little," said Thorndyke. "Apparently, the notice in The Times was a false notice, but why it should have been inserted it is difficult to guess."

"Unless," I suggested, "he was living under an assumed name and that name was given to the registrar, the true name being published for the information of the family."

Thorndyke shook his head. "I don't think that will do, Jervis," said he. "The person who sent the notice to The Times knew his proper name, age and description. There is no imaginable reason why a person having that knowledge should give a false name to the registrar, and there are the best of reasons why he should not."

"Is it possible," I suggested, "that he may have committed suicide and sent off the notice himself before completing the job?

"It is possible, of course," replied Thorndyke, "but, in the absence of any positive fact indicating the probability of its having occurred, the mere possibility is not worth considering."

"No," agreed Brodribb, "it is of no use guessing. The important truth that emerges is that his death, which has been accepted all these years by the family as an established fact, has now become extremely doubtful. At any rate, there is no legal evidence that he is dead. No court would entertain a mere obituary notice unsupported by any corresponding entry in the register of deaths. Legally speaking, Gervase is presumably still living, and it is not at all improbable that he is actually alive."

"Then, in that case," said I, "why do you say that David has a good claim to be the heir?"

"Because he is here and visible--extremely visible; whereas the very existence of Gervase is problematical. David's claim is good unless it is contested by Gervase. In Gervase's absence, I think David would have no difficulty in taking possession. Who could oppose him? If I did, as executor (and I think I should have a try), the probability is that his claim would be admitted, subject to the chance that Gervase or his heir might come forward later and endeavour to oust him."

"And meanwhile?" asked Thorndyke.

"Meanwhile, I propose setting on foot some enquiries by which I hope to be able to pick up some trace of Gervase on the Continent. It isn't a very hopeful task, I must admit."

"I can't imagine any less hopeful task," said I, "than searching for a man who has been lost to sight for over sixteen years, who was probably living under an assumed name and whose place of abode at any time is utterly unknown. I don't see how you are going to start."

"I am not very clear, myself," Brodribb admitted; and with this, as it was now growing late, he rose, and, having gathered up his hat and stick, shook our hands despondently and took his departure.

CHAPTER V:

FINE FEATHERS MAKE FINE BIRDS

(Jasper Gray's Narrative)

THE providence that doth shape our ends is apt to do so by methods so unobtrusive as entirely to escape our notice. Passively we float on the quiet stream of events with no suspicion as to whither we are being carried until at last we are thrown up high and dry on the shore of our destiny, the mere jetsam of unnoted circumstances.

When I drew up my truck at the shabby door of a studio in a mews near Fitzroy Square and pulled the bell-handle no intelligible message was borne to me by the tintinnabulation from within; nor, when the door was opened by a pleasant-faced grey-haired woman in a blue overall, did I recognise the chief arbiter--or shall I say arbitress?--of my fate. I merely pulled off my cap and said: "A roll of paper, madam, from Sturt and Wopsalls."

"Oh, I'm glad you've come," she said. "Shall I help you to carry it in?"

"Thank you, madam," I replied, "but I think I can manage without troubling you."

It was an unwieldy roll of cartoon paper, six feet long and uncommonly heavy. But I was used to handling ponderous and unshapely packages, and I got the roll on my shoulder without difficulty. The lady preceded me down a passage and into a great, bare studio, where, according to directions, I laid the roll down on the floor in a corner.

"You seem to be very strong," the lady remarked.

"I'm pretty strong, thank you, madam," I answered; adding that I got a good deal of exercise.

Here a second lady, rather younger than the first, turned from her easel to look at me.

"I wonder if he would help us to move that costume chest," she said.

I expressed my willingness to do anything that would be of service to them; and being shown the chest, a huge box-settle with an upholstered top, I skilfully coaxed it along the bare floor to the place by the wall that had been cleared for it.

"Would you like a glass of lemonade?" the elder lady asked when she had thanked me.

I accepted gratefully, for it was a hot day; though, for that matter, I believe a healthy boy of seventeen would drink lemonade with pleasure at the North Pole. Accordingly a glass jug and a tumbler were placed on a little table by the settle and I was invited to sit down and refresh at my leisure; which I did, staring about me meanwhile with the lively curiosity proper to my age. It was a great barn of a place with rough, white washed walls, which were, however, mostly covered with large paper cartoons, on which life-size figure subjects were broadly sketched in charcoal. There were also a number of smaller studies of heads and limbs and some complete figures--complete, that is to say, excepting as to their clothing; and the strangely aboriginal state of these, even allowing for the heat of the weather, occasioned profound speculations on my part.

As I sat sipping the lemonade and gaping at the pictures with serene enjoyment, the two ladies conversed in low tones and disjointed scraps of their conversation reached my ears, though I tried not to listen.

"Yes" (this was the elder lady), "and not only so handsome but so exactly the correct type. And a rare type, too. Even the colouring is absolutely perfect."

"Yes," agreed the other; "it is typical. So clean-cut, refined and symmetrical. A little severe, but all the better for that; and really quite distinguished--quite distinguished."

Here I happened to glance at the ladies and was dismayed to find them both looking very attentively at me. I blushed furiously. Could they be talking about me? It seemed impossible. Sturt and Wopsall's parcels-boy could hardly be described as a distinguished person. But it almost seemed as if they were, for the elder lady said with an engaging smile: "We want to see how you would look in a wig. Would you mind trying one on?"

This was a staggerer, but of course I didn't mind. It was rather a "lark" in fact. And when the lady produced from a cupboard a golden wig with long ringlets, I sniggered shyly and allowed her to put it on my head. The two women looked at me with their heads on one side and then at one another.

"It's the very thing, you know," said the younger lady.

The other nodded, and, addressing me, said: "Would you just frown a little and put on a rather haughty expression?"

Needless to say, I grinned like a Cheshire cat, and, a heroic effort to control my features only ended in violent giggles. The two ladies smiled good-humouredly, and the elder said, in a wheedling tone:

"I wonder if you would do me a very great favour."

"I would if I could," was my prompt and natural reply.

"It is this," she continued. "I am painting a picture of an incident in the French Revolution to be called 'An Aristocrat at Bay'. I suppose you have heard of the French Revolution?"

I had. In fact I had read Carlyle's work on the subject--and didn't think much of it--and the "Tale of Two Cities" which I had found greatly superior.

"Very well," my new friend went on, "then I will show you the sketch for the picture;" and she led me to a great easel with a handle like that of a barrel-organ, on which was a large canvas with a sheet of cartoon paper pinned on it. The sketch, which was roughly put in with charcoal and tinted in parts with an occasional smear of pastel or wash of water-colour, showed a lady standing in a doorway at the top of a flight of steps around the foot of which surged a crowd of revolutionaries.

"My difficulty," the lady continued, "is this. I have got a model for the figure of the Aristocrat but I can't get a suitable model for the head. Now you happen to suit perfectly and the question is, will you let me paint the head from you?"

"But it's a woman!" I protested.

That lady knew something about boys. "I know," she said; "but a man would do as well if he was clean-shaved and wore a wig. You will say yes, now, won't you? Of course it is a business arrangement. You will be paid for your time."

Eventually it was settled that I should sit from six to eight every morning--I wasn't due at the warehouse until half-past eight--and breakfast in the studio afterwards. I didn't much like this latter arrangement for Pontifex and I always breakfasted together and the old gentleman would miss me. My employer suggested that he should come to breakfast too; but this would not do. Poor old Ponty would have pawned my boots if the whisky had run short, but he took no favours from strangers. However, my salary was to be twelve shillings a week, Sunday sittings to be extra pro rata, and that would have to compensate. I agreed to the terms and the arrangement was fixed.

"Your hair is rather long," said my employer. "Would you mind having it cut short, so as to let the wig set more closely?"

Would I mind! For, twelve shillings a week I would have had my head shaved and painted in green and red stripes. As a matter of fact I went that very evening to a barber and made him trim me until my head looked like a ball of brown plush. Which must have made Providence wink the eye that was fixed on my destiny.

The sittings--or rather standings--began two days later, when I took up my pose on the model's throne, rigged out in the full costume of a royalist lady and an aristocrat; my first appearance in either character. After the sitting we all had breakfast in a corner of the studio, and the two ladies crammed me until I was ready to burst with nourishment and gratitude. They were dear women. I loved them both from the very beginning, with a slight preference, perhaps, for my employer, Miss Vernet; though, to be sure, the younger lady, Miss Brandon, was a lovable creature, too. But I must not linger on their perfections. Reluctantly I must leave them for a while to relate a most singular adventure that arose in part out of my employment by them.

It was, I think, on the day of my fourth sitting that I had a stroke of luck; a parcel--and not a very large one, either--to deliver to a bibliophile who kept a private press somewhere out Tottenham way and close to the river Lea. It was virtually a day's holiday with a railway fare thrown in, and I set forth jubilantly with the parcel on my shoulder, whistling an operatic air as I went. The train bore me luxuriously to Black Horse Road Station, I found the house of the bibliophile, delivered my parcel, a then, free as air, struck out across the fields towards the river.

Along the shallow, winding stream that runs parallel to the 'Lea Navigation' I wandered with the ecstatic delight of the thoroughbred Londoner in rural scenes, be they never so homely. It was a day of wonders. I had hardly ever been in the country before and this mere suburb--though it was more rural then than now--gave to my urban eyes a veritable glimpse of Paradise. I looked into the few inches of running water and saw actual fish. I watched an angler and saw him land, with elaborate artifice, what looked like a piece of cheese. For the first time in my life I looked upon a living frog and chased it to its lair under the bank. And then I came on a group of urchins, disporting themselves, as naked as cherubim, in the shallows; and Providence closed its left eye firmly.

It was a roasting day. Those urchins were certainly naked and wet and probably cool. How delicious! And why not? There was no one about, and there was plenty of cover. Five minutes later I had shed my garments beside a willow bush and was lying on my stomach in four inches of water making frantic efforts to swim.

I waded joyfully up the stream, sometimes almost knee-deep, and impersonated characters suitable to the scenery. Now I was some sort of Indian and impaled fish--which weren't there--with an imaginary barbed spear. There I discovered a curious lurking-place under a large pollard and between two clumps of willow-bush; and forthwith I tucked myself into it, becoming instantly--as I persuaded myself--invisible to mortal eyes. I was now an Indian no longer. My role had changed to that of some unclassified species of water-sprite; at least I think so, though I am not quite clear; for the fact is that, at this moment, a nursemaid with two children hove in sight on the bank facing me, and, having sauntered along with exasperating slowness, finally sat down exactly opposite my hiding-place and produced a novelette which she began to read with much composure and satisfaction.

I watched her balefully; and I watched the children. Especially, I watched the children. And meanwhile I sat up to my hips in water, finding it delightfully cool and shady beneath the pollard.

The minutes wore on. It was still cool. Surprisingly so, considering the heat of the sun outside. In fact my teeth presently began to chatter slightly and an urgent desire to sample the sunshine once more made itself felt. But there I was, and there I must stay until the young lady opposite moved on; for I was a modest youth with a rather exaggerated notion of the delicacy of young women. And, after all, the situation was of my own making.

At last, one of the children observed me and pointed me out with a yell of ecstasy. "Oh! Look, Nanny! What's that hiding in the water over there?

"It's nothing, dear," replied Nanny, without raising her eyes from her novelette; "only a frog."

"But it looks like a man," the young viper protested.

"I know, dear. They do," and Nanny went on serenely with her reading.

The child was evidently dissatisfied and continued to stare at me with large, devouring eyes, and was presently joined by his fellow demon. But now a new object appeared, to divert their attention and mine. A man came along the bank just behind them, walking quickly and breaking now and again, into a shambling trot. I watched him at first without special interest; but when he had passed, and a back view was presented, I found myself viewing him with suddenly-awakened curiosity. What first attracted my attention was a patch in the rear of his trousers. For my own trousers had a precisely similar patch: I had sewn it in myself, so I knew it thoroughly. It was an extraordinary coincidence. The two patches were identical in shape and colour, but more than this; the pattern of the man's trousers was absolutely the same as the pattern of mine. There could be no doubt about it. They were made from the same piece; or else--Yes! The horrible conviction forced itself on me--they were my trousers!

But that was not all. A glance at the coat, Yea! and even the cap, revealed familiar traits. The fellow was walking off in my clothes!

For a brief space, modesty, anger and chilly horror struggled for mastery; and in that interval the man disappeared over a fence. Then modesty was "outed" and I stood up. The children howled with joy; the nursemaid bounced up and retreated, making audible references to a "disgusting creature," and I ran splashing through the shallows towards the spot where I had undressed. For it was fairly certain that the man had not come to this place unclothed. He must have left some sort of exuvium in place of mine. But if the exchange had been worth his while--well! my expectations expressed themselves in a premonitory impulse to scratch myself, for whatever the clothes were like, I should have to put them on.

The reality turned out to be better and worse than my anticipations. The clothes were good enough; better than mine, in fact, though the colour--a dusty buff--was disagreeable. But it was the decoration that spoiled them. Some misguided person had covered them with a pattern that recalled the device on a bench mark. The broad arrow, to put it in a nutshell. My absent friend was a run-away convict.

I huddled the wretched garments on as quickly as I could, for I was chilled to the marrow; and as I stood up in that livery of shame, I was sensible of a subtle influence that exhaled from it, impelling me to skulk in unfrequented places and to sneak from cover to cover. Of course the mistake could be explained if I was arrested; but I didn't want to be arrested. I was safer at large. The better plan was to get home if possible, or make for Sturt and Wopsalls, where I was known. But how was I to get home? My return ticket was in the pocket of the vanished trousers in company with a clasp-knife and eighteen-pence, and miles of town lay between me and safety.

I crept stealthily round the meadows away from the river, keeping under the cover of hedges and fences and reviewing anxiously my chances of escape, which seemed hopelessly remote. Ahead of me, near the side of a meadow, were a couple of hayricks, like enormous loaves; and the narrow space between their ends looked a likely place in which to conceal myself while I thought over my plans. Accordingly I crept along under the hedge until I was opposite the ricks, when I dashed out across the open, darted into the space between the ricks, and nearly fell over a man who was lying there smoking a pipe.

"I beg your pardon," I stammered. "I didn't know you were here."

"Don't mention it," he replied suavely. "If I'd expected yer I'd ha' told the footman to announce yer." He sat up, and, regarding me attentively, asked: "And how goes it? Doin' a bit of a skyboozle I guess?" I assented vaguely, not being perfectly clear as to the nature of a skyboozle, and he then enquired: "How did yer git out o' the jug?"

"I didn't get out at all. I wasn't ever in."

"Lor!" he exclaimed. "Wasn't yer? Where did yer git them pretty clothes from?"

I described the disastrous circumstances of the exchange and he listened to my story with a foxy smile.

"Well I'm blowed!" was his comment. "What bloomin' impidence, to take and prig a young gentleman's clothes. I call it actially rude. And he seems to 'ave cut yer 'air, too. He oughtn't to 'a done that. He'll 'ave to be spoke to."

At this reference to my closely cropped hair, I started violently. That was an added danger that I had overlooked, and I was so much disturbed by it that I have no recollection of my friend's further remarks; only I know that they were few and brief, for he shortly rose, and, knocking out his pipe (against the rick), looked at me with profound attention.

"Well," he said, at length, "I must be movin' on or I shall be late for lunch. You'd best lay down 'ere and 'ave a good rest, 'cos you may have to make a bolt for it any minute, and the fresher you are the quicker you'll be able to leg it. So long."

With these words of sage advice, he turned and sauntered away with funereal slowness, looking back once or twice to see if I had profited by his counsel. I sat down--not where he had been lying--and when he looked back again and observed this, he nodded approvingly and changed his direction slightly, so that he passed out of view. But the influence of that livery of dishonour had made me wary. After waiting a few seconds, I crept on all fours to the corner of the rick and peeped round; and behold! my friend's pace was funereal no longer; he was running across the meadow like a slip-shod, disreputable hare. And I had no difficulty in guessing at his destination.

I let him get well out of sight and then I followed his example in the opposite direction. Skirting the adjoining meadow, I came to a hedge that bordered a by-road; and here I lurked awhile, for a van was approaching, though it was still some distance away, and I was afraid to cross the road until it had passed. I watched the vehicle wistfully as it drew nearer. Through the opening of the tilt I could see that it was empty, or nearly so; and, from the conduct of the driver, who lolled in the corner of his seat and chanted a popular ballad, I judged that he had finished his delivery and was homeward bound.

Nearer and nearer drew the van at a steady jog-trot. Now I could see the driver's face and hear the words of his song. I could also make out the tops of one or two cases--probably empties--rising above the back of his seat; and I crouched by a gap in the hedge, my heart thumping violently and my knees trembling. At last the van came rumbling by. I had a brief view of a familiar name and of the words "Theobald's Road" painted on the tilt, and it had passed.

I looked out of the gap. Besides the carter there was not a soul in sight. The tail-board of the van was up, its body was half empty, and the driver's back was towards me. In a moment I was out through the gap and padding along swiftly in my soft prison shoes after the van. I had my hands on the tail-board, I gave a light spring, remained poised for a moment on the edge, and then stealthily crawling over, crept silently into the space between two empty cases. For the moment I was saved.

The van rattled along and the driver, all unconscious of his passenger, carolled blithely. From my retreat I could see out at the back by peeping round a case, and so ascertain our direction; and I was somewhat alarmed presently to observe that the road took a sharp turn towards the place where the tramp had disappeared. This made me so uneasy that I risked craning up to look out through the front of the van; and when I did so, I got a most terrible shock. Far away along the road, but coming towards us, was a small crowd of men, and, as we mutually approached, I could make out at least one constable in uniform among them. A little nearer and I was able to recognise the tramp, walking by the constable and evidently acting as guide. I broke out into a cold perspiration. Would that constable stop the van and search it? It was quite possible; it was even likely. And again I craned up and peeped at my enemies.

We were getting quite near when the tramp stopped and pointed at the ricks, no doubt. Then he climbed over the fence that bordered the road. The constable followed him and the others followed the constable; and so they passed out of view.

But they came into sight again shortly from the back of the van, and now I could see the ricks, too. The crowd had deployed out into a long, curved line and were advancing, in the highest style of strategy, under the direction of the tramp and the constable. It reminded me of the formation of the Spanish Armada, as that great fleet swept up-channel. I didn't see the end of it. The line was still deploying out to encircle the rick when the van turned sharply and rumbled over a bridge. I was sorry to miss the denouement; but perhaps it was better so. After all, my business was to get clear away.

The van rumbled on at its quiet jog-trot and all seemed plain sailing. Through the northern suburbs and gradually into the town by way of Stamford Hill and Stoke Newington. And still all went well until we came out of the Essex Road and drew nigh unto the Angel at Islington; when the Devil entered into the carman and caused him to draw up by a public house and inspect the interior of the van.

Of course he saw me at once though I squeezed myself into the farthest corner between the cases, and with a sort of gruff reluctance, he ordered me to clear out.

I begged to be allowed to travel with him as far as Theobald's Road, and began to tender explanations; but he shook his head decidedly.

"I'd be in chokee myself if I let you," said he, "and I can't afford that with a wife and family to keep."

There was nothing more to be said. Reluctantly and with deep misgivings, I bundled out and began to walk away briskly along the crowded pavement. But I didn't get far. Before I had gone a hundred yards, two tall men who were walking towards me suddenly roused and, darting at me, seized me by the arms.

"Have you got a pair of darbies about you, Sims?" one of them asked the other. Fortunately Mr. Sims had not but suggested that "this young feller" did not look like giving trouble, whereupon, the two officers began to walk me along briskly in the direction of the Angel.

There was no lack of public recognition. I had already gathered quite a nice little following when I met the detectives, and my retinue increased so rapidly that before we reached the Angel we had become the centre of a hurrying hallooing crowd. At this point, my captors decided to cross the road.

Now the traffic about the cross roads by the Angel is usually pretty dense. On this occasion, I think it was denser than usual, and when our procession launched itself from the kerb, it reached a superlative degree of density. Vans, omnibuses, hansoms, all manner of vehicles slowed down that their drivers might get a better view of the man in motley. For the moment the roadway seemed to be completely choked with vehicles and foot-passengers, and from the closely-packed throng there arose a very babel of shouts and cheers. Thus we were standing in the road-way, jammed immovably, when above the universal uproar, rose a new sound; a thunderous rattle, jingling of small bells and a quick succession of shouts. The omnibuses, vans and hansoms began to back hurriedly towards the pavements, their drivers cheering lustily and flourishing their whips; the mob surged to and fro, a cloud of smoke and sparks arose behind them; there was a vision of gleaming brass helmets and of galloping horses bearing down apparently straight on us; the rattling, jingling and shouting swelled into a deafening roar, and the crowd surged away to the right and left.

"Look out, Sims!" yelled the other detective. "They'll be on top of us." He thrust his shoulder into the crowd and dragged me out of the track of the oncoming engine. The horses dashed by within a few inches; the rushing wheels grazed our very toes and still I kept a cool head. With eyes dazzled by the scarlet glare, the glitter of brass and the flying sparks, I watched for my chance and took it. As the shining boiler whizzed past, I made a quick snatch at the big brass rail that supports the foot-plate, and at the same moment, jumped forward. The sudden wrench nearly dislocated my arm; but it was a strong arm and I held on. The jerk whisked me clean out of the grasp of the two officers; I swung round behind the engine and, grabbing the engineer with my other hand, hauled myself on to the foot-plate. A single, instantaneous glance backward showed me two plain-clothes officers lying on their backs with their feet in the air. Of course they could not have maintained that position permanently, but I saw them only for the fraction of a second and that was how they appeared.

The engine rattled on. The coachman and his two satellites had naturally seen nothing; and the four men who sat back to back on the body of the engine also appeared to be unaware of my arrival though, oddly enough, they were all on the broad grin and their "Hi, hies!" tended at times to be tremulous. Even the engineer, whom I clasped fondly by the waist, seemed to be oblivious of my presence and stolidly shovelled coal into the little furnace.

We swept round the corner at the "Angel," and never shall I forget the way in which we thundered down Pentonville Hill with our brakes on and our horses at full gallop. I think I have never enjoyed anything so thoroughly. The engine skidded to and fro, the firemen yelled themselves purple, houses and lamp-posts flashed by and far ahead, even unto King's Cross, an expectant crowd awaited us with welcoming bellows. We passed through the narrow strait at the foot of the hill like a royal procession; our arrival was respectfully anticipated at the crossing by the Great Northern, and we thundered down the Euston Road between ranks of waiting omnibuses like the leaders in a chariot race. We were approaching Tottenham Court Road when the engineer observed placidly, apparently addressing his remark to the pressure gauge, that "there was such things as telegraph wires and it might be as well to hop off." I accepted the friendly hint, and as we turned into the latter thoroughfare I dropped from the foot-plate and made a bolt down Warren Street. The engine gave me a send-off, for it attracted so much attention that I was, at first, almost unnoticed; it was only when I had covered half the length of Warren Street, that juvenile and other loafers, deciding that a convict in the hand is worth two fire engines in the bush, turned to follow my fortunes, or misfortunes, as the case might be.

What manner of crowd it was that howled at my heels, I cannot say, for I did not look back. I was on familiar ground and I now had a definite objective. Miss Vernet's studio backed on a mews, and there was a large window which was usually left open. That was my port of salvation. Swiftly I zigzagged up and down the narrow streets, keeping my pursuers at a respectable distance, and gradually drawing nearer to the vicinity of the mews. At length I shot round the last corner and, diving into the entrance of the mews, padded furiously over the rough cobbles. The place was fortunately empty, for it was now late afternoon, and half-way down, the open window yawned hospitably. Setting my foot on a brick plinth, I sprang up, grasped the window-sill and shot in through the opening like a harlequin.

My arrival on all-fours on the studio floor was hailed by startled shrieks from my two friends who were hard at work at their easels. But, of course, they recognised me at once, and a few words of breathless explanation enabled them to grasp the state of affairs.

"Get into the dressing-room instantly," said Miss Vernet, "and put on your costume."

"Yes, and throw us out those horrible clothes," added Miss Brandon.

I shot into the dressing-room, and peeling off the garb of infamy with the speed of a quick-change artist, threw the garments out and whisked the costume down from its pegs; and even as the roar of many voices from the mews outside announced the arrival of my pursuers, I dropped the gown over my head, secured the fastenings with trembling fingers and clapped the ringlets on my stubbly pate. When I came out into the studio Miss Brandon had just closed the costume chest, on the lid of which she was piling palettes, paint-tubes and sheafs of brushes, and Miss Vernet was standing at her easel.

"Now," she said briskly, "get on the throne and take up your pose; and pull your gloves on. They mustn't see your hands."

I had just struggled into my long gloves and taken up the pose when the murmur of voices announced the return of my pursuers from an unsuccessful quest at the end of the mews. There was a scrambling sound and a disreputable head and shoulders framed itself in the window, and the eyes appertaining thereto glared inquisitively into the studio. Then it disappeared with a suddenness suggestive of outside assistance; the scrambling sound was renewed and a helmeted head rose majestically in its place. The constable gazed in enquiringly, and had just opened his mouth as if about to speak, when he caught the stern and for bidding eye of Miss Vernet, which seemed to paralyse him completely.

"What are you doing at my window, sir?" the lady demanded acidly.

The constable's mouth opened once more and this time with more result.

"I beg your pardon, madam," said he, "but there is an escaped convict--" here the constable disappeared with the same suddenness as the previous observer, his toes having apparently slipped off the brick coping. He did not reappear, but I heard a voice, which seemed to be his, enquiring irritably: "Where's the dam door?"

Somebody must have shown him the "dam door", for after a brief pause, the studio bell rang and Miss Brandon, smothering her giggles, went out and returned accompanied by two constables and two elderly gentlemen. The latter came in in a state of hilarity that contrasted strongly with the solemnity of the officials.

"I hear you've got a convict hiding in here," said one of them, a fresh-faced farmer-like looking gentleman.

"What's that?" demanded Miss Vernet, whisking round from her easel.

"Yes, madam," said one of the constables, staring hard at the picture and then glaring at me. "A convict who has escaped from Pentonville is believed to have climbed in at your window."

"At my window!" shrieked Miss Vernet, "but what a frightful thing, and how disgraceful of you to let him. I call it a perfect scandal that a respectable householder, paying police rates, should be subjected to the annoyance and danger of having hordes of convicts and criminals swarming in at all the windows if they happen to be left open."

"Oh, droar it mild, madam," protested the constable. "It ain't as bad as that. There's only one of them."

"If there's one there may be a dozen," Miss Vernet replied, rather illogically, I thought, "and I insist on your searching the premises and removing every one of them."

"Is that the window?" asked the gentleman who had spoken before. The constable admitted that it was. "But, my good man," the gentleman protested, "how could anyone have got in without being seen?"

The constable suggested that the ladies might have been looking the other way at the time, at which both the old gentlemen laughed aloud and shook their heads.

"At any rate," said Miss Vernet, laying down her palette, "I must insist on having the premises searched thoroughly," and thereupon she and Miss Brandon conducted the two constables out through the doorway that led to the kitchen and offices. As soon as they were gone, the two gentlemen settled themselves to examine the picture, and from the canvas they presently turned their attention to me with an intentness that made my flesh creep. The farmer-like gentleman seemed particularly interested, and having minutely compared me with the figure on the canvas, turned suddenly to his companion.

"This is a most extraordinary coincidence, Brodribb," said he; and as he spoke I was dimly aware of something familiar in the sound of the name.

The other gentleman--a fine, jovial-looking old cock with a complexion like that of a Dublin Bay prawn and hair like white silk--looked about him a little vaguely and then asked: "What is?

"That figure in the picture," his friend replied. "Doesn't it recall anything to your mind?"

Mr. Brodribb looked at the canvas with a frown of concentration and an air of slight perplexity, but apparently without the desired effect on his memory, for, after a prolonged stare, he shook his head and replied: "I can't say that it does."

"Come and stand here," said the other, stepping back a couple of paces, "and look carefully at the central figure only, taking the architrave of the door way as the picture frame. Is there no portrait that you have ever seen that it reminds you of?"

Again Mr. Brodribb looked and again he shook his head.

"Dear, dear," exclaimed the farmer-like gentleman, "and to think how many dozens of times you must have looked on it! Don't you remember a portrait that hangs over the fireplace in the small drawing room at Bradstow? A portrait by Romney of, I think, a Miss Isabel Hardcastle."

Mr. Brodribb brightened up. "Yes, yes, of course," said he, "I remember the portrait that you mention. Not very well, though. But what about it?

"Why, my dear Brodribb, this figure is an almost exact replica. The dress is of the same character and the pose is similar, though that might easily be in an historical picture of the same period. But the most astonishing resemblance is in the face. This might be a copy."

Mr. Brodribb looked interested. "I remember the picture," said he, "and I recognise the general resemblance now you point it out, though I can't recall the face. I am not a portrait painter, you see, Sir Giles, so I haven't your memory for faces. But if the facial resemblance is as strong as you say it is in the two portraits, a very interesting fact seems to follow; for as this portrait is an excellent likeness of this young lady," (here the old gentleman bowed to me deferentially, whereupon I grinned and turned as red as a lobster) "she must be extremely like the subject of the other portrait, is it not so?"

Sir Giles laughed a fine, jolly, agricultural laugh. "Q.E.D., hey, Brodribb. Very acutely argued. Discreetly, too, as we can't put the other lady in evidence. But, of course, you're right."

At this point the two ladies returned, accompanied by the constables, who were both looking into the interiors of their helmets and bore a subtle suggestion of having taken refreshment. They departed with thanks and apologies, and the two ladies and the gentlemen then engaged in a spirited discussion on the composition of the picture. I was glad when it came to an end and the two gentlemen took their leave--each with a valedictory bow to me, which I returned to the best of my ability--for I was tired and hungry and wanted to get home.

"Now, Jasper," said Miss Vernet, when she had shown them out, "the question is how we are to get you away from here. You can't wear the prison clothes and you can't go home in your costume. What are we to do, Lucy?"

Miss Brandon reflected awhile and then suggested: "There's that widow's costume, you know. That would fit him."

"Yes, of course," agreed Miss Vernet, "it's the very thing. He shall put it on and I will walk home with him, myself."

And so the tragedy ended. Less than an hour later, a tall and gawky-looking widow might have been seen--but fortunately was not--sneaking up the stairs to the third floor of the house in Great Ormond Street. Pontifex was out shopping and came in later with a bottle under his arm. But by that time, my widowhood had come to an end. The resources of my wardrobe were slender, but they included two suits which I had outgrown before they had degenerated into mere scarecrow's costume, and into one of these I insinuated myself cautiously and with some misgivings as to its tensile strength. But, of course, it was impossible. Even Sturt and Wopsall's packer revolted at the sight of four inches of visible sock above my boots, and besides, I didn't dare to stoop. Miss Vernet had delicately hinted as we walked home at a desire to replace my lost garments, but, grateful as I was to her the thing was not to be thought of when I had five golden sovereigns hidden away. Accordingly, the very next day, I disinterred two of them and, making my way to a shop of which I knew in the vicinity of Convent Garden, procured in exchange for them a most admirable second-hand suit, in which I came forth proudly with my outgrown exuvium under my arm. Never before had I been so well dressed. When I returned to the warehouse, the packer raised his brown-paper cap and made me a deep bow; and even Pontifex, who was not ordinarily acutely observant, eyed that suit in silence and with an evidently unsuccessful effort of memory.

But there was a fly in the ointment--or perhaps I should say that there was a fly--a butterfly--missing from the ointment. I hastened to sew in at the back of the waistcoat a commodious secret pocket. But alas! that pocket was empty. The miserable wretch who had absconded in my patched and threadbare clothes, had, all unconsciously, been the bearer of a priceless treasure. In the agitation of the moment, I had forgotten the emerald that reposed at the back of his--or rather my--waistcoat. Now, too late, the realisation of my loss was borne in on me and remained for weeks a deep and abiding sorrow.

CHAPTER VI:

A VISIT TO STRATFORD ATTE BOW

(Dr. Jervis's Narrative)

THE mystery surrounding the disappearance of Sir Edward Hardcastle was solved in a very startling and tragic manner; if, indeed, that can be called a solution which was even more mysterious than the problem which it solved. The news was brought to us late one afternoon by Mr. Brodribb, who burst into our chambers in a state of such extreme agitation that we were at once prepared for some tidings of disaster.

"Here is a terrible thing, Thorndyke!" he exclaimed, dropping into a chair and mopping his face with his handkerchief. "Sir Edward has made away with himself."

Thorndyke was evidently surprised at the news, as also was I, but he made no comment beyond a half-articulate "Ha," and Brodribb continued: "I have just had the information from the police. Superintendent Miller was kind enough to call on me and give me the report himself. He had no details but--to put the horrible affair in a nutshell--Sir Edward's body was found this morning hanging from a beam in an empty house at Stratford."

"At Stratford!" Thorndyke repeated, incredulously. For if the news of the suicide itself was surprising, the alleged circumstances were amazing.

"Yes," said Brodribb, "it is an astonishing affair. I can't imagine what can have taken him to Stratford. But I suppose that people in the state of mind that is associated with self-destruction are apt to behave in a rather unaccountable way. Perhaps some kind of explanation will be forthcoming at the inquest, which I understand from the Superintendent is to take place to-morrow. It appears that there are some circumstances that make it desirable to hold the inquiry as soon as possible."

We had no difficulty in guessing what those circumstances were, but neither of us made any comment.

"I shall have to go," Brodribb continued; "in fact the Superintendent warned me, but I should like you to be present to watch the proceedings, if you can manage it. Not that there is any real necessity, since there is no insurance question to raise and there seems unfortunately to be no doubt of the facts. But inquests are quite out of my province and I should feel more satisfied if I had your views on the affair."

"Very well," said Thorndyke. "I will attend the inquest on your instructions.

But I think I had better be present at the post mortem, too. I should wish to have an opportunity of forming a direct judgement on the facts as well as hearing the evidence of the medical witness."

Brodribb nodded approvingly. "That is what I like about you, Thorndyke," said he. "You are so thorough--even beyond the necessities of the case. You take nothing on trust. But there is another matter. The Superintendent urged me--in fact, I may say that he ordered me--to go down to Stratford this evening and identify the body. He said that it was most important that the question of identity should be settled at once, and I suppose he is right. But it is frightfully unpleasant."

I suspected that it would be more unpleasant than he was aware of, but I kept my suspicions to myself; and he continued: "I don't see why the identification couldn't have been done by Weeks, Sir Edward's butler. They have summoned him by telegraph--I left his name and address with Miller, you remember--and I suppose he will have to see the body. However, the Superintendent insisted that I ought to go this evening, so there is no help for it. I suppose you couldn't come down with me?" he added, wistfully.

"Yes," Thorndyke replied, promptly, "I will come with you, and perhaps Jervis will keep us company."

He looked enquiringly at me, and, when I had assented--which I did readily enough--he resumed: "But there is one thing that must be done, at once, since there may not be time to-morrow. I must get a letter from the Home Office asking the coroner to give me the necessary facilities. Otherwise I may be refused permission to be present at the post mortem."

"Would that matter?" asked Brodribb. "There can't be much question as to the cause of death."

"That is impossible to say," replied Thorndyke. "If I am to attend I may as well be in a position to check the medical evidence. That, in fact, is my proper function."

"But you won't find anybody at the Home Office now," Brodribb objected.

"I think I shall," said Thorndyke. "There is always some responsible person on late duty to attend to urgent business. I suggest that you two go on to Stratford and wait for me at the police station."

"No, we won't do that," said Brodribb. "We will wait for you at my office and then we can all go down together."

To this arrangement Thorndyke agreed and took his departure forth en route for Whitehall, while Brodribb and I, in more leisurely fashion, made our way out into Fleet Street and so, by way of Carey Street to New Square. We did not, however, go into Brodribb's office; for our old friend was in a state of nervous unrest, and now that he was to have our company on his distasteful errand, was all impatience to start. Accordingly we walked together up and down the pavement of the quiet square, exchanging now and again a few words but mostly occupied with our own thoughts.

What Brodribb's thoughts were I cannot guess, but my own were fully occupied by the communication that he had made to us. For, brief and sketchy as it was, it contained matter that certainly invited reflection. Thorndyke, I could see, was, if not actually suspicious, at least very definitely on his guard. His determination to check the official medical evidence by independent observation showed clearly that in his view there might be more in the case than might meet the eye of a routine investigator. And I found myself in complete agreement with him. The alleged facts carried a distinct suggestion of fishiness. As to the probability of Sir Edward's committing suicide I could form no opinion; but the circumstances in which the suicide had occurred called aloud for inquiry. I was, indeed, somewhat surprised at the easy-going fashion in which the usually astute Brodribb had accepted them. But perhaps I was doing him an injustice. Possibly he was purposely withholding his own doubts the better to test Thorndyke's attitude.

I had reached this point in my reflections when, on making a quarter-deck turn, I perceived my colleague advancing swiftly up the pavement from the Carey Street gate. We stepped out to meet him and, as he joined us, Brodribb greeted him with the comprehensive question: "Well, what news?"

"I have got a letter for the coroner asking for facilities, and a hansom waiting opposite the gate."

"Hm," grunted Brodribb, "it will be a damned tight fit."

And I must admit that it was. Three large men, one of whom was distinctly of "a full habit" were more than the coach-builder had made allowance for. However, Thorndyke and I bore the brunt of the squeeze, and the journey was not a long one. In due course we unpacked ourselves at Liverpool Street Station and presently boarded a train bound for Bow and Stratford.

We travelled for the most part in silence, and what conversation passed was not connected with our present quest. There was, in fact, no opportunity for interchange of talk on confidential matters as our carriage contained, besides ourselves, three passengers, apparently businessmen returning, at the end of the day's work, not indeed to Stratford, but to some of the more savoury localities in the neighbourhood of Epping Forest. At length a strange and repulsive effluvium which began to filter in at the windows, suggestive of soap-boiling, glue-making and other odoriferous forms of industry, announced our approach to the classical neighbourhood of Stratford atte Bow, and a minute or two later we disembarked, Brodribb snorting disgustedly and holding a large silk handkerchief to his nose. From the railway station we made our way to that of the police, to which Mr. Brodribb had been directed by Superintendent Miller; and presenting ourselves to the sergeant on duty in the outer office and stating our business, were duly conducted into the inner office and the presence of the Station Superintendent.

The latter turned out to be an eminently helpful officer. Possibly the Home Office letter (which, though it was addressed to the coroner, was shown to the Superintendent) requesting that Dr. Thorndyke should be given such facilities as he might reasonably require, might have influenced him, to say nothing of our virtual introduction by Superintendent Miller. But apart from this, he was a capable, businesslike man, quite free from any tendency to red tape officialism and naturally inclined rather to help than to obstruct. Accordingly, when we had presented our credentials and explained our connection with the case, he proceeded to give us, without reserve, all the information that he possessed.

"The discovery," he began, "was made this morning about nine o'clock by a man named Holker, a retired ship's steward who owns a good deal of low-class weekly property about here--mostly small houses that he has picked up cheap and put in some sort of repair himself. He's what you'd call a handy man, able to do a job of bricklaying or plastering or joinery, so it doesn't cost him much to codge up these old derelicts that he buys. Now, some time ago he bought a row of half a dozen little houses that some fool had built on a bit of waste land down by Abbey Creek. He got them for next to nothing as they had never been inhabited and were in a ruinous condition and stood by an unmade road that was often half under water. He meant to do them up and let them at low rents to some of the labourers at the works. In fact he started work on one of them--Number Five--about a month ago, that is how we are able to fix the dates. The last time he was working there was Sunday, the twenty-first of June, and he is quite sure that nothing had happened then because he went all over the house. On Sunday night he was offered, and accepted, a temporary job on one of his old ships which traded to Marseilles; and on Monday morning he dropped in at the house to fetch away his tools. As he was in a hurry, he only went into the front room, where the tools had been left, but he could see that someone had been in the house by the fact that a glove was lying on the floor. He thought it queer, but, as I said, he was in a hurry and as it was an empty house with nothing in it to steal, he didn't trouble to look into the matter but just got his tools and came away.

"That was three weeks ago--this is the fourteenth. Now, Holker got back from his trip yesterday, and this morning he went round to get on with his work at the house. As soon as he got there he noticed the glove still lying on the floor. And then he noticed--well he noticed that there was something wrong about the house, so he went through to the kitchen and from there to the wash-house; and the first thing he saw when he opened the wash-house door was a man hanging from a tie-beam. There was no doubt that the man was dead and that he had been dead a pretty long time. Holker didn't stop to cut the body down. He just bolted out and came up here to report what he had seen. I happened to be here at the time so I thought I had better go along and see into the affair, though the job didn't sound much of a catch from what Holker said. And I can tell you it wasn't. However, I needn't go into that. You can imagine what it was like for yourselves.

"Well, there was the body hanging from the beam and an old, broken-backed windsor chair capsized on the floor underneath. Evidently he had stood on the chair to tie the rope to the beam and when he had fixed the noose round his neck he had kicked the chair over and left himself dangling. It was all pretty obvious, fortunately, for one didn't want to spend a lot of time in that wash-house making observations. I just cut the rope when the constables had got the stretcher underneath and they lowered the body on to it, covered it up and carried it away."

"Concerning the rope," said Thorndyke, as the Superintendent paused; "I presume deceased found that on the premises?

"No," the officer replied, "he must have brought the rope with him for it wasn't Hiker's. It was a smallish, brown rope--looked like coir--and he'd brought more than he wanted, for there was a spare end about four feet long."

"And with regard to the glove that was mentioned--?"

"Yes, I saw that in the front room. The fellow one was on the wash-house floor. I picked them both up and I've got them here."

"By the way," said Thorndyke, "how do you suppose the deceased man got into the house?"

"He must have got in by the window. He didn't get in by the front door, for Holker is sure he shut it when he left on Sunday and he found it shut when he went there on Monday morning. Of course, the lock is only a cheap builder's night-latch that anyone used to locks could open easily enough. But I don't suppose the deceased gentleman was accustomed to picking locks; and he didn't open it with a key because he hadn't a key of any sort about him."

"I don't suppose," Thorndyke remarked, "that he was much accustomed to getting in at windows."

"Probably not," the officer agreed. "But, you see, sir, he got in somehow; and Holker found the sitting-room window unfastened on the Monday morning. So it would have been easy enough for anyone to get in. The window-sill is only about two feet six above the ground. And you remember that the one glove was lying on the sitting-room floor. As a matter of fact, it was just under the window."

There was silence for a few moments. Then Brodribb remarked: "The officer from Scotland Yard mentioned that the body had been identified by some letters that were found in the pockets. I suppose there were some other things?"

"Yes, but mighty few considering the man's position; and yet enough to show that the body had not been robbed. I've got the things here if you would like to see them."

He stepped over to a nest of drawers which stood on a massive shelf, and, unlocking one of the drawers, drew it out bodily and brought it over to the table at which we were sitting. "There's the collection," said he. "It isn't quite what you'd expect to find on the person of a baronet. Look at that watch, for instance. Sort of thing that you could pick up at a cheap jeweller's for seven and six. What is rather odd, too, is that there are no keys. Not even a latch-key."

"He left his keys and his gold watch and some other valuables at his club," said Brodribb as he ran a gloomy eye over the contents of the drawer.

"Ah! Did he? Yes, very natural and very proper, too, having regard to what he intended to do. I'll make a note of that. It will be an important point for the coroner."

Brodribb was evidently sorry that he had spoken, but he did not lose his presence of mind. "Yes," he agreed. "The secretary of the club, Mr. Northbrook, will be able to tell you about it. I suppose you will have to summon him as a witness as Sir Edward was staying at the club."

"Yes, we shall want his evidence, and in fact, a summons has been served on him," the Superintendent replied, adding with a faint smile, "I take it that you'd rather not be called. But I'm afraid it can't be helped. You know more about his private and financial affairs than anybody else. The butler has been summoned, but he can't tell us what state the deceased's affairs were in, whereas you can give any information that is wanted. My sergeant, here, is the coroner's officer and he will hand you the summons when he takes you over to the mortuary."

"Do you really think it necessary for me to go there?" Mr. Brodribb protested with evident discomfort. "The butler will be able to testify to the identity."

"Yes," the officer agreed, "that is so. But for our own information, now, we should like to know whether this is or is not Sir Edward's body. You had better run over and just take a glance at it."

Brodribb acquiesced with a faint groan and the Superintendent then reverted to the contents of the drawer. "Do you recognise any of these articles?" he asked.

Brodribb looked them over once again before replying. They comprised the watch, a pair of wash-leather gloves, a shabby leather cigar-case--empty--a small silver match-box, an old and well-worn pigskin purse, containing, as the officer demonstrated, three sovereigns, a handkerchief marked E. H., a lead pencil, a fountain-pen, a small pocket-knife, some loose silver and coppers and a letter-case, containing two five-pound notes and one or two letters in envelopes, addressed to "Sir Edward Hardcastle, Bart., Bradstow, Kent."

"No," Brodribb replied, at length. "I don't recognise any of these things. The handkerchief is marked with Sir Edward's initials, as you can see; and the envelopes bear his name and address, as you can also see. That is all. Would you like me to look through the letters?"

"There is no need," the officer replied. "The coroner will read them and he will ask you anything that he wants to know about them. And now you would like to step across to the mortuary? I will tell the sergeant to take you over."

He rose, and, having replaced the drawer in its nest, passed through into an adjoining office and returned almost immediately accompanied by his subordinate, who bore in his hand a small blue paper.

"Here," said the Superintendent, "is your summons, Mr. Brodribb. Is there anything else that I can do for you?"

"There is one little matter, Superintendent," said Thorndyke. "I should like, if possible, to have an opportunity to inspect the house in which the body was found. I presume there is no objection?"

"None whatever," was the reply. "But you are not thinking of going there to-night? Better go to-morrow morning by daylight, before you attend at the post mortem. I'll see that there is someone to show you the place and let you in, and then we can tell you what time to turn up at the mortuary. But you'll waste your time at the house, for there is nothing to see but the end of a cut rope and an overturned chair."

"Well," said Thorndyke, "we will inspect them. It is a mere formality, but it is a good rule to see everything."

"So it is, sir," the Superintendent agreed; and with this he glanced at the sergeant, who forthwith opened the door and launched us into the street, the gathering darkness of which was tempered by the light of the lamp over the doorway.

"A pleasant night, gentlemen," he remarked as he led us across the road; "a trifle warm, perhaps, but that is seasonable, though for my part, I prefer rather cooler weather for mortuary jobs."

At this, Mr. Brodribb shuddered audibly, and, as I observed that he had taken Thorndyke's arm, I suddenly realised that what was for me and my colleague a matter of mere daily routine was to our poor old friend a really distressing and horrible experience. Evidently, Thorndyke had realised it too, for when the sergeant had unlocked a door at the bottom of a narrow alley and entered before us to light the gas, I heard him say in a low tone: "I'll go in first, Brodribb. You had better wait here till I call you."

The light from the large, shaded gas-lamps shone down brightly on the shrouded figure that lay on the central table and lit more dimly and fitfully the side benches, the great porcelain sink and the white washed walls. Thorndyke and I, with the sergeant, advanced to the table and the latter drew back the sheet, exposing the head and shoulders of the corpse. It was not a pleasant spectacle, but, still, immeasurably less repulsive than I had expected from my experiences of the "found drowned" corpses that I had seen in riverside mortuaries; and what was more to the point, it appeared to be quite recognisable. For a few seconds we stood looking down at the shrunken, discoloured face. Then Thorndyke drew up the sheet and having arranged it so that the face alone was visible, called out to Brodribb; who thereupon entered, walking quickly and a little unsteadily, and stepped up to the table by Thorndyke's side.

A single horrified glance apparently disposed of any doubts or hopes that he may have entertained, for he turned away quickly, muttering, "Dear Lord! What an end!" and began to walk towards the door.

"Can you identify the body, sir?" the sergeant asked in matter-of-fact tones.

"I can," replied Brodribb, relapsing, despite his agitation, into legal precision. "The body is that of Sir Edward Hardcastle of Bradstow in Kent"; and having made his statement, he walked out into the dark alley.

We followed almost immediately, for there was nothing to see that would not be better seen by daylight on the morrow. At the top of the alley we wished the sergeant "good night" and while he hurried away in the direction of the office, we turned our steps towards the station.

During the short walk, hardly a word was spoken. Brodribb strode forward with his chin on his breast and his gaze bent on the ground, absorbed in gloomy reflections, while Thorndyke and I silently turned over in our minds the significance of what we had seen and heard. It was not until we were seated in a first-class carriage--of which we were the only occupants--that our friend came out of his "brown study." Then, as the train moved out of the station, he turned to my colleague and asked abruptly: "Well, Thorndyke; what do you think of it?"

Thorndyke considered a few moments before replying. "It is early," he said, at length, "to express, or even to form an opinion. At present, we have no technical data. All that we can do is to form a provisional opinion based on the facts now known to us. That you can do as well as Jervis and I can."

"Perhaps," said Brodribb. "All the same, I should like to hear what the facts convey to you."

"Then I may say," Thorndyke responded, "that they convey to me principally the urgent necessity of getting more facts. At present we are confronted by two sets of conflicting probabilities, and we await further facts to throw greater weight on the one or the other. For instance, the mode of death is markedly characteristic of suicide. When a man is found hanging, the probability is that he has hanged himself. The possible alternatives are accident and homicide. Accidental hanging is rare and is usually obvious on inspection. Homicidal hanging is extremely rare. So that the mode of death, in the absence of any elucidatory evidence, establishes a strong presumption of suicide. Evidence of motive or intention would turn that presumption into something approaching certainty. Absence of such motive would reduce the probability; but the presumption would remain. At present we have no evidence of motive or intention."

"You are not forgetting that he emptied his pockets of all valuables?" Brodribb objected.

"No, I am not. The exact significance of that proceeding is not obvious but it does not appear to me to indicate an intention to commit suicide."

"Does it not? Do you not find a certain congruity between that action and the place and circumstances in which the body was found?"

"Undoubtedly I do," replied Thorndyke. "But the place and circumstances have no natural connection with suicide. That is what I mean by conflicting probabilities. If Sir Edward had been found hanging from a peg in his bedroom the ordinary presumption of suicide would have existed, because suicides commonly act in that way. But here we have a man making preparations (as it appears to me) to go into some place where property on the person is not safe and being later found dead in a remote part of the town which we should suppose to be quite unknown to him. The circumstances are so abnormal and the conduct so strikingly unlike the usual conduct of suicides that the ordinary presumption based on the mode of death cannot be accepted."

"Then," said Brodribb, "what is it that you are suggesting?"

"At present, I am suggesting nothing excepting that I am not prepared to accept the Superintendent's account at its face value. Beyond that it is useless to go until we have heard what transpires at the inquest."

Brodribb nodded gravely. "Yes," he agreed. "Discussion at this stage is merely academic. But probably the evidence at the inquest will clear matters up. I suppose the post-mortem will settle the question of suicide?"

"It may," Thorndyke replied, guardedly, "in a negative sense, by showing the absence of any alternative suggestion. But the conditions are not favourable for forming positive and definite opinions as to the exact circumstances in which death occurred."

"Well, you will be there, so, if it is possible to establish the fact of suicide--or to exclude it--by an examination of the body, we may say that the question will be decided to-morrow."

To this statement Thorndyke made no rejoinder; and as Brodribb relapsed into silent meditation and my colleague showed no inclination for further discussion, I followed their example, and, as I smoked my pipe, turned the situation over in my mind.

In the colloquy to which I had listened, two things had impressed me rather forcibly. For the first time in my experience of him, Brodribb had appeared unprepared to defer to Thorndyke's judgement. It was evident that in his opinion the suicide of Sir Edward was virtually an established fact, and that in his view Thorndyke's scepticism was merely a manifestation of the specialist's tendency to see things through the medium of his own specialty. On the other hand it had struck me that Thorndyke had made little effort to influence his opinion. He had, it is true, fairly answered Brodribb's questions; but it was quite obvious to me that he had not put the case against suicide with nearly the force that was possible even with the few facts that we had. This might have been due to his habit of avoiding anything like premature conclusions, but I had the feeling that he was not unwilling that Brodribb should continue to take the case, as he had expressed it, at its face value.

At the terminus we separated, Brodribb setting forth alone in a hansom while Thorndyke and I decided to restore our circulations by a brisk walk homewards through the city streets on which the quiet and repose of evening had now descended. Having seen Brodribb fairly launched, we turned out of the station, and, crossing Liverpool Street, started at a swinging pace up New Broad Street. For a minute or two we walked on in silence while I debated inwardly whether or not I should propound my views to Thorndyke. Finally deciding in the affirmative, I began, cautiously: "Brodribb appears to me to have made up his mind definitely on this case. He seems quite convinced that Sir Edward hanged himself."

"Yes, that was what I gathered from his remarks on the case."

"I wonder why. He is a lawyer, and a pretty shrewd one, too."

"Yes; but not a criminal lawyer. His experience is all on the civil side and principally in relation to property. Still, he may have reasons for his views of the affair which he has not disclosed. He knew Sir Edward pretty intimately and he knows all about the family. There may be some highly pertinent facts connected with the dead man's personality and the family history which we know nothing about. I take it that you don't agree with Brodribb?"

"I do not; and neither, I suspect, do you."

"You are quite right, Jervis. I do not. But we must not allow ourselves to come to any sort of conclusion before we have seen and heard the evidence. We must try to approach to-morrow's investigation with a perfectly open mind, and I am not sure that we ought to be discussing it now."

"There is no harm," said I, "in just going over the ground--without prejudice."

"Perhaps not," he agreed; "and since my learned friend seems to have arrived at certain provisional conclusions, it would be interesting to hear his exposition of the case as it presents itself to him."

I reflected for a few moments, trying to arrange my ideas in an orderly sequence. At length I began: "Taking the points for and against the theory of suicide in this case, I know of only one in favour of it; the one that you mentioned--that unofficial hanging is usually suicidal. On the other hand, there are several reasons against it.

"First, there is the fact that he came to London. Why should he, if he had been intending to commit suicide? The natural thing, according to precedent, would have been to hang himself in his own bedroom or in a garret."

"There are precedents of the opposite kind, though," objected Thorndyke. "I recall a case of a lady who poisoned herself in a very secluded wood on a common or in a park near London and whose body was not discovered for some months. Still, I agree that the probabilities are with you. What is the next point?"

"It is the fact that he unloaded his pockets of all valuables before he set out from the club. Why did he do that? If it is suggested that it was to provide against the chance that his body might be robbed, the obvious answer is that he could have avoided that possibility by committing suicide on his own premises. And the way in which the things were hidden under his shirts strongly suggests an intention to return and recover them. By Brodribb this incident seems to have been accepted as proof of an intention to commit suicide; but to me it has quite the opposite significance. Your own suggestion, made at the time, that he was expecting to go to some place and among some people where he might expect to be robbed, seems to meet the case perfectly; and Brodribb's suggestion that where property on the person is not safe, the person is probably also in some danger seems to receive corroboration. You and Brodribb suggest in advance the possibility of his being exposed to danger of personal violence, and the next thing that happens is that he is found dead, having admittedly died a violent death."

Thorndyke nodded approvingly. "Yes," he admitted, "I think that is quite fairly argued."

"The next point," I continued, "is the place in which the body was found. It is an empty house in an obscure and remote part of a region which is quite unknown to the immense majority of Londoners and almost certainly unknown to the deceased. How on earth did he get there and what could have been his object in going there? He could hardly have strayed thither by chance, for the place is difficult of access and right off the track to any more likely locality. On the other hand, the choice of this particular house suggests some local knowledge--knowledge of the existence of that desolate row of houses and of the fact that they were all uninhabited and likely to be left undisturbed and unexamined for months. The whole set of circumstances seems to me profoundly suspicious."

"There I am entirely with you," said Thorndyke. "That empty house on the edge of no-man's-land wants a deal of explaining."

"Then," I resumed, "there is that new, cheap watch, evidently bought as a substitute for the watch that he had left at the club. The purchase of that watch seems to me utterly to exclude the state of mind of a man intending immediately to commit suicide. Then, finally, there is a point which, strangely enough, seems to have been overlooked by Brodribb--the seal. That seems to me the most suspicious of all the elements in the case. The sealed letter was posted on the Saturday, but we have evidence that the hanging could not have occurred before Sunday night at the earliest. Now, it is fair to assume that the letter was not sealed by Sir Edward."

"It is extremely unlikely," Thorndyke interposed, "but we can't say that it is impossible. And if we accept the hypothesis of suicide, it is not even very improbable. It might be suggested that Sir Edward adopted that method of announcing his death. But I may say that I agree with you in assuming that the letter was almost certainly sealed and posted by some other person."

"Then, in that case, Sir Edward's signet ring must have been in the possession of some other person at least twenty-four hours before the earliest moment at which he could have hanged himself in the empty house. That is a very remarkable and significant fact."

"Has it occurred to you, Jervis," Thorndyke asked, "that Sir Edward might have been wearing his ring that day, or some other day after he left the club, and that it might have slipped off his finger and been picked up by some chance stranger? We have been told that it was a very loose fit."

"That did occur to me," I replied, "but I think we must reject that explanation. You remember that Sir Edward usually carried the ring in a little leather case or bag in his pocket. Now, if he had lost the ring off his finger, the empty case would have been in his pocket. But apparently it was not. I looked for it carefully among the things in the drawer that the Superintendent showed us and it was not there. And it could hardly have been overlooked in a careful search of the pockets."

"No," Thorndyke agreed, "I think we may take it that the case was not there, though we shall have to verify its absence, since, as you say, the point is an important one and opens up some very curious possibilities. But here we are at our journey's end. Your masterly summing-up of the evidence has made the miles slip by unnoticed. I must compliment you on the completeness of your survey. And we shall be none the worse for having gone over the ground in advance, provided that we approach the actual investigation to-morrow without prejudice or any expectation as to what we are likely to discover."

As he concluded, we turned in at our entry and mounted the stairs to our landing. The door of our chambers was open, giving us a view of the lighted room, in which Polton was adding a few final touches to the supper table.

CHAPTER VII:

NUMBER FIVE PIPER'S ROW

(Dr. Jervis's Narrative)

FROM my long association with Thorndyke, I was often able to deduce something of his state of mind and his intentions from observation of his actions. Particularly interesting was it to me to watch him (as unobtrusively as possible) packing his green canvas "research case" in preparation for some investigation, for, by noting carefully the appliances and materials with which he provided himself, I could form a pretty clear idea as to the points that he thought it necessary to elucidate.

Thus, on the morning on which we were to set forth for our second visit to Stratford, I stood by with an attentive eye on his proceedings as he put into the case the various articles which he thought might be needed. I was specially interested on this occasion because, while I viewed the case with the deepest suspicion, I could think of no method of attack on the undoubtedly plausible prima facie appearances. Possibly Thorndyke was in the same position; but one thing became clear to me as I watched him. He was taking nothing for granted. As I observed him putting into the case the chemically clean bottles with stoppers prepared for sealing, I realised that he was prepared for signs that might call for an analysis. The little portable microscope and the box of blank-labelled slides, the insufflator, or powder-spray, the miniature camera and telescopic tripod, the surveyor's tape and small electric lamp, each indicated certain points which were to be subjected to exact tests and measurements, and the rubber gloves and case of post-mortem instruments showed that he contemplated taking an active part in the actual necropsy if the opportunity should present itself. The whole outfit suggested his habitual state of mind. Nothing was to be taken on trust. The one undoubted fact was that Sir Edward Hardcastle was dead. Beyond that Thorndyke would accept no suggestion. He was going to begin at the beginning as if no cause of death had been hinted at.

One item of the outfit did certainly puzzle me considerably--a box of keys from Polton's rather doubtfully legal collection. The fact is that our worthy laboratory assistant held somewhat obscure views on certain aspects of the law; but on one subject he was perfectly clear. Whatever legal restrictions or obligations might apply to common persons, they had no application to "The Doctor." In his view, his revered employer was above the law. Thus, in the assumed interests of that employer, Polton had amassed a collection of keys that would have been enough to bring a "common person" within hail of penal servitude, and a portion of his illegal hoard I now saw going into the research case. I examined them with profoundly speculative eyes. The collection included a number of common latch-keys, a graded set of blanks (how on earth had Polton managed to acquire those blanks, so strictly forbidden by the law?) and a bunch of skeleton keys of the pipe variety, simple in construction but undeniably felonious in aspect.

I asked no questions concerning those keys, reserving to myself the prospective entertainment of seeing them produced and put to their mysterious use; as to which I could form no sort of surmise. They were certainly not to let us into the house, for we had already been promised free admittance. But it was useless to speculate. The explanation would come all in good time, and now the research case, having received its lading, was closed and fastened and we were due to start.

At Stratford, we found the Superintendent ready to receive us and in the same helpful spirit as on the preceding day.

"You are full early, gentlemen," he remarked, "as matters stand. The inquest opens, as you know, at four p.m., and the doctor has fixed two p.m. for the post-mortem. So you'll have plenty of time to survey the 'scene of the tragedy,' as the newspapers call it, though I don't fancy that you'll spend your time very profitably. However, that's your affair. You are acting for the executor, as I understand, so I suppose you have got to make a show of doing something."

"Exactly," Thorndyke agreed. "A specialist must make a demonstration of some kind. You gave my letter to the coroner?"

"Yes, sir. And it is just as well that you had it. Otherwise I don't fancy you'd have got many facilities. He's rather a touchy man and he seemed disposed to resent your coming here to hold what he calls 'an unofficial inquiry of your own.' However, it is all right. I am to let you see anything that you want to see, and the medical witness--he is the police surgeon's deputy--has got the same instructions. And now I expect you would like to start. I've got the key here, but I can't give it to you in case the coroner wants to inspect the place himself. Besides, you'll want someone to show you where it is."

He stepped to the door, and, looking into the adjoining office, called out: "Marshall, just take these two gentlemen down to number five Piper's Row. You needn't stay. Just let them into the house and bring the key back to me."

As he spoke, he produced from the nest of drawers a key with a wooden label attached to it which he handed to the constable; and I noticed that, as it passed from hand to hand, Thorndyke bestowed a quick glance on it, and I suspected that he was memorising its shape and size. It was, however, but a momentary glance, for the key disappeared immediately into the constabulary pocket and the officer, with a salute to his superior, turned and led the way out into the street.

The town of Stratford is not strikingly prepossessing in any part. There is nothing of the residential suburb about it. But the district to which we were conducted by Constable Marshall seemed to reach the very limit of what is attainable in the way of repulsive squalor by the most advanced developments of modern industry. Turning out of the High Street by Abbey Lane, we presently emerged from the inhabited areas on to a dreary expanse of marsh, on which a few anaemic weeds struggled to grow in the interstices of the rubbish that littered every open space. Gas works, chemical works, pumping stations and various large buildings of the mill or factory type arose on all sides, each accompanied by its group of tall chimney-shafts, all belching forth smoke and each diffusing the particular stench appropriate to the industry that it represented. A few rough roads, like urbanised cart tracks, flanked by drainage ditches, meandered across this region, and along one of these we picked our way until it brought us to the place where, as the Superintendent bluntly but justly expressed it, "some fool had built" Piper's Row.

"Not much to look at, are they, sir?" Constable Marshall remarked in comment on our disparaging glances at the unspeakably sordid, ruinous little hovels. "Mr. Holker bought them for a song, but I fancy he's going to lose his money all the same. This is the one."

He halted at a decaying door bearing the number 5, fished the key out of his pocket, inserted it, gave it a turn and pushed the door open. Then, as we entered, he withdrew the key, wished us "good morning," closed the door and took his departure.

For some moments Thorndyke stood looking about the tiny room--for there was no hall, the sitting-room opening directly on the street--letting his eye travel over its scanty details; the rusty grate, the little cupboard in the recess, the small, low window and especially the floor. He stepped across and tried the door of the cupboard, and, finding it locked, remarked that Holker had probably used it to stow away his tools.

"You notice, Jervis," he added, "that the appearance of the floor does not seem to support the theory that the house was entered by the window. There are footmarks under the window, certainly, but they are quite faint, whereas there are well-marked prints of muddy feet, two pairs at least, leading from the street door to the next room, which I suppose is the kitchen."

"Yes, I see that," I replied; "but as we don't know whose foot-prints they are or when they were made, the observation doesn't carry us very far."

"Still," he rejoined, "we note their existence and observe that they proceed, getting rapidly fainter, direct to the kitchen."

He passed through the open doorway, still narrowly examining the floor, and halted in the kitchen to look round. But, beyond the faint marks on the floor, there was nothing to attract notice, and, after a brief inspection, we went on to the wash-house, which was what we had actually come to see.

Apparently, the place had been left in the condition in which it had been found by Holker, for the decrepit Windsor chair still lay on its side, while almost directly above it a length of thinnish brown rope hung down from a short beam that connected the principal pair of rafters. At this Thorndyke, when he had finished his scrutiny of the floor, looked with an expression of interest that it hardly seemed to warrant.

"The Superintendent," he remarked, "spoke of a tie beam. It is only a matter of terminology, but this is rather what architects would call a collar beam. But the fact is of some interest. A tie beam, in a building of this size, would be within comfortable reach of a short man. But this beam is fully eight feet above the floor. Even with the aid of the chair, it is not so very accessible."

"No. But the rope could have been thrown over and pulled taut after the knot was tied. It is made fast with a fisherman's bend, which would run up close when the rope was hauled on."

"Yes," he agreed, "that is so. And, by the way, the character of the knot is worth noting. There is something rather distinctive about a fisherman's bend."

He stood looking up thoughtfully at the knot, from which a long end hung down beside the 'standing part', which had been cut, as if the rope had been longer than was necessary for the purpose. Then he took the cut end in his hand and examined it minutely, first with the naked eye and then with the aid of a pocket lens. Finally, slipping on a glove, he picked up the chair, and, mounting on it, began deliberately to untie the knot.

"Is that quite in order, Thorndyke?" I protested. "We had permission to inspect the premises, but I don't think we were expected to disturb anything."

"We are not going to disturb anything in any essential sense," he replied. "When we have finished, we shall re-tie the knot and put the chair as we found it. That will be good enough for the coroner's jury. You might give me the tape out of the case."

I opened the case and took out the long tape, which I handed to him and watched him as he carefully measured the rope and entered the length in his note book. It seemed an unaccountable proceeding, but I made no comment until he had re-fastened the rope and stepped down from the chair. Then I ventured to remark: "I should like to know why you measured that rope, Thorndyke. It seems to me that its length can have no possible bearing on anything connected with the case that we are investigating. Evidently I am wrong."

"When we are collecting facts," he replied, "especially when we are absolutely in the dark, we are not bound to consider their relevancy in advance. The length of this rope is a fact and that fact might acquire later some relevancy which it does not appear to have now. There is no harm in noting irrelevant facts, but a great deal of harm in leaving any fact unnoted. That is a general rule. But in this case there is a reason for ascertaining and recording the length of this piece of rope. Look at it attentively and see what information it yields."

I glared at the rope with concentrated attention, but all the information that it yielded to me was that it was a piece of rope.

"I am looking at it attentively," I said, doggedly, "and what I see is a length--about a fathom and a half--of thinnish coir rope, the thinnest coir rope, I think, that I have ever seen. It is made fast at the end with a fisherman's bend and the other part has been cut."

"Why 'the other part'? I mean what is the distinction?

"It is obvious," I replied. "The end proper has got the whipping on it."

"Exactly," said Thorndyke. "That is the point. Incidentally, it is not a coir rope. It is a hemp rope dyed, apparently with cutch. But that is a detail, though a significant one. The chief point is that the end is whipped. A rope with cut ends is a rope of no determinate length. It is simply a piece of rope. But a rope with whipped ends has a determinate length. It is a definite entity. It may be a boat's painter, a sheet, a halyard, a waterman's towing-rope; in any case it is a thing, not a part of a thing. Here we have a piece of rope with a whipping at one end. We haven't seen the other part. But we know that when it was complete it was whipped at both ends. And we know that, somewhere, there is a counterpart to this fragment and that the two together make up a known length."

"Yes," I agreed, "there is no denying the truth of what you have said, but it is a mere exposition of theory. Undoubtedly there does exist a piece of rope which is the complement to this piece. But as we have no idea where it is and there is not the remotest chance that we shall ever meet with it, or that we should recognise it if we did, your measurement is a mere demonstration of a principle without any utility what ever."

"Our chance of meeting with that complementary portion is small enough, I must admit," said Thorndyke, "but it is not so infinitesimal as you think. There are some points which you have overlooked; and I think you have not fully taken in the immense importance of tracing the origin of this rope. But we must not waste time in discussion. This chair is the next subject for investigation. On the hypothesis that Sir Edward hanged himself, there should be prints of his fingers on some part of it; and if he did not, then there should be prints of the fingers of some other person."

"I think we can take it that there will be plenty of finger-prints on it," said I, "if they are not too old to develop. The latest must be at least three weeks old."

"Yes, it is rather a poor chance, but we will try our luck."

He opened the research case and brought out the insufflator with one of the powder containers which was filled with a pure white powder. Having fitted the container to the spray-producer, he placed the chair where the light fell on the front aspect of it and began to work the bellows, keeping at some distance from the chair, so that the cloud of white powder met the surface quite gently. Very soon the whole of the front of the chair became covered with a thin, uniform coating of the impalpably fine white dust. Then the chair was turned about by pushing and pulling the lower parts of the legs and the other aspect coated with powder. When this process was completed Thorndyke proceeded to tap each of the legs very lightly and quickly with the handle of a large pocket-knife. At once, in response to the faint jarring strokes, the white dust began to creep down the perpendicular surfaces, and in a few seconds there came into view a number of rounded, smeary shapes on the broad, flat top rail of the chair-back. Still, as the light, quick tapping went on, the powder continued to creep down, leaving the shapes more and more conspicuous and distinct. Finally, Thorndyke transferred his operations to the top of the chair-back, gradually increasing the force of his blows until practically the whole of the powder had been jarred off, leaving the shapes--now unmistakable finger-prints--standing out strongly against the dingy, varnished surface.

"Not a very promising lot," Thorndyke commented, after a preliminary inspection. "Several hopeless smears and several more super-imposed. Those won't be much use even to the experts."

With the aid of his pocket lens, he made a more critical survey of the one side while I examined the other, reinforcing the feeble light with the electric lamp.

"They are a very confused lot," I remarked. "The trouble is that there are too many of them on top of one another. Still, there are several that show a distinguishable pattern. I should think the finger print experts will be able to make something of them."

"Yes," Thorndyke agreed, "I think so. It is surprising to see what shockingly bad prints they manage to decipher. At any rate, we will give them a chance."

Between us, we got out the little camera, mounted it on its tripod and placed it in position by means of its wire sighting frame. Having measured the distance with the tape and set the focusing-scale, Thorndyke stopped the lens down to F. 16, and, taking out his watch, gave the long exposure that was demanded by the weak light and the small stop. Then, when, as a measure of safety, he had made a second exposure, we turned the chair round and repeated the operation on the opposite side.

"Are you going to leave the powder on the chair?" I asked as we re-packed the camera.

"No," he replied. "The police have had their opportunity. Perhaps they have taken it. At any rate it will be best for us to keep our own counsel as to our private investigations. And the photographs will be available if they are wanted."

With this he carefully dusted away all traces of the powder and when he had laid the chair in the place and position in which we had found it, he picked up the research case and we went back to the front room.

"Well," I said, moving towards the door, "I think we have seen everything here and we have picked up one or two crumbs--pretty small ones as far as I am concerned. But perhaps there is something else that you want to see?"

"Yes," he replied, "there are two more points that we ought to consider before we go. First there are those wheel-ruts. You noticed them, I suppose?

"I observed some ruts in the road as we came along. Deuced uncomfortable they were to a man with thin shoes. But what about them?"

"Apparently you did not notice them," said he, "excepting as a source of physical discomfort. Come out now and take a careful look at them."

He opened the street door and we stepped out on to the strip of rough ground that served as the footpath or 'side-walk'. The unmade road that passed the houses was bumpy with obscure impressions of feet that had trodden it when the surface was moist and there were faint suggestions of old ruts. But in addition to these was a pair of deep, sharply-defined ruts with clear hoof-marks between, which I now remembered having seen as we came out of Abbey Lane.

"I can't quite make up my mind as to the class of vehicle," he said. "What do you make of it?"

"A two-wheeled cart of some kind," I suggested. "A largish one, to judge by the space between the ruts."

"Yes, it is rather wide for a light cart. My provisional diagnosis was a good-sized gig or dog-cart--more probably a gig. It was evidently a light, high vehicle, as we can tell by the narrowness of the rims and the large diameter of the wheels."

"I can see that the rims were narrow, but I don't see how you arrive at the diameter of the wheels."

"It happens," he explained, "to be quite easy in this case. There is a notch in the edge of the near tyre; rather a surprising feature if you consider the strength of an iron tyre. It must have been caused by striking a sharp angle of granite or iron at some corner."

"I should have thought," said I, "that a blow that would notch the tyre would have broken the wheel."

"So should I." he agreed. "However, there it is, and it leaves a small, triangular projection at the side of the rut; and of course, the distance between two such projections is the circumference of the wheel. We may as well measure that distance, and the width between the two tracks and the width of the rims. Fortunately, there is no one here to spy on us."

I looked round as I unfastened the research case and handed out the tape. There was not a human creature in sight. Piper's Row might as well have been in the midst of the Sahara.

Taking advantage of the solitude, we went out on to the road and made the three measurements at our ease; and as I held one end of the tape while Thorndyke stretched it and took the reading, I speculated vaguely as to the object of the proceeding.

"The tyres are one inch and a half wide," he reported as he put away his notebook, "the width between the outside edges of the tyre-marks is fifty-seven inches and the circumference of the wheels is thirteen feet ten inches. That makes the diameter about four feet seven and a half, that is fifty-five and a half inches.

"Yes," I agreed without much enthusiasm, "that will be about right. But why are we taking all this trouble? Is there anything particularly interesting about this cart?

"The interest attaching to this cart," he replied, "lies in the fact that it stopped at number five Piper's Row."

"The deuce it did!" I exclaimed. "That is rather remarkable, seeing that Number Five is an empty house."

"Very remarkable," he agreed. "It was quite a short halt," he continued, "unless the horse was more than usually patient. But there is no doubt about it. You can see where the tracks swerve in slightly towards the house. Then there is the spot where the ruts lose their regularity and broaden out somewhat, and there is quite plainly the re-duplication of the hoof-marks where the horse has trodden two or three times in nearly the same place. That could have happened only when the cart was stationary."

I was still looking down at the impressions to verify his statements when I was aroused by the slamming of a door. I looked up quickly and saw that a gust of wind had caught the door of Number Five and shut us out.

"Well, Thorndyke," I remarked with a faint grin, "that seems to put the stopper on that further point that you were going to elucidate."

"Not at all," he retorted. "I would say rather that it introduces it in a particularly opportune way. Do you mind opening the research case?"

I did so; and when he had replaced the tape in its compartment, he took out the box of keys which had so stimulated my curiosity. Opening it, he extracted the bunch of skeleton keys, and, glancing from them to the keyhole, he deliberately selected one and inserted it. It entered quite easily and when he gave it a turn and a slight push, the door opened and we walked in.

"You see, Jervis," he said, withdrawing it from the keyhole and holding it out to me, "here is a perfectly elementary skeleton key, made by simply cutting away the whole of the bit excepting the top and the bolt edge. I selected it with Constable Marshall's key in my mind."

"That was a ward key, I think?"

"Yes, it had three vertical slits in the bit, which ostensibly corresponded to three concentric wards in the lock."

"Why 'ostensibly'?"

"Because I suspect that they are not there. But in selecting the skeleton key I assumed that they were there, and you saw the result. Also you see the weakness of a ward lock. The wards are obstructions placed in the path of the key. The key which fits a particular lock has slits corresponding to the wards, so that it can turn and let the wards pass through. But it isn't necessary for the slits to fit the wards. All that is necessary is a hole in the key-bit large enough to let it pass the wards. The simplest plan is, as in this key, to cut out the whole of the bit excepting the distal edge--which enters the notch, or 'talon' of the bolt and moves it--and the top edge which joins it to the key stem. I am speaking, of course, of comparatively simple locks."

"And you think that this lock hasn't any wards at all?"

"It is a mere guess based on the generally shoddy appearance of the fittings. But we can easily settle the question."

Once more he opened the key box and this time took out a locksmith's 'blank', which he compared with the skeleton key. Finding their bits about the same width, he tried the blank in the lock. It entered as easily as the skeleton had, and when he turned it, it made its circuit in the same manner and duly drew in the bolt.

"That," said Thorndyke, "makes it perfectly clear. This blank could not possibly have passed a ward. It follows that this lock contains nothing but a spring bolt. Consequently it could be opened by practically any key that would enter the keyhole and that was long enough in the bit to reach the notch of the bolt."

"By the way," said I, "if there are no wards, what is the function of those slits that you described in the key?"

"Their function, I take it, is purely commercial--a matter of salesmanship; to produce a certain moral effect on the purchaser. He sees a somewhat intricate key and naturally infers a corresponding intricacy in the lock. The ethics of commerce are sometimes a little difficult for the uncommercial mind to follow."

"Yes, by Jove," said I. "That dummy key does seem uncommonly like a fraud. But with regard to this lock: it is all very curious and interesting but I don't quite see the purpose of these experiments. Obviously they have some bearing since you took the trouble to bring that collection of keys."

"Yes," he replied as he returned the box to the green canvas case and fastened the latter, "they have a bearing. We can discuss it as we walk back to the town; and I propose that we follow the tracks of the cart and see where it went to. It is bound to go our way, as this area of marsh is enclosed on the other three sides by the creeks."

We went out of the dismal little house, slamming the door behind us, and set forth along the rough footway in the direction in which the cart had gone. We walked a short distance in silence; then Thorndyke returned to my question.

"The bearing of what we have ascertained about that lock is this; we are invited to believe that entrance was effected into the house by the window because the door was shut and locked. But the fact, which we have established, that the lock is one which can be opened with almost any key--or even with a piece of stiff wire--makes any such supposition unnecessary. The house was accessible to anybody by way of the door."

"As far as Sir Edward was concerned," said I, "you remember that he had no keys on him at all."

"Yes. And that fact may have influenced the Superintendent. But it doesn't influence us. If Sir Edward went into that house of his own free will it is of no concern to us whether he got in at the window or climbed down the chimney. But if we assume--as I take it we both do, without prejudice as to what may transpire at the inquest--that he was taken into that house forcibly, or in a state of unconsciousness, or actually dead, then the facility of access becomes a material fact. For the proceedings would necessarily be hurried. There would be no time for the manipulation of windows or picking of locks. Entry would have to be effected at once."

"That means," said I, "that the person or persons who entered knew what sort of lock was on the door."

"Undoubtedly," he agreed. "The house must have been known to at least one of the parties, and would, presumably, have been visited and explored. The plan must have been arranged and prepared in advance to enable it to be carried out quickly."

"What do you suppose to have been the actual modus operandi?" I asked.

"From what we have seen, I should reconstruct events somewhat thus: First, a scout would come to the place, try the lock and ascertain that a particular key would open it, explore the house and select the place where the victim could be most conveniently hanged. Then, at the appointed time, the victim--who must almost necessarily have been either dead or insensible--would be put in the cart and covered up; the three men--possibly two, but much more probably three--would mount to the seat and the cart would be driven to the house pretty late at night, so as to secure complete darkness.

"On arriving at Number Five, one man would jump down and open the door. The victim and the rope would then be handed down and carried in and the door shut. The cart would then be driven off, possibly to wait at some rendezvous outside the immediate neighbourhood. The two men, having concluded the business, would come out and walk to the rendezvous and the whole party would then return whence they came."

"Yes," I said, "that sounds very complete and consistent. But aren't we taking rather a lot for granted? I admit that the stopping of that cart opposite Number Five is a highly suspicious circumstance--and here we are, back at Abbey Lane and here are the cart-tracks back with us. So the cart must have made the round expressly to call at Number Five, which strongly supports your theory. But still, we are assuming that the cart made that very suspicious call on that particular night. Of course, it is extremely probable that it did; and if it did, it almost certainly conveyed Sir Edward, alive or dead. The fatal flaw in the evidence is that we can't fix the date on which the cart called at the house."

"But I think we can, Jervis. One doesn't like to use the word certainty, but I think I can fix the date with the very highest degree of probability."

"Then," said I, "if you can do that, I accept your hypothetical reconstruction as almost certainly representing what actually happened. But I should like to hear the evidence."

"The evidence," he replied, "is based on two factors; one is the state of the road when the tracks were made; the other is the time at which the road could have been in that particular state. Let us consider factor one.

"You saw the ruts and the hoof-prints. They were deep and sharp but by no means dead sharp. There was a slight blurring of the edges of the impressions. The soil of the road was an impure clayey loam. Now, since the impressions were deep, the road must have been quite soft; but since the impressions were fairly sharp, the mud could not have been liquid or diffluent, for liquid or semi-liquid mud does not retain impressions. It could not have been raining when the impressions were made, for in the soft state of the road, rain would have largely obliterated them. For the same reason, no appreciable rain could have fallen after they were made.

"On the other hand, the road could not have dried enough to become plastic or semi-solid, or--on soil of this kind--the impressions would have been dead sharp. So it comes to this: the ruts were made after heavy rain--heavy enough to swamp the road. But there was an interval after the rain, long enough to allow the semi-liquid stage to pass off but not long enough to allow the mud to pass into the plastic or semi-solid stage.

"Now let us take the second factor--the time factor. I need not remind you of the long drought that has prevailed this summer. It began, as you probably remember, at the very end of May, and it still continues. In that drought there has been up to the present only a single break--a single, dramatic break. On Sunday, the twenty-first June, a tremendous storm burst over the London area, and for more than an hour the rain fell in torrents. The storm clouds came up quite suddenly about half-past four in the afternoon and the rain ceased and the clouds rolled away with almost equal suddenness about six o'clock. And forthwith the drought resumed its sway. A hot, dry easterly wind followed the storm and the pavements dried up as if the water on them had been spirit.

"Now, during that heavy rain, these roads across the marshes must have been flooded. For the time being, their surfaces must have been just liquid mud. But we must remember that under that liquid mud, only a few inches down, was soil baked dry by weeks of drought. Before midnight the surface water would have soaked in, bringing the soil to the consistency shown by these ruts. By the following morning, or at least by noon, the plastic stage would have been reached, while by evening, after a day's hot sunshine and dry wind, the surface would have become too firm to yield deep impressions like these with their surrounding ridges. As I say, one doesn't like to use the word certainty; but I submit that we are justified in assuming with considerable confidence that these ruts were made on the night of Sunday, the twenty-first of June, probably after ten o'clock."

"More probably in the small hours of the morning," I suggested.

"The state of the road would admit of that view," he replied, "but other considerations suggest an earlier hour--say from eleven to half-past. A party of men with a dead or insensible man in a cart would not wish to attract notice or run the risk of being stopped and questioned. Up to midnight they would be pretty safe, but in the small hours a cart prowling round an unfrequented neighbourhood or travelling along a road that leads nowhere might excite the curiosity of an alert and enterprising policeman. However, that is mere surmise and not at present of special interest to us. The important point is the date and the approximate time."

"By the way, Thorndyke," I asked, "how do you manage to remember all these details? I recollect the storm, of course, and now that you mention it, I think I can corroborate the date and the time. But it is a mystery to me how you keep these dates and times in your memory, ready to be produced at a moment's notice."

"The solution of that mystery," he replied, "is quite simple. I don't. I keep a diary; a highly condensed affair, but I note in it everything that may need to be recalled. And I always enter the state of the weather, having learned from experience that it is often a vitally important means of fixing the time of other happenings, as in the present case. I looked it up last night, principally in connection with the possibility of finding muddy foot-prints in the house."

"After reading me a lecture on the impropriety of discussing the case in advance," I said with a grin; "and now you have built up a complete reconstruction of the events before we have even seen what the post mortem has to tell, to say nothing of the inquest."

He smiled deprecatingly. "We had no choice, Jervis. We could only observe the facts in the order in which they were presented. But, still, I hope we shall approach the inquest without prejudice; and it is possible that we may get a surprise from the evidence of Brodribb or Weeks, but especially Brodribb. I suspect that he has something in his mind that he has not disclosed to us."

"The deuce!" I exclaimed. "You think there may have been reasons for anticipating the possibility of suicide? It will be a bit of an anti-climax if evidence of that kind is given, for it will knock the bottom out of your elaborate reconstruction."

"Not necessarily," he replied; "opinions and expectations are no answer to observed facts; and you must not forget, Jervis, that a known intention or tendency to commit suicide makes things uncommonly easy for a murderer. But it is time that we turned our attention to the subject of food. We are due at the mortuary at two o'clock, and it will not be amiss if we get there a few minutes before our time. How will this place do?"

He halted opposite a restaurant of somewhat fly-blown aspect, the fascia of which bore an Italian name. In the window, a 'set piece' (consisting of two glass dishes of tomatoes flanking the head of a calf, who appeared from his complexion to have died of pernicious anaemia) was exhibited to whet the appetites of passers-by, while through the open doorway an unctuous odour suggestive of thick soup stole forth to mingle with the aroma from an adjacent soap-boiler's.

"Well," I said, "the soup inside smells better than the soap outside. Let us go in." Accordingly we went in.

CHAPTER VIII:

SIR EDWARD HARDCASTLE, BART., DECEASED

(Dr. Jervis's Narrative)

THORNDYKE'S reasons for wishing to arrive at the mortuary a few minutes before the appointed time were not difficult to guess at. But they became crystal clear as soon as the constable, deputed by the Superintendent, had admitted us and retired. As soon as the door shut behind the officer, he stepped quickly across to the long shelf on which the clothing had been deposited, and, picking up the shoes, turned them over, took a single glance at the soles, and then, without comment, held them out for my inspection.

No comment was needed. The soles were, relatively speaking, perfectly clean. There was not a trace of mud or any sign whatever of their having been damp. On the contrary, there still clung to them a certain amount of light dust, and this was still more evident on the welts and uppers. The condition of those shoes proved with absolute certainty that however and whenever Sir Edward Hardcastle had got into that empty house, he had not walked there on the night of Sunday, the twenty-first of June.

There was no time, however, to dwell on this striking confirmation of our previous conclusions. Thorndyke already had the research case open and had taken out the little finger-print box and produced from it the ready-inked copper plate, a piece of soft rag and a couple of smooth cards. The latter he handed to me, and together we moved over to the great table and uncovered the hands of the corpse.

"We shan't get normal prints," he remarked, as he wiped the finger-tips one after the other and then touched them with the inked plate, "but they will be clear enough to compare with our photographs of those of the chair-back."

They were certainly not normal prints, for the finger-tips were shrunken and almost mummified. But, distorted as they were, the ridge-patterns were fairly distinct and quite decipherable, as I could see by the quick glance that I took at each print after pressing the inked finger-tip on the card.

"Yes," I agreed, "there will be no difficulty about these. I only wish the photographs were half as clear."

I handed them to him and he immediately slipped them into the grooved receptacle with which the box was provided. Then he closed the latter and replaced it in the research case.

"I am glad we were able to get that done unobserved," said he. "Now we can make our observations at our ease."

He took out of the research case a pair of rubber gloves and a case of post-mortem instruments which he placed on a vacant spot on the great table. Then he brought out the tape and carefully measured the length of the corpse.

"Sixty-five inches," he reported. "Five feet five. You remember the height of that beam. Now we will have another look at those shoes."

He took them up once more and turned them over slowly to bring each part into view. Adhering to one heel was a small flat mass of some material which had apparently been trodden on, and which Thorndyke detached with his pocket-knife and deposited in an envelope from the research case.

"Looks like a small piece of soap," he remarked as he wrote "heel of right shoe" on it and put it back in the case, "but we may as well see what it is. You notice several rubbed places on these shoes, but especially on the backs, as if deceased had been dragged along a fairly smooth surface. Perhaps the back of his coat may tell us something more."

He laid the shoes down and, taking up the neatly folded coat, carefully unfolded it and held it up.

"I think you are right, Thorndyke," said I. "The coat is pretty dirty all over, but the back is noticeably more dusty than the other parts. It looks as if it had been dragged along a dirty floor; and those two bits of cotton sticking to it suggest indoor rather than outdoor dirt. And the same is true of the trousers," I added, holding them up for inspection. "There is a definitely dusty area at the back, and here is another piece of cotton sticking to the cloth."

"Yes, I think that point is clear," he said, "and it is an important point. The cotton is, as you say, definitely suggestive of a floor rather than an out-of-door surface." He picked off the three fragments, and, as he bestowed them with the other 'specimens', remarked: "There is nothing very distinctive about cotton, but we may as well take them for reference. I wish we had time to go over the clothing thoroughly, but we had better not show too conspicuous an interest."

Nevertheless, he looked over each garment, quickly, but with intense scrutiny, passing each to me before taking up the next. Over one object only--the collar--did he seem disposed to linger; and certainly its appearance invited notice; for not only was it extremely dirty and crumpled, but it seemed to be uniformly stained as if with weak tea. Moreover, as I held it in my hands, it gave me the impression of a sort of harsh stiffness unaccounted for by the material, for it was a collar of the kind known as 'semi-stiff' which usually becomes quite limp after a day's wear. But now Thorndyke had passed on to an examination of the rope noose and I laid down the collar to join him.

"Evidently," said he, "as they were able to remove it without cutting it, the knot must have slipped open pretty easily. And you can see why. The noose was made with a running bowline, a rather unsuitable and unusual knot for the purpose. We will venture to untie it and measure its length, to add to our other measurement. You notice that both ends are cut, so that the whole length is only a part of the complete rope, whatever it was."

He rapidly unfastened the knot and measured the length of the piece, and when he had made a note of the measurement, he produced his pocket-knife and cut off a portion about eight inches long which he dropped into the research case. Meanwhile, I carefully re-tied the bowline and had just replaced it where we had found it when the door opened somewhat abruptly and a stout, well-dressed, middle-aged man bustled in and deposited a hand-bag on a side bench.

"I must really apologise to you, gentlemen," he said, civilly, "for keeping you waiting, but you know how difficult it is for a G.P. to keep appointments punctually. Inquests are the bane of my life."

He hung his hat on a peg by the door, and then, as he turned, his glance lighted on Thorndyke's rubber gloves and instrument case.

"Those your tools?" he asked; and when Thorndyke admitted the ownership, he enquired with evident interest: "Were you thinking of taking a hand in this job?"

"I came prepared to offer any assistance that might be acceptable," Thorndyke replied.

"That is very good of you--my name is Ross, by the way. Of course I know yours--very good of you, indeed. I don't mind confiding to you that I hate post-mortems; and really, they are not very suitable jobs for a man who is going in and out of sick-rooms and examining living people."

"I quite agree with you," said Thorndyke. "Medicine and pathology do not mix kindly; and as I am a pathologist and not in medical practice, perhaps you would like me to carry out the actual dissection?"

"I should, very much," Dr. Ross replied. "You are an experienced pathologist and I am not. But do you think it would be in order?

"Why not?" Thorndyke asked. "You are instructed to make a post-mortem inspection. You can do that without performing the dissection. The observations and inferences on which you will give evidence will be your own observations and inferences."

"Yes, that is true," agreed Ross. "But perhaps I had better make, say, the first incision. If I do that, I can say truthfully that I made the post-mortem with your assistance. That is, if I am asked. The whole affair is a mere formality."

"Very well," said Thorndyke; "we will make the autopsy jointly," and with this he took off his coat, rolled up his shirt sleeves, drew on the rubber gloves, opened his instrument case and removed the sheet with which the body had been covered.

I was somewhat amused at our colleague's casuistry and also at the subtlety of Thorndyke's tactics. The sort of examination that our friend would have made, on the assumption that the cause of death was obvious and the autopsy "a mere formality," would not have served Thorndyke's purpose. Now he would conduct the investigation in accordance with what was in his own mind.

Dr. Ross ran his eye quickly over the corpse. "It is not an attractive body," he remarked, "but it might easily have been worse after three weeks. Still, all those post-mortem stains are a trifle confusing. You don't see anything abnormal about the general appearance, do you?

"Nothing very definite," replied Thorndyke. 'Those transverse stains on the outer sides of the arms might be pressure marks, or they might not."

"Precisely," said Ross. "I should say they are just post-mortem stains. They are certainly not bruises. What do you think of the groove?"

"Well," replied Thorndyke, "as we know that the body was hanging for three weeks, we can hardly expect to learn much from it. You notice that the knot was at the back and that it was a rather bulky knot."

"Yes," said Ross. "Wrong place, of course, and wrong sort of knot. But perhaps he hadn't had much practice in hanging himself. Shall I make the incision now?"

Thorndyke handed him a scalpel and he made an incision--a very tentative one. Then he retired to the open window and lit his pipe.

"You don't want to supervise?" Thorndyke enquired with a faint smile.

"What is the use? You are an expert and I am not. If you will tell me what you find, that will satisfy me. I accept your facts without question, though I shall form my own conclusions."

"You don't consider an expert's conclusions as convincing as his facts?" I suggested.

"Oh, I wouldn't say that," he replied. "But, you see, a medico-legal expert tends to approach an inquiry with a certain bias in favour of the abnormal. Take this present case. Here is an unfortunate gentleman who is found hanging in an empty house. A melancholy affair, but that is all that there is to it. Yet here are you two experts, with an enthusiasm that I admire and respect, voluntarily and cheerfully undertaking a most unpleasant investigation in search of something that pretty certainly is not there. And why? Because you utterly refuse to accept the obvious."

"It isn't exactly the function of a medico-legal expert to accept the obvious," I ventured to remind him.

"Precisely," he agreed. "That is my point. Your function is to look out for the abnormal and find it if you possibly can. To you, a normal case is just a failure, a case in which you have drawn a blank."

I was on the point of suggesting that his own function in this case was, in effect, the same as ours. But then, as I realised that his easy-going acceptance of surface appearances was making things easy for Thorndyke, I refrained and proceeded to "make conversation" along other lines.

"Your work as police surgeon must give you a good deal of medico-legal experience," I remarked.

"I'm not the police surgeon," he replied; "at least only by acting rank. The genuine artist is away on leave and I don't care how soon he comes back. This job is a hideous interruption of one's ordinary routine. But I see that the pathologist has made a discovery. What is the specimen that you are collecting?" he added as Thorndyke replaced the stopper in a bottle and stood the latter on a side bench.

"It is some fluid from the stomach," Thorndyke replied. "There was only an ounce or so, but I am surprised to find any in a half-mummified body like this."

"And you are preserving it for analysis, I suppose?" said Ross.

"Yes, just a rough analysis as a matter of routine. Would you write the label, Jervis?"

"Any particular reason for preserving that fluid?" asked Ross. "Any signs or suggestions of poison, for instance?

"No," replied Thorndyke. "But it will be just as well to exclude it definitely. The stomach is better preserved than I should have expected and less red."

"You don't suspect arsenic?"

"No, certainly not as a cause of death; nor, in fact, any other poison. The routine analysis is just an extra precaution."

"Well, I expect you are right, from your point of view," said Ross. "And, of course, poison is a possibility. The ways of suicides are so unaccountable, I heard of a man who took a dose of oxalic acid, then cut his throat, ineffectually, and finally hanged himself. So this man may have taken a dose and failed to produce the desired effect; but he undoubtedly finished himself off with the rope, and that is all that matters to the coroner's jury."

"There are a number of small bodies which look like fish-scales sticking to the walls of the stomach," Thorndyke reported. "No other contents excepting the fluid."

"Well," Ross protested, "there is nothing very abnormal about fish-scales in the stomach. The reasonable inference is that he had been eating fish. What do you mean to suggest?"

"I am not suggesting anything," replied Thorndyke. "I am merely reporting the facts as I observe them. The lungs seem slightly cedematous and there is just a trace of fluid in them--only a trace."

"Oh, come," Ross expostulated, "you are not going to hint that he was drowned! Because he wasn't. I've seen some drowned bodies and I can say quite positively that this is not one. Besides, let us keep the facts in mind. This man was found hanging from a beam in a house."

"Once more," Thorndyke replied, a little wearily, "let me repeat that I am offering no suggestions or inferences. As we agreed, I report the facts and you form your own conclusions. There are one or two of these little bodies--fish-scales or whatever they are--in the air-passages. Perhaps you would like to look at them."

Dr. Ross walked over to the table and looked down as Thorndyke demonstrated the little whitish specks sticking to the sides of the bronchial tubes, and for the moment he seemed somewhat impressed. But only for a moment. Unlike the medico-legal expert, as his fancy painted him, Dr. Ross evidently approached an inquiry with a strong bias in favour of the normal.

"Yes," he said, as he returned to the window, "it is queer how they can have got into the lung. Still, we know he had been eating fish, and there must have been particles in the mouth. Perhaps he had an attack of coughing and got some of them drawn down his trachea. Anyhow there they are. But if you will excuse me for saying so, these curious and no doubt interesting little details are just a trifle beside the mark. The object of this examination is to ascertain the cause of death--if it isn't obvious enough from the circumstances. Now, what do you say? You have made a pretty complete examination--and uncommonly quick you have been over it. I couldn't have done it in twice the time. But what is the result? The alleged fact is that this man hanged himself. If he did, he presumably died of asphyxia. Is the appearance of the body consistent with death from asphyxia? That is the question that I shall be asked at the inquest; and I have got to answer it. What do you say?

"One doesn't like to dogmatise," Thorndyke answered, cautiously. "You see the state of the body. Most of the characteristic signs are absent owing to the drying and the other changes. But making all the necessary allowances, I think the appearances are suggestive of death from asphyxia. At any rate there are no signs inconsistent with that cause of death and there is nothing to suggest any other."

"That is what I wanted to know," said Ross, "and if you can give me one or two details, I will run off and put my notes in order so that I can give my evidence clearly and answer any questions."

Thorndyke dictated a brief description of the state of the various organs which Ross took down verbatim in his note-book. Then he put it away, got his hat from the peg and picked up his hand-bag.

"I am infinitely obliged to you two gentlemen," he said. "You have saved me from a task that I hate and you have done the job immeasurably better than I could have done it and in half the time. I only hope that I haven't victimised you too much."

"You haven't victimised us at all," said Thorndyke. "It has been a matter of mutual accommodation."

"Very good of you to say so," said Ross; and having thanked us once more, he bustled away.

"I hope that you have not misled that good gentleman," I remarked as Thorndyke proceeded to restore, as far as possible, the status quo ante and render the corpse presentable to the coroner's jury.

"I have not misled him intentionally," he replied. "I gave him all the observed facts. His interpretation of them is his own affair. Perhaps, while I am finishing, you would complete the labels. That corked tube filled with water contains the fish-scales, as I assume them to be."

"Shall I write 'fish-scales' on the label?"

"No; just write 'from lungs, mouth and stomach'; and perhaps you might look through the beard and the hair and see if you can find any more."

"The hair!" I exclaimed. "How on earth could they get into the hair?"

"Perhaps they did not," he replied. "But you may as well look. We are not adopting Ross's interpretation, you know."

I took a pair of dissecting forceps and searched among the rather short hair of the scalp, speculating curiously as to what Thorndyke could have in his mind. But whatever it was, it evidently agreed with the facts for my search brought to light no less than six of the little, white, lustrous objects.

"You had better put them in a separate tube," said Thorndyke, when I reported the find, "in case they are not the same as the others. And now it would be as well to have another look at the coat."

He had drawn the sheet over the whole of the body excepting the head and neck and now proceeded to clean and dry his rubber gloves and instruments. While he was thus occupied, I took up the coat and made a fresh and more detailed inspection.

"It is extraordinarily dirty at the back," I reported, "and there seems to be a slight stain on the collar and shoulders as if it had been wetted with dirty water."

"Yes, I noticed that," he said. "You don't see any foreign particles sticking to it or to any of the other garments?"

I looked the coat over inside and out but could find nothing excepting a tiny fragment of what looked like black silk thread, which had stuck to the flap of a pocket. I picked it off and put it in the envelope with the ends of cotton. Then I turned my attention to the other garments. From the trousers nothing fresh was to be learned, nor from the waistcoat--the pockets of which I searched to make sure that the little leather ring-case had not been overlooked--excepting that, like the coat, it showed signs on its collar of having been wetted; as also did the blue and white striped cotton shirt. I was examining the latter when Thorndyke, having finished 'tidying up', came and looked over my shoulder.

"That stain," he remarked, "hardly looks like water, even dirty water, though it is surprising how distinct and conspicuous a stain perfectly clean water will sometimes make on linen which has been worn and exposed to dust."

He took the garment from me and examined the stained part intently, felt it critically with finger and thumb and finally held it to his nose and sniffed at it. Then he laid it down and picked up the collar, which he examined in the same manner, by sight, touch and smell, turning it over and opening the fold to inspect the inside.

"I think," he said, "we ought to find out, if possible, whether this was water or some other fluid. We don't know what light the knowledge might throw on this extraordinarily obscure case."

He was still standing, as if undecided, with the collar in his hand when the sound of footsteps approaching down the alley became audible; whereupon he turned quickly, and, dropping the collar into the research case, closed the latter and took his hat down from the peg. The next moment the door opened and the sergeant looked in.

"Jury coming to view the body, gentlemen," he announced; and with a critical look towards the table, he added: "I thought I had better come on ahead and see that they shouldn't get too bad a shock. Juries are sometimes a bit squeamish, but I see that the doctor has left everything tidy and decent. You know where the inquest is to be held, I suppose?"

"We don't," replied Thorndyke, "but if we lurk outside and follow the jury we shan't go far wrong."

We walked up to the top of the alley, where we met a party of rather apprehensive-looking men who were being personally conducted by a constable. We waited for them to return, which they did with remarkable promptitude and looking not at all refreshed by their visit, and we turned and followed in their wake, the sergeant, as coroner's officer, hurrying past us to anticipate their arrival at the place where the inquiry was to be held.

"It seems almost a waste of time for us to sit out the proceedings," I remarked as we walked along in the rear of the procession. "We have got all the material facts."

"We think we have," replied Thorndyke, "and it is not likely that we shall hear anything that will alter our views of the case. But, still, we don't know that something vital may not turn up in the evidence."

"I can't imagine anything that could account for the state of the dead man's shoes," said I.

"No," he agreed, "that seems conclusive, and I think it is. Nevertheless, if it should transpire in evidence that Sir Edward was seen in the neighbourhood before the rain started, the absence of mud on his shoes would cease to have any special significance. But here we are at the court. I expect Brodribb is there already and it will probably be best for him and for us if we select seats that are not too near his. He will want to give his whole attention to his own evidence and that of the other witnesses."

We watched the last of the jurymen enter the municipal office in which the proceedings were to take place; then we went in and took possession of a couple of chairs in a corner, commanding a view of the table and the place in which the witnesses would stand or sit to give their evidence.

CHAPTER IX:

THE CROWNER'S QUEST

(Dr. Jervis's Narrative)

DURING the brief preliminary period, while the jury-men were taking their places and the court was pervaded by the hum of conversation and the rustle of movement, I looked about me to see who was present and if possible to identify the prospective witnesses. Brodribb was seated near the coroner's chair, and, by his rather unhappy, preoccupied look, I judged that Thorndyke, with his usual tact, had pretty accurately gauged his mental state. He caught my eye once and acknowledged my silent greeting with a grave nod, but immediately relapsed into his previous gloomy and meditative condition.

Seated next to him was an elderly--or perhaps I should say an old--man, for he looked well over sixty, who was, in appearance, such a typical example of the old-fashioned better gentleman's servant that I instantly placed him, correctly, as it turned out, as Mr. Weeks, Sir Edward's butler. Behind the coroner's chair was our friend the Superintendent, who was carrying on a whispered conversation with Dr. Ross. Our colleague struck me as looking a little nervous and sheepish and I noticed that he held a paper in his hand and glanced at it from time to time. From which I inferred that he was conning over his notes with a view to the prompt and confident delivery of his evidence.

At this point my observations were brought to an end by a premonitory cough on the part of the coroner, which had somewhat the effect of the warning rattle of a striking clock, as giving the company to understand that he was about to begin his address. Thereupon, silence fell on the assembly and the proceedings opened. Quite briefly and in general terms, he indicated the nature of the case which was the subject of the inquiry, and, having sketchily recited the leading facts, proceeded to call the witnesses.

"It is the common practice," he said in conclusion, "to begin with the medical evidence, as the state of the body is usually the principal means of determining the cause of death and of answering the questions, How, When and Where that death was brought about. But in the present case the circumstances surrounding the discovery of the body have so important a bearing that I think it better to take the evidence on that point first. The first witness will be James Holker."

In response to the implied summons, a well-dressed, capable-looking man rose and approached the table. Having been sworn, he deposed that his name was James Holker, that he was by calling a ship's steward but now retired and living chiefly on the proceeds of certain house property that he owned. Among other such property was a row of houses known as Piper's Row; and it was in one of these houses, Number Five, to wit, that he made the discovery.

"On what date was that?" the coroner asked.

"On Tuesday, the fourteenth of July. Yesterday morning, in fact."

"Tell us exactly what happened on that occasion."

"I went round to Number Five to go on with some repairs that I had begun. I went straight into the front room--that is the living-room--and then I noticed a glove lying on the floor under the window. I remembered having seen that glove before. But now I noticed something very unpleasant about the air of the place and there seemed to be an unusual number of flies and blue-bottles about. So I went through to the kitchen and it was worse there. Then I opened the door of the wash-house and looked in; and there I saw a man hanging from a roof-beam. I didn't stop to examine him. I just bolted straight out of the house and ran up to the police station to report what had happened."

"You had no doubt that the man was dead?"

"None whatever. I could see at a glance that he had been dead a week or two. And it wasn't a matter of eyesight only--"

"No. Quite so. Now, have you any means of judging how long he had been hanging there?"

"Yes. I judge that he had been hanging there a little over three weeks."

"Tell us how you are able to arrive at that time."

"Well, sir, it was this way. On Sunday, the twenty-first of June, I put in a fairly full day's work at the repairs on Number Five; and nothing could have happened on that day, because I went all over the house. I worked on there all the afternoon up to getting on for five, and then, as I saw that it was coming on wet, I stowed my tools in a cupboard in the front room and ran off home as hard as I could go through the rain.

"That night, the captain of an old ship of mine, the _Esmeralda_, called to ask me to take a trip with him to Marseilles, as his steward had to go into hospital. I thought I'd like the trip, and I was glad to oblige the captain, so I said 'Yes' and set to work to pack my kit. Next morning, Monday, I ran round to Number Five to fetch my tools away. As I was in a hurry, I only went into the front room, where my tools were. But I could see that someone had been in the house, because there was a glove lying on the floor just under the window; and I noticed that the window was unfastened and slightly open. If I had had time I would have had a look round the house; but, as I was in a hurry to get on to the docks, and there was nothing in the house that anyone could take, I just took up my tools and came away."

"Did you pick up the glove?"

"No. I left it as it was; and when I went to the house yesterday, it was lying in the same place."

"Is there anything else that you can tell us about the case?"

"No, sir. That's all I know about it."

The coroner glanced at the jury. "Are there any questions that you wish to ask the witness, gentlemen?" he enquired. "If not, we will next take the evidence of Superintendent Thompson."

The Superintendent marched briskly up to the table and having disposed, with business-like brevity, of the preliminary formalities, gave his evidence with a conciseness born of long experience.

"At ten-fifteen yesterday morning, that is Tuesday, the fourteenth of July, the previous witness, James Holker, came to the police station and reported to me that a dead man was hanging in a house of his, Number Five Piper's Row. I gave instructions for a wheeled stretcher to be sent there and then proceeded forthwith to the house in company with Holker and Constable Marshall.

"On entering, I went straight through to the wash-house, where I saw the dead body of a man hanging by a rope from a roof-beam. Nearly underneath the body but a little to one side was an overturned chair; and close to the chair a wash-leather glove was lying on the floor and a little farther off a soft felt hat. A walking-stick was standing in the corner by the door. Deceased had no collar on, but I found the collar, afterwards, in his pocket, very dirty and crumpled. The rope by which the body was hanging was a small coir rope, a trifle thinner than my little finger. It was tied very securely to the beam above and the noose had a rather large knot, which was at the back of the neck."

"Could you form any idea as to how long the body had been hanging?" the coroner asked.

"I could only form a rough estimate. Judging by the advanced state of decomposition I concluded that it must have been hanging at least a fortnight, and I thought it probable that Holker's account, making it three weeks, was correct."

"Did there appear to be anything unusual in the method used by deceased?"

"No. The way in which the suicide was carried out seemed quite simple and ordinary. Apparently, when he came into the wash-house, he stood his stick in the corner, threw down his hat and glove, took off his collar and put it in his pocket. Then he probably made the noose, stood on the chair and tied the rope to the beam, put the noose round his neck, pulled it fairly tight, drew up his legs and kicked the chair over so that he was left swinging free. That was what it looked like."

"Is there any evidence as to how deceased got into the house?"

"I think there is no doubt that he got in by the front room window. He couldn't have got in by the street door, because it was locked--at least, so I am informed by Holker, who is quite sure that he shut it when he left the house on Sunday evening, the twenty-first of June--and deceased had no keys on him. But there is positive evidence that he got in by the window; for when I went into the front room, I found the window unfastened and open a couple of inches, and just underneath it I found a wash-leather glove on the floor, which was evidently the fellow of the glove that was lying on the wash-house floor under the body."

"And with regard to the rope. Did deceased find that on the premises?"

"No. He must have brought it with him. I questioned Holker about it and he informed me that it was not his, that he had never seen it before and that there was no rope of any kind in the house."

"Were there any signs that the body had been robbed?"

"No; and I think I can say definitely that it had not. There was not much in the pockets, considering the deceased gentleman's position, but there were things in them that no thief would have left. For instance, there was a purse containing three sovereigns and a letter wallet with two five-pound notes in it. And the small value of the contents of the pockets seems to be satisfactorily accounted for, as Mr. Brodribb has informed me that deceased had emptied his pockets of most of his valuables, including his gold watch, before he left the club."

"Ah," said the coroner, "that is a significant fact. We must get the details from Mr. Brodribb. Are there any further facts known to you that ought to be communicated to the jury?"

"I think I ought to mention that deceased's clothing was extraordinarily dirty and tumbled. The collar was excessively dirty and seemed to have been wetted, and so did the shirt at the neck; and the coat and trousers were very dusty at the back, as if deceased had been lying on a dirty floor."

"What do you suggest as to the significance of those facts?"

"Taken with the fact that deceased left the club (as I am informed) on Wednesday, the seventeenth of June, and could not have entered the empty house before Sunday night, the twenty-first of June, the state of his clothes suggests to me that he had been wandering about in the interval, perhaps spending the nights in common lodging-houses or sleeping in the open, and that he had washed himself at pumps or taps and got his head and neck wet. Of course, that is only a guess."

"Quite so. But it seems probable and certainly agrees with the known circumstances. Is there any thing more that you have to tell the jury?"

"No, sir. That is all the information that I have to give."

"Any questions, gentlemen?" the coroner asked, glancing at the jury. "No questions. Thank you, Superintendent. Perhaps, before we hear the next witness we had better recall Mr. Holker in order that he may confirm on oath those of his statements which have been quoted by the Superintendent."

Holker was accordingly recalled and formally confirmed those passages of the officer's evidence (referring to the door and the rope) when they had been read out by the coroner from the depositions. This formality having been disposed of, the coroner glanced through his notes and then announced: "We will take the medical evidence next so that the doctor may be able to get away to his patients. Dr. Ross."

Our colleague approached the table with less obvious self-possession than the experienced officer who had preceded him. But he was quite a good witness. He had made up his mind as to what he was going to say and he said it with a confident, authoritative air that carried conviction to the jury.

"You have made a thorough examination of the body of deceased?" the coroner said, when the witness had been sworn and the other preliminaries despatched.

"I have," was the reply.

"And what was the result of your examination? You understand, doctor, that the jury don't want you to go into technical details. They just want the conclusions that you arrived at. To begin with, how long should you say the deceased had been dead?"

"I should say that he had been dead not less than three weeks."

"Were you able to ascertain the cause of death?"

"I was able to form a very definite opinion. The condition of the body was so very unfavourable for examination that I hardly like to go beyond that."

"Quite so. The jury have seen the body and I am sure they fully realise its condition. But you were able to form a decided opinion?"

"Yes. I found distinct signs of death from asphyxia and I found nothing whatever to suggest any other cause of death."

"Well," said the coroner, "that seems to be sufficient for our purpose. Was there anything to account for the asphyxia?

"There was a deep groove encircling the neck, marking the position of the rope by which deceased had been suspended."

Here the foreman of the jury interposed with the request that the witness would explain exactly what he meant by asphyxia.

"Asphyxia," the doctor explained, "is the condition which is produced when a person is prevented from breathing. If the breathing is completely stopped, death occurs in about two minutes."

"And how may the breathing become stopped?" the foreman asked.

"In various ways. By hanging, by strangling, by covering the mouth and nose with a pillow or other soft object, by drowning or by immersion in a gas such as carbonic acid."

"What do you say was the cause of the asphyxia in this case?"

"As hanging causes asphyxia and deceased was undoubtedly hanged, the asphyxia was presumably due to the hanging."

"That seems fairly obvious," said the coroner; "but," he added, looking a little severely at the foreman, "we mustn't ask the doctor to provide us with a verdict. He is giving evidence as to the facts observed by himself. It is for you to decide on the significance of those facts. He tells us that he observed signs of death from asphyxia. We have heard from other witnesses that deceased was found hanging; the connection of those facts is a question for the jury. Is there anything else that you have to tell us, doctor?"

"No, I observed nothing else that is relevant to the inquiry."

"Does any gentleman wish to ask the doctor any further questions?" the coroner asked, glancing at the jury; and as no one expressed any such desire, he continued: "Then I think we need not detain the doctor any longer. The next witness will be Herbert Weeks."

On hearing his name pronounced, Mr. Weeks rose and took his place at the table. Having been sworn, he stated that he had been butler to deceased, whose father, Sir Julian, he had served in the same capacity. He had known deceased practically all his (deceased's) life and they were on very intimate and confidential terms.

"Had you ever any reason to expect that deceased might make away with himself?" the coroner asked.

"No," was the reply. "Such a thing never occurred to me."

"Have you noticed anything of late in his manner or his apparent state of mind that might account for, or explain his having made away with himself? Has he, for instance, seemed worried or depressed about anything?"

Mr. Weeks hesitated. At length he replied, with an air of weighing his words carefully: "I don't think he was worried about anything. So far as I know, there was nothing for him to worry about. And I should hardly describe him as being depressed, though I must admit that he had not very good spirits. He had never really recovered from the shock of losing his wife and his son--his only child."

"When did that happen?"

"About ten years ago. They were both carried off by influenza within a few days, and Sir Edward himself nearly died of the same complaint. When he began to get better, we had to break it to him and I thought it would have killed him; and though he did at last recover, he was never the same man again."

"In what respect was he changed?"

"He seemed to have lost interest in life. When her ladyship and the young gentleman were alive, he was always cheerful and gay and full of schemes and projects for the future. He was constantly planning improvements in the estate and riding about the property with his son to discuss them. He was very devoted to his wife and son, as they were to him; a most affectionate and united family. When they died, it seemed as if he had lost everything that he cared for. He took no further interest in his property but just left it to the bailiff to manage and turned his business affairs over to Mr. Brodribb."

"And you say that he was changed in manner?"

"Yes. All his old high spirits went, though he was just as kind and thoughtful for others as he had always been. But he became grave and quiet in his manner and seemed rather dull and aimless, as if there was nothing that he cared about in particular."

The coroner reflected for a few moments on these statements. Then abandoning this line of enquiry, he asked: "When did deceased leave home?"

"On Tuesday, the sixteenth of June."

"Did he inform you what his intended movements were?"

"Yes. He said that he was going to spend a couple of days in London and that he expected to return home on Thursday afternoon. He told me that he intended to stay at his club as he usually did when visiting London."

"Did you notice anything unusual in his manner on that occasion?"

"I thought that he seemed rather preoccupied, as if he had some business on hand that he was giving a good deal of thought to."

"He did not strike you as unusually depressed or anxious?"

"No; only that he gave me the impression that he was thinking out something that he did not quite understand."

"Was that the last time that you saw him alive?"

"Yes. I stood at the main door and watched him walk away down the drive, followed by one of the gardeners carrying his suit-case. I never saw him again until this morning, when I saw him in the mortuary."

Mr. Weeks delivered these statements in quiet, even tones, but it was easy to see that he was controlling his emotion with some difficulty. Observing this, the coroner turned from the witness to the jury.

"I think," he said, "Mr. Weeks has given us all the material facts known to him, so, if there are no questions, we need not prolong what is, no doubt, a very painful ordeal for him." He paused, and then, as no question was asked, he thanked the witness and dismissed him. A brief pause followed during which the coroner glanced quickly through his notes. Then Mr. Brodribb's name was called; and, bearing Thorndyke's prediction in mind, I gave his evidence my very special attention.

"What was the exact nature of your relations with deceased?" the coroner asked, when the introductory matter had been disposed of.

"I was his solicitor. But in addition to my purely legal functions, I acted as his adviser in respect of the general business connected with the management of his property. I am also the executor of his will."

"Then you can tell us if there were any embarrassments or difficulties connected with his property that were causing him anxiety."

"I can. There were no embarrassments or difficulties whatever. His financial affairs were not only completely in order but in a highly favourable state. I may say that his estate was flourishing and his income considerably in excess of his expenditure. He certainly had no financial anxieties."

"Had he any anxieties of any kind, so far as you know?"

"So far as I know, he had none."

"You heard Mr. Weeks's description of the change in his manner and habits caused by his bereavement. Do you confirm that?"

"Yes; the loss of his wife and son left him a broken man."

"You attribute the change in him to the grief due to his bereavement?

"Principally. The loss of those so dear to him left an abiding grief. But there was a further effect. Sir Edward's lively interest in his estate and his ambition to improve it and increase its value were based on the consideration that it would in due course pass to his son, and probably to his son's son. Like most English landowners, he had a strong sense of continuity. But the continuity of succession was destroyed by his son's death. The present heir-presumptive is a distant relative who was almost a stranger to Sir Edward. Thus deceased had come to feel that he was no more than a life-tenant of the estate; that, at his death, it would pass out of the possession of his own family into the hands of strangers and there was no knowing what might happen to it. As a result he, not unnaturally, lost all interest in the future of the estate. But since, hitherto, this had been the predominant purpose of his life, its failure left him without any strong interest or aim in life."

The coroner nodded, as one who appreciates a material point of evidence.

"Yes," he said, "this loss of interest in life seems to have an important bearing on our inquiry. But beyond this general state of mind, did you ever notice any more particular manifestation. In short, did you ever observe anything that caused you to entertain the possibility that deceased might make away with himself?"

Mr. Brodribb hesitated. "I can't say," he replied, after a pause, "that the possibility of suicide ever entered my mind."

"That, Mr. Brodribb, seems a rather qualified answer, as if you had something further in your mind. Am I right?"

Apparently the coroner was right, for Mr. Brodribb, after a few moments' rather uneasy reflection, replied with obvious unwillingness: "I certainly never considered the possibility of suicide; but, looking back, I am not sure that there were not some suggestions that were at least susceptible of such an interpretation. I now recall, for instance, a remark which deceased made to me some months ago. We were, I think, discussing the almost universal repugnance to the idea of death when deceased said (as nearly as I can remember), 'I often feel, Brodribb, that there is something rather restful in the thought of death. That it would be quite pleasant and peaceful to feel oneself sinking into sleep with the certain knowledge that one was never going to wake up.' I attached no weight to that remark at the time, but now, looking at it in the light of what has happened, it seems rather significant."

"I agree with you," the coroner said, emphatically. "It seems very significant indeed. And that suggests another question. I presume that you are pretty well acquainted with the affairs of deceased's family?"

"Very well indeed. I have been connected with the Hardcastle estate during the whole of my professional life, and so was my father before me."

"Then you can tell us whether any instances of suicide have occurred among any of deceased's relatives."

Once more Mr. Brodribb hesitated with a slightly puzzled and reluctant air. At length, he replied, cautiously: "I can only say that no instance of suicide in the family is known to me, or even suspected by me. But it seems proper that I should acquaint you with the rather mysterious and highly eccentric conduct of deceased's brother, Gervase. This gentleman became, unfortunately, rather intemperate in his habits, with the regrettable result--among others--that he was deprived of a fellowship that he held at Oxford. Thereafter, he disappeared and ceased to communicate with his family, and all that is known of him is that he was, for a time, living in poverty, and apparently in something like squalor, in Paris and other foreign towns."

"Had his family cast him off?"

"Not at all. Sir Edward's feelings towards him were quite friendly and brotherly. He would willingly have provided the means for his brother to live comfortably and in a manner suitable to his station. The self-imposed ostracism on Gervase's part was sheer perversity."

"And what became of this brother? Is he still living?"

"His death was announced in the obituary column of The Times about sixteen years ago without any address other than Brighton. Of the circumstances of his death, nothing whatever is known."

"Have you any reason to suppose that he made away with himself?"

"I have not. I mentioned his case merely as an instance of voluntary disappearance and generally eccentric behaviour."

"Exactly; as furnishing a parallel to the voluntary disappearance of deceased. That is quite an important point. And now, as a final question, I should like to ask you to confirm what the Superintendent told us as to deceased having emptied his pockets of things of value before leaving the club."

"The Superintendent's statement is, in the main, correct. When examining his bedroom at the club, I found in a locked suit-case--which I was able to unlock--a gold watch and chain, a valuable pearl tie pin, a bunch of keys and a few private letters, which I glanced through and which threw no light on his disappearance."

"Ah," said the coroner, "a very significant proceeding. No doubt it struck you so?"

"It did, coupled with the fact that the owner was missing; and I communicated the facts at once to the police."

"Yes. Very proper. And that, I think, is all that we wish to ask you, unless there is anything else that occurs to you or unless the jury desire to put any questions."

Mr. Brodribb intimated that he had nothing further to communicate, and, as the jury made no sign, the witness was allowed to retire to his seat.

The next name called was that of Mr. Northbrook, the secretary of the club; but as his evidence for the most part, merely confirmed and amplified that of the preceding witnesses, I need not record it in detail. One new fact, however, emerged, though it did not seem to me, at the time, to have any particular significance.

"You say," said the coroner, "that you saw deceased leave the club?"

"Yes. I was in the porter's office at the time, and, as deceased passed the open door, I wished him 'good morning.' But apparently he did not hear me, for he passed out without taking any notice."

"And that, I take it, was actually the last time he is known to have been seen alive?

"Not absolutely the last time. He was seen a few minutes later by one of the club waiters, getting into a hansom cab. I have brought the waiter with me in case you wished to hear his account first hand."

"That was very thoughtful of you," said the coroner, "and I am glad you did. We should certainly wish to have the evidence of the last person who saw deceased alive."

The waiter was accordingly called and sworn, when it transpired that his name was Joseph Wood and that he had mighty little to tell. That little may as well, however, be given in his own words.

"I was coming along Piccadilly from the west when I caught sight of Sir Edward Hardcastle, coming towards me. He was a good distance off, but I recognised him at once. I wait at the table that he always used, so I knew him very well by sight. While I was looking at him, a hansom drew up by the pavement and he got in, and then the hansom drove away. I didn't see him hail it, but he may have done. I couldn't see if there was anyone else in the cab, because its back was towards me, and as soon as he got in it drove away. I didn't see him say anything to the cabman, but he may have spoken up through the trap. The cab drove off in an easterly direction--towards the Circus. I did not notice the number of the cab. There was no reason why I should."

This was the sum of his evidence, and it was not clear to me why he had been brought so far to tell so little, for the trivial circumstance that he deposed to appeared to have no bearing whatever on the case; and I was not a little surprised to observe that Thorndyke took down his statements, apparently verbatim, in shorthand; a proceeding that I could account for only by bearing in mind his invariable rule that nothing could be considered irrelevant until all the facts were known.

The waiter, Joseph Wood, was the last of the witnesses, and, when he had concluded his evidence, the coroner, having announced that all the known facts were now in the jury's possession, made a brief inspection of his notes with a view to his summing-up. At length he began: "It is not necessary, gentlemen, that I should address you at great length. We have given to this painful case an exhaustive consideration which was called for rather by reason of the deceased gentleman's position and the interests involved than by any inherent difficulties. The case is, in fact, quite a simple one. All the material circumstances are known to us, and there is not the slightest conflict of evidence. On the contrary, all the witnesses are in complete agreement and the evidence of each confirms that of the others.

"The time at which this sad affair occurred is fixed beyond any possible doubt by Mr. Holker's evidence. Deceased must have entered the house, in which his body was subsequently found, during the evening or night of Sunday, the twenty-first of June; and this date is confirmed by the medical evidence. Thus, the questions, When and Where are answered conclusively. Mr. Holker and the Superintendent both saw the dead body suspended from a beam; and the medical witness found signs of death from asphyxia, as would be expected in the case of a man who had died by hanging.

"The question of motive seems to be solved as completely as we could expect by the evidence of Mr. Weeks and especially by that of Mr. Brodribb. The terrible bereavement which deceased suffered, the shipwreck of all his hopes and ambitions and the desolate state in which he was left, if they could not be properly regarded as conditions predisposing to suicide, furnish a reasonable explanation of it after the event.

"There is one feature in the case which did, at first, appear very strange and difficult to explain, and which, I may admit, occasioned this very rigorous inquiry. That feature is the extraordinary surroundings in which the body was discovered. How, one asked oneself, is it possible to account for the appearance of a man in deceased's position in an empty house in the purlieus of Stratford? It seemed an insoluble mystery. Then came the evidence of the Superintendent and Mr. Brodribb. The one finds traces that, to the expert eye, tell of ramblings in sordid neighbourhoods and waste places, of nights spent in doss-houses or in the open. The other tells us of a relative--actually a brother of deceased--who, in a strangely similar manner, had disappeared from his usual places of resort, cut himself off from family and friends and, by deliberate choice, had lived--and perhaps died--in surroundings of sordid poverty. I will not say that this evidence explains the proceedings of deceased. Probably they will never be completely explained. But I do say that our knowledge of the brother's conduct makes that of deceased perfectly credible.

"I will add only one further observation. If you find that deceased made away with himself, as the evidence seems to prove, I think you will agree with me that, at the time and for some days previously, he was not in his right mind. If that is your view, I will ask you to embody it in your verdict."

At the conclusion of the coroner's address, the jury consulted together. But their consultation occupied only a minute or two. Apparently they had already made up their minds, as they might well have done, taking the evidence at its face value. When the whispered conference came to an end, the foreman announced that they had agreed on their verdict and the coroner then put the formal question: "And what is your decision, gentlemen?

"We find," was the reply, "that deceased committed suicide by hanging himself while temporarily insane."

"Yes," said the coroner, "I am in entire agreement with you, and I must thank you for the care and attention with which you have considered the evidence."

As the proceedings came to an end, Thorndyke and I rose and made our way out, leaving Brodribb in conversation with the coroner and the Superintendent.

"Well," I said as we halted outside to wait for our friend, "it has been quite entertaining, but I don't see that we have got much for our attendance."

"We have got one fact, at least," replied Thorndyke, "that was worth coming for. We now know that Holker was in the house until after the rain had begun to fall. That clears away any uncertainties on a point of vital importance. But we had better not discuss the case now. And I think--though it seems rather scurvy treatment of our old friend--but I think we had better keep our own counsel. Brodribb accepts the suicide as an established fact, and perhaps it is as well that he should. If we are going to work at this case, it will be all to the good that we hold the monopoly of the real facts. It will be a difficult and obscure case, but the difficulty will be materially reduced if we can watch the development of events quietly, without anyone suspecting that we are watching. This was no crime of sudden impulse. It was premeditated and arranged. Obviously there was, behind it, some perfectly definite motive. We have, among other things, to discover what that motive was. The criminals at present believe themselves to be entirely unsuspected. If they maintain that belief, they will feel at liberty to pursue their purpose without any special precautions; and we--also unsuspected--may get our chance. But here comes Brodribb."

I must confess that Thorndyke's observations appeared to me so cryptic as to convey no meaning whatever. That, I recognised, was owing to my own 'slowness in the uptake'. However, there was no opportunity to seek elucidation, for Brodribb had seen us and was now bearing down on us. He replied to our greeting with something less than his usual vivacity, and we set forth on our way to the station in almost uninterrupted silence.

CHAPTER X:

A SUMMARY OF THE EVIDENCE

(Dr. Jervis's Narrative)

MR. BRODRIBB'S taciturn mood persisted even after we had taken possession of an empty first-class smoking compartment and lit our pipes. Evidently his recent experiences had depressed him profoundly; which, after all, was no matter for surprise. An inquest is not a jovial function under the most favourable conditions, and the conditions in the recent inquiry had been far from favourable for the friends of the deceased.

"It was a ghoulish business," he remarked in semi-apologetic explanation of his low spirits, "but, of course, it had to be; and the coroner managed it as decently as possible. Still, I had rather that he had managed without me."

"If he had," said I, "he would have missed what he regarded as most important evidence."

"Yes, I know," replied Brodribb. "That was what I felt, though I hated giving that evidence. The affair had to be cleared up, and I have no doubt that the jury were right in their verdict. I know you don't agree with me, Thorndyke, but I think your special experience has misled you for once."

"There is always the possibility," Thorndyke admitted, "that professional bias may influence one. In any case, our divergence of views does not affect the position in practice. The death of Sir Edward is an established fact and the ambiguity of your legal status is at an end."

"Yes," Brodribb agreed, "there is that very unsatisfactory compensation. I am now the executor and can act as I think best. I could only wish that the best course of action were a little more easy to decide on."

With this, he relapsed into silent reflection, possibly connected with the difficulties suggested by his last sentence; and as Thorndyke and I were unable to discuss before him the matters that were occupying our thoughts, we followed his example and devoted ourselves to the consideration of our own affairs.

Suddenly Brodribb sat up with a start and began to rummage in his inside breast-pocket. "Bless my soul!" he exclaimed. "What a fool I am! Clean forgot this. Ought to have mentioned it in my evidence."

Here he brought out a letter wallet, and, taking from it an envelope, opened the latter and tipped some small object out on to his palm.

"There!" he said, holding out his open hand to Thorndyke. "What do you think of that?"

Thorndyke picked up the object, and, having examined it, held it up to the light, when I saw that it was a little oval plate of a bright transparent green bearing an engraved device which I recognised instantly.

"The missing seal!" I exclaimed, taking it from Thorndyke to inspect it more closely. "Then we may assume that the great mystery is solved."

"Indeed, you may assume nothing of the kind," said Brodribb. "On the contrary, the mystery is more profound than ever and the chance of a solution more remote. I will tell you all about it--all that I know, that is to say. It is a queer story. Your friend, Superintendent Miller, brought it to me yesterday afternoon to compare with my seals and for formal identification by me (which I thought very kind and courteous of him), and this is the account he gave of its discovery.

"It seems that, about a week ago, a man escaped from Pentonville Gaol. I understand that he got away in the evening, and in some miraculous fashion--you know where the prison is; right in the middle of a populous neighbourhood--he kept out of sight until it was dark, which wouldn't have been much before eleven at this time of year. Then, with the same miraculous luck, he managed to slip away through the streets, right across the northern suburbs to the neighbourhood of Temple Mills by the River Lea.

"There he was lurking the next afternoon when he had another stroke of luck. Some devotee of the simple life had elected to take a bath in the river, and he must have strayed away some distance from his clothes, for our Pentonville sportsman found them unguarded. Possibly he may have watched the other sportsman taking them off. At any rate, he seized the opportunity; slipped off the prison clothes and popped on the others. Then he nipped off across the meadows in the direction of Tottenham. And there it was that his luck deserted him; for, by the merest chance, a plain clothes officer who knew him by sight, happened to meet him, and, as the hue and cry was out, he collared him forthwith.

"And now comes one of the quaint features of the story. At Tottenham Police Station they went through his pockets--they were really the other fellow's, of course--with mighty little result. The next day they took him back to Pentonville, and once more he was put into uniform. The clothes that were taken off him were put aside until they could be disposed of in some way. But a couple of days ago it occurred to one of the officers to go over them carefully to see if he could find out the lawful owner. And then he made a discovery. Apparently, the owner of those clothes was a pickpocket, for there was a secret receptacle in the back of the waistcoat, which had been overlooked at the first search; and in that secret pocket the officer found this stone."

"And what happened to the other man?" I asked.

"Ah!" chuckled Brodribb, quite recovering his natural spirits for the time being, "that's the cream of the joke. He found the gaol-bird's discarded garments in place of his own clothes and of course he had to put 'em on, since he couldn't go about naked. It was a lovely situation; almost as if he had walked into prison and locked himself in. However, as soon as he was dressed in his proper character, he made a bolt for it; and he had even better luck than the other fellow. In some perfectly incredible manner, he made his way, in broad daylight, right across North London and came to the surface at the Angel, of all unlikely places."

"At the Angel!" I repeated, incredulously.

"At the Angel," Brodribb reiterated, joyously. "Just picture to yourselves an escaped convict in full uniform, elbowing his way through the crowd at the Angel! Well, of course, it couldn't go on. A couple of plain-clothes men saw him and pounced on him in an instant. It looked as if his luck had given out. But apparently his wits were as nimble as his heels, for he got just a dog's chance and he took it. At the moment when the two constables were taking him across the road, a fire-engine came thundering along and they had to scuttle back out of the way. But as it flew past, our friend made a grab at the rail of the foot-plate and held on. The momentum of the engine whisked him out of the clutches of his captors and sent them sprawling; and when they got up, their prisoner was standing on the foot-plate and fading in the distance before their eyes. Of course, it is no use shouting after a fire-engine.

"Now the odd thing is," Mr. Brodribb continued in a slightly shaky voice, "that none of the fire-men on the engine seem to have noticed him; and the constables couldn't telephone a warning until they had found out where the fire was. So our friend stuck on the engine until it turned down Tottenham Court Road, when he hopped off and made a bolt down Warren Street. Naturally, he soon picked up some followers, but he kept ahead of them, flying up one street and down another until he arrived at Cleveland Mews with half the town at his heels. He turned into the mews, still well ahead, and shot down it like a rocket. And that was the last that was seen of him. The crowd and the police surged in after him, and as the mews is a blind alley, they were quite cocksure that they'd got him. But when they came to the blind end, there was not a sign of him. He had vanished into thin air. And he had vanished for good, you observe. For, as nobody knew who he was, nobody could identify him when once he had changed his clothes."

"No," I agreed, "he has got clear away, and I must admit that I think he deserved to."

"I am afraid that I agree with you," said Brodribb. "Very improper for a lawyer, but even lawyers are human. But the police were very puzzled; not only as to how he had managed to escape, but, when the real convict was captured, they couldn't make out why he ran away. Of course, when the seal was found in the pocket, they understood."

"I wonder how he did get away," said I.

"So do I," said Brodribb. "It was a remarkable exploit. I examined the place myself and could see no apparent way of escape."

"You examined the place?" I exclaimed in surprise.

"Yes. I forgot to mention that, by a remarkable coincidence, I happened to be there at the very time. I took Sir Giles Farnaby to see a client of mine who has a studio that fronts on the mews. When we arrived the police were actually searching the studio. They thought the fugitive might have got in at the open window, unnoticed by the two ladies who were at work there. So they went all over the premises. Just as well for our friend that they did; for while they were searching the studio premises he had time to make his little arrangements at the bottom of the mews. And now we shall never know how he came by that seal, though, as he seems to have been a pickpocket, we can make a pretty likely guess."

"Yes," Thorndyke agreed a little dryly, "it is always possible to guess. But guesses are not very valuable evidential assets. The police guessed that this man was a pickpocket, and we can guess that, being a pickpocket, he obtained the seal in the practice of his art. That guess is supported by the fact that the ring is the only article known to be missing from his person, and that the leather case in which it was usually carried, is also missing. On the other hand, it is not in agreement with the fact that the stone had been dismounted from the ring and that the ring was not found with it. The pickpocket usually takes his booty to the receiver as he finds it. It is the receiver who extracts the stones and melts down the metal. That is the usual procedure, but, naturally, there are exceptions."

"At any rate," said Brodribb, "what matters to us is that the man has vanished and no one knows who he is."

On this conclusion neither Thorndyke nor I made any comment, and the discussion was brought to an end by our arrival at Liverpool Street, where we saw Mr. Brodribb into a hansom and then embarked in another for the Temple.

During the meal which we found awaiting us at our chambers, I endeavoured to extract from Thorndyke some elucidation of the statement that had seemed to me so obscure. But he was not willing to enter into details at present.

"The position at the moment, Jervis," said he, "is this. We have no doubt whatever that Sir Edward Hardcastle was murdered. We have evidence that the murder was premeditated and the methods planned in advance with considerable care and some ingenuity. It was carried out by more than one, and probably several persons. It was, in fact, of the nature of a conspiracy. The purpose of the murder was not robbery from the person. The perpetrators, or at least some of them, were apparently of a low class, socially; and the victim seems to have walked, not entirely unsuspecting, into some sort of ambush.

"That is all that we know at present, and it doesn't carry us far. What we have to discover, if we can, is the identity of the murderers. If we can do that, the motive will disclose itself. If, on the other hand, we can uncover the motive, that will probably point to the murderers. We must proceed along both lines if we can. We must endeavour cautiously to ascertain whether Sir Edward had any enemies who might conceivably have been capable of a crime of revenge; and we must watch the consequences of his death and note who benefits by them."

"It is evident," said I, "that someone is going to benefit to the extent of a title and an uncommonly valuable estate."

"Yes, and we shall bear that in mind. But we mustn't attach undue weight to it. Whenever a well-to-do person is murdered, the heirs benefit; but that fact--though it furnishes a conceivable motive--does not cast suspicion on them in the absence of any other evidence. In practice, as you know, I like to leave the question of motive until I have got a lead in some definite direction. It is much safer. The premature consideration of motive may be very misleading, whereas its use as corroboration may be invaluable."

"Yes, I realise that," said I, "but in this case I don't see how you are going to get a lead. The murderers left plenty of traces of a kind; but they were the wrong kind. There was nothing personal about them--unless the finger-prints can be identified, and I doubt if they can. They were very confused and obscure. And even if they could be made out, they would be of no use unless they were the prints of criminals known to the police and recorded at the register."

Thorndyke laughed grimly. "My learned friend," he remarked, "is not disposed to be encouraging. But never mind. We have made many a worse start and yet reached our goal. Presently we will examine our material and see what it has to tell us. Perhaps we may get a lead in some direction from an unexpected source."

At the actual examination I was not present, for our expeditions to Stratford had left me with one or two unfulfilled engagements. Accordingly, as soon as we had finished our supper (or dinner--the exact status of our evening meal was not clearly defined), I went forth to despatch one of them, my regret tempered by the consideration that I should miss nothing but the mere manipulations, most of which were now fairly familiar to me, and that on my return I should find most of the work done and the results available.

And so it turned out. Re-entering our chambers about half-past ten and finding the sitting-room untenanted, I made my way up to the laboratory where a glance around told me that the final stage of the investigation had been reached. On one bench was a microscope and a row of slides, each bearing a temporary or permanent label; on the chemical bench a sand-bath stood over a bunsen burner and bore a small glass evaporating dish, and one or two large watch-glasses containing fluid with a crystalline margin had apparently had their turn on the bath. Beside them in a beaker of fluid--presumably water--was the collar that had been abstracted from the mortuary by Thorndyke, who was at the moment gently prodding it with a glass rod, while his familiar demon, Polton, was engaged in vigorously wringing out the end of rope in a basin of hot liquid which exhaled the unmistakable aroma of soft soap.

"We have nearly finished," said Thorndyke, "and we haven't done so badly, considering that this is only the beginning of our investigation. Have a look at the specimens and see if you agree with the findings."

I went over to the microscope bench and ran my eye over the exhibits. As I did so, I was once more impressed by the wonderfully simple, orderly and efficient plan on which my colleague worked. For years past, indeed, from the very earliest days of his practice, it had been his habit to collect impartially examples of every kind of natural and artificial material and to make, wherever it was practicable, permanent microscopic preparations of each. The result was an immense and carefully classified collection of minute objects of all kinds--hairs, feather insect scales, diatoms, pollen, seeds, powders, starches, textiles, threads, fibres--any one of which could be found in a moment and used for comparison with any new 'find', the nature of which had to be determined. Thus he was, to a great extent, independent of books of reference and had the great advantage of being able to submit both the new specimen and the 'standard' to any kind of test with the micrometer or polariscope or otherwise.

In the present case, the specimens were laid out in pairs, the new, unknown specimen with a 'certified' example from the collection; and an eye-piece micrometer was in position for comparing dimensions. I took up one slide, labelled 'E. H. decd. 15. 7. 03. From Rt. Bronchus', and placed it on the stage of the microscope. Instantly the nature of the object became obvious. It was a fish-scale; but, of course, I could not say what fish. Then I laid on the stage the companion slide from the collection, labelled 'Scale of Herring', and made a rough comparison. In the shape of the margins, the concentric and radiating markings and all other characters, the two specimens appeared to be identical. I did not make an exhaustive examination, assuming that this had been done by Thorndyke, but went on to the other specimens. All the fish-scales were alike, as might have been expected, and I gave them only a passing glance. Then I picked up a slide labelled 'From Trachea' and placed it on the stage. The specimen appeared to be a small piece of a leaf of some kind; a rather large leaf, as I judged by the absence of any indication of form, and by its thickness, and I observed that it seemed to have one cut edge.

Taking up the 'reference' slide I read, 'Cuticle of Cabbage'.

"I don't remember this scrap of leaf, Thorndyke," said I.

"No," he replied. "I did not draw Ross's attention to it. It was wearisome to keep pointing out facts to a man who had already made up his mind. It seems to be a fragment of cabbage leaf, but it is of no special importance. The fish-scales prove the entrance of water to the lungs, which is the really significant fact."

"And this little melted fragment from the heel of the boot? It doesn't look like soap."

"It isn't. It is beeswax. I put that fragment on the slide to observe the melting-point."

The other two specimens were the scraps of cotton and silk thread that we had picked off the clothes. The silk thread was clearly shown, by comparison with the 'reference specimen' to be a fragment of 'buttonhole twist'. The white cotton corresponded exactly with a reference specimen of basting cotton; but here the identification was less certain owing to the less distinctive character of the thread.

"Yes," Thorndyke agreed when I remarked upon this, "white cotton threads are a good deal alike, but I haven't much doubt that this is basting cotton. Still, I shall take the specimens to a trimmings-dealer and get an expert opinion."

"Have you made any analysis of the fluids from the stomach and lungs?" I asked.

"No," he replied, "only a preliminary test. But I think that has given us the essential facts, though as a measure of safety, I shall have a complete examination made. What I find is that both fluids contain a considerable amount of sodium chloride. They appear to be, and I have no doubt are, just simply salt water. We can't tell how salt the water was when it was swallowed and drawn into the lungs owing to the drying that had occurred in the body. But the salt is there, and that is the important point."

"You haven't yet tested the water in which you have soaked the collar?"

"No. We will do that now."

He poured a little of the water from the beaker in which the collar had been soaking, through a filter into a test-tube. Then, with a pipette, he dipped up a small quantity of a solution of silver nitrate from a bottle and let it fall, drop by drop, into the test-tube. As each drop fell into the clear liquid it gave rise to a little milky cloud, which became denser with each succeeding drop.

"Chloride of some kind," I observed.

"Yes," said he, "and we may take it, provisionally, that it is sodium chloride. And that finishes our preliminary examination of our material. Have you got that rope clean, Polton?"

"Yes, sir," replied Polton, producing the end of rope from a towel in which he had been squeezing the last remains of moisture from it. "It is quite clean, but a good deal of the colour has come out. I think you are right, sir. It looks like cutch."

He exhibited the discoloured water in the basin and handed the piece of rope to Thorndyke, who passed it to me.

"Yes," I said, "I see now that it is a hemp rope. But it is odd that they should have been at the trouble of dyeing it to imitate coir, which is an inferior rope to hemp."

He made no reply, but seemed to look at me attentively as I turned the rope over in my hand, and finally took it from me without remark. I had the feeling that he had expected me to make some observation, and I wondered vaguely what it might have been. Also, I wondered a little at his interest in the physical characters of this rope, which really seemed to have no bearing on our inquiry; and even as I wondered, I had an uneasy suspicion that I had missed some significant point.

"How have the photographs come out?" I asked.

"I haven't seen them yet," he replied. "They are in Polton's province. What do you say, Polton? Is it possible to inspect them?"

"The enlargements are now washing," Polton replied. "I'll fetch them in for you to see."

He went through into the dark room and presently returned with four porcelain dishes, each containing a half-plate bromide print, which he laid down on the bench under the shaded light. All the four prints were enlargements to the same scale--about three times the natural linear size.

"Well," I remarked, as we looked them over together, "Sir Edward's finger-prints are clear enough, though they look a little odd, but the chair-back groups are a most unholy muddle. Most of the prints are just undecipherable smears."

"Yes," Thorndyke admitted regretfully, "they are a poor lot and too many superimposed and obliterating one another. But, still, I have some hopes. Our expert friends are wonderfully clever at sorting out imperfect prints; and some of these seem to me to have enough visible detail for identification. At any rate, one important negative fact can, I think, be established. I see no print that seems to resemble any of Sir Edward's."

"Neither do I; and, of course, if they were there, they would be more distinct than any of the others, being the most recent. But it would be a facer if the experts should find them there. That would fairly knock the bottom out of the entire case."

"It would, certainly," Thorndyke agreed. "But the probability is so negligibly remote that it is not worth considering. What is of much more interest is the chance of their being able to identify some of the prints as those of known criminals."

"Supposing they can?" said I. "What then?"

"In that case," he replied, "I think we should have to take Miller into our confidence. You see, Jervis, that our present difficulty is that we are dealing with a crime in the abstract, so to speak. The perpetrators are unknown to us. We have--at the moment--no clue whatever to their identity. But give us a name; turn our unknown criminals into actual, known persons, and I think we have enough evidence to secure a conviction. At any rate, a very little corroboration by police investigation would make the case complete."

"The deuce it would!" I exclaimed, completely taken aback. "I had no idea that the case had advanced as far as that. I thought it was rather a matter of strong suspicion than of definite evidence. But evidently your examination of the material has brought some new facts to light. Is it not so?"

"We have elicited a few new facts; nothing very startling, however. But the evidence emerges when we put together, in their proper order, the facts that we already knew with the new ones added. Shall we go over the evidence together and see what we really know about the case?"

I assented with enthusiasm, and, having filled my pipe, disposed myself in the rather ascetic laboratory chair in a posture of attention and receptivity; and I noticed that Polton had unobtrusively drawn a stool up to the opposite bench, and, having stuck a watchmaker's glass into his eye, was making a shameless pretence of exploring the 'innards' of an invalid carriage clock.

"Let us begin," said Thorndyke, "by taking the evidence in order without going into much detail. In the first place we have established that Sir Edward Hardcastle was drowned in salt water in which considerable numbers of herring-scales were suspended."

"You think there is no doubt about the drowning?"

"I think it is practically certain," he replied. "The presence in the lungs of salt water and herring-scales, together with the presence of similar salt-water and herring-scales in the stomach is nearly conclusive. That the herring-scales were water-borne and not the remains of food eaten is proved by our finding them in the hair. Add to this the fairly definite signs of asphyxia and no signs of any other cause of death; and the fact that deceased's head and neck had been immersed in salt water containing suspended herring-scales, as proved by the scales which you found in the hair, by the stains on the neck of his shirt and on his collar and by the salt which I extracted from that collar; and I think we have very complete and conclusive evidence of drowning."

"I agree," said I. "Excuse my interrupting."

"Not at all," he replied. "I want you to challenge the evidence if you do not find it convincing. To proceed; we find that, Sir Edward's body, dead or alive, had been lying on, and apparently dragged along, the dirty floor of a room. Among the litter on that floor were short pieces of basting-cotton and button-hole twist and a fragment of beeswax. These materials suggest a room in which garments were being made; probably a tailor's work-room, though other people besides tailors use these materials.

"Next we find that the body was conveyed in a two-wheeled vehicle, which may have been a cart or gig, or perhaps a hansom cab--"

"Surely not a hansom, Thorndyke," I interrupted. It had iron tyres."

"That doesn't absolutely exclude it," said he. "You occasionally meet with iron-tired hansoms even to this day. I saw one at Fenchurch Street Station only a few weeks ago--a shabby old crock with the old-fashioned, round-backed dickey, probably driven by the owner. The reason that I incline to the hansom is that the dimensions of this vehicle coincide exactly with those of a hansom. I looked them up in my notes on the dimensions of various vehicles. The wheels of a hansom are fifty-five and a half inches in diameter. The tyres, when of iron, are one and a half inches wide, on a rim which is slightly thicker and which widens inwards towards the spokes. The track, or distance between the wheels, measured at the ground level from the outer edge of one tyre to the outer edge of the other, is fifty-seven inches. Now, these are exactly the dimensions that we noted in our measurements of the track of the unknown vehicle. It isn't by any means conclusive, but we are bound to take note of the coincidence."

"Yes, indeed," I assented. "It is a decidedly striking coincidence; a sort of Bertillon measurement, at least so it appears, though I don't know to what extent the dimensions of vehicles are standardised."

"At any rate," said he, "we note the possibility that this vehicle may have been a hansom cab; and whatever it was, it served to convey the body of Sir Edward to Five Piper's Row on Sunday, the twenty-first of June, at some time in the evening or night, but most probably between eleven and twelve. The body was carried into the house by at least two persons, one of whom appears to have been a waterside or sea-faring person."

"Is it clearly established that there was more than one person?" I asked.

"Yes. There were at least two sets of muddy foot-marks--and apparently only two--on the floor leading from the front door to the kitchen. They were not Holker's, for he arrived with dry feet; they were certainly not Sir Edward's, as we know from the state of his shoes, apart from the ascertained fact that he was dead when he was taken into the house. There were undoubtedly two men; and we can take it that neither of them was the driver of the vehicle since that made merely a pause at the house and not a prolonged stay.

"The body, then, was carried into the house by these two persons, one of whom--probably the nautical person--had brought with him a piece of rope which had been cut off a longer complete rope and which bears visible evidence of having been stolen."

"What do you mean by visible evidence?" I demanded. "Surely a rope which has been stolen is not visibly different from any other rope! The act of stealing a rope does not impress on it any new distinguishable properties."

"That is true," he admitted; "and yet it may be possible to recognise a stolen rope by its visible properties. Did you ever hear of a 'rogue's' yarn?

"Not to my knowledge."

"It is a device that used formerly to be employed in the Navy to check the stealing of cordage. Every rope that was made in the Royal Dockyards had one yarn in one of the strands which was different from all the others. It was twisted in reverse, and, if the rope was a white rope, the rogue's yarn was tarred, while in a tarred rope the tell-tale yarn was left white. Later, the special yarn was replaced by a single coloured worsted thread, which was spun into the middle of a yarn and so was not visible externally, but only at the cut end. This was a better device, as each dockyard had its own colour, so that when a stolen rope was discovered it could be seen at once which dockyard it belonged to.

"But the plan of marking rope in this way is not confined to the Navy. Many public, and even private bodies which use rope, have it made up with some distinctive mark--usually a coloured thread in one of the yarns. And that happens to be the case with this particular rope. It is a marked rope; evidently the property of some public or private body." He took the washed 'specimen' from the bench, and, handing it to me, continued: "You see this is a four-strand rope, and in two of the strands is a yarn in which has been twisted a coloured cotton thread, a red thread in the one and a green thread in the other."

I examined the little length of rope closely, and, now that I had been told, the coloured threads were easy enough to see, though only at the cut ends. Now, too, I understood Thorndyke's intense interest in the rope. But there was another thing that I did not understand at all.

"I suppose," said I, "that it was these coloured threads that made you give so much attention to this rope?"

"Undoubtedly," he replied; "and you must admit that they were calculated to attract attention."

"Certainly, I do. But what puzzles me is how you came to see them at all. They are extremely inconspicuous, and must have been still more so before the rope was cleaned."

"There is no mystery about that," said he. "I saw them because I looked for them. You remember that you--like the Superintendent--took this rope for a coir rope. So did I, at first. Then I saw that the texture did not agree with the colour; that it was really a hempen rope dyed to imitate coir. Then I asked myself the question that you asked just now: Why should anyone dye a hemp rope to imitate the less valuable coir? The natural suggestion was that the rope had been disguised to cover unlawful possession. It was probably a stolen rope. This idea suggested the possibility that it might be a marked rope. Accordingly I carefully examined the cut end, and behold! the two coloured threads; very inconspicuous, as you inferred, but visible enough when looked for."

"But this is a very important fact, Thorndyke," said I.

"It is," he agreed. "It is by far the most valuable clue that we hold. In fact, if the finger-prints fail us, it is the only clue that leads away from generalities to a definite place and set of surroundings. We shall almost certainly be able to trace this rope to the place from which it was stolen, and that alone will tell us something of the person who stole it."

"Mighty little," said I.

"Probably. But if we are able to add only a little to what we know, that little may be very illuminating."

"What do we know about these men?" I asked.

"Perhaps I should have said 'infer' rather than 'know'; but our inferences are fairly safe. First, we find a person evidently accustomed to handling cordage, and probably a seaman or waterside character; a person, probably the same, who has a stolen rope in his possession; a person who is in some way connected with a tailor's work-room or some similar establishment; and a person who uses, drives and probably owns some two-wheeled vehicle, either a gig, a light cart or possibly a hansom cab, and if the latter, an old cab, probably in poor condition and distinguished by the unusual character of iron tyres. Then there is the choice of Piper's Row. The selection of this particular house could hardly have been made by a complete stranger. It suggests a person with some knowledge of the place and of its usually undisturbed condition. Assuming the object to be the disposal of the body in some place where it would not be discovered until all traces of the crime--of the actual method of the murder--had disappeared, the hiding-place was extraordinarily well chosen. But for the mere accident of Holker's picking out this house for repairs, the body might have remained undiscovered for months and the plan have succeeded perfectly."

"It has succeeded pretty perfectly as it is," said I, "so far as the coroner and the police are concerned."

"Yes. But in another month the cause of death would have been completely unascertainable. But you notice that however long the interval might have been, the body would still have been identifiable by the contents of the pockets and the marking of the clothes. That seems to be worth noting."

"You mean that the intention was that the body should ultimately be identified?"

"I mean that there was no attempt to conceal the identity. The significance of that--such as it is--lies in the fact that in an ordinary murder the safety of the murderers is much greater if the identity of the murdered person is unknown, since, in that case, the police usually have nothing to indicate the identity of the murderer. But I doubt if there is much in it. The intention evidently was, in this case, that the death should not be recognised as a murder at all."

"Yes, and they were very near to bringing it off. In fact, they have brought it off so far. They are still very decidedly birds in the bush. And the inquest was an absolute walk-over for them. All the evidence seemed to point to suicide, and that of Weeks and Brodribb must have been most convincing to people who already had a bias in that direction. By the way, did you pick up anything from the evidence besides that statement of Holker's?

"Nothing very definite," he replied. "There were certain hints and suggestions in the evidence of Weeks and in that of Joseph Wood, the waiter. Weeks, you remember, had evidently had the feeling that there was something unusual in the air when Sir Edward started from home that morning; and Wood seemed to me to have the impression that there was someone in the cab which drew up for Sir Edward to enter. He didn't say so, in fact he said that he did not know, but he mentioned pointedly that he did not see Sir Edward hail the cab or give any directions to the driver. Taking what was implied rather than stated by these two witnesses, there seems to be a suggestion that one, at least, of the murderers was known to Sir Edward; and the fact that he went away in a hansom, whether alone or with some other person, is certainly significant as pointing to a definite destination. It is quite inconsistent with the Superintendent's suggestion of aimless wandering.

"But we are straying away into a consideration of the general aspects of the case. To come back to the question that we were discussing, you see now what our position is at the moment. If Miller can give us the name of a person who has handled that chair at Piper's Row, we can give him sufficient information to enable him to put that person on trial for murder. Of course he would not do so off-hand. Before he moved, he would fill in detail and seek corroborative evidence. But there would be very little doubt of the result.

"On the other hand, if Miller cannot produce a known person, we shall be left with a very complete case of murder against some persons unknown. Then it will be our task to convert those unknown persons into known persons; and to do that we shall need to acquire some further facts."

There were some other points that I should have liked to raise. But Thorndyke's very definite conclusion seemed to put an end to the discussion; so much so that Polton threw off all pretence, and, removing the eyeglass from his eye, deliberately carried the clock to a cupboard and there deposited it as a thing that had served its purpose.

CHAPTER XI:

ASHDOD REVISITED

(Jasper Gray's Narrative)

A GOOD old proverb assures us that we may be sure our sins will find us out. I will not make the customary facetious commentary on this proposition. That joke has now worn rather thin. But the idiotic booby-trap that I set for poor old Ponty, rebounding on me again and again like a self-acting, perpetual motion boomerang, illustrated the proverb admirably, while the encounter on my very doorstep with a dry-faced, plain-clothes policeman, illustrated the joke. Most inopportunely, my sins had found me at home.

He must have had a description of me for he addressed me tentatively by name. I acknowledged my identity and he then explained his business.

"It's about that counterfeit half-crown that your father passed by mistake. I want to know, as well as you can remember, how it came into your possession."

Now, of course I ought to have told him all I knew. I realised that. But my recollections of Mr. Ebbstein's establishment were so exceedingly unpleasant that I boggled at the idea of being any further mixed up with it. And then there was Miss Stella. I couldn't endure the thought of having her name dragged into a disreputable affair of this sort. Wherefore I temporised and evaded.

"The man who gave it to me was a complete stranger," said I.

"Naturally," said the officer. "You didn't hear his name by any chance?"

"I heard another man call him 'Jim'."

"Well, that's something, though it doesn't carry us very far. But how came he to give it to you? Was it payment?"

I described the transaction with literal truth up to the point of the delivery of the coin but said nothing of the subsequent events. I think he must have been a rather inexperienced officer, for he assumed that the payment concluded the business and that I then came away. I didn't say so.

"You took the case up in Mansell Street. Do you remember what number?"

"No, but I remember the house. It was on the right-hand side, going from the High Street, just past a tobacconist's shop--next door, in fact. The shop had a figure of a Red Indian on a bracket outside."

He entered this statement in a large, black-covered note-book and then asked:

"You took the case to Byles's Wharf, you say. Whereabouts is that? Isn't it somewhere down Wapping way?"

"Yes, this end of Wapping."

"And do you think you would know the man again?"

"I am sure I should."

He noted this down and reflected awhile. But having missed all the really relevant questions, he didn't seem able to think of any others. Accordingly, after a spell of profound thought, he put his note-book away and closed the proceedings.

I went on my way greatly relieved at having, as I hoped, at last shaken myself free of that accursed make-believe, but yet by no means satisfied with my conduct of the affair. I knew that, as a good citizen, I ought to have told him about 'Chonas', and my default rankled in my bosom and again illustrated the proverb by haunting me in all my comings and goings. But the oddest effect of the working of my conscience was to develop in me a most inconsistent hankering to make my incriminating knowledge more complete. I became possessed by an unreasonable urge to revisit the scene of my adventure, to go down again into Ashdod, and turn my confused recollections into definite knowledge.

The opportunity came unexpectedly. I had to deliver a parcel of stationery at an office appertaining to a large warehouse in Commercial Road East. It was a heavy parcel, but not heavy enough to demand the use of the truck. I carried it on my shoulder, and when I had at length dumped it down in the outer office and taken my receipt for it, I was free and unencumbered. And the weight of the parcel seemed to justify me in taking a little time off to spend on my own affairs.

As I strolled back along Commercial Road East, I kept a sharp look-out for landmarks of that memorable journey with the hansom. Presently I came to the corner of Sidney Street, which I remembered having passed on that occasion, and which gave me what mariners call a "departure." I turned back, eastward, and, taking the first turning on the right (southerly), left the broad thoroughfare behind and entered a maze of small streets. They were rather bewildering. But it is difficult thoroughly to bewilder a seasoned Londoner who is accustomed to wandering about the town on foot (people who ride in conveyances don't count. They never become real Londoners). Presently I came to a corner which was marked at the kerb by an angular granite corner-stone. I remembered that stone. I had reason to (and so had the owner of the cab). Taking a fresh departure from it, I soon arrived at a little street at the end of which was a seedy-looking public-house distinguished by the sign of a lion and an inscription in Hebrew characters which suggested that the royal beast aforesaid was none other than the Lion of Judah.

I now had my bearings. This was the place where I had found and purloined the hansom. Just round the corner was the empty house from which Miss Stella and I had dropped down into the court. That was the last house in the street which I had come to identify, the street which was made illustrious by the residence therein of Mr. Ebbstein and his tenant, the ingenious 'Chonas', to say nothing of the old villain whom I had knocked on the head.

I sauntered round the corner, keeping my eyes skinned (as our packer would have expressed it) but carefully avoiding any outward manifestation of interest. The illustrious street I learned from a half-illegible name-plate rejoiced in the romantic name of Pentecost Grove. Strolling along it, I took in the numbers--where there were any--with the tail of my eye, keeping account of them, since so many were missing, until I arrived exactly opposite the mews, or stable-yard, which I had seen from the window of my prison. Thereby I learned that Mr. Ebbstein resided at Number Forty-nine, and the person whose cranium I had damaged was to be found--if still extant--at Number Fifty.

If I had been content with this enlargement of my knowledge and taken myself off, all would have been well. But at this point, my intelligent interest over powered my caution. The stable-yard opposite, bearing the superscription, 'Zion Place', yawned invitingly and offered an alluring glimpse of a hansom cab, horseless and apparently in dry dock. I couldn't resist that hansom cab. Without doubt, it was the identical hansom with which I had scattered the howling and blaspheming denizens of Ashdod. Of course, it didn't matter a 'snide' half-crown whether it was or not. But I was sensible of an idiotic impulse to examine it and try to verify its identity. Accordingly I crossed the street and sauntered idly into Zion Place, gradually edging towards the object of my curiosity.

It was an extraordinarily shabby old vehicle and seemed to be dropping to pieces from sheer senile decay. But it wasn't really. The actual robustness of its old age was demonstrated by the near wheel, which memory impelled me to inspect narrowly. On the rim including the tyre, was a deep, angular notch, corresponding, as I grinningly realised, with that sharp granite corner-stone and recalling the terrific lurch that had nearly jerked me from my perch. The notch was an honourable scar on which the builder and wheel wright might have looked with pardonable pride.

I had just reached this conclusion when I became aware of a face protruded round a stable door and a pair of beady eyes fixed very attentively on me. Then the face emerged, accompanied by a suitable torso and a pair of thin, bandy legs, the entire outfit representing the Jehu whom I remembered as bearing the style and title of Louis. He advanced towards me crab-wise and demanded, suspiciously: "Vell. Vat you vant in here?"

I replied that I was just having a look round.

"Ah," said he, "zen you shall take your look outside."

I expressed the hope that I had not intruded, and, turning about, strolled up the yard and out into the street. He followed closely at my heels, not only up the yard, but along the street. Finding him still clinging to me, I quickened my pace, deciding now to get clear of the neighbourhood without delay. Heading towards The Lion, I was approaching the corner when two men came round it. One of them, whose head was bound with a dirty rag, instantly riveted my attention and stirred the chords of memory. Apparently, my appearance affected him in a like manner, for, as soon as he saw me he stopped, and, after regarding me for a moment with an astonished glare, flung up his arms and uttered a loud cry which sounded to me like "Hoya!" At the same moment, his companion started forward as if to intercept me.

That uncanny, Oriental alarm-cry, repeated now and echoed by the other two men, instantly warned me of my danger. I remembered its effect last time; indeed, the aid of memory was needless, for already a dozen windows were thrown up and a dozen shaggy heads thrust out, with open mouths repeating that ill-omened word, whatever it might be. Pocketing my dignity, I evaded the attempt to head me off and broke into a run with the cab-driver and the other man yelling at my heels.

Past the Lion of Judah I bolted and along the street beyond for some fifty yards; but now my imperfect recollection of the neighbourhood played me false. For, coming to a narrow turning on my right, I assumed it to be the one by which I had come, and did not discover my error until I had covered more than half its length, when a sharp turn revealed a blind end. But the discovery came too late. Already the place was humming like an overturned hive, and, when I spun about to retrace my steps, behold! the end of the little street was blocked by a yelling crowd.

There was nothing for it but to go back, which I did at a brisk walk; and when the mob came forward to meet me with the obvious intention of obstructing my retreat, I charged valiantly enough. But, of course, it was hopeless. A score of dirty hands grabbed at me as I strove to push my way through and in a few moments I was brought to a stand with both my arms immovably held, and then began to be slowly pushed and dragged forward; and all around me were those strange, pale, greasy, alien faces with their high cheek bones and beady eyes, all jabbering vociferously in an uncouth, alien tongue. Suddenly, out of this incomprehensible babel issued the welcome sound of some thing resembling English speech.

"Wot's the good of makin' all this rumpus? Give the bloke a clout on the 'ed and let 'im go."

I looked round at the speaker and instantly recognised the man who had given me the 'snide' half-crown at Byles's Wharf; and even in my bewilderment, I could see that he was obviously nervous and uneasy.

"Let 'im go!" exclaimed a flat-faced, hairy alien who was hanging on to my arm. "You do not know zat he have try to kill poor Mr. Gomorrah!"

"I know," said the other. "'E 'it 'im on the 'ed. And wot I says is, 'it 'im on the 'ed and let 'im 'ook it. Wot's the good of raisin' a stink and bringin' the coppers round?"

"He shall pay for vot he 'ave done, Mr. Trout," the other replied, doggedly; and at this moment, my acquaintance with the bandaged head pushed his way through the crowd and stood for a few moments gloating over me with an expression of concentrated vindictiveness; and certainly, the presence of the bandage after all these weeks suggested that he had some excuse for feeling annoyed with me. I thought that he was about to take 'consideration for value received' forthwith, but then he altered his mind, and, with a savage grin, directed his friends (as

I gathered) to bring me along to some more convenient place.

"Don't be a fool, Gomorrah," urged my friend--whose name appeared to be Trout. "You'll get yourself and the rest of us into the soup if you ain't careful. This 'ere is England, and don't you forget it."

His warnings, however, had no effect, and, once more an effort was made to propel me in the desired direction. It was clear to me that I was being led to the slaughter--not, however, like a lamb (whose policy I have always considered a mistaken one), for I proceeded to make things as uncomfortable as possible for the men who were holding me; who, to do them justice, retaliated effectively in kind. The proceedings became distinctly boisterous with considerable wear and tear of my clothing and person, and our progress was neither dignified nor rapid. Suddenly, the man who was clinging to my right wrist, breathlessly addressed the still-protesting Trout.

"Here come Mr. Zichlinsky. Now ye shall see."

I looked anxiously at the new-comer who was thrusting through the crowd, and, as he came into view, I had two instantaneous impressions. First, in spite of his shabby, ill-fitting clothes, he was obviously of a totally different social class from the others. Secondly, though he was certainly a stranger, his face seemed to awaken some dim and vague reminiscence. It was a villainous face--dead white with a pair of strangely colourless eyes of the palest grey; and the pallor of eyes and skin was intensified by a brush of jet-black hair that stood straight up on his hatless head. Though not actually uncomely, his appearance and expression were evil to the point of repulsiveness.

These were but momentary impressions of which I was but half aware; for there was matter enough of another kind to keep my attention fully occupied. As soon as Mr. Zichlinsky had worked his way through to me, he introduced himself by slapping my face and remarking, with a sort of wild-cat grin: "So you haf come to see us again. Zis time you shall haf a brober velcome."

With this he slapped my face again, and then grabbing a handful of flesh and clothing together, helped the others to drag me along. Mr. Trout made yet one more appeal.

"For Gawd's sake, Mr. Zichlinsky, don't go and do nothing stoopid. This ain't Russia, yer know--"

Zichlinsky turned on him as if he would have bitten him. "Have I ask for you to tell me vot I shall do? Keep your hands out of my business!"

But there was yet another protestor. I could not see him, and, though I could hear his voice--speaking in barbarous French--I could make out only a word or two. But of those words, two--"la pucelle"--conveyed to me the gist of the matter.

Zichlinsky answered him less savagely and in excellent French: "It is not only revenge, though this beast has robbed me of a fortune. But he knows too much, and you can see for yourself he is a spy."

Here he refreshed himself again by slapping my face, and then, apparently goaded to fury by the recollection of his wrongs, snarled and bared his teeth like a dog, and, seizing my ear, began to pull and twist it with the ferocity of a madman. The pain and consequent anger scattered the last remains of my patience and caution. Wrenching my left hand free, I shot out my fist with the full strength of an uncommonly strong arm.

My knuckles impinged on his countenance exactly between his eyes, and the weight of the blow flung him backward like a capsized ninepin. If there had been room, he would have measured his length on the ground. As it was, some of his friends caught him, and he leaned against them motionless for a few seconds apparently dazed, while from the crowd a deafening yell of execration arose. Then he recovered himself, and, with a horrid, womanish shriek, came at me with all his teeth exposed. And now I could see that he held a long, pointed knife in his hand.

I suppose that, until my time comes, I shall never be so near death as I was at that moment. The man was within a foot of me and his arm was swung out to strike. The nearest wretches in the crowd glared at me with gloating, fascinated eyes while my own followed the outward swing of the knife.

And then, in an instant, the fateful thing happened: A pair of strong hands--I think they were Trout's--seized and held the outswung arm. The din of triumphant yells died down suddenly, giving place to a strange silence. The hands which gripped my arms relaxed their hold so that I could shake myself free. I cast a bewildered glance around, and then I saw the cause of this singular change. Above the heads of the crowd appeared two constabulary helmets, and in another moment two stalwart policemen (the police patrol in pairs in neighbourhoods of this type) pushed their way to the centre of the throng. Zichlinsky hurriedly put away his knife--but not before one of the policemen had observed it--and was in the act of withdrawing when a stern official voice commanded him to stay.

"Now," said the constable who had noticed the knife, "what's going on here?"

Mr. Trout hastened to explain. "It's a parcel of foolery, constable, that's what it is. A silly mistake. They took this young man for somebody else and they was going to wallop 'im."

"Seem to have done a fair amount of walloping already," the constable remarked apropos of my rather dishevelled condition. "And one of them," he added, fixing an accusing eye on Zichlinsky, "was going to do the walloping with a knife. I saw you putting it away. Now what might your name be?"

The question was evidently anticipated for Zichlinsky replied, promptly: "Jacob Silberstein."

"And where do you live?"

"I lodge with Mr. Gomorrah."

"Oh," said the constable, "you live with old Solomon Gomorrah, do you? That isn't much of a testimonial."

He produced a large, black-covered note-book in which he entered the particulars while the other constable peered curiously over his shoulder.

"What's that?" the latter asked. "Did he say he lived at Sodom and Gomorrah?"

"No," his colleague explained. "Solomon Gomorrah is a man--at least he'd pass for one in the monkey-house at the Zoo. One of these cag-mag tailors. Makes shoddy trousers. What they call in Whitechapel a kickseys builder. You'll know all about Solomon when you've been a little longer on this beat." He ran an expert eye over the remaining bystanders (the production of the note-book had occasioned a rapid dwindling of the assembly, though curiosity still held the less cautious) and demanded: "But what was it all about? What did they want to wallop this young fellow for?"

Mr. Trout would have essayed to explain, but he was forestalled by an elderly Jewess who looked as if she might have been "collected" from the Assyrian room at the British Museum. "He is a vicked man! He have try to kill poor Mr. Gomorrah."

"Nothing of the sort!" said Trout. "T'wasn't this bloke at all. They thought 'e was 'im, but it wasn't. It was another cove altogether. 'E 'it 'im on the 'ed."

The constable's unsympathetic comment on this slightly confused explanation was that it probably served him right; "but," he asked, "where is Gomorrah?"

"Seems to have hooked it," said Trout, looking round vaguely, and I then observed that Zichlinsky had also taken the opportunity to fade away. The constable turned to me somewhat wearily and asked:

"What is your name, sonny, and where do you live?"

"My name," I replied, "is Jasper Gray, and I live at 165, Great Ormond Street."

"Quite a treat to hear a Christianlike name," said the officer, writing it down. "So you don't belong to this select residential neighbourhood; and if you will take my tip, you'll clear out of it as quickly as possible. Better walk with us up to Commercial Road East."

I accepted the invitation gladly enough, and we turned away together from the now silent and rapidly emptying street, and as we went, the senior constable put a few judicious questions. "Do you know what the rumpus was about? Why did that man Silberstein want to knife you?"

"He said I had robbed him of a fortune. I don't know what he meant. I have never seen him before, to my knowledge. But his name is not Silberstein. It is Zichlinsky. I heard them call him by that name."

"Oh, Zichlinsky, is it?" said my friend, fishing out the note-book again. "Probably a 'wanted' name as he gave a false one. We must see who he is. And now, here we are in Commercial Road East. You'd better have a penn'orth on a bus. Safer than walking. Got any coppers?"

He was slipping his hand into his trousers pocket, but I assured him that I was solvent to the extent of twopence, whereupon, waving away my thanks, he hailed a west-bound Blackwall omnibus and stood by to see me safely on board.

I was not sorry to sink down restfully on a cushioned seat (the constable had directed me to travel inside) for I had had a strenuous finish to a rather fatiguing morning. And as the omnibus rumbled along west ward I reflected on my late experiences, and once more the voice of conscience made itself heard. Evidently, Pentecost Grove was a veritable nest of criminals of the most dangerous type. Of those criminals I knew enough to enable the police to lay hands, at least on some and probably on all. Hitherto I had, for purely selfish reasons, kept my knowledge to myself. Now it was time for me to consider my duties as a citizen.

So I reflected as the leisurely omnibus jogged on along the familiar highway, and the sordid east gradually gave place to the busy west. When I dropped off opposite Great Turnstile my mind was made up. I would seek out the guardians of the law and tell them my story.

But once more Fate intervened. The guardians of the law forestalled my intentions; and the ears into which my story was delivered were not those of the mere official police.

CHAPTER XII:

OF A HANSOM CAB AND A BLACK EAGLE

(Dr. Jervis's Narrative)

WHEN I came down to breakfast on the day after the inquest, I found the table laid for one; a phenomenon which Polton explained by informing me that "the doctor" had gone out early. "In a hansom," he added with a crinkly and cunning smile. "I fancy he's got something on. I saw him copying a lot of names out of the directory."

I followed his knowing glance to a side table, whereon lay a copy of the Post Office Directory, and had no doubt that he was right. The Post Office Directory was one of Thorndyke's most potent instruments of research. In his hands, and used with imagination and analytical feeling, it was capable of throwing the most surprising amount and kind of illumination on obscure cases. In the present instance, its function, I had no doubt, was quite simple; and so, on examination, it turned out to be. Although closed, the volume had two places conspicuously marked by slips of paper, one at the page devoted to rope manufacturers and the other at the list of ship chandlers; and a number of light pencil marks opposite names in the two lists showed that a definite itinerary had been made out.

"The doctor said I was to show you this," said Polton, laying an open envelope beside my plate.

I drew out the enclosed letter, which I found to be a short and civil note from Mr. Northbrook, inviting us informally to lunch at the Clarendon Club. The invitation was for the current day, and the note was endorsed by Thorndyke: "I have accepted, and shall be at the club at one o'clock. Come if you can."

I was a little surprised, for Thorndyke was evidently full of business, and I suspected that Northbrook merely wanted to extract comments on the inquest; but it was quite convenient for me to go, and, as Thorndyke clearly wished me to--quite possibly for some definite reason--I strolled forth in good time and made my way to the rendezvous by the pleasant way of St. James's and the Green Park.

Northbrook's intentions were as I had supposed, and I have no doubt that, in the course of a very pleasant lunch, he may have elicited some interesting comments on the previous day's proceedings. But Thorndyke was an extremely difficult man to pump; the more so as he had the manner of discussing affairs without any appearance of reservation. But I noted that no inkling was conveyed to Northbrook of any dissent from the finding of the jury.

I found myself speculating from time to time on Thorndyke's object in wasting rather valuable time on this leisurely and apparently purposeless conversation. But towards the end of the meal I received a sudden enlightenment. "This," he said, "I take to be the table at which Sir Edward usually took his meals?"

"Yes," replied Northbrook, "and a very pleasant table it is, looking out right across the Green Park. You judged, no doubt, by the fact that Joseph Wood is waiting on us?"

"You are quite right," said Thorndyke; "and that reminds me that I should like to have a word or two with Joseph Wood, presently."

"But certainly, my dear sir. You shall have an opportunity of interviewing him in the strictest privacy."

"Oh, that is not necessary at all," said Thorndyke. "There are no secrets. I merely wanted him to amplify one of the points in his evidence. Perhaps I may ask him now, as I see he is coming with the coffee."

"Do so, do so, by all means," said Northbrook, evidently delighted at the chance of hearing the "amplification."

Thus invited, Thorndyke addressed the waiter as he placed the coffee on the table.

"I wanted to ask you one or two questions about your evidence at the inquest concerning the hansom in which Sir Edward drove away."

"Yessir," said Wood, standing stiffly at attention.

"It seemed to me that you had an impression that there was someone in it when it drew up for him to get in."

"Yessir. I had. I didn't say so at the inquest, because I was there to tell what I saw, not what I thought."

"You were perfectly right," said Thorndyke. "It was for the coroner to ask for your opinions if he wanted them. But you did think so?"

"Yessir. I didn't see Sir Edward hail the cab, and I don't think he did. He just stopped and the cab drew up. Then he got in and the cab drove away. I didn't see him speak to the cabman, and I don't believe he did, for the man started off and whipped up his horse as if he knew where he had to go."

"You said you didn't notice the number of the cab. Of course, you would not."

"No, sir. I hadn't no occasion to."

"Did you notice what the cab was like--whether there was anything unusual in its appearance?

"Yessir, I did notice that. You couldn't help noticing it. That cab," he continued solemnly, "must have been the great-grandfather of all the cabs in London. You never see such a shabby old rattle-trap. Got an old round dickey with a sheet-iron back, like I remember when I was a boy, and, if you will believe me, sir, iron tyres! Iron tyres in this twentieth century! Why that cab must have been fifty years old if it was a day."

"Why didn't you say that in your evidence, Wood?" Northbrook demanded.

"Nobody asked me, sir," was the very reasonable reply.

"No. And, after all, I suppose it didn't very much matter what the cab was like. Do you think so, doctor?

"It would have been helpful if we could have identified the cab and ascertained if anyone was in it and where it went to. That might have enabled us to fill in the picture. However, we can't; but, all the same, I must thank you, Wood, for telling me what you noticed."

After this little episode, I was not surprised when Thorndyke became suddenly conscious of the passage of time.

"Dear me!" he exclaimed with a glance at his watch, "how the minutes slip away in pleasant society! We shall have to get on the road, Jervis, and let Mr. Northbrook retire to his office. It was most kind of you to invite us, Mr. Northbrook, and we have both enjoyed a very agreeable interlude in the day's work."

He finished his coffee and we both stood up; and after a few more exchanges of compliments, we took our departure. As we descended the steps, a disengaged hansom approached and drew up in response to Thorndyke's hail. I stepped in, and, as my colleague followed, I heard him give the destination: "New Scotland Yard, Whitehall Gate."

"That waiter man's information was rather startling--at least, it was to me," I remarked as the cab horse padded away to the accompaniment of his softly tinkling bell.

"It is a very valuable addition to our small stock of facts," Thorndyke replied. "And how extraordinarily opportune Northbrook's invitation was. I was casting about for some way of getting a talk with Wood without making a fuss, and behold! Northbrook solves the difficulty in the simplest fashion. What did you think of the other point; the possible presence of some other person in the cab?

"I think it is more than merely possible. I should say it is very highly probable, especially in view of the peculiarity of the cab. And, of course, this new information confirms very strongly your suspicion that the Stratford vehicle was really a hansom."

"It does," he agreed; "in fact I am assuming as a working hypothesis that the cab which bore Sir Edward away from the club, conveyed his body to Piper's Row. On that assumption I am now going to Scotland Yard to find out what facilities there are for tracing a cab the number of which is unknown. I should like to see Miller in the first place if we are lucky enough to catch him."

By this time our 'gondola' was turning from Trafalgar Square into Whitehall, and I was noting how strikingly it contrasted with the 'rattle-trap' that Wood had described. This was a typical West End hansom, as smart and clean as a private carriage; furnished with gay silken blinds and at each side with a little mirror and a flower-holder containing a bunch of violets; and it slid along as smoothly as a sleigh, without a sound beyond the gentle and musical tinkle-tinkle of the bell on the horse's collar.

"If you want to catch Miller," said I, as we approached the main gateway of the Police Head quarters, "you are just in time. I see him coming out across the courtyard."

In effect, the Superintendent emerged into Whitehall just as we got out of the hansom, and, observing us, stopped to wait for us.

"Were you wanting to see me?" he asked with an inflection that subtly conveyed the earnest hope that we were not. Thorndyke evidently caught that faint overtone, for he replied: "Only for a moment. Which way are you going?"

"Westminster Station--underground."

"So are we; so we can talk as we go. What I want to know is this: there are still in London a few old hansom cabs with unconverted iron tyres. Now, could your people produce a list of those cabs?"

Miller shook his head. "No," he replied. "The register doesn't give particulars of the furnishing of particular cabs. Of course, we could find out by means of what they call an ad hoc investigation. But it would be a troublesome business. Possibly Inspector Radcliffe might be able to give you some information. He is our principal specialist in public vehicles."

He paused and seemed to reflect for a few moments. Then, suddenly, he emitted a soft laugh as if he had remembered something amusing. Which, in fact, turned out to be the case, for he resumed: "Talking of iron-tired cabs, Radcliffe told me a rather quaint story some time ago. Nothing much in it, but your question brought it to mind. It seems that a certain constable whose beat included Dorchester Square was going his round rather late one evening when he noticed a hansom cab drawn up about the middle of the south side of the square. There was no sign of the driver, and no one minding the horse; and as this was not quite according to Cocker, it naturally attracted his attention. But what specially tickled him was the way the horse was secured. The reins were made fast to a lamp-post with a clove hitch, just as a waterman makes fast his boat's painter to a railing or a thin iron post. The constable was a Margate man and familiar with the ways of boatmen, so it struck him as rather funny to see a cab moored to the lamp-post like a boat.

"However, he didn't take any notice but went off on his beat. When he came round the square the next time, the cab was still there and there was still no sign of the driver. He began to think it a bit queer, but he didn't want to make a fuss unnecessarily. But when he came round the third time and found the cab still there, he began to look into things. First he noticed that the cab was a most shocking old ramshackle--battered old round-backed dickey and iron tires--sort of cab that Queen Elizabeth might have driven about in; and then he looked at the horse and saw that it looked ready to drop with exhaustion. Just then as the sergeant happened to come round, the constable drew his attention to the cab, and the sergeant detailed another constable to take it round to a livery stable. There they gave the poor old horse a drink and a feed, and they say that he went for the oats as if he'd never tasted any before and nearly swallowed the nose-bag.

"Next morning, having found out from the register that the cab came from a little private yard down Mile End way, one of our men took it there and interviewed the owner, who drove it himself. It was a queer affair. The owner was a Polish Jew, about as unlike a horsey man as you can imagine. But what struck our man principally was that the fellow seemed to be in a blue funk. His story was that he had gone into a pub to get a drink, leaving the cab in charge of a man who happened to be loafing outside, and when he'd had his drink and come out, the cab was gone. Asked why he hadn't given information to the police, he said he hadn't thought of it, he was so upset. And that was all our man could get out of him. But as it was obvious that there was something behind the affair, our man took the fellow's name--though it was on the register--and reported the incident to Radcliffe.

"That's the story. I don't know whether it is of any interest to you, but if it is, I will tell Radcliffe to let you have particulars if you care to look him up. And he might be able to tell you about some other cabs with iron tyres."

Thorndyke thanked the Superintendent and said that he would certainly avail himself of the assistance thus kindly offered. Then, as the train began to slow down he rose. (I have not interrupted Miller's narrative to describe our movements but I may explain that, at Westminster, we had all taken tickets, Miller's being for Bishopsgate and ours for the Monument and that we had all boarded the same eastbound train.) When the train stopped we shook hands with the Superintendent and got out, leaving him to pursue his journey.

"That Polish gentleman sounds suspiciously like one of our friends," I remarked as we made our way out of the station.

"He does," Thorndyke agreed. "The man and the cab seem to fit the circumstances. It remains to be seen whether the date will. But I shall take an early opportunity of calling on Inspector Radcliffe and getting more precise details."

"Where are we going now?" I asked, having noted that our course seemed to be riverward.

"The Old Swan Pier," he replied, "whence we shall embark for a short voyage. The object of that voyage will, I hope, appear later."

As Thorndyke's answer, while withholding the explanation, did not deprecate speculation on my part, I gave the possibilities due consideration by the light of our further proceedings. From the Old Swan Pier we boarded one of the excellent and convenient river steamers which plied on the Thames in those days, by which we were borne eastward beneath the Tower Bridge and down the busy Pool. Cherry Gardens Pier was reached and left behind without supplying any hint, nor was I any the wiser when, as the boat headed in towards The Tunnel Pier, Wapping, my colleague rose and moved towards the gangway.

From the head of the pier, Thorndyke turned west ward along High Street, Wapping, commenting on our surroundings as he went.

"A queer, romantic old neighbourhood, this, Jervis; dull and squalid to look at now but rich in memories of those more stirring and eventful days which we think of fondly with the advantage of not having had to live in them. We are now passing Execution Dock, still, I believe, so called though it is now a mere work-a-day wharf. But a century or so ago you could have stood here and looked on a row of pirates hanging in chains."

"I shouldn't mind if you could now," I remarked, "if I could have the choosing of the pirates."

Thorndyke chuckled. "Yes," he said, "there was no nonsense about legal procedure in those days. If the intermediate stages were not all that could be desired, the final ones had the merit of conclusiveness. Here we approach The Town of Ramsgate Inn and Wapping Old Stairs, the latter a little disappointing to look at. The art of seasoning squalor with picturesqueness seems to have been lost. This is the goal of our pilgrimage."

As he spoke, he turned in at the gateway of a small dock and began to walk at a reduced pace along the quay. I looked around in search of some object that might be of interest to us but my glance met nothing beyond the craft in the basin--mostly lighters and Thames barges--the dreary dock buildings, the massive mooring-posts and bollards and here and there a life-buoy stand. Suddenly, however, I became aware that these last, which my eye had passed almost without notice, were not viewed with the same indifference by Thorndyke, for he walked straight up to the nearest one and halted before it with an air of obvious interest. And then, in a moment, I saw what we had come for.

The lifebuoy stand was in the form of a screen supported on two stanchions. In the middle of the screen, under a little pent-house, was a massive wooden hook on which was hung the life-buoy and a coil of smallish rope. Neither the buoy nor the rope was secured in any way, but either or both could be freely lifted off the hook. I thought at first that Thorndyke was about to lift off the coil, but he merely sought one of the ends of the rope, and, having found it, looked at it for a few moments with close attention. Then, having spread out with his thumb the little brush of fibres that projected beyond the whipping, he made a more minute examination with the aid of his pocket lens. Finally, without comment, he handed the end of the rope and the lens to me.

A moment's careful inspection through the glass was sufficient.

"Yes," I said, "there is no doubt about it. I can see the red and the green threads plainly enough through the lens though they are mighty hard to see with the naked eye. Which is unkind to the thief as giving him a false sense of security."

"It is for the thief, like the rest of us, to know his job," said Thorndyke, producing from his pocket the invaluable calliper gauge. He took the rope from me, and having measured the diameter, continued: "The agreement is perfect. This is a four-strand rope three eighths of an inch in diameter and having the two 'rogues' threads' of the same colour and similarly placed. So we may say that the place of origin of the Piper's Row rope is established beyond doubt."

At this moment an amphibious-looking person in a peaked cap who had been approaching slowly and with a somewhat stealthy manner, made his presence known.

"What's the game?" he enquired, and then, by way of elucidation: "What are yer up to with that rope?"

Thorndyke faced him genially.

"You, I take it, are the dock keeper?"

"I ham," was the concise reply. "And what abaat it?"

"I should like, if you would not mind," said Thorndyke, "to ask you one or two questions. I may explain that I am a lawyer and am, at the moment, rather interested in the subject of rope-stealing. These life-lines look to me very exposed and easy to steal."

"So they are," our friend replied in a slightly truculent tone, "but what else can you do? Make 'em fast with a padlock, I suppose! And then you'd be in a pretty fine 'ole if a bloke went overboard and nobody hadn't got the key."

"Very true," said Thorndyke. "They must be free to lift off at a moment's notice. I see that. But I expect you find one missing now and again."

"Now and again!" repeated the dock-keeper. "I tell you, the way them ropes used to disappear was somethink chronic."

"That was before you took to marking them, I suppose?"

"How did you know we marked 'em?" our friend enquired suspiciously; and as Thorndyke silently held up the free end, he continued: "If you spotted them marks, you won't be much good to the spectacle trade. But you are quite right. Before we took to marking 'em they used to go one after the other. Couldn't keep one no how. And we lost one or two--three altogether--after we took to the marks. But we got back two of 'em and dropped on the coves that pinched one of 'em; and now they've ogled that there's something wrong with our ropes and they leaves 'em alone--leastways they have for the last week or two."

Here he paused, but neither of us made any comment. Guided by long experience, we waited for the inevitable story to emerge; and sure enough, after a brief interval, our friend resumed:

"Three ropes we lost after the marks was put in, and we got back two. The first one I found in a junk shop in Shadwell 'Igh Street. The bloke said he bought it of a stranger, and p'raps he did. Nobody could say he didn't, so there was no use in makin' a rumpus. I just collared the rope and told him to keep a sharper look out in future. The second rope I spotted laying in a boat alongside Hermitage Stairs. Nearly missed it, I did, too, for the artful blighters had gone and dyed it with cutch. Made it look just like a ky-ar rope. But I looks at it a bit hard and I thinks it looks uncommon like our rope, barrin' the colour; four strands, same size, looked about the same length as ours--ten fathoms, that is, to a inch--and it seemed to be laying spare in the boat. So I jumps down--there wasn't nobody in the boat at the time--and I has a look at the cut end. And there was our marks quite plain in spite of the cutch.

"Now it happened that while I was overhauling that rope, a bobby came out on the head of the stairs and stood there a-twiggin' of me.

"'That your boat?' he says.

"'No,' I says, 'it ain't.'

"'Then,' he says, 'what are you doin' with that rope?' he says.

"So I nips up the stairs with the rope in my hand and tells him how things is and who I am.

"'Well,' says he, 'are you goin' to charge this man with stealin' the rope?'

"'No,' I says, 'I ain't,' I says. 'I'm a-goin' to pinch this rope,' I says, 'and you've caught me in the very act, and you're goin' to run me in, and you're goin' to bring this bloke along to make the charge and to swear to his property.'

"The copper grins at this. 'You seem to be a pretty fly old bird,' he says, 'but it's a sound wheeze. You'll catch him on the hop if he swears to the rope.'

"Just then two blokes come down to the stairs. They take a long squint at me and the copper and then down they goes to the boat. One of 'em was a regler Thames water rat and the other was one of them foreign sheenies--hair down on his shoulders and a beard what looked as if he'd pinched it out of a horse hair mattress. The copper grabs hold of my wrist and runs me down after them.

"'Here,' he says to the water rat, 'is this your boat?'

"Water rat didn't seem quite sure whether it was or not, but at last he said he supposed it was.

"'Well,' says the copper, 'I've just caught this man stealing rope out of your boat, and I'm going to take him along to the station, and you two have got to come along with me to identify your property.'

"Then I saw that my wheeze wasn't going to work. Water rat bloke had rumbled me--seen me at the dock, I expect.

"'Wot property are yer talkin' about,' says he, beginning to cast off his painter from the ring. 'That there rope don't belong to me. Someone must have dropped it into the boat while we was up at the pub.'

"The copper reaches out and grabs the painter so that they couldn't hike off and he says: 'Well, it's somebody's rope and it's been pinched, and you've got to come along to the station to tell us about it.'

"I thought those coves was going to give trouble, but just then a Thames Police gig came along and the copper beckoned to 'em. So they pulls in and one of the water police helped us to take the two blokes to the station. I went along quite quiet, myself. When we got there, the Inspector asks the water rat what his name was. Water rat didn't seem quite sure about it but at last he says: 'Frederick Walker,' he says, 'is my name,' he says.

"'No, it isn't,' says the Inspector. 'Think again,' he says. 'Last time you was James Trout and you lived in King David Lane, Shadwell. Live there still?'

"'Yus,' says Trout. 'If you knowed, what did you ask me for?'

"'We don't want any of your sauce,' says the Inspector; and then he turns to the sheeny. 'What's your name and address?' he says.

"The sheeny shakes his head like as if he was trundling a mop. 'No speak Anglish,' says he.

"'Oh, rats!' says the Inspector, 'you can't have forgot the English language in a couple of months. Last time you was Solomon Gomorrah and you lived in Pentecost Grove and was a tailor by trade. Any change?'

"'No,' says Solomon. 'It vas chust ze same.'

"'Well,' says the Inspector, 'you'll have to stay here while I send a man round to see that the addresses are correct. Sure you don't want to make any change?'

"They said no; so I left the rope with the Inspector and came away."

"And what was the end of it?" Thorndyke asked.

"That was," our friend replied. He expectorated scornfully and continued: "Both of 'em swore before the beak that it wasn't their rope, and we couldn't prove that it was, so he dismissed the case and told 'em to be more careful in future."

"And with regard to the third rope that you lost?"

"Ah," said the dock-keeper, regretfully, "I'm afraid that's a goner. Now that they know it's got a secret mark, they'll most likely have traded it away with some foreigner."

"You haven't done so badly," said Thorndyke. "I must compliment you on the smart way in which you found the lost sheep. And we needn't despair of the third rope. If you can give me the exact dates and the names and addresses, I may be able to help you, and you will certainly help me. I want to get a list of these rope thieves."

Our friend hereupon produced from his pocket a portentous note-book, the leaves of which he turned over rapidly. Having at last found the entry of the transaction, he read out the particulars, which Thorndyke duly entered in his own note-book.

"The length of these ropes, you say, is ten fathoms?"

"Ten fathoms exactly to a inch. I cut 'em off the coil myself and put on the whippings at the ends."

"I should have thought you would want them longer than ten fathoms," Thorndyke remarked.

"Why?" our friend demanded. "It's long enough for a man overboard. Of course, if he was going for a channel swim that would be a different matter. We haven't provided for that."

"Naturally," said Thorndyke. "And now, perhaps I had better make a note of your name and address in case I have any information to give you."

"My name," said the dock-keeper, "is Stephen Waters, and any letters addressed to me at the office here--Black Eagle Dock, Wapping--will find me. And I may as well have your name and address, if you don't mind."

Thorndyke produced a card from his case and handed it to Waters with the remark: "Better not mention to anyone that you have been in communication with me. The less we tell other people, the more we are likely to learn."

Mr. Waters warmly agreed with these sentiments (though his own practice had not been strikingly illustrative of them), and when we had thanked him for having so far taken us into his confidence, we bade him adieu and made our way out of the dock premises.

"Well," I exclaimed as we turned out into the High Street, "this has been a regular windfall. But how did you discover the place?"

"Oh, that was simple enough," replied Thorndyke. "I just took a list of rope-merchants and ship chandlers from the Post Office Directory and started systematically to call on them. One was bound, sooner or later, to strike the right one. But I was lucky from the beginning, for the second rope-merchant whom I called on gave me the name of a rope-maker who made a speciality of private ropes of unusual construction and particularly of marked ropes. So I went straight off to that maker and gave him the description of our rope, when it turned out that it was one of his own make. He had a big coil of it actually in stock and was good enough to give me a sample (when I had given him my card) as well as a direction to Black Eagle Dock. That was a stroke of luck, for I obtained, after a couple of hours' search, information that I had been prepared to spend a week on. But this meeting with Waters is a much bigger stroke of luck. We could, and should, have discovered eventually all that he has told us, but it would have involved a long and tedious investigation. This has been an excellent day's work."

"By Jove, it has!" I exclaimed. "With the Polish-Hebrew cab-driver and Mr. William Trout and the venerable Sodom-and-Gomorrah, we seem to have gathered up the whole party."

"We mustn't let our conclusions get ahead of our facts," Thorndyke protested. "We are doing extremely well. Our great need was to give to certain unknown persons 'a local habitation and a name.' We seem to have done that; but we have to make sure that it is the right habitation and the right name. Possibly the finger-prints may dispose of that question definitely."

Unfortunately, however, they did not. As we entered the Temple by the Tudor Street gate, we perceived Superintendent Miller advancing towards us from the direction of the Mitre Court entrance. He quickened his pace on seeing us and we met almost on our own threshold.

"Well, Doctor," he said as we turned into the entry together, "I thought I would come along and give you the news, though it isn't very good news. I'm afraid you've drawn a blank."

"Finger-prints unknown or undecipherable?" asked Thorndyke.

"Both," replied Miller. "Most of the marks are just smears, no visible pattern at all. There are two prints that Singleton says he could identify if they were in the records. But they are not. They are strangers. So that cat won't jump. Then there is a print--or rather part of a print, and bad at that--which Singleton thought, at first, that he could spot. But he decided afterwards that it was only a resemblance. You do get general resemblances in finger-prints, of course, but they don't stand systematic checking, character by character."

"And this one failed to pass the test?" asked Thorndyke.

"Well, it wasn't that so much," replied Miller. "It was a bad print and the identification was very uncertain; and when we came to look up the records, it didn't seem possible that the identification could be right. The print in the register that it resembled was taken from a man named Maurice Zichlinsky who was tried under extradition procedure for conspiracy to murder. The alleged crime was committed at St. Petersburg, and, as the extradition court convicted him, he was handed over to the Russian police, and a note on the record says that he was tried in Russia and sentenced to imprisonment for life. Consequently, as he is presumably in a Russian prison at this moment, it seems to be physically impossible that this print can be his. That is, if these are recent finger-prints."

"They are," said Thorndyke. "So I am afraid it is an absolute blank. Can you show me which are the possible prints?"

"Yes," replied Miller. "Singleton marked them on the photograph and wrote the particulars on the back. Here they are," he continued, laying the photograph on the table; "these are the two possibles and this one, numbered 'three', is the one that might have been the Russian's."

"And with regard to the second photograph?"

"Ah," said Miller, producing it from his pocket, "Singleton was rather interested in that. Thought the prints looked as if they had been taken from a dead body."

"He was quite right," said Thorndyke. "They were; and the question was whether there was any trace of them on the other photograph."

"There was not," said Miller. "Of course, negative evidence is not conclusive, but Singleton couldn't find the least sign of them and he is pretty sure that they are not there. You see, even a smear may give you a hint if you know what you are looking for."

"Then," said Thorndyke, "we have not drawn an utter blank. We can take it that our known prints are not among the group, and that is something gained."

I now inducted the Superintendent into an easy chair while Thorndyke placed by his side a decanter of whisky, a siphon and a box of cigars. It has sometimes struck me that my learned colleague would have made an excellent innkeeper, judging by the sympathetic attention that he gave to the tastes of his visitors in the matter of refreshments. Brodribb delighted in a particular kind of dry and ancient port and Thorndyke kept a special bin for his exclusive gratification. Miller's more modern tastes inclined to an aged and mellow type of Scotch whisky and a particular brand of obese and rather full-flavoured cigar; and his fancy also received due consideration.

"I was going to ask you," said Thorndyke, when the Superintendent's cigar was well alight, "at what time Radcliffe is usually to be found in his office."

"You needn't find him at all," replied Miller. "I thought you would probably want particulars of that hansom I told you about, so I got them for you when I saw him this afternoon."

"That was very thoughtful of you, Miller," said Thorndyke, watching with lively interest the extraction of a large pocket-book from the Millerian pocket.

"Not a bit," was the reply. "You are always ready to give me a bit of help. The driver's name, which is also that of the owner, as they are one and the same person, is Louis Shemrofsky--there's a name for a hansom cab driver!--and he keeps his blooming antique at a stable yard in Pentecost Grove; that is one of those little back streets somewhere between Commercial Road East and Shadwell--a pretty crummy neighbourhood, if you ask me--full of foreign crooks and shady Jews and what they call refugees."

"I suppose," said Thorndyke, "you didn't happen to note the date on which the cab was found in Dorchester Square?"

"Oh, didn't I?" replied Miller. "Do you suppose I don't appreciate the importance of dates? The cab was found in the Square on Friday, the nineteenth of June, at about ten-fifteen p.m."

Thorndyke probably experienced the faint sense of disappointment of which I was myself aware. For, of course, it was the wrong date. Meanwhile, Miller watched him narrowly, and, after a short interval, was fain to let the cloven hoof come plainly into view.

"That interest you particularly?" he asked with suppressed eagerness.

Thorndyke looked at him thoughtfully for a few moments before replying. At length he answered:

"Yes, Miller, it does. Jervis and I have a case in hand--a queer, intricate case with very important issues, and I think that this man, Shemrofsky, comes into the picture. We have quite a lot of evidence, but that evidence is in isolated patches with wide spaces between."

"Why not let me try to fill up some of the spaces," said Miller, eagerly, evidently smelling a case with possibilities of glory.

"I am going to ask for your collaboration presently," Thorndyke replied. "But just at the moment, the case is more suitable to my methods than to yours. And there is no urgency. Our activities are entirely unsuspected."

The Superintendent grinned. "I know," said he. "I've seen you do it before. Just work away out of sight until you are ready and then pounce. Well, Doctor, when you want me you know where to find me, and meanwhile, I'll do anything you want done without troubling you with inconvenient questions."

When the Superintendent had gone, I ventured to raise a question that had arisen in my mind during the conversation.

"Aren't you a little over-critical, Thorndyke? You spoke of spaces between patches of evidence but it seems to me that the case comes together very completely."

"No, Jervis," he replied. "It does not. We are getting on admirably, but we have not made out a coherent case. We have facts and we have probabilities. But the facts and the probabilities do not make complete contact."

"I do not quite follow you," said I.

"Let us look at our evidence critically," he replied. "The vehicle which went to Piper's Row was probably a hansom. Very probably but not certainly. That probable hansom was probably Shemrofsky's hansom and probably driven by Shemrofsky. We have to turn those probabilities into certainties. Again, the rope which was used to hang Sir Edward was stolen from Black Eagle Dock. We may treat that as a fact. It was dyed with cutch. That again is a fact. The rope found in the possession of Trout and Gomorrah was stolen from Black Eagle Dock and it was dyed with cutch. That is a fact. That it was stolen by, and was the temporary property of, one or both of them is highly probable but cannot be proved. The magistrate dismissed it as unproved. Gomorrah lives in Pentecost Grove. Shemrofsky's cab is kept in Pentecost Grove. Those are facts. The inference that Gomorrah and Trout and Shemrofsky were concerned in conveying that dyed rope (together with the body) to Piper's Row is very highly probable, but it cannot be certainly connected with the known facts.

"Again, the murder of Sir Edward we may regard as a known fact. He was probably murdered in a house in which is a tailor's work-room. Therefore he was probably murdered in Gomorrah's house. Still it is only a probability. And here there is a considerable space in our evidence. For Sir Edward was murdered by being drowned in salt water in which numerous herring-scales were suspended. Now, we have not traced that salt water or those herring-scales."

"No, we have not; and I can't even make a guess at what they may have been. Have you formed any theory on the subject?"

"Yes, I have a very definite opinion. But that is of no use. We have an abundance of excellent inferences. What we want is some new facts."

"But surely, Thorndyke," I protested, "a body of facts such as you have here, affording a series of probabilities all pointing in the same direction, is virtually equivalent to proof?"

"I don't think so," he answered. "I distrust a case that rests entirely on circumstantial evidence. A learned judge has told us that circumstantial evidence, if there is enough of it, is not only as good as but better than direct evidence, because direct evidence may be false. I do not agree with him. In the first place, direct evidence which may possibly be false is not evidence at all. But the evil of circumstantial evidence is that it may yield false inferences, as it has often done, and then the whole scheme is illusory. My feeling is that circumstantial evidence requires at least one point of direct evidence to establish a real connection of its parts with the question that is to be proved.

"For instance, if we could prove directly that Shemrofsky's cab was actually at Piper's Row on that Sunday night, we should link up all the other facts. Or again, if we could establish the fact of personal contact between Sir Edward and any of these suspected persons, that would connect the other facts with the murder. Or again, if we could prove by direct evidence that the remainder of that rope was or had been in the possession of Gomorrah or Trout or Shemrofsky, the other facts, and our inferences from them, would immediately become of high evidential value.

"And that is what we have got to do. We have to obtain at least one undeniable fact which will establish incontestably the actual connection of one or more of these persons with Sir Edward or with Number Five Piper's Row."

"Yes," I admitted, "I suppose you are right. It is an obscure case, after all. And there is one curious feature in it that puzzles me. I can't understand what object these men could have had in murdering Sir Edward. Nor can I imagine how he came to be in any way mixed up with a parcel of ragamuffins like these."

"Exactly, Jervis," said he. "You have struck the heart of the mystery. How came Sir Edward to be in this neighbourhood at all? We infer that he came voluntarily in Shemrofsky's cab to Pentecost Grove, probably with some other person. But why? And who was that other person? When we ask ourselves those questions, we cannot but feel that there is something behind this murder that we have not yet got a glimpse of."

"This seems to have been a conspiracy carried out by a gang of East End criminals of the lowest class. Legally speaking, they are no doubt the principals in the crime. But I have the feeling--the very strong feeling--that behind them was some person--or some persons--of a very different social class, who were pulling the strings. The motive of this crime has not yet come into sight. Probably if we can secure the actual murderer or murderers, the motive will be revealed. But until it is, our work will not be completed. To lay hands on the criminal puppets will not be enough. We have to secure the master criminal who has furnished at once the directing and the driving force."

CHAPTER XIII:

MR. BRODRIBB'S DISCOVERY

(Dr. Jervis's Narrative)

I AM not quite clear how the matter arose. We had, I remember, been discussing with Mr. Brodribb some of the cases in which a contact occurs between legal and scientific theory, and eventually the conversation drifted towards the subject of personal identity in connection with blood relationship and heredity. Mr. Brodribb quoted a novel, the title of which has escaped me, and asked for an opinion on the problem in heredity that the story presented.

"I have rather forgotten the book," he said, "but, so far as my memory serves me, the story turns upon the appearance in a certain noble or royal family of a man who is completely identical in appearance and outward characteristics with a more or less remote ancestor--so completely identical that he can be passed off as a survival or re-incarnation of that very person. Now, I should like to know whether such a thing can be, in a scientific sense, admitted as possible."

"So should I, and so would a good many other people," I interposed. "But I don't think you will get Thorndyke to commit himself to a statement as to the possibility or impossibility of any particular form of inheritance."

"No," Thorndyke agreed. "A scientist is chary of declaring anything to be absolutely impossible. It is better to express it in terms or probability. Evidently a probability of one to a thousand millions is in practice equivalent to impossibility. The probability is negligible. But the statement keeps within the limits of what is known and can be proved."

"Hm," grunted Brodribb. "Seems rather a hair splitting distinction. But what is the answer to my question in terms of probability?"

"It is not at all simple," replied Thorndyke. "There are quite a number of different lines of probability to follow. First there is the multiplication of ancestors. A man has two parents, to both of whom he is equally related; four grandparents, eight great-grandparents, and so on by a geometrical progression. The eighth ancestral generation contains two hundred and fifty-six ancestors, to all of whom he is equally related. Then the first question is, what is the probability of his completely resembling one of these two hundred and fifty-six and bearing no resemblance to the other two hundred and fifty-five?"

"Of course," said Brodribb, "the probability is negligible. And since de minimis non curat lex we may say that it doesn't exist."

"So it would seem," Thorndyke agreed. "But it is not quite so simple as that. Have you given any attention to the subject of Mendelism?

"Mendelism?" repeated Brodribb, suspiciously. "What's that? Sounds like some sort of political claptrap."

"It is a mode of inheritance," Thorndyke explained, "by which certain definite characteristics are transmitted unchanged and undiminished from generation to generation. Let us take the case of one such characteristic--colour-blindness, for instance. If a colour-blind man marries a normal woman, his children will be apparently normal. His sons will be really normal but of his daughters some will be carriers of colour-blindness. A proportion of their sons will be colour-blind. If these sons marry, the process will be repeated; normal sons, daughters who are carriers and whose sons may be colour-blind. Tracing the condition down the generations, we find, first a generation of colour-blind men, followed by a generation of normal men, followed by a generation of colour-blind men, and so on for ever. The defect doesn't die out, but it appears only in alternate generations. Now see how this affects your question. Supposing that, of my two hundred and fifty-six ancestors of the eighth generation, one had been colour-blind. That could not affect me, because I am of the odd generation. But my father--who would have been of the even generation--might have been colour-blind; and if I had had married sisters, I might have had colour-blind nephews."

"Yes, I see," said Brodribb, in a slightly depressed tone.

"And you will also see," pursued Thorndyke, "that this instance will not fit your imaginary case. The inheritance is masked by continued change of family name. Colour-blind Jones has normal sons, and colour blind grandsons. But those grandsons are not named Jones. They are his daughter's sons. Suppose his daughter has married a Smith. Then the defect has apparently moved out of the Jones family into the Smith family. And so on at each reappearance. It always appears associated with a new family name. But this will not do for the novelist. For his purpose inheritance must usually be in tail male to agree with the devolution of property and titles.

"But even now we have not opened up the whole problem. We have to consider what characteristics go to the making of a visibly distinguishable personality and how those characteristics are transmitted from generation to generation."

"Yes," Brodribb admitted, wearily, "it is damned complicated. But there is another question, which I was discussing the other day with Middlewick. How far is a so-called family likeness to be considered as evidence of actual relationship? What do you say to that?"

"If the likeness were real and would bear detailed comparison," replied Thorndyke, "I should attach great importance to it."

"What do you mean by a real likeness?" asked Brodribb.

"I mean, first, that subtle resemblance of facial character that one finds in families. Then special resemblance in particular features, as the nose and ears--especially the ears--the hands and particularly the finger-nails. The nails are nearly as distinctive as the ears. If, added to these resemblances, there were similarities of voice and intonation and of gait and characteristic bodily movements, I should think that these agreements as a whole established a strong probability of blood relationship."

"That was Middlewick's view, though he did not present it in so much detail. I have always had rather strong doubts as to the significance of apparent personal likeness and I have recently met with a very striking case that serves to justify my rather sceptical attitude. I told Middlewick about it, but, of course he was not convinced, as I could not produce my example for his inspection."

"We aren't as unbelieving as Middlewick," said I. "Tell us about your case."

Brodribb fortified himself with a sip from his glass and smiled reminiscently. "It was an odd experience," said he, "and quite romantic in a small way. You remember my telling you about a visit that I paid with Sir Giles Farnaby to the studio of my friend and client, Miss Vernet?

"I remember. It was in connection with the adventure of the disappearing pickpocket in the convict suit."

"Yes, that was the occasion. Well, while Miss Vernet was assisting the police to search the premises, Sir Giles and I examined the picture that she was at work on. It was a large subject picture, called 'An Aristocrat at Bay,' showing a French noblewoman of the Revolution period standing in a doorway at the top of a flight of steps around which a hostile mob had gathered. Miss Vernet was apparently then working at the principal figure, for she had a model posed on the studio throne in the correct costume.

"Now, as soon as Sir Giles clapped eyes on the picture, he uttered an exclamation of surprise, and then he drew my attention to what he declared to be a most extraordinary coincidence. It seemed that the picture of the French lady was an exact counterpart of a portrait by Romney that hangs in the small drawing-room at Bradstow, the architrave of the doorway representing the frame of the portrait. It was not only that the costume was similar and the pose nearly the same--there would have been nothing very astonishing in that; but he declared that the facial resemblance was so perfect that the figure in the picture might have been copied from the portrait. I wasn't able to confirm this statement at the time, for, although I remembered the portrait and recognised the general resemblance, I hadn't his expert eye or his memory for faces. But what I could see was that the figure that Miss Vernet was painting was a most excellent likeness of the very handsome young lady who was posing on the throne.

"A few days later, however, I had to go down to Bradstow to see the bailiff and I then took the opportunity to have a good look at the portrait--which represented a Miss Isabel Hardcastle; and I assure you that Sir Giles's statement was absolutely correct. The figure in Miss Vernet's picture might have been a portrait of Isabel Hardcastle. But that figure, as I have said, was a perfectly admirable portrait of the young lady who was acting as the model."

"That is very interesting, Brodribb," said I. "Quite a picturesque incident as you say. But what is it supposed to prove?"

Brodribb looked at me fiercely. "The testimony of a reputable eye-witness," said he, "is good enough for a court of law. But apparently you won't accept anything short of the production in evidence of the actual things; the portrait, the picture and the model. Must see them with your own eyes."

"Not at all," I protested. "I am not contesting your facts. It is your logic that I object to, unless I have misunderstood you. I ask again, what is your instance supposed to prove?"

"It proves," Brodribb replied severely, "that your theory--and Thorndyke's and Middlewick's--that personal resemblance is evidence of blood-relationship, is not supported by observed facts. Here is a portrait of Isabel Hardcastle, by a famous painter and presumably like her; and here is a young lady, the model, a perfect stranger, who is exactly like that portrait, and therefore, presumably, exactly like Isabel Hardcastle."

"But," I objected, "you have only proved half of your case. What evidence have you that this young lady--Miss Vernet's model--is not a blood-relation of Isabel Hardcastle?"

Brodribb turned as red as a lobster (boiled) and began to gobble like a turkey. Then, suddenly, he stopped and gazed at me with his mouth slightly open.

"Yes," he said, "I suppose you are right, Jervis. Of course I was taking that for granted."

With this he let the argument drop and seemed to lose interest in the subject for he sat sipping his wine with a profoundly reflective air but speaking no word. After sitting thus for some time, he roused himself by a visible effort, and, having emptied his glass, rose to take his leave. But even as he shook our hands and moved towards the door, I had the impression that he was still deep in thought, and I seemed to detect in his bearing a certain something suggestive of a settled purpose.

"I am afraid, Jervis," said Thorndyke, as our friend's footsteps died away on the stairs, "you have given Brodribb a sleepless night and perhaps sent him off to explore a mare's nest. I hope he has not taken you too seriously."

"If you come to that," I retorted, "you are the real offender. It was you who tried to prove that ancestral characteristics might reappear after several generations--and you didn't do it."

"No," he admitted, "the argument came to a premature end. Mendelian factors were too much for Brodribb. But it is an interesting problem; I mean the question as to the number of factors that go to the making of a recognisable personality and the possibilities of their transmission. The idea of a more or less complete re-incarnation is attractive and romantic, though I am afraid that the laws of chance don't offer much encouragement. But to return to Brodribb; I deeply suspect that you have sent him off in search of a re-incarnated Isabel Hardcastle. I only hope that he won't be too seriously disappointed."

"I hope so, too. When I saw how he took my objection, I was sorry I had spoken. For poor old Brodribb would give his eyes to discover some hitherto unknown Hardcastle whose claim he could set up against that of the present heir presumptive, though I don't see that a young lady would help him, seeing that the settlement is in tail male."

"No; but he is probably looking farther afield. We may safely assume the existence of at least one male relative, alive or dead."

"Yes, she certainly must have, or have had, a father. But there again one doesn't see any loophole for Brodribb. There can't be any unknown members of the family nearer to Sir Edward than David Hardcastle, unless he is thinking of the elusive Gervase. Perhaps he is."

"I have no doubt that he is," said Thorndyke, "and I wish him luck though it doesn't look like a very hopeful quest. But time will show."

In effect, time did show and the time was not very long. Our suspicions as to Brodribb's activities were fully justified. He had 'gone a-angling'. But the fish that he landed was as great a surprise to himself as to us.

The news reached us four days after the conversation which I have recorded. It was brought by him in person, and even before he spoke, we knew by the way in which he danced into the room, fairly effervescing with excitement, that something of more than common import had happened.

"Congratulate me, gentlemen," he exclaimed. "I have made a discovery, thanks to Jervis's confounded leg-pulling."

He flopped down in a chair, and, when we had made suitable demonstrations of curiosity, he continued: "I have been making enquiries about the young lady who was posing as the Aristocrat for Miss Vernet."

"Ah!" I exclaimed. "And who is she?"

"That I can't say exactly at the moment. But, to begin with, she is a he. The young lady turns out to be a boy."

"Ha!" said I, "we smell a mystery."

"You smell the solution of a mystery," he corrected. "The young lady is not only a boy. She is the boy."

"The boy?" Thorndyke repeated enquiringly.

"Yes, the boy. The disappearing pickpocket. The gentleman in the convict suit. The police were quite right, after all. He had popped in through the open studio window. But I had better begin the story at the beginning.

"It appears that this lad--Jasper Gray by name--is employed by a firm of wholesale stationers, Sturt and Wopsalls, to deliver parcels. He seems to be a highly respectable youth--"

"With a secret pocket in the back of his waistcoat," I murmured.

"Yes, that is a queer feature, I must admit," said Brodribb. "But both the ladies seem to have the highest opinion of his character."

"Plausible young rascal, I expect," I said. "Naturally, he would be able to bamboozle a pair of innocent spinsters."

"That is quite possible," Brodribb admitted, "and he is certainly most unusually good-looking. I saw that, for myself, though the wig and the costume may have helped. But to continue; he came to the studio to deliver a roll of paper, and Miss Vernet was so struck with his appearance that she persuaded him to pose for the principal figure in her picture. It was a regular arrangement. He came and took up the pose every morning before going to work.

"Now you see how the escape was managed: When he found himself in the Tottenham Court Road in a prison suit, he simply made a bee-line for the studio. He knew about the open window and made straight for it and sprang in. Then the two women bundled him into the dressing-room where he made a quick change into his costume. They hid the prison clothes and he took up his pose on the throne. By the time the police arrived he had become transformed into a lady of the old noblesse. It was a delightful comedy. Now I can appreciate the solemn way in which Miss Vernet conducted the two unsuspecting constables over the premises to search for the missing convict."

"Can you?" said I, with mock severity. "I am surprised at you, Brodribb, a respectable solicitor, chortling over a manifest conspiracy to defeat the ends of justice. You are not forgetting that secret pocket or the fact that Sir Edward Hardcastle's seal was found in it?"

"Of course I am not," he replied. "That is the importance of the discovery. I expect he picked the seal up, though as you say, there is the secret pocket to be accounted for. But we shall soon know all about it. Miss Vernet has arranged for him to meet me at the studio the day after to-morrow. He was quite willing and he is prepared to tell me anything I want to know. I suggested that you might come with me and there was no objection to that, so I hope you will be able to come. It ought to be quite interesting to us all. What do you say?"

There was no doubt in my mind as to what Thorndyke would say, for, evidently, this young scallywag was one of the indispensable missing links.

"I will come with you with the greatest pleasure," he replied, "and no doubt Jervis will come too and add to the gaiety of the proceedings."

"Good," said Brodribb. "I will let Miss Vernet know." And with this he took his departure with an appearance of satisfaction that seemed to me to be somewhat disproportionate to the results of his embassy. For, whereas to us the tracing of the seal held untold potentialities of enlightenment, to Brodribb it could appear no more than a matter of curious and trivial interest.

"Yes," Thorndyke agreed when I commented on Brodribb's remarkable self-complacency. "I had the same impression. Believing as he does, that Sir Edward made away with himself, he can have no reason for attaching any special significance to the fact that the seal was in the lad's possession. But he is obviously extremely pleased with himself; and I suspect we shall find that he has not disclosed to us the whole of his discovery. But we shall see."

And in due course we did see.

CHAPTER XIV:

NEW LIGHT ON THE PROBLEM

(Jasper Gray's Narrative)

IT was while I was carrying out some improvements on the studio skylight that Miss Vernet made her momentous communication. Of course, she didn't know that it was momentous. Neither did I. You never do. Providence has a way of keeping these little surprises up its sleeve and letting them fly at you when you are looking the other way.

But it was not only her communication that held such unsuspected potentialities. My very occupation, trivial and commonplace as it appeared, was fraught with a hidden significance which it was presently to develop together with that of other seemingly trifling actions.

At the moment, I was standing on the top of a rickety pair of steps which Miss Vernet was anxiously steadying while I fastened a rope to a swinging fan light. Hitherto that fan-light had been clumsily adjusted from below with the aid of a sort of boat-hook. Now, by means of the rope and a cleat on the wall, it could be conveniently set at any angle and securely fixed.

As I came down the steps, having completed the job, Miss Vernet murmured her thanks, mingled with expressions of admiration at the ingenuity of the arrangement. Then, after a pause, she said a little hesitatingly: "I have a confession to make, Jasper. I hope you won't be angry, but I have to a certain extent broken your confidence."

I looked at her in surprise but made no comment. There was nothing to say until I knew what she meant, so I waited for her to continue.

"Do you remember Mr. Brodribb?" she asked.

"I think so," I replied. "Isn't he the gentleman with beautiful silky white hair who came with Sir Giles to look at your picture?"

"Yes," she said eagerly. "I am glad you remember him. Well, for some reason, he is greatly interested in you. He came here yesterday on purpose to ask me about you. He put quite a lot of questions, which, of course, I couldn't answer, but I did let out about your coming here in those prison clothes."

"Is that all?" I exclaimed. "What does it matter? I don't mind his knowing. I don't care who knows now that the affair is over and we have sent the clothes back." (I had addressed the parcel myself to the Governor of Pentonville Prison and delivered it in person at the gate.)

She was obviously relieved at my attitude, but I could see that there was something more to come.

"I don't know why he is so concerned about you," she continued, "but he assures me that his interest is a proper and legitimate interest and not mere curiosity. He would very much like to meet you and ask you one or two questions. He thinks that you might be able to give him some information that would be very valuable and helpful to him. Do you think you would mind meeting him here one day?"

"Of course I shouldn't. Why should I? But I think he must be mistaken if he thinks I could tell him anything that would matter to him."

"Well, that is his affair," said she, "and naturally you won't tell him anything that you don't want to. I am sure, when you meet him, you will like him very much. Everybody does."

Accordingly we proceeded to arrange the date of the meeting which was fixed for the ensuing Thursday afternoon, subject to my obtaining leave of absence from Sturt and Wopsalls; and then, as an afterthought, Miss Vernet mentioned that Mr. Brodribb would like to bring a friend and fellow lawyer with him. This sounded rather portentous, but I made no objection; and when I went away (having secured the rope on its cleat) I left Miss Vernet happy in having success fully carried out the negotiations on Mr. Brodribb's behalf.

Sturt and Wopsalls raised no difficulties about the afternoon off, it being the first time that I had ever made such a request. I cleared up most of the deliveries in a strenuous morning, and, having made myself as presentable as the resources of my wardrobe permitted, presented myself at the studio punctually at three o'clock in the afternoon. I was the first arrival and thereby was enabled to assist the two ladies in setting out a tea-table that made my mouth water; and I was amused to observe that, of the three, I was the only one who was not in a most almighty twitter.

But even my self-possession sustained a slight jar when the visitors arrived; for Mr. Brodribb had gone beyond the contract and brought two friends with him; both, as I assumed, lawyers. But it appeared that I was mistaken, for it turned out that they were doctors. And yet, later, it seemed as if they were lawyers. It was rather confusing. However, they were all very agreeable gentlemen and they all addressed me as "Mr. Gray," which caused me to swell with secret pride and induced in Miss Brandon a tendency to giggles.

One thing which astonished me was their indifference to the delicacies with which the table was loaded. I had seen such things in pastry cooks' windows and had wondered sometimes if they tasted as well as they looked. Now I knew. The answer was in the affirmative. But these gentlemen trifled negligently with those incredible cakes and pastries as if they had been common 'tommy', and as for Mr. Brodribb he positively ate nothing at all. However, the delicacies weren't wasted. Miss Vernet knew my capacity for disposing of nourishment and kept a supply moving in my direction.

Of course, there were no questions asked while we were having tea. The gentlemen mostly talked with the ladies about pictures and painting and models, and very entertaining their conversation was, only I found myself wishing that Mr. Brodribb had taken something to eat to distract his attention from me. For whenever I glanced at him, I met his bright blue eye fixed on me with an intensity of interest that would have destroyed my appetite if the food had not been so unusually alluring. Not that he was the only observer. I was distinctly conscious that his two friends, Dr. Jervis and Dr. Thorndyke, were 'taking stock of me', as our packer would express it; but they didn't devour me with their eyes as Mr. Brodribb did.

As the closing phases of the meal set in, the conversation turned from the subject of pictures and models in general to Miss Vernet's picture and her model in particular, and while the two ladies were clearing away, I was persuaded to go to the dressing-room and put on my costume for the visitors' entertainment. When I came forth and took up my pose on the throne, my appearance was greeted with murmurs of applause by all, but especially by Mr. Brodribb.

"It is perfectly amazing," he exclaimed. "I assure you Thorndyke, that the resemblance is positively photographic."

"Do you think," Dr. Thorndyke asked, "that you are making full allowance for the costume and the pose?

"I think so," Mr. Brodribb answered. "To me the facial resemblance seems most striking. I should like you to see the portrait for yourself. Nothing short of that I know will convince you."

"At any rate," said Dr. Thorndyke, "we can understand how those unfortunate constables were deluded. I am all agog to hear Mr. Gray's account of that comedy of errors."

On this hint I retired once more to shed my gorgeous plumage and when I returned to the studio, I found half a dozen chairs arranged and the audience in waiting.

"Now, Jasper," said Miss Vernet, "you understand that Mr. Brodribb wants you to tell us the story in full detail. You are not to leave anything out."

I grinned a little uncomfortably and felt my face growing hot and red. "There isn't much to tell," I mumbled, "I expect Miss Vernet has told you all there is."

"Never mind," said Mr. Brodribb, "we want the whole story. To begin with, what took you to the River Lea?"

I explained about the parcel and the railway journey, and having thus broken the ice, and got fairly started, I went on to recount the successive events of that day of mingled joy and terror, gradually warming to my task under the influence of the genuine interest and amusement that my audience manifested. So great was their appreciation that--my shyness being now quite dissipated--I was quite sorry when I had brought my adventures down to the moment when I changed into my costume and took up my pose. For that was the end of my story--at least I thought it was. But my legal friends soon undeceived me. The end of the story was the beginning of the cross-examination.

Mr. Brodribb started the ball. "When that convict ran off with your clothes did he take anything of value with them? Anything in the pockets, I mean."

"Yes," I answered. "There was my return ticket in the trousers' pocket and an emerald in a secret pocket at the back of the waistcoat."

"An emerald?" said Mr. Brodribb.

"Well, it was a green stone of some kind and it must have come out of a signet ring, because it had a seal engraved on it; a little castle with a motto underneath--'Strong in Defence'--and above it the head of some sort of animal that looked rather like a crocodile."

"What is known in heraldry as a Wyvern, I think. Now would you recognise an impression of that seal?"

I assured him that I most certainly should, where upon he carefully extracted from a pocket letter-case an envelope on which was a black seal.

"Now," said he, handing it to me, "just look at that seal and tell me if you think it was made with the stone that you had."

I looked at the seal and glanced at the address on the envelope, and then I grinned.

"I am quite sure it was," I answered, "because I made it myself."

"The deuce you did!" exclaimed Mr. Brodribb. "How was that?"

I described the incident of the dropped letter and was rather surprised at the amount of amusement it created, for I didn't see anything particularly funny in it. But they did; especially Dr. Jervis, who laughed until he had to wipe his eyes.

"Excuse me, gentlemen," said he, "but the recollection of the great pow-wow in New Square was too much for me. Mr. Gray had us all guessing that time."

"Yes," chuckled Mr. Brodribb, "we were a trifle out of our depth, though I would remind you that Thorndyke gave us practically the correct solution. But, now, I wonder if you would mind, Mr. Gray, telling us how that seal stone came into your possession?"

I had been expecting this question, and obviously it had got to be answered. For the seal had probably been stolen and I had to make it clear that it had not been stolen by me. It would not he enough merely to say that I had found it.

"I have no objection at all," said I, "but it is rather a long story."

"So much the better," said Dr. Jervis, "if it is as amusing as the last. But tell us the whole of it."

"Yes," urged Dr. Thorndyke, "begin at the beginning and don't be afraid of going into detail. We want to know all about that seal."

My recent experience in Pentecost Grove had completely cured me of any tendency to reticence. Here was an opportunity to expose that nest of criminals and I resolved to take it. Accordingly, in obedience to Dr. Thorndyke's directions, I began with the incident of the truck and the egg-chest and recounted in full detail all the adventures and perils of that unforgettable day.

"Bless the boy!" exclaimed Miss Vernet, as I described my entry into the egg-chest on the schooner's deck, "he is a regular Sindbad the Sailor! But don't let me interrupt."

She did interrupt, nevertheless, from time to time, with ejaculations of astonishment and horror. But what interested me especially was the effect of my story on the three men. They all listened with rapt attention, especially Dr. Thorndyke; and I had the feeling that they were comparing what I was telling them with something that they already knew. For instance, when I described Ebbstein's house and the work-room with the goose on the fire and the sour smell and the big tub of herrings and cabbage, Dr. Jervis seemed to start; and then he turned to Dr. Thorndyke, and looked at him in a most singular way. And Dr. Thorndyke caught his eye and nodded as if he understood that look.

When I came to my escape from Ebbstein's house I hesitated for a moment, being, for some reason, a little unwilling to tell them about Miss Stella. But I had promised to give them the whole story and I felt that perhaps this part, too, might mean more to them than it did to me. So I described the rescue in detail and related how we had escaped together. And very glad I was that I had not held anything back. For I could see at once by Dr. Jervis's manner and expression that there was more in my story than I had understood.

"I hope," Miss Vernet interrupted as I was describing the escape from the empty house, "that you didn't kill that unfortunate wretch. It would really have served him right, but still--"

"Oh, it's all right," I reassured her. "I didn't kill him. I've seen him since."

This statement Dr. Thorndyke noted in a book which he had produced from his pocket and in which I had observed him jotting down short notes from time to time with a view, as I discovered later, to cross-examination, and to avoid interrupting my narrative. He was evidently deeply interested; much more so, I noticed, than Mr. Brodribb, who, in fact, listened with an air of rather detached amusement.

I now went on to describe our meeting with the hansom; and at the mention of that vehicle and the driver's name, Louis, Dr. Jervis uttered an exclamation of surprise or excitement. But the climax, for me, came when I brought my story to a close with our arrival at Miss Stella's house. Then, in an instant, Mr. Brodribb's detached interest gave place to the most intense excitement. He sat up with a jerk, and, having stared at me in astonished silence for a few moments, demanded:

"Dorchester Square, you say? You don't remember the number, I suppose?"

"It was number sixty-three," I replied.

"Ha!" he exclaimed; and then, "You didn't happen to learn the young lady's name?"

"I heard the footman refer to her as Miss Stella."

"Ha!" said Mr. Brodribb again. Then he turned to Dr. Thorndyke and said in a low, deeply impressive tone: "Stella Hardcastle. Paul's daughter, you know."

Dr. Thorndyke nodded. I think he had already guessed who she was--and for a little while no one spoke. It was Mr. Brodribb who broke the silence. "I've been a fool, Thorndyke. For the first--and last--time, I have set my judgement against yours. And I was wrong. I see it plainly enough now. I only hope that my folly has not caused a fatal hindrance."

Dr. Thorndyke looked at him with an extraordinarily pleasant smile as he replied: "We assumed that you would alter your mind when some of the facts emerged, and we have been working on that assumption." Then, turning to me, he said: "I have quite a number of questions to ask you, Mr. Gray. First of all, about that rope. You mentioned that you threw it on the foot board of the cab. Did you leave it there?"

Now, I had already noticed Dr. Thorndyke looking rather hard, now and again, at the rope that hung from the skylight, so I wasn't surprised at his question. But what followed did surprise me most uncommonly.

"No," I answered. "I brought it away with me."

"And what has become of it?"

I grinned (for I was pretty sure that he had 'ogled' it, as our packer would say), and pointed to the rope. "That is it," said I.

"The deuce it is!" exclaimed Dr. Jervis. "And a brown rope, too. This looks like another windfall, Thorndyke."

"It does," the latter agreed; and, rising, he stepped over to the cleat and taking the two ends of the rope in his hands, looked at them closely. Then he brought a magnifying-glass out of his pocket and had a look at them through that.

"Were both of these ends whipped when you found the rope?" he asked as Dr. Jervis took the glass from him and examined the ends through it.

"No," I answered. "Only one end was whipped. I did the other end myself--the one with the white whipping."

He nodded and glanced at Dr. Jervis, who also nodded. Then he asked: "Do you think, Miss Vernet, that we might have this rope down to examine a little more completely?"

"But, of course," she replied. "Jasper will--"

I didn't hear the finish, for I was off, hot-foot for the steps. Evidently there was mystery in the air and it was a mystery that I was concerned with. I had the rope down in a twinkling and handed it to Dr. Thorndyke, who had just taken possession of the studio yard measure, which he now passed to Dr. Jervis.

"Measure the rope carefully, Jervis, and don't pull it out too taut."

I helped Dr. Jervis to take the measurement, laying the rope on the table and pulling it just taut but not stretching it, while Mr. Brodribb and the two ladies looked on, mightily interested and a good deal puzzled by the proceedings. When we had made the measurement, Dr. Jervis wrote the length down on a scrap of paper and then did the measurement over again with practically the same result. Then he laid the yard measure down and asked: "What do you say the length is, Thorndyke?"

"If the whole remainder is there," was the reply, "it should be forty-six feet, four and a half inches."

"It is forty-six feet, five inches," said Dr. Jervis, "which we may take as complete agreement."

"Yes," said Dr. Thorndyke, "the difference is negligible. We may take it as certain that this is the remainder."

"The remainder of what?" demanded Mr. Brodribb. "I see that you have identified this rope. What does that identification tell you?"

"It tells us," Dr. Thorndyke replied, "that this rope was stolen from Black Eagle Dock, Wapping, when it was sixty feet long; that a piece thirteen feet, seven inches long was cut off it; that that piece was taken in a two-wheeled vehicle--probably a hansom cab--on the night of Sunday, the twenty-first of June, to Number Five, Piper's Row, Stratford. Those facts emerge from the identification of this rope, from Mr. Gray's story and from certain other data that we have accumulated."

"Good God!" exclaimed Mr. Brodribb. "Then this was the very rope! Horrible, horrible! But, my dear Thorndyke, you seem to have the whole of the case cut and dried! Can you give the villain a name?"

"We shall not mention names prematurely," he replied. "But we haven't finished with Mr. Gray yet. I think he has something more to tell us. Isn't it so? You said just now that you had seen the man whom you knocked on the head on some later occasion. Would you mind telling us about that?"

I didn't mind at all. On the contrary, I was only too delighted to put my new knowledge into such obviously capable hands. Therefore I embarked joyfully on a detailed narrative of my journey of exploration, to which Dr. Thorndyke listened with the closest attention, jotting down notes as I proceeded but never interrupting. Others, however, were less restrained, particularly Mr. Brodribb, who, when I had described the murderous attempt of the man with the knife, broke in excitedly: "You say that this man spoke in French to the other."

"Yes, and quite good French, too."

"Then we may take it that you understand French?"

"Yes, I speak French pretty fluently. You see, I was born in France or Belgium--I am not quite sure which--and we lived in France until I was nearly four. So French was the first language that I learnt. And my father speaks it perfectly, and we often converse in French to keep up our knowledge of the language."

He nodded as if the matter were quite important. Then he asked: "You say that this man accused you of having robbed him of a fortune?"

"Yes"; and here I repeated the exact words that the man had used.

"Have you any idea what he meant?"

"Not the least. So far as I know, I had never seen him before."

"You didn't by any chance hear what his name was?"

"Yes, I did. He gave the name of Jacob Silberstein to the policeman. But that was not his name. I heard two of the people call him Mr. Zichlinsky."

At this Mr. Brodribb fairly exploded. I have never seen a man so excited. He spluttered two or three times as if he was going to speak, and then, whisking an envelope out of his pocket, scrawled something on it, and, apologising to the rest of us, passed it to Dr. Thorndyke, who glanced at it and handed it to Dr. Jervis, remarking: "This is extremely valuable confirmation of what we had inferred. It seems definitely to establish the fact that Maurice Zichlinsky is in England--assuming this to be Maurice, of which I have little doubt."

Mr. Brodribb stared at him in astonishment. "How did you know that his name was Maurice?" he demanded.

"We have been looking into matters, you know," said Dr. Thorndyke. "But we mustn't interrupt Mr. Gray or he may overlook something important."

I had not, however, much more to tell, and when that little was told, I waited for the inevitable cross-examination.

"There are one or two points that I should like to have cleared up," said Dr. Thorndyke, glancing at his notes. "First, as to the cab that you saw in the yard. You seem to have had a good look at it. I wonder if you noticed anything unusual about the near wheel?"

"I noticed one thing," said I, "because I looked for it. There was a deep notch on the edge of the tyre. I fancy I made that notch when I bumped the cab over a sharp corner-stone. The tyre was worn very thin. I wonder that the jolt didn't break the wheel."

"It is a mercy that it didn't," said he. "However, the notch was what we wanted to know about. And now, as to the names and addresses of these people. Can you give us those?"

"The street that I went to is Pentecost Grove. Ebbstein, and Jonas, the coiner, live at Number Forty nine. Gomorrah lives next door, Number Fifty, the house in which I found Miss Stella. Zichlinsky lives there, too. He lodges with Gomorrah. The cab-yard turns out of Pentecost Grove just opposite Ebbstein's house. It is called Zion Place. I don't know where Trout lives."

"He lives in Shadwell," said Dr. Thorndyke. "We have his address." On hearing which, Mr. Brodribb chuckled and shook his head. I think he found the doctor as astonishing as I did. He seemed to know everything. However, this seemed to finish the cross-examination, for Dr. Thorndyke now rose to depart and took leave of the ladies with polite acknowledgments of their hospitality. As he shook hands with me, he gave me a few directions concerning the rope.

"You had better put it away in a safe place," said he, "and remember that it is of the greatest value, as it will be produced in evidence in an important case. When the police take possession of it, which they will probably do very shortly, they will want you to certify to its identity. I will send you a rope to replace it for the skylight."

Finally, he took down my address in case he might have to write to me, and then he turned to Mr. Brodribb.

"You are not coming with us, are you?" he asked. "No," replied Mr. Brodribb. "I want to have a few words with Mr. Gray on another matter. Perhaps, if he is going homeward, I may walk part of the way with him."

On this hint, I, too, made preparations for departure, and we issued forth together in the wake of the two doctors.

"I want you to understand," said Mr. Brodribb as we walked up the mews, "that I am not poking my nose into your affairs from mere curiosity. If I seem to ask impertinent questions, believe me I have very good reasons."

"I quite understand that, sir," said I, wondering what the deuce was coming next. Nothing came for a little while, but at length he opened fire.

"You mentioned just now that you lived abroad in your early childhood. Have you any recollection of how and where you lived?"

"Very little. I was quite a small child when we came to England. I remember seeing dogs harnessed in carts and I have a dim recollection of an old woman in a big white cap who used to look after us. I expect we were very poor, but a little child doesn't notice that."

"No," said Mr. Brodribb with a sigh. "There are many advantages in being young. You don't remember your mother?"

"No. She died when I was quite an infant. But she must have been a very good woman, for my father once said to me that she had been a saint on earth and was now an angel in heaven. I think he was very devoted to her."

Rather to my surprise, Mr. Brodribb appeared to be deeply moved by my reply. For some time he walked on in silence, but at length, he asked: "Did you ever hear what your mother's name was?"

"Yes. Her Christian name was Phillipa."

"Ha!" said Mr. Brodribb in a tone of deep significance; and I wondered why. But I was quite prepared for his next question. "Your father, I take it, is a man of considerable education?"

"Oh, yes, sir. He is quite a learned man. He is a classical tutor--crams fellows for examinations in classics and mathematics."

"Do you happen to know if he was always a tutor, or if he ever had any other vocation?"

"I have an idea," said I, "that he was at one time a clergyman."

"Yes. Probably. Clergymen often do become tutors. You haven't any idea, I suppose, why he abandoned his vocation as a clergyman?"

I hesitated. I didn't like the thought of disclosing poor old Ponty's failings, but

I remembered what Mr. Brodribb had said. And, obviously, there was something behind these questions.

"I suppose, sir," I said, at length, "there is no harm in my confiding in you. The fact is that my father is not very careful in the matter of stimulants. He doesn't ever get intoxicated, you know, but he sometimes takes a little more than would be quite good for a clergyman. I expect it is due to the rather dull, lonely life that he leads."

"No doubt, no doubt," said Mr. Brodribb, speaking with a singular gentleness. "I have noticed that classical tutors frequently seem to feel the need of stimulants. And it is, as you say, a dull life for a man of culture."

He paused, and seemed to be in a little difficulty, for after an interval he resumed in a slightly hesitating manner: "I have a sort of idea--rather vague and indefinite--but I have the feeling that I may have been slightly acquainted with your father many years ago, and I should very much like, if it could be managed, to see whether my memory is or is not playing me false. I don't suppose your father cares much for encounters with strangers?"

"No, he does not. He is extremely reserved and solitary."

"Exactly. Now if I could get an opportunity of seeing him without making any formal occasion--just a casual inspection, you know, even by passing him in the street--"

"I think you might have a chance now, sir," said I. "He has a teaching appointment from four to six on Thursdays and usually comes straight home. It is now a few minutes to six, so if we step out, we shall probably meet him. If we do, I will point him out to you and then you would like me to leave you, I expect."

"If you don't mind, I think it would be better," said he; "and if I may make a suggestion, it would be as well, for the present, if you made no mention of this conversation or of your having met me."

I had already reached this conclusion and said so; and for a while we walked on at a slightly quickened pace in silence. As we crossed the top of Queen Square by the ancient pump that stands in the middle of the crossing, I began to keep a sharp look-out, for Ponty was now due; and we had hardly crossed to the corner of Great Ormond Street when I saw the familiar figure turn in from Lamb's Conduit Street and come creeping along the pavement towards us.

"That is my father, sir," said I; "that old gentleman with the stoop and the walking-stick."

"I see," said Mr. Brodribb. "He has something under his arm."

"Yes," I answered; and there being no use in blinking the fact, I added: "I expect it is a bottle. Good evening, sir."

He shook my hand warmly and I ran on ahead and dived into our entry. But I didn't run up the stairs. A reasonable and natural curiosity impelled me to linger and see what came of this meeting. For some thing told me that Mr. Brodribb could, if he chose, enlighten the mystery of my father's past on which I had often vaguely speculated, and that these presentproceedings might not be without some significance for me.

From the entry I watched the two men approach one another and I thought they were going to pass. But they did not. Mr. Brodribb halted and accosted Ponty, apparently to ask for some direction, for I saw my father point with his stick. Then, instead of going on his way, Mr. Brodribb lingered as if to ask some further questions. A short conversation followed--a very short one. Then the two old gentlemen bowed to one another ceremoniously and separated. Mr. Brodribb strode away down the street and Pontifex came creeping homeward more slowly than ever with his chin on his breast and something rather dejected in his manner.

He made no reference to the meeting when he entered the room, whither I had preceded him, but silently placed the bottle on the mantelpiece. He was very thoughtful and quiet that evening, and the matter of his thoughts did not appear to be exhilarating. Indeed he seemed to be in such low spirits that I found myself wishing that Mr. Brodribb had taken less interest in our affairs. And yet, as I watched poor old Pontifex despondently broaching the new bottle, my thoughts kept drifting back to that meeting and those few words of conversation; and again the suspicion would creep into my mind that perhaps the shadows of coming events were already falling upon me.

CHAPTER XV:

THORNDYKE'S PLAN OF ATTACK

(Dr. Jervis's Narrative)

"A MOST astonishing experience, Thorndyke," I commented as we walked away from Miss Vernet's studio after our meeting with Jasper Gray (recorded above in his own words).

"Yes," he agreed; "and not the least astonishing part of it was the boy himself. A truly Olympian errand boy. I have never seen anything like him."

"Nor have I. As an advertisement of democracy be would be worth his weight in gold to a propagandist. If he could be seen strolling across the quadrangle of an Oxford College, old-fashioned persons would point him out as a type of the young British aristocrat. Yet the amazing fact is that he is just a stationer's errand boy."

Thorndyke chuckled. "I am afraid, Jervis," said he, "that as a demonstration of the essential equality of men he would fail, as demonstrations of that kind are apt to do on going into particulars. Our young friend's vocabulary and accent and his manners and bearing, while they fit his personal appearance well enough, are quite out of character with his ostensible social status. There is some mystery in his background. But we needn't concern ourselves with it, for I can see that Brodribb's curiosity is at white heat. We can safely leave the private enquiries to him."

"Yes. And I suspect that he is pursuing them at this moment. But, speaking of Brodribb, I think you rather took his breath away. He was positively staggered at the amount of knowledge that you disclosed. And I don't wonder. He was hardly exaggerating when he said that you had the whole case cut and dried."

"I wouldn't put it so high as that," said Thorndyke. "We can now be confident that we shall lay our hands on the murderer, but we haven't done it yet. We have advanced our investigations another stage and I think the end is in sight. But we have yet another stage before us."

"It is surprising," I remarked, "how our knowledge of the case has advanced step by step, almost imperceptibly."

"It is," he agreed, "and an intensely interesting experience it has been, to watch it closing in from the vaguest generalities to the most complete particularity. We began with a purely speculative probability of murder. Then the murder became an established fact and its methods and procedure ascertained. But the perpetrators remained totally unknown to us and even unguessed at. Then, as you say, step by step, our knowledge advanced. One figure after another came into view, first as mere contacts with the known circumstances, then as possible suspects, until at last we seem to have the whole group in view and can begin to assign to each his place in the conspiracy."

"It seems to me," said I, "that Jasper Gray's information should help us to do that off-hand."

"It is extremely valuable," he replied. "But the enormous importance of what he has told us is really tactical. He has placed an invaluable weapon in our hands."

"What weapon do you mean?" I asked.

"I mean the power to make an arrest whenever we please. And that, when the moment comes, will be the very keystone of our tactics."

"I don't quite see either point; how we have the power or what special value it is. You wouldn't suggest an arrest before you are prepared to prove the murder charge against a definite person."

"But that, I suspect, is precisely what we shall have to do. Let me explain. The abduction of Miss Hardcastle is a new fact. It is very illuminating to us, but we can't prove that it was connected with the murder of Sir Edward. Nevertheless, it is a crime, and we actually know two of the guilty parties, Shemrofsky and Gomorrah. With Gray's assistance, we could lay a sworn information now; and on his and Miss Stella's evidence, we could secure a conviction. Of course, we shall not do anything of the kind. We have got to make sure of the woman who lured the girl away. Brodribb evidently suspects that she is Mrs. David Hardcastle--at least that is what I gathered when he wrote down her maiden name, Marie Zichlinsky, for our information--and I think he is probably right. You remember that she had a brother who was convicted in Russia of a conspiracy to murder. He also thinks that the Zichlinsky who tried to murder Gray is that brother. And again I suspect that he is right.

"But these are only suspicions, and we cannot rush into action on suspicions. We have to prove them right or wrong. If we can turn our suspicions into demonstrable truths, we shall have our whole case complete and can act at once and with confidence."

"Then what do you propose to do?"

"First, I propose to settle the question, if I can, as to whether the Zichlinsky of Pentecost Grove is the Maurice Zichlinsky whose finger-prints are in the records at Scotland Yard. If he is the same man, I shall then try to ascertain if the convict, Maurice Zichlinsky, is Mrs. David Hardcastle's brother."

"But I understood Brodribb to say that he was."

"So did I," said Thorndyke. "But I must get a categorical statement with particulars as to the date of the extradition proceedings. If Brodribb can confirm his implied statement, then I shall have to test our suspicion that the woman who managed the abduction of Miss Stella was Marie Zichlinsky, alias Mrs. David Hardcastle."

"You will have your work cut out," I remarked. "I don't see how you are going to prove either proposition."

"There are no insuperable difficulties in identifying the woman," he replied, "though I have not yet made a definite plan. As to Zichlinsky, I shall ask Singleton to re-examine our finger-print."

"But he has already said that he can't identify it."

"That was not quite what I understood. I gathered that he recognised the print, but then rejected his identification on extrinsic evidence. He realised that a man who is in a Russian prison cannot make a finger print in London. But if I re-submit the print with the information that the man is believed to be in London and that there are circumstances which make it probable that the print was made by him, we may get an entirely different report; especially if I have previously communicated the facts to Miller."

I laughed with malicious glee. "Really, Thorndyke," I chuckled, "I am surprised at you! Actually, you are going to set Miller on to ginger up Singleton and induce him to swear to a doubtful finger-print. And this after all your professions of scepticism regarding finger-print evidence!"

"My dear Jervis," he replied with an indulgent smile, "let us be reasonable. If this finger-print conforms in pattern to the one at the Record Office, it is Zichlinsky's finger-print. There is no question of forgery. It is obviously a real finger-print. The only problem is its identity of pattern. And we are not proposing to ask for a conviction on it. We shall use it merely to enable us to secure the person of Zichlinsky and charge him with the crime. Nor need you be uneasy about Singleton. He won't swear to the print unless he is prepared to prove its identity in court, factor by factor, on an enlarged photograph."

"No, I suppose he won't. But what plan of action is in your mind? Assuming that all our suspicions are confirmed, including the finger-print; what do you propose to do?"

"I propose to make arrangements with Miller that the whereabouts of each of the parties shall be ascertained and an overwhelming force kept ready for action at a moment's notice. Then, at the appointed time, we shall swoop down on the whole crowd simultaneously--Mrs. David, Zichlinsky, Gomorrah, Shemrofsky, Ebbstein, and, if it seems practicable, James Trout."

"But," I protested, "you could never charge all these people with the murder. The magistrate would insist on your making out a prima facie case; and you couldn't do it."

"No," he replied. "But that is where Jasper Gray's information is so invaluable. We don't need a prima facie case for the charge of murder against any of these persons, excepting Zichlinsky. And in his case, the finger-print, which we are assuming to be provable, will be enough. In all the other cases, we shall proceed on different charges, on which we can make out a prima facie case. Mrs. David, Gomorrah and Shemrofsky will be charged with the abduction. Ebbstein--against whom we have nothing but deep suspicion--will be roped in as an accessory of the felonous proceedings of his lodger, Mr. Jonas, the ingenious manufacturer of half-crowns. As to Trout, I am not sure whether we can get him on suspicion of having stolen the rope. I should like to. He would be extremely useful. I must see what Miller thinks about it."

"But when you have got all these people by the heels? What then?"

"Ah, then we shall allow the subject of the murder to leak out; and it will be remarkable if, among this gang of rascals, there is not, at least, one who will be prepared to volunteer a statement. Take the case of Shemrofsky; he was probably a principal in the second degree as to the murder. It is unlikely that he took part in the actual killing; and if he did not, he will probably be very willing to clear himself of the major charge by giving evidence as to who actually committed the murder. Again there is Trout. He probably selected the house at Stratford. He probably stole the rope, and the fisherman's bend and the running bowline look like his work. He is an associate of Gomorrah's, but it is very unlikely that he had a hand in the murder. If he could be charged, he would almost certainly make for safety by putting the onus on the shoulders of the actual murderers."

"It seems a rather unsatisfactory method," I objected. "You are going to depend very largely on bluff."

"It is unsatisfactory," Thorndyke admitted, "but what else can we do? We know that these people conspired together to commit the murder. One or more of them did actually commit the murder; the rest are principals in the second degree. The only proceeding open to us is to charge them all and let them sort themselves out."

"But supposing they don't sort themselves out? What can you prove independently?"

"Let us see," he answered, "what sort of case we could make out. I am assuming that Singleton can identify the finger-print and that Stella and Gray can identify Mrs. David, because without that evidence we should not proceed at all. We should require further investigation. But, assuming those identifications, we shall proceed somewhat thus:

"First, we charge Mrs. David, Shemrofsky and Gomorrah with the abduction; and observe that we here bring into evidence the motive--the elimination of the principal beneficiary under Sir Edward's will, with reversion to the husband of Mrs. David. That charge we can prove conclusively.

"We then charge the whole group with conspiracy to commit murder. Here, again, the motive comes into view. The murder of Sir Edward leaves--or is believed to leave--the succession to the property and title open to the husband of Mrs. David."

"What about David, himself?"

"At present he doesn't seem to come into the picture, though, naturally, he lies under suspicion of complicity. We have no direct evidence against him. But to continue. The abduction, with its apparent motive, connects itself with the murder, of which the motive is similar. Mrs. David stands to gain by the success of both crimes. But we have proved her to be guilty of one of the crimes. This is presumptive evidence of her guilt in respect of the other crime, since the two crimes appear to be parts of the same transaction. Then the evidence against Zichlinsky operates against her since he is her brother and has no motive excepting that of benefiting her.

"Gomorrah is implicated by the facts that the rope used to hang the deceased is known to have been in his possession; that Zichlinsky was his lodger; that he is proved to have been concerned in the abduction and was therefore a confederate of Mrs. David.

"Shemrofsky was concerned in the abduction and is thus implicated in the conspiracy. We can bring weighty evidence to prove that he was at Piper's Row on the night of Sunday, the twenty-first of June, and that he assisted to convey the body of the victim to that house.

"Zichlinsky is proved, by his finger-print, to have been in the Stratford house and to have handled the chair. He is Mrs. David's brother and so stands to benefit, indirectly, by the deaths of Stella and Sir Edward. His statement, overheard by Jasper Gray, would be admitted as evidence of his being an interested party.

"As to Trout, all that is actually against him is his connection with the rope. But, if the police could definitely connect him with the neighbourhood at Stratford, that would be a material point. The importance of getting him charged is that, although he was almost certainly an accessory, it is most improbable that he had any hand in the murder; and from what Gray has told us as to his efforts to restrain Zichlinsky and Gomorrah, we may suspect that he disapproved of their violent proceedings and would not be prepared to take any risk in shielding them. He is really an outsider of the gang."

"Well," I said, "you have a better case than I thought, though it isn't up to your usual standard."

"No," he admitted, "but it is the best that we can do. And probably we shall get some further detail. We have not yet ascertained how much Miss Stella will be able to enlarge our knowledge. But, in any event, we have a substantial case to start with. We can prove the fact of the murder and the conveyance of the body to the house at Stratford; and by means of the rope, we can definitely connect this group of persons with the crime. Moreover, we can prove that one, at least, of those persons had a very strong motive for committing the murder and was known to have committed another crime--the abduction--apparently with the same motive."

"To say nothing," said I, "of the fact that the circumstances of the abduction strongly suggest an intention to commit another murder."

"Exactly," he agreed. "Zichlinsky's remark that he had been robbed of a fortune makes that fairly clear."

"I suppose," said I, after a pause, "that you now have a tolerably complete picture in your mind as to the actual course of events?"

"Yes," he replied. "Of course, it is largely inferential; but I think I can reconstruct the whole crime in outline with considerable confidence that my reconstruction is broadly correct. Perhaps it would be helpful to go over it and see exactly what we shall have to prove."

"It would be extremely helpful to me," I said, "seeing that it is, in effect, the case for the prosecution."

"Then," said he, "we will begin quite at the beginning and adopt the narrative style to save words. First some communication was made to Sir Edward, probably verbally and probably by some confidential envoy of Mrs. David's, begging him to grant an interview to some person who was unable to come to him. This person may have been her brother, who, being a fugitive from Russia, might naturally be in hiding and might be living in an otherwise unlikely neighbourhood. Sir Edward consented, with some misgivings, as we may judge from Weeks's description of his preoccupied state when he left home. It was arranged that Mrs. David should meet him with a hansom at an appointed place near his club and convey him to the place where the person was living. The approximate whereabouts of this person's place of abode was mentioned, as suggested by Sir Edward's precautions in leaving his valuables at the club; which also suggests that he was not without suspicions as to the nature of the transaction.

"On his arrival at Pentecost Grove, in Shemrofsky's cab, he was introduced to Zichlinsky; and, probably almost at once, the attack was made on him. I am disposed to think that the original intention was to hang him, but that, suddenly during the struggle, it became necessary to silence him. A knock on the head was not practicable as it would have produced a recognisable injury, and made the pretence of suicide untenable. The alternative, adopted on the spur of the moment, was to thrust his head into the brine tub; and this having been done, he was held there until he was dead."

"They must have been savage brutes!" I exclaimed. "But their savagery was their undoing. If they had hanged him, it would have been difficult to prove the murder, if not impossible."

"Hardly impossible, Jervis," said he. "You will remember that we had virtually decided against suicide before we saw the body. And then there were the shoes and the wheel-tracks. Still, the drowning made the case much more conclusive."

"By the way," said I. "You mentioned that you had a hypothetical explanation of the salt and the herring scales. Was it a brine tub that was in your mind?"

"It occurred to me as a possibility, and the only one I could think of. I happened to know that it is the habit of low-class East European aliens to keep in their living or working rooms a tub of brine containing herrings and cut cabbage. The crime seemed to be associated with that part of London in which colonies of these people are settled, and it had a certain crude atrocity that was unlike English crime. Then the appearances agreed with this supposition and with no other. The man had been drowned, but only his head and neck had been wetted. He might have been held over the side of a boat or a landing-stage; but that theory would not account for the salt and the herring scales. But a receptacle containing salt water and herrings met the conditions exactly. And that little shred of cabbage gave strong confirmation. Still, it was only a hypothesis; and even now it is but an inference. It remains to be proved."

"I don't think there is much doubt of it," said I, "though it had never occurred to me. Of course, when Jasper Gray mentioned the tub of herrings and cabbage floating in brine, the explanation came in a flash. But go on with your reconstruction."

"There isn't much more to say. The body was kept at Gomorrah's house--or Ebbstein's, whichever it was. Ebbstein's house fits the conditions perfectly but Gomorrah's is probably exactly similar--until Sunday night, perhaps because then there would be fewer people about down by the creeks. Then one man--probably Trout--was sent on ahead to get the house open and see that all was clear. The body was put into Shemrofsky's cab--probably it was placed upright, sitting on the seat--and accompanied by one of the murderers, who was almost certainly Zichlinsky. Then, as it had been a wet evening, the glass front could be let down without appearing remarkable, and the two occupants, the living and the dead, would thus be practically invisible from the outside.

"On the arrival of the cab at the house, the advance man--call him Trout--would give the signal 'all clear' and the body and the rope would then be quickly carried in by him and Zichlinsky. Probably Trout made the rope fast to the beam and prepared the noose while Zichlinsky held up the body. As soon as it was suspended, they would turn the chair over and make the other arrangements. Then they would go into the front room, open the window and drop the glove under it. Finally, they would look out to see that there was no one about and then come away and make for the rendezvous where Shemrofsky would be waiting for them with his cab. Or he may have driven straight home, leaving them to follow on foot or in an omnibus.

"That is how I think the plan was carried out, and that is the account that I shall give to Miller as the basis of enquiries and of such questions as he may think fit to put to the prisoners."

"And what do you propose to do at the moment?"

"My first proceeding," he replied, "will be to see Miller and try to get the finger-print question settled. Then I shall consult with Brodribb as to the best way of ascertaining whether the woman who captured Miss Stella was or was not Mrs. David Hardcastle. I have a plan in my mind, but as it involves Brodribb's co-operation, I can't decide on it until I have secured his agreement."

"My impression is," said I, "that Brodribb will agree gladly to anything that you may suggest."

"That is my impression, too," said Thorndyke. And subsequent events proved that we were both right.

CHAPTER XVI:

MRS. DAVID HARDCASTLE

(Jasper Gray's Narralive)

My premonitions of some impending change in the conditions of my life, dimly associated with Mr. Brodribb, were revived some days later when I saw that gentleman coming out of our office in earnest conversation with Mr. Wopsall. The apparition caused me some surprise, and when Mr. Wopsall beckoned to me, I came forward with alacrity, bubbling over with curiosity.

"You are going off duty for a day or two, Gray," said Mr. Wopsall. "Mr. Brodribb wants you to attend at his office to-morrow and perhaps afterwards. He will give you your instructions, and you will understand that they have my full concurrence; and I need hardly suggest that you smarten yourself up a bit and try to do us credit."

With this he shook hands with Mr. Brodribb and retired to his office, leaving us together; and we drifted out into the street to pursue our business. However, he had not much to say. In effect, he wished me to present myself at his abode in New Square, Lincoln's Inn, punctually at ten o'clock on the following morning, when he would give me more detailed instructions; and having delivered himself of this request and satisfied himself of my ability to find my way to his office, he shook my hand warmly and went his way with an air of deep satisfaction.

As he had given me no hint as to the nature of the business on hand, it was natural that I should spend the remainder of the day in speculating with the most intense curiosity on the circumstances that called for my presence in a place so remote from the scene of my customary activities; and it was equally natural that I should make my appearance in the place of assignation with more than common punctuality. Indeed, the word 'punctuality' understates the case; for, although I had spent a full hour operating on my clothes with a sponge, a nail-brush and a flat iron, I strolled into the Square from Chancery Lane at the moment when the hands of the big clock showed a quarter past nine. (I say 'the hands' advisedly, for the joker who put up that clock had omitted the figures on the dial, substituting for them a dozen exactly similar marks.)

I stood for some time inspecting that eccentric clock-face with mildly surprised interest. Then I transferred my attention to a fine pear-tree that some rural-minded lawyer had trained up the side of his house; and I was still contemplating this phenomenon when I became aware of a somewhat chubby gentleman in a broad-brimmed straw hat and slippers who was sauntering up the pavement smoking a very large pipe. At the moment, his head was inclined forward so that the hat-brim concealed his face; but as we approached, he raised his head, and, the hat ascending with it, disclosed the countenance of Mr. Brodribb.

"Ha!" he exclaimed as he caught sight of me, "You are a little before your time, which is a good fault, if that is not a contradiction of terms. The early bird catches the worm, as the rather ambiguous proverb has it--ambiguous, I mean, as to the moral to be conveyed. For while the early rising is obviously advantageous to the bird, it is obviously disadvantageous to the worm. He had better have stayed in bed a little longer. However, here you are, and it will be all to the good if we get our arrangements completed in advance."

He pulled out a prosperous-looking gold watch (apparently, he didn't trust the clock) and having looked at it thoughtfully, continued: "I shall want you to sit at a desk in my outer office, and you are to try to look as if you'd been there all your life. You are supposed to be one of my clerks. Do you understand?"

I assured him (but not in those words) that I 'rumbled him', as our packer would say, and he went on: "I am expecting some visitors presently. They will come to the outer office and you will take down their names on a slip of paper and then come into my office and announce them. And while you are taking down their names, I should like you to have a good look at them so that you will be able to recognise them if you should see them again."

This sounded agreeably mysterious, and once more, I assured him--in suitable terms--that I 'ogled' perfectly.

"If anyone asks you any questions," he continued, "be as evasive as you can. Don't give any information."

I remarked that I hadn't much to give, to which he replied that perhaps I had more than I realised. "But in any case," said he, "keep your own counsel. If they should ask you who you are, say you are my clerk."

"That won't be quite correct, sir," I ventured to remind him.

"Bless the boy!" he chuckled, "we aren't as particular as that in the law. But, in fact, you are my clerk. I appoint you to the post this very instant. Will that satisfy your scruples?"

I agreed that it would, though the appointment was obviously a legal fiction, and, the preliminaries being thus arranged, I was presently inducted into the outer office, of which I seemed to be the sole occupant, and installed at a handsome mahogany desk, furnished with blotting-pad, an inkstand with three ink bottles--black, green and red--a pile of paper slips and a number of quill pens.

At ten o'clock precisely, Mr. Brodribb entered his private office and shut the door; and there descended on the premises a profound silence, through which I could hear faintly the sound of movement in the inner office with an occasional squeak of a quill pen; by which I judged that the communicating door was by no means sound-proof. But I discovered later that there was a second, baize-covered door which could be shut when required to ensure privacy.

The minutes ran on. Soon the novelty of the situation exhausted itself. I began to be bored by the continued occupancy of the leather-seated stool and to be sensible of a faint yearning for a parcel to deliver. Sitting still was well enough when one was tired, but it was no sort of occupation for an active youth at ten o'clock in the morning. However, it had to be; so failing any opportunity for physical exercise, I directed my attention to the quill pens and the three bottles of ink. I had never used a quill pen and had no consider able experience of coloured inks. Now I proceeded to make a few experiments and was greatly pleased with the results. Beginning with a spirited portrait of Mr. Gomorrah, I discovered the surprising potentialities of a polychromatic medium. The green ink enabled me to do full justice to his complexion, while the red ink imparted a convincing surgical quality to his bandaged head.

I was adding the finishing touches to this masterpiece of portraiture when I became aware of sounds penetrating the door--not Mr. Brodribb's door, but another which apparently gave access to an adjoining room. The sounds conveyed the impression of several persons moving about on an oil-clothed floor and were accompanied by the dragging of chairs. But after a short time these sounds died away, and I had just returned to my polychrome portrait when the crescendo music of a pair of creaky boots informed me that someone was approaching the outer door. A moment later, that door was flung open and a largish gentleman with a puffy face, not unadorned with pimples, stamped into the room, and having bestowed on me a disparaging stare, demanded: "Is Mr. Brodribb disengaged?"

I sprang up from my stool and spluttered at him ambiguously. Meanwhile he stood, holding the door open and looking out into the lobby.

"Come along!" he exclaimed impatiently addressing some person outside; whereupon the person addressed came along, and in a moment completed my confusion.

I recognised her instantly, which was the more remarkable since she was strikingly changed since I had last seen her; changed as to her habiliments and even in her person, for then her hair had been jet black whereas now it was of a glaring red. But I knew her all the same. Hers was a face that no make-up could disguise. And if her hair had changed, her eyes had not; and now I saw why they had appeared different in colour. The pupil of the left eye, instead of being a round black spot, was drawn out to the shape of a key hole. Nor did her handsome clothing make any essential change in her appearance. From the moment when my glance fell on her as she entered the room, I never had the shadow of a doubt that she was the ill-omened nurse at whom I had peered through the gutter-hole in Pentecost Grove.

I suppose I must have gone even beyond Mr. Brodribb's instructions to 'have a good look at' the visitors, for the odd silence was broken by her voice demanding angrily and with a faint foreign accent: "Well! what are you staring at me like that for?"

I mumbled a semi-articulate apology which she ignored, continuing: "Go at once to Mr. Brodribb and tell him that Mr. and Mrs. Hardcastle wish to see him."

I pulled myself together rapidly, but incompletely, and, dimly recalling Mr. Brodribb's directions concerning the slips of paper, I grabbed up the portrait of Gomorrah, and, blundering into his private office without knocking, slapped it down on his writing-table. He regarded it for a moment with a stupefied stare and then exclaimed: "What the dev--"

But at this point his eye caught the two visitors, who, waiving ceremony, now appeared in the doorway. He rose to receive them, and I hastily made my escape, leaving the door open; an omission the enormity of which I realised when I saw--and heard--Mr. Hardcastle ostentatiously slam it.

I crept back to my stool and drew a deep breath, conscious that I had made rather a hash of the business, so far. Well, every man to his trade. One couldn't expect the practice of parcels delivery to produce expertness in the duties of a lawyer's clerk. Still, I must manage the next visitors better; and having formed this resolution, I fell, naturally enough, into deep reflection on the astonishing thing that had just happened.

So this woman's name was Hardcastle. But Miss Stella's name was Hardcastle too. Very odd, this. They must be relatives, but yet they had seemed to be strangers, for Miss Stella had referred to her simply as "a woman." But at this point my train of thought was interrupted by Mr. Hardcastle's voice, penetrating the door. He was speaking in a loud, excited tone--not to say shouting--and I could hear quite distinctly what he was saying.

"But, damn it, Brodribb, the man is dead! Been dead a matter of fifteen years or more. You know that as well as I do."

There followed a sudden silence, and then I heard the thud of a closing door which I judged to be the baize inner door of Mr. Brodribb's office; a conclusion that was confirmed by the fact that, thereafter, Mr. Hardcastle's rather raucous voice percolated through only in a state of extreme attenuation. Even this I tried to ignore, and I had just resumed my speculations on the possible relationship of Mrs. Hardcastle and Miss Stella when I was rendered positively speechless by a new, and even more astonishing, arrival. For, without any warning of premonitory foot-falls, the outer door opened softly and gave entrance to none other than Miss Stella herself.

She was not alone. Closely following her was a very pleasant-looking lady whom I judged, from a recognisable resemblance, to be her mother, and who asked me if Mr. Brodribb was at liberty. Before I could collect my wits to reply, Miss Stella uttered a little cry of surprise and ran to me holding out her hand.

"You haven't forgotten me, have you?" she asked, as I took her hand rather shyly.

"No, indeed, miss," I answered emphatically. "I shouldn't be likely to forget you."

"This is fortunate!" she exclaimed. "I was afraid that I should never see you again and never be able to thank you."

Here she turned to the other lady, who was gazing at us in evident astonishment, and explained: "This is the gentleman who rescued me and brought me home that night. Let me introduce my knight-errant to my mother."

On this, the elder lady darted forward and seized both my hands. I thought she was going to kiss me, and shouldn't have minded if she had. What she was about to say I shall never know, though it is not difficult to guess; for at this moment the door of Mr. Brodribb's office flew open and Mr. Hardcastle's voice, raised to an infuriated shout, was heard proclaiming: "It's a damned conspiracy! You are setting up this impostor for your own ends. But you had better have a care, my friend. You may find it a dangerous game."

He stamped out, purple and gibbering with wrath, and close behind him came his wife. Her ghastly white face was indescribable in its concentrated malice and fury; but as soon as I caught sight of it, I knew why Zichlinsky's face had stirred my memory. She might have been his sister. But this recognition came only in a half-conscious flash, for the sight of her strung me up to readiness for the inevitable clash. And the next moment it came. Mr. Hardcastle had pushed roughly past the two ladies and his wife was following, when, just as they came abreast, Miss Stella turned her head and looked at the woman. As their eyes met, she uttered a cry of terror and shrank back, seizing my arm and making as if she would have taken shelter behind me.

For a moment there was a strange effect of arrested movement in the room, all the figures standing motionless as in a tableau. Mr. Hardcastle had turned and was staring in angry astonishment; his wife stood glaring at the terrified girl, and Mr. Brodribb looked on with frowning curiosity from the doorway of his office. It was he who broke the silence. "What is it, Miss Stella?"

"The woman," she gasped, pointing at Mrs. Hardcastle. "The nurse who took me to that dreadful house."

"What the devil does she mean?" demanded Mr. Hardcastle, looking in bewilderment from Miss Stella to his wife.

"How should I know?" the latter snarled. "The girl is an idiot. Let us get away from this den of swindlers and lunatics."

She moved towards the door with an assumed air of unconcern, though I could see that she was mightily shaken by the encounter. Mr. Hardcastle preceded her and wrenched the door open. Then he stood for a moment with the open door in his hand looking out.

"Don't block up the door like that, man," he said, irritably. "Come in or get out of the way."

The unseen person elected to come in, and having come in, he promptly shut the door and turned the key. Mr. Hardcastle looked at him fiercely and demanded: "What the devil is the meaning of this, sir?

"I take it," replied the newcomer, "that you are Mr. David Hardcastle?"

"And supposing I am. What then?"

"And this lady is Mrs. David Hardcastle, formerly Marie Zichlinsky?"

Mrs. Hardcastle glared at him with an expression that reminded me of a frightened cat. But she made no reply. The answer came from Mr. Brodribb.

"Yes, Superintendent, she is Mrs. David Hardcastle; and she has been identified by Miss Stella Hardcastle, who is here."

The woman turned on him furiously. "So," she exclaimed, "this is a trap that you had set for us, you sly old devil! Well, Superintendent, what do you want with Mrs. David Hardcastle?"

The Superintendent looked at Miss Stella and asked:

"What do you say, Miss Hardcastle? Do you recognise this lady, and if so, what do you know about her?"

"She is the woman who was dressed as a nurse and who enticed me by false pretences to a house where I was imprisoned and bound with rope and from which this gentleman rescued me."

If a look could have killed, 'this gentleman' would have been a dead gentleman. As it was, he was only a deeply interested gentleman.

"This," exclaimed Mrs. David, "is a parcel of foolery. The girl is mistaking me for some other person if she isn't merely lying."

"We can't go into that here," said the Superintendent. "We are not trying the case. I am a police officer and I arrest you for having abducted and forcibly detained Miss Stella Hardcastle, and I caution you that anything that you say will be taken down and may be used in evidence against you."

Mrs. Hardcastle was obviously terrified but she maintained a certain air of defiance, demanding angrily: "What right have you got to arrest me? Where is your warrant?"

"No warrant is necessary in a case of abduction," the Superintendent explained civilly.

"But you have only a bare statement. You cannot arrest without an information given on oath."

The lady struck me as being remarkably well informed in the matter of police procedure. But the Superintendent knew a thing or two for he replied, still in the same patient and courteous manner: "Miss Hardcastle has already laid a sworn information as to the facts. I assure you that the arrest is perfectly regular and the less difficulties you make, the less unpleasant it will be for us all."

During these proceedings Mr. Hardcastle had looked on with an air of stupefaction. All the bluster had gone out of his manner and his puffy face had suddenly turned white and haggard. He now broke in with the bewildered enquiry: "What is this all about? I don't understand. What are they talking about, Marie?"

She gave him a single wild, despairing look, and then she made a sudden dash for the door of communication. In a moment she had wrenched it open, only to reveal the presence of two massive plain-clothes officers standing just inside. For one moment she stood gazing at them in dismay; then she turned back and faced the Superintendent. "Very well," she said, sullenly. "I will come with you if I must."

"I am afraid you must," said he; "and, if you take my advice, you will not make a disagreeable business worse by any sort of resistance."

He glanced at the two officers and asked: "Have you got a cab waiting?" and on receiving an affirmative reply, he said, addressing the older of them; "Then you will take charge of this lady, and of course, you will avoid any appearance of having her in custody, provided she accompanies you quietly. You know where to go."

As the two officers entered the room and shut the door Mr. Hardcastle turned to the Superintendent. "Is it possible for me to accompany my wife?" he asked.

The Superintendent shook his head. "I am afraid that is quite impossible," said he; "but you can attend at the police court and apply for her to be admitted to bail. I will give you the necessary directions presently."

Here the senior of the two officers indicated to Mrs. Hardcastle that he was ready to start; whereupon her husband stepped towards her, and, laying his hands on her shoulders, kissed her livid cheek. She pushed him away gently without looking at him, and, with a set face and a firm step, followed the first officer out of the room and was in turn followed by the other.

As soon as they were gone Mr. Hardcastle looked at my employer, gloomily, but with none of his former bluster. "Is this your doing, Brodribb?" he asked.

Mr. Brodribb, who looked considerably upset by what had just happened, replied gently: "There was no choice, Mr. Hardcastle. If there had been, you would have been spared the distress of witnessing this catastrophe."

"Yes," said the Superintendent, who had taken possession of my desk and was writing on one of the paper slips, "we are all very sorry that this trouble has fallen on you. But the trouble was not of our making. Now, here are the particulars that you will want and the directions as to what you had better do. But I must warn you that the magistrate may refuse bail. Still, that is his affair and yours. The police can't accept bail in a case of this kind."

He handed the paper to Mr. Hardcastle, who glanced through it, put it in his pocket, and, without another word, walked dejectedly to the door and passed out of our sight. And with his disappearance there seemed to come a general relaxation of tension. Mr. Brodribb especially appeared to feel the relief, for, as the door closed, he drew a deep breath and murmured: "Thank God that's over!"

"Yes," said Miss Stella's mother, "it was a dreadful experience, though it is difficult to feel any sort of sympathy except for her unfortunate husband. May I take it, Mr. Brodribb, that this was the business that required my presence here and Stella's?"

"Yes," was the reply. "There were some other matters, but they will have to wait. But I shall hope to do myself the honour of calling on you in the course of the next day or two."

"Then our business here is finished for to-day?"

Mr. Brodribb glanced at the Superintendent, who replied: "I shall want Miss Hardcastle to identify one or two of the persons who will be charged with the abduction, but it is not urgent, as we have Mr. Gray here and enough evidence of other kinds to cover the arrests. So we need not detain these two ladies any longer."

The two ladies accordingly made their adieux to Mr. Brodribb and then bade me a very cordial farewell. As she shook my hand, the elder lady said with a smile: "We have found you at last, Mr. Gray, and we are not going to lose sight of you again. We shall hold Mr. Brodribb responsible for you."

With this and a gracious bow to the Superintendent, she passed out of the door which I held open for her, her arm linked in Miss Stella's, and both acknowledged my bow with a valedictory smile.

"Now," said the Superintendent, glancing at his watch, "it is time for us to be moving, Mr. Brodribb. I told Dr. Thorndyke that we should be there by half-past eleven and it's nearly that now."

Mr. Brodribb went into his office where, besides securing his hat and stick, he apparently rang a bell, for a dry-looking gentleman--a genuine clerk--made his appearance from a communicating door and looked at his employer enquiringly.

"I am going now, Bateman," said Mr. Brodribb. "Did you order the cab?"

"The cab is now at the door, sir," replied Mr. Bateman; on which the Superintendent went out and Mr. Brodribb followed, pushing me in front of him. I was naturally somewhat curious as to our destination, but, as I had only to wait until our arrival to satisfy my curiosity, I wasted no effort on speculation, but gave my attention to my fellow passengers' conversation; from which, however, I did not gather very much.

"I don't know why you want me to come," Mr. Brodribb remarked. "I don't know anything but what Dr. Thorndyke has told me."

The Superintendent chuckled. "You are in much the same position as the rest of us," said he. "But you may as well see how far we can confirm his information. We've got most of these birds in the hand now, and it remains to be seen how much we shall get out of them."

"But you can't interrogate prisoners concerning the crimes that they are charged with."

"No, certainly not. But we can let them talk after they have been cautioned, and we can let them make statements if they want to."

"Do you think they will want to?" asked Mr. Brodribb.

"I shall be very surprised if some of them don't. You see, out of this batch, one or two, or perhaps three, are the actual principals. The rest are accessories. But an accessory, when he sees the rope dangling before his nose, is going to take uncommon care that he isn't mistaken for a principal in the first degree. He'll probably lie like Ananias, but it is tolerably easy to sort out the lies and separate the facts."

At this point the cab, which had been rumbling down Whitehall, turned in at a large gateway and drew up at the entrance to a building which I decided to be the police headquarters, judging by the constabulary appearance of all the visible occupants. Here we disembarked and made our way to a barely furnished room containing a large table, furnished with writing materials, and a few chairs. Seated at the table with their backs to the windows were Dr. Thorndyke, Dr. Jervis, and a gentleman whom I did not know. Exactly opposite the table was a door, at each side of which a police officer in uniform stood stiffly on guard, which led me to surmise that 'the birds in hand' were not very far away.

"Now," said the Superintendent when the brief greetings had been exchanged, "the first thing will be for Mr. Gray to identify the various parties. It is a mere formality, but it is necessary to connect his statements with actual persons. You will just look at the prisoners, Mr. Gray, and if you recognise any of them, you will tell us who they are and what you know about them."

With this, he led me to the door, which was then thrown open by one of the guardians.

CHAPTER XVII:

SOME STATEMENTS AND A TRAGEDY

(Jasper Gray's Narrative)

As I stood for a moment in the open doorway and looked through into the large room beyond, I was sensible of an uncomfortable thrill. The grim spectacle on which I looked was an impressive illustration of the omnipotence of the law and its inexorable purpose when once set in motion. The room was as bare as the other, containing only a central table and a number of chairs ranged along the walls, on six of which, spaced at wide intervals, the prisoners were seated, each guarded by two constables. A single comprehensive glance took them all in; and then my eyes wandered back to Mrs. Hardcastle, and I hoped that Mr. Brodribb had not seen her.

She sat, rigid and ghastly, a very image of despair. The misery and deadly fear that her haggard face expressed wrung my heart in spite of my knowledge of her wickedness, though, to be sure, the whole extent of her wickedness was not then known to me. But even if it had been, her dreadful condition would still have shocked me.

"I recognise this lady," I said huskily in answer to the Superintendent's question. "I saw her in Pentecost Grove the day I escaped with Miss Stella Hardcastle. She was then dressed as a nurse."

"It is a lie!" she exclaimed, casting a tigerish glance at me. "This young fool has mistaken me for some stranger."

The Superintendent made no comment and we passed on to the next chair.

"This is James Trout," said I. "All I know about him is that he gave me a bad half-crown and that he tried to prevent the other man from stabbing me."

"Have you ever seen this man before?" the Superintendent asked when we came to the next prisoner. The man looked at me wolfishly, and as I answered in the affirmative, he uttered a sort of snarl. And again I was struck by his resemblance to Mrs. Hardcastle.

"He gave the name of Jacob Silberstein to the policeman," said I, "but I heard some of the people address him as Mr. Zichlinsky."

The three remaining prisoners were Ebbstein, Gomorrah, and the cab-driver, Louis, and when I had identified them we went back to the other room and once more the door was shut. The Superintendent took his seat at the table between Dr.

Thorndyke and Mr. Brodribb, the strange gentleman laid a large note-book on the table before him and uncapped a fountain-pen, and I was given a chair next to Mr. Brodribb and provided with a blotting-pad, paper and pens and ink.

"You will listen to any statements that are made, Mr. Gray," said the Superintendent, "and if any of them appear to you to be incorrect you will make no remark but write down the correction for our information later. And I need not say that you are to regard anything that you may hear as strictly secret and confidential."

I signified that I clearly understood this, and the Superintendent then addressed Dr. Thorndyke.

"I think we had better begin with Trout. He is the most likely subject."

As Dr. Thorndyke agreed, the Superintendent gave the name to one of the constables on guard, who then opened the door, and, entering the large room, presently returned accompanied by Trout, who was given a chair opposite the middle of the table and facing the Superintendent. The latter looked at him doubtfully for a moment or two as if considering how he should begin; but Trout solved the problem by opening the proceedings himself.

"You are makin' a rare to-do about that bit of rope, sir," he complained. "I don't see why I've been brought here along o' them foreign crooks. Suppose I did pinch that rope--which I didn't. But suppose I did. It's nothin' to make all this fuss about."

"You are quite right, Trout," said the Superintendent. "The mere stealing of the rope is no great matter. We could let the dock company deal with that. It is a much more serious matter that we are concerned with; and the way the rope question comes into it is this: a piece cut off that rope--how long did you say that piece was, Doctor?"

"Thirteen feet," Dr. Thorndyke replied.

"A piece thirteen feet long was cut off that rope, and this piece was taken to a house at Stratford--Number Five, Piper's Row."

He paused and looked steadily at Trout, who in his turn gazed at the Superintendent with an expression of astonishment and unmistakable alarm.

"The persons who took that piece of rope to that place," the Superintendent continued, "also conveyed there the body of a man who had been murdered and they used the rope to hang that body from a beam."

"But," protested Trout, "that man hadn't been murdered. The inquest found that he hung himself."

"Yes, but we have since ascertained that he was murdered--drowned in a very unusual way. Now wait a moment, Trout. Before you say anything I must caution you that whatever you say will be taken down in writing and may be used in evidence against you at your trial."

"My trial!" gasped Trout, now evidently terrified. "What do you mean, sir? Why are you cautioning me like this?"

"Because I now charge you with the murder of this man, Sir Edward Hardcastle, whose body was found in that house."

"Me!" shrieked Trout, turning as pale as a bladder of lard. "You charge me! Why I don't know nothin' about it!"

"You are charged," the Superintendent continued in calm, even tones, "together with Maurice Zichlinsky, Solomon Gomorrah, Louis Shemrofsky and Marie Hardcastle, with a conspiracy to murder the person I have named. Now, remember my caution. You are not bound to say anything and you had better think carefully before you do say anything. If you wish to make a statement you can do so, and it will be taken down in writing and you will be required to sign it. But there is no need for you to say anything at all."

Trout reflected with an alarmed eye on the officer. Evidently he was thunderstruck by the turn of events and mightily puzzled how to act. At length, he said cautiously: "Supposing I was prepared to make a statement--though I don't know nothin' about the affair, mind you--"

"If you don't know anything, your statement wouldn't help us much," the Superintendent remarked dryly.

"Well, if I was able to tell you anything at all, would you drop this charge against me?"

"No," was the prompt reply. "I can make no promise or bargain with you. But if you are innocent, it will clearly be to your advantage that the true facts should be known. But don't decide hastily. You had better go into the other room and think it over; and while you are considering whether you would like to make a statement, we will have Shemrofsky in."

"Don't you take no notice of what Shemrofsky says," Trout implored with obvious apprehension. "He's the biggest liar as ever drove a cab."

"Very likely," said the Superintendent. "But we shall have to listen to him if he wants to say anything. And if he chooses to tell lies, that is his look-out."

Here the Superintendent nodded to Trout's custodian and uttered the single word, "Shemrofsky," whereupon the officer conducted his charge back to the other room and shut the door. There followed a short interval, during which we all sat looking at the closed door, awaiting the emergence of the other prisoner. Suddenly, a murmur of voices and a confused sound of movement was audible from within. Then the door flew open and a constable rushed out.

"The woman prisoner, sir!" he exclaimed in a dismayed tone. "There's something the matter--"

Before he could finish, the Superintendent and the two doctors had sprung to their feet and darted in through the open doorway. From where I sat I got a glimpse of a row of prisoners and constables craning forward with horrified faces, and opposite to them Mrs. Hardcastle supported by two officers. When I first saw her, she was sitting bent forward with her head nearly on her knees; but then the officers raised her until she leaned back in her chair, when her arms fell down at her side, her head fell back and her chin dropped, leaving her mouth wide open. That was the last that I saw of her, for at that moment the door closed; and when, after a considerable interval, it opened again, her chair was empty.

As the Superintendent and the two doctors returned to their places Mr. Brodribb looked at them enquiringly.

"Too late," said the Superintendent. "She was dead when the doctor got to her."

"Dear, dear!" Mr. Brodribb murmured in a shocked tone. "Poor creature! I suppose her deathwas not--er--"

"Natural?" said Dr. Thorndyke. "No. It was apparently cyanide poisoning. She must have kept a little supply concealed on her person in case of an emergency. Probably one or two tablets."

"Yes," growled the Superintendent, "and we might have expected it. Ought to have had her searched. However, it's too late to think of that now."

But in spite of these expressed regrets, I had the feeling that he was less disturbed by the tragedy than I should have expected. And so with the others. Even the sensitive, soft-hearted Mr. Brodribb took the catastrophe with singularly calm resignation. Indeed, it was he who gave voice to what was probably the general view.

"A shocking affair. Shocking. And yet, perhaps, in view of what might have been--"

He did not finish the sentence, but I gathered that he was rather more relieved than shocked by what had happened. And, later, I understood why.

After a decent pause, the business was resumed. Once more the door opened and now the cabman, Louis, was led out by an officer and brought up to the table; and a glance at him told me that, on him, at least, the recent tragedy had fallen with shattering effect. His face was blanched to a tallowy white and damp with sweat, his eyes stared and his thin, bandy legs trembled visibly.

The Superintendent regarded him with a critical eye, and addressed him in passionless but not unfriendly tones.

"Sit down, Shemrofsky. The officer who arrested you has cautioned you that anything that you say may be used in evidence against you. Now, bear that caution in mind."

"Yes," replied Shemrofsky, "I shall remember. But zere is noding against me. I drive a cab. Zere is no harm to drive a cab."

Mr. Miller nodded but made no comment, and Shemrofsky continued: "Zey say I take avay ze young lady, but zat is not true. Ze young lady get into ze cab by herself. Madame tell me vere to drive and I drive zere. Ze young lady get out of ze cab and go into ze house. I do not make her go. Madame could tell you I know noding of vot she do. But now Madame is dead and zere is nobody to speak for me."

"Very well," said the Superintendent. "We will let that pass. But there is another charge; and I caution you again that anything you say may be used in evidence against you. Don't forget that."

Shemrofsky turned, if possible, paler and stared apprehensively at the officer. "Anozer charge!" he exclaimed.

"Yes. It refers to a gentleman who was brought from Piccadilly, near Dover Street, to Number Fifty Pentecost Grove. In that house he was murdered, and his body was taken to Number Five Piper's Row, Stratford. The murder was committed by Maurice Zichlinsky, Solomon Gomorrah and certain other persons; and I charge you with being one of those other persons. Now, remember my caution."

For a few moments Shemrofsky gazed at the Superintendent in speechless consternation. Then he broke out, passionately: "You charge me zat I help to kill zat chentleman! I tell you I haf noding to do vid zat. I did not know zat anybody kill him. Somebody tell you lies about me. If Madame vas here, she vould tell you zat I chust drive ze cab vere I am told. Zat is all. I know noding of vot zey do."

The Superintendent wrote down these statements, though the gentleman at the end of the table was apparently the official scribe. But he made no remark, and presently Shemrofsky continued: "Somebody have tried to put ze blame on me. But I shall tell you all zat I know. Zen you vill see zat I haf noding to do vid killing zis chentleman."

"Do you mean," said the Superintendent, with ill-concealed satisfaction, "that you wish to make a statement? You are not bound to say anything, you know. But if you wish to make a statement, you may; and it will be taken down in writing, and, when you have read it and find it correct, you will be required to sign it. But do exactly as you think best."

"I shall tell you all vot I know," said Shemrofsky, whereupon the Superintendent glanced at the recording officer--who took a fresh sheet of paper--and advised the prisoner to stick to the truth and begin at the beginning.

"You had better start," said he, "by telling us what you know as to how this gentleman came to Pentecost Grove."

"He came in my cab." said Shemrofsky. "I vill tell you how it vos. Vun morning--it vas a Vednesday--Madame say to me zat a friend is coming to see Mr. Zichlinsky--zat vas her broder--and as he vould not know ze vay she vould fetch him in my cab. So she get in ze cab and tell me to drive to Dover Street, Piccadilly. Ven ve get zere, I valk ze horse slowly. Zen ze chentleman come. Madame push up ze trap vid her umbrella and I stop. Ze chentleman get into ze cab and I drive to Pentecost Grove as I haf been told. Madame and ze chentleman get out and go into Mr. Ebbstein's house."

"Ebbstein's!" exclaimed the Superintendent. "I understood it was Gomorrah's."

"No, it vos Ebbstein's. Vel, zey go in and I take my cab to ze yard. I see ze chentleman no more and I hear noding about him. Zen, on Sunday, Gomorrah come to me and say zat Mr. Zichlinsky want me to take ze chentleman to Stratford. He tell me to come for him at night a liddle before eleven. Ven I come to ze house--Mr. Ebbstein's--Gomorrah tell me ze chentleman haf got drunk. He vos very drunk; so Gomorrah and Ebbstein haf to help him out to ze cab."

"What do you mean by 'help him out'?" asked the Superintendent. "Was he able to walk?"

"No, he vos too drunk. Zey haf to carry him out. Zey sit him in ze cab and zen Mr. Zichlinsky get in and sit by his side. Zey tell me to let down ze glass front, so I let it down and zen I drive to Stratford. Zey tell me to go up Stratford High Street, and ven I get zere I pull up ze trap and Mr. Zichlinsky tell me vich vay to go. Presently ve come to a row of houses vich seem to be empty, all but vun, vere I see a man standing at an open door. He make a sign to me and I stop and pull up ze glass front. Zen ze man get in and help Mr. Zichlinsky to take ze chentleman out of ze cab and carry him into ze house. Zey shut ze door and I drive avay and go home."

"Was there any light in the house?" the Superintendent asked.

"Zere vos a lantern on ze floor chust inside."

"With regard to this man," said Mr. Miller. "Was he anyone that you knew?"

"It vos very dark," Shemrofsky replied, evasively. "I could not see him plainly."

"Still," said the Superintendent, "he was quite close to you when he got into the cab. I don't want to press you, but if you know who he was you had much better say so."

"Vell," Shemrofsky replied, reluctantly, "it vos very dark. I could not see vell, but ze man seem to look a liddle like Mr. Trout."

"Ha! And what happened after that?"

"Noding. I go home and zat is all I know." The Superintendent reflected awhile. Then he held out his hand to the scribe, who passed him the written statement. When he had glanced through it he read it slowly aloud, including the questions.

"Now, Shemrofsky," he said, "is that all you know? Or would you like to add anything to it?"

"Zat is all I know," was the reply; whereupon "the deponent" was provided with a pen, an instrument with which he seemed unfamiliar, but with which he contrived to make some sort of mark, which the Superintendent countersigned as witness. Then Shemrofsky was conducted back to the other room, whence Trout was brought forth to take his place.

"Well, Trout," the Superintendent said, genially. "Have you thought it over?"

"Yus," was the reply: "and I am going to make a statement. I ain't going to lump in with them foreign crooks. I don't 'old with their ways and I've told 'em so over and over again."

"Then I take it that you are going to tell us all that you know about this affair and that you are going to make a true statement."

"I am," replied Trout, "though, mind you, I don't know anything but what I've been told."

"What you have been told," said the Superintendent, "is not evidence. Still, it is your statement, so you can say what you please. You had better begin at the beginning and take the events in their proper order."

"The beginning of the affair, as I understand," said Trout, "was when this gent came to Ebbstein's house. He came in Shemrofsky's cab with Madame--she was Zichlinsky's sister, I believe. They went in together, but Madame came out again almost at once and went into Gomorrah's house. Shemrofsky told me this. The rest of the story I had from Gomorrah.

"It seems that Madame took the gent into Ebbstein's work-room. There was no work being done there that day, so the women what worked for him had been given a day off. There was three men there: Zichlinsky, Ebbstein and Gomorrah; and as soon as Madame was gone, the whole three set about the gent. But he gave 'em more trouble than they had bargained for. They had meant to hang him and they'd got the rope ready, but they couldn't manage him; and all the time, he was fairly raising Cain--hollering 'murder!' fit to fetch the roof off. Just then a woman runs in and says there was two coppers coming up the street. Ebbstein wanted to knife the gent straight away, but Zichlinsky wouldn't let him; but as they was close to the pickle tub, they got him bent down and Zichlinsky shoved his head down into the brine and held it there while the other two lifted his legs. They held on like that until the coppers had passed out of the street, and when they took his head out of the brine he was dead."

"You had better say what you mean by 'the pickle tub'," said the Superintendent.

"It is a big tub of brine what they pickles their herrings and cabbage in. There wasn't much in it but brine just then. They filled it up with fish and cabbage the next day."

"And about this rope that you say they had ready. What do you know about that?"

"It was a bit about a couple of fathoms long that was cut off a rope that belonged to Gomorrah. I don't know where he got it. But I know the rope because he brought the piece to me and asked me to show him how to make a noose in it. That was the day before they did the gent in. Of course, I didn't know what he wanted it for, so I made a running bowline in the end just to show him."

"I see," said the Superintendent (and no doubt he did); "what happened next?"

"Well," replied Trout, "when they'd done him in, they'd got to dispose of the body. For the time being they stowed it away in the cellar, and a rare fright they got while it was there; for some coves brought an egg-chest to the house in a mighty hurry. They thought Powis was inside it, but when they opened it a strange young man popped out. I fancy it was this young gentleman," he added, indicating me, "and a pretty narrow squeak he had; for Ebbstein thought he was a spy, and, being in a blue funk about the body that he'd got in his cellar, he wanted to do the young man in to make things safe. But the bloke what had brought the case wasn't going to be mixed up with any throat slitting--of course, he didn't know anything about the body downstairs--so they locked the young man up in Jonas Markovitch's room, and he got out of the window and hiked off.

"However, that's another story. To come back to this job: the night they did the gent in, Gomorrah comes to me and says that him and Ebbstein is in difficulties. He says the gent was took ill--had a stroke, or somethink--and died suddenly, and they don't know what to do with the body. He asks me if I know of any safe place where they could plant it, where it wouldn't be found for a little while. Of course, he didn't say anything about the murder at that time. If he had, I wouldn't have had anything to do with the business. But as it seemed to be just an accident, I didn't see no harm in giving 'em a bit of advice.

"Now, I happened to know Stratford pretty well. Got a married sister what lives there. And I knowed about those empty houses in Piper's Row, so I told Gomorrah about them and he thought they'd suit to a 'T'. So he asked me to take Zichlinsky and Shemrofsky down to the place and show 'em the way; and he gave me a bunch of skeleton keys and some tools to get in. But I didn't want 'em; for when I went down there that night with Zichlinsky and Shemrofsky and picked out a likely-looking house, I found I could open the door with my own latch-key. So I told Zichlinsky that I would lend him the latch-key when he wanted to get into the house. And I did. I lent him the key on the Sunday afternoon and he give it me back the next morning."

"You didn't go with him to Stratford when he took the body there?"

"Me! Not much. He wanted me to, but I wasn't going to be mixed up in the business."

"Do you know who did go with him?"

"No. I don't know as anybody did. Anyhow, it wasn't me."

"When did you first hear about the murder?"

"Not until after the body was found. When I heard about it being found hanging in the wash'us, I smelt a rat. So I asked Gomorrah about it and then he let on by degrees. He wasn't quite himself just then on account of a knock on the head that he got from this young gentleman. First he put it all on to Zichlinsky, but afterwards I got the whole story out of him."

The Superintendent waited for some further observations, but as none were forthcoming, he asked: "Is that all you've got to tell us?"

"That's the lot, sir," Trout replied with cheerful finality, adding, "and quite enough too."

"Not quite enough, Trout," the Superintendent corrected. "There's one other little matter that we want some information about. Have you got that small object about you, Mr. Brodribb?"

Mr. Brodribb had, and presently produced it from an envelope which he took out of his letter case. As he laid it down on the clean, white blotting pad, I recognised with something of a thrill my long-lost and deeply lamented emerald.

Mr. Trout regarded it stolidly, and, when the Superintendent asked him what he could tell us about it, he promptly replied: "Nothing."

"That isn't much," the officer remarked. "Perhaps if I tell you something about it you'll remember something more. You probably know that Powis is in detention awaiting his trial. Now, this stone was in his possession, and he says that you sold it to him."

"Well," protested Trout, "supposing I did. It ain't got nothin' to do with this other business."

"But it has a great deal," said the Superintendent. "This stone was in a ring which is known to have been on the person of the gentleman who was murdered. This is the ring that it came from" (here the Superintendent took from his pocket and laid on the blotting pad a rather massive gold ring in which was an empty oval space); "and this ring was found in the possession of Jonas Markovitch, who says that he bought it from you."

"He's a liar," exclaimed Trout, indignantly. "He sold me the stone, himself. He took it out of the ring because it wasn't no good to him, as he was going to melt down the metal. I gave him a bob for it and I sold it to Powis for five bob. Markovitch told me he found the ring on the work-room floor."

"Well, why didn't you say so at first, Trout?" said the Superintendent in a tone of mild reproach.

"I forgot," replied Trout, adding irrelevantly: "besides, I couldn't see that it mattered."

As it appeared that he had nothing further to communicate, his statement was read over to him, and, when he had suggested one or two trifling alterations, he signed it with considerable effort and the addition of two good-sized blots which he endeavoured to lick up. The addition of the Superintendent's signature completed the formalities and the prisoner was then conducted back to the other room. As the door closed behind him, the Superintendent uttered a grunt of satisfaction.

"Not so bad," said he. "With your evidence, Doctor, and Mr. Gray's and these two statements, we may say that we have a complete case."

"You think these two men will be willing to go into the witness box?" asked Mr. Brodribb.

"Oh, they will be willing enough," replied the Superintendent, "seeing that their evidence tends to clear them of being directly concerned in the murder."

"What about Singleton?" Dr. Thorndyke asked. "Will he swear to Zichlinsky's finger-print?

"Yes," the Superintendent answered. "He would have sworn to it before, only that it seemed impossible, and that he has such a holy terror of you since that Hornby case. But now he is ready to swear to it and give details as to the agreement of the separate features. So we have got a strong case even without these statements. But, Lord! Doctor, you haven't left us much glory. Here is your information" (he took a paper from his pocket and opened it before him), "describing the whole crime in close detail, and here are these two statements; and, making allowance for a few obvious lies, they are identical. The only weak spot was the murder charge against 'Madame,' as they call her; and she has solved that difficulty by throwing in her hand. Her suicide almost amounts to a confession--for although she hadn't been charged with the murder, she must have seen that she was going to be--and it will have put the fear of God into the others."

"Speaking of the others," said Dr. Thorndyke, "do you propose to offer the three principals the opportunity to make voluntary statements?"

"Of course, they can if they like," the Superintendent replied, "but I have advised them to say nothing until they have consulted their Rabbi or a lawyer. As they will be on trial for their lives, it would not be proper to encourage them to talk at this stage. No doubt they will elect to give evidence at their trial, and each of them will try to clear himself by incriminating the others. But that is their look-out."

"With regard to David Hardcastle," said Mr. Brodribb, "I assume that you take the same view as I do: that he had no hand in the affair at all."

"That is so," was the reply. "We have nothing against him. He seems to be right outside the picture. He would be, you know. This is not an English type of crime. It is pretty certain that Madame kept him entirely in the dark about the whole affair. And now, gentlemen, I think we have finished for the present and I am very much obliged to you for your help. You will be kept informed as to any further developments."

With this, the meeting broke up; and as it seemed that my valuable services were no longer in demand at Mr. Brodribb's office, I was released (with a substantial fee for my attendance), after a cordial hand-shake with the four gentlemen, and went forth to view the neighbourhood of Westminster and to reflect upon the surprising circumstances in which I had become involved.

CHAPTER XVIII:

THE WHEEL OF FORTUNE

(Jasper Gray's Narrative)

To most of us a retrospect of life presents a picture of a succession of events each of which is visibly connected with those that have gone before. Times change indeed and we change with them; but the changes are gradual, progressive, evolutionary. The child grows up to manhood and in so doing reacts on his environment in such a way as to set up in it responsive changes. But he remains the same person and his environment remains substantially the same environment. Though both alter insensibly from day to day and from year to year, there is no point at which the connection of the present with the past is definitely broken.

This is the common experience; to which my own offers a striking exception. For into my life there came a break with the past so sudden and complete that in a few moments I not only passed into a totally new environment but even seemed, in a sense, to have acquired a new personality.

The break came on the third day after my attendance at the police headquarters. I can recall the circumstances with the most intense vividness; as well I may, for, with the material gain was linked an irreparable loss that has left a blank in my life even unto this day. I was still on leave from Sturt and Wopsalls, 'standing by' at Mr. Brodribb's request, for possible, and unknown, duties, and having nothing to do on this particular morning had taken up my position in a reasonably comfortable chair to listen while Pontifex expounded the Latin language to one of his pupils.

How clearly the picture rises before me as I write! The shabby room, ill-furnished and none too clean; the deal table--its excessive dealiness partially cloaked by a threadbare cover--invitingly furnished with one or two books and a little pile of scribbling paper; and the two figures that faced one another across the table--Pontifex, sitting limply in his Windsor elbow-chair and looking strangely old and frail, and the stolid pupil with eyes sullenly downcast at his book. I watched them both, but especially Pontifex, noting uneasily how he seemed to have aged and withered within the last week or two and wondering how much of the change was attributable respectively to Mr. Brodribb or Johnny Walker; and noting, further, that the latter was conspicuously in abeyance at the moment.

Mr. Cohen, the present recipient of instruction, was not a promising pupil. It was not that he was a fool. By no means. I had seen him conducting the business of the paternal pawnbroker's shop and could certify as to his being most completely on the spot; so much so that my mission (as Ponty's agent) turned out a financial failure. But Mr. Cohen's genius was exclusively commercial. As a classical scholar he was hopeless. Poor Ponty groaned at the sound of his footsteps on the stair.

This morning the subject of study was Virgil's Georgics, Book Four, of which the opening paragraph had been dealt with, painfully and incompletely, in the previous lesson.

"Now, Mr. Cohen," said Pontifex, with a cheerful and encouraging air, "we begin with verse eight, which introduces the subject of the poem. Principio sedes apibus statioque pelenda. Let us hear how you render that into English."

Mr. Cohen glared sulkily at his book, but rendering there was none beyond certain inward mutterings which had a suspiciously expletive quality. Pontifex waited patiently awhile, and then, as no further sound was forthcoming, he made a fresh start.

"Perhaps we shall simplify matters if we attack the translation word by word. Let us take the first word, Principio. How shall we translate Principio, Mr. Cohen?"

Mr. Cohen reflected and at length pronounced the word "Principal," possibly influenced unconsciously by some reminiscence of the three golden balls.

"No," said Pontifex, "that will hardly do. Possibly, if you recall the opening sentence of the Gospel of St. John in the Vulgate. In principio erat verbum--ahem--" here Ponty pulled up short, suddenly realising that Mr. Cohen was probably not familiar with the Gospel of St. John in the Vulgate or any other form. After a short pause he continued: "Shall we say 'to begin with' or 'in the first place'?"

"Yes," Mr. Cohen agreed promptly, "that's all right."

"Very well," said Ponty. "Now take the next word, sedes."

"Seeds," suggested Mr. Cohen.

"Not seeds," Ponty corrected mildly. "We must not allow ourselves to be misled by analogies of sound. Think of the word sedentary. What is the distinguishing characteristic of a sedentary person, Mr. Cohen?"

"Doesn't take enough exercise," was the reply.

"Very true," Ponty admitted; "and for the reason that he usually occupies a seat. 'Seats' is the word we want, not seeds. 'In the first place seats' statioque--seats and a--and a what, Mr. Cohen?"

"Station," was the confident answer.

"Excellent!" exclaimed Ponty. "Perfectly correct. Seats and a station petenda," he paused for a moment and then, despairing of Cohen's grammar, translated, "must be procured, or more correctly, sought. In the first place, seats and a station must be sought apibi the--for the what, Mr. Cohen?"

"Apes," replied Cohen, promptly.

"No, no," protested Ponty. "Not apes. Similarities of sound are misleading us again. Think of the English word, apiary. You know what an apiary is, Mr.

Cohen?"

Mr. Cohen said that he did, and I didn't believe him. "Well now," said Ponty, persuasively, "what does one keep in an apiary?"

"Apes," was the dogged answer.

What the end of it would have been I shall never know, for at this point footsteps became audible, ascending the stairs. Pontifex listened uneasily and laid down his book as they reached the landing. There was a short pause, and then a soft, apologetic tapping at the door. I sprang up, and, crossing the room, threw the door open, thereby disclosing the astonishing apparition of Mr. Brodribb and Miss Stella's mother.

For a moment, I was so disconcerted that I could only stand, holding the door open and staring vacantly at our visitors. Not so Pontifex. At the first glance he had risen and now came forward to receive them with a dignified and rather stiff bow, and having placed chairs for them excused himself and turned to his gaping and inquisitive pupil.

"I am afraid, Mr. Cohen," said he, "that we shall have to suspend our studies for this morning."

"Right you are," replied Cohen, rising with unscholarly alacrity. Gleefully he snatched up his book and was off like a lamplighter. As his boots clattered down the stairs, Pontifex faced Mr. Brodribb with an air of polite and rather frosty enquiry; and the latter, who had not seated himself, showed less than his usual self-possession.

"I feel, sir," he began hesitatingly, "that I should apologize for what must appear like an intrusion, especially after your clearly expressed desire to be left untroubled by visitors."

"You need have no such feeling," replied Pontifex, "since I have no doubt that I am indebted for the honour of this visit to some unusual and sufficient circumstances."

"You are quite right, sir," rejoined Mr. Brodribb. "Circumstances have arisen which have made it imperative that I should communicate with you. I should have hinted at them when I had the pleasure of meeting you the other day, but your reception of me was not encouraging. Now, I have no choice, and I have ventured to ask Mrs. Paul Hardcastle to accompany me in the hope that her presence may--ha--lessen the force of the impact."

Pontifex bowed to the lady and smiled a frosty smile. I looked at him in astonishment. The familiar Ponty seemed to have suffered some strange transformation. This cool, dignified, starchy old gentleman was a new phenomenon. But Mrs. Paul would have none of his starch. Starting up from her chair, she ran to him impulsively and took both his hands.

"Why are you so cold to us, Sir Gervase?" she exclaimed. "Why do you hold us at arm's length in this way? Are we not old friends? It is true that the years have drifted in between us. But we were friends when we were young, and nothing has ever befallen to weaken our friendship. We both loved dear Phillipa and we both treasure her memory. For her dear sake, if for no other, let us be friends still."

Pontifex softened visibly. "It is true, Constance," he said, gently, "that my heart should warm to you for the sake of that sweet saint, of whose devotion I was so unworthy. Pardon a crabbed old man who has made the world his enemy. One does not gather gratefully the harvest of one's own folly. Forgive me, cousin, and let us hear about your mission."

"It is not my mission, Sir Gervase," she replied. "I came because Mr. Brodribb thought that my presence might make things easier for you."

"That was most kind of you," said he. "But why do you call me Sir Gervase?"

"The answer to that question," interposed Mr. Brodribb, "explains the occasion of this visit. I have to inform you with deep regret that your brother, Sir Edward, died some weeks ago. If I had then known your whereabouts, I should, of course, have communicated with you, not only as his brother but as his heir."

Pontifex looked at Mr. Brodribb in a queer, bewildered fashion and then seemed to fall into a sort of half-conscious dreamy state.

"Dear, dear," he muttered, "so brother Edward is gone--and I am left. My old playmate gone and no word of farewell spoken."

Suddenly he came out of his reverie and addressed Mr. Brodribb sharply. "But you spoke of me as his heir. How can that be? He had children."

"He had one child," said Mr. Brodribb, "a son. That son died some ten years ago. Consequently, the title and the settled estate devolve on you. I may say, have devolved, since there is no question as to the succession."

Pontifex listened to him attentively, but with the same curiously bewildered air. He seemed thunderstruck. After a moment or two he dropped into his chair and sat slowly shaking his head and muttering. Presently he looked up at Mr. Brodribb, and said in a weak, shaky voice: "No, no, Mr. Brodribb. It is too late. This is not for me."

I stood somewhat in the background, watching Pontifex with growing anxiety. Like him, I was astounded by Mr. Brodribb's news. But in that matter I did not feel deeply concerned at the moment. My entire attention was concentrated on the change which had come over my father. It had begun in the very instant when our visitors had appeared in the open doorway. In spite of his cool, stiff bearing, I could see by his sudden change of colour, and the trembling of his hands, that he was intensely agitated. And now, Mr. Brodribb's announcement had inflicted a further shock. It was evident to me that the sudden accession to rank and fortune, so far from giving him pleasure or satisfaction, was profoundly repugnant. And dear Mrs. Paul, with the kindest intentions, did but make matters worse and intensify the shock.

"It is not too late, cousin," said she. "How can it be when there are years of prosperity and ease before you? Think, dear Sir Gervase, think of the bright future which begins from to-day. You will leave all this"--she glanced round the shabby room--"the poverty and ill-paid labour and the struggle for mere daily bread, and go to live in modest affluence in your own fine house with your park and woodlands around you and your servants to minister to your comfort. And you will come back to take your place among your own people in the station of life which properly belongs to you. Think, too, of this dear boy--Phillipa's own boy, and so like her--who, in his turn, shall carry on the honourable traditions of our family. And think of her, who loved you and him and would have been so rejoiced to see you both come back to the inheritance of your fathers."

Pontifex listened to her gravely, and, as she concluded, he looked at me with one of his rare, affectionate smiles.

"Yes, Constance," he said weakly, "you are right. He is Phillipa's own boy. Faithful and loving and good like his mother."

Once more, he lapsed into reverie and I stood gazing at him in dismay with a growing terror at my heart. For a horrible pallor was spreading over his face and even his poor old nose had faded to a sickly mauve. I think my alarm began to be shared by the others, for an uneasy silence settled on the room. And even as we looked at him he seemed to shrink and subside limply into his chair with his chin upon his breast, and so sat for a few moments. Then he rose slowly to his feet, his face turned upward and his trembling hands thrust out before him as one groping in the dark. I heard him murmur, "Domine non sum dignus!" and sprang forward to catch him in my arms as he fell.

* * * * *

How shall I write of that time of sorrow and desolation? Of the emptiness that came upon my little world now that my earliest and dearest companion--almost, as he had sometimes seemed, my child--was gone from me for ever? But need I write of it at all? My tale is told; the tale of the destiny that came to me, all unsuspected, in the egg-chest. My father's death wrote Finis to one volume of my life. With that the old things passed away and all things became new. Jasper Gray was dead, and Sir Jasper Hardcastle had stepped into his shoes.

Yet must I not make my exit too abruptly. The world which I had left lived on, and the drama in which I had played my part still claimed me as a dramatis persona. I pass over the quiet funeral and the solemn procession to the great vault in the shadow of the flint-built tower of the village church at Bradstow; my translation to the house at Dorchester Square, where the white-headed footman (whose deceptive powder I now detected) shattered my nerves by addressing me as "Sir Jasper," and where my cousin, Stella, openly worshipped me as her incomparable Galahad. It was all encompassed by an atmosphere of unreality through which I wandered as one in a dream.

More real was the scene at the Old Bailey--the grimly sordid old Sessions House that is now swept away--where I gave my evidence amidst a breathless silence and afterwards, as the representative of the deceased, sat with Mr. Brodribb at the solicitors' table and listened to Dr. Thorndyke as, with deadly clarity, he set forth the crushing tale of incriminating facts. Quite unmoved, I remember, by any qualm of pity, I heard those five wretches frantically striving to cast the guilt on one another and each but hurrying himself to his own doom. Clearly, but still without a qualm, I recall the pusillanimous shrieks for mercy as the black-capped judge consigned the three murderers to the gallows; and the blubberings of Shemrofsky and the sullen protests of Trout as their terms of penal servitude were pronounced.

It was a memorable experience, and it affected me with a curious, impersonal interest. As I sat at the table, I found myself again and again reflecting on the irony of it all; on the singular futility of this crime. For it was the means of defeating, finally and completely, its original object. The wretched woman who, in her greed and impatience to possess, had planned and directed it, had extinguished her husband's claim for ever. If she had but held her hand, poor Pontifex would have lived and died in his hiding-place, his very existence unsuspected, and she would in due course have become the Lady of Bradstow. It was the murder of my uncle Edward that brought my father into view.

The years have rolled away since these events befell. They have been prosperous years of sober happiness; as they must needs have been; for a man can hardly fail to achieve happiness who is a hero in his wife's eyes. And such is my lot, though undeserved. To this day I am Stella's incomparable Galahad.

Yet, though I would not under-value the gifts of Fortune, I am fain often to reflect on the inconsiderable part that mere material possessions play in the creation of human happiness. As I survey the fine old mansion, the shady park and the wide domain which is all my own, I find them good to look upon and to possess. But, nevertheless, there are times when I feel that I would gladly give much of them to look once more on dear old Ponty, sitting in his shabby dressing-gown, delicately tending the frizzling scallops. How little it cost to give us pleasure in those days! Mr. Weeks's salary would have made us rich, and we could have had scallops every night. But perhaps the habitual scallop would not have had the same flavour.

THE END

Lector House believes that a society develops through a two-fold approach of continuous learning and adaptation, which is derived from the study of classic literary works spread across the historic timeline of literature records. Therefore, we aim at reviving, repairing and redeveloping all those inaccessible or damaged but historically as well as culturally important literature across subjects so that the future generations may have an opportunity to study and learn from past works to embark upon a journey of creating a better future.

This book is a result of an effort made by Lector House towards making a contribution to the preservation and repair of original ancient works which might hold historical significance to the approach of continuous learning across subjects.

HAPPY READING & LEARNING!

LECTOR HOUSE LLP
E-MAIL: lectorpublishing@gmail.com

9 789353 366834

Lightning Source UK Ltd.
Milton Keynes UK
UKHW010802120421
381772UK00002B/285

9 789353 366834